SETH

A Small Town, Enemies to Lovers, Military Protector Romance

Ghost Ops
Book 3

LYNN RAYE HARRIS

H.O.T. Publishing, LLC

Printed in the United States of America

First Printing, 2025

For rights inquires, visit www.LynnRayeHarris.com

ISBN: 979-8-89117-044-5

CALLIE STARED AT THE DATA ON HER SCREEN. SOMETHING wasn't right, but she didn't know what. She'd been over the lines of code more than once, and it seemed fine. But there was a heaviness that weighed on her soul, as if she was missing something obvious.

She wasn't, though. The code was fine. So what else could it be?

A sound startled her as the lines of code blurred. She jerked her head up, gazing around the office. The lab was secure with no windows and only one door, but she knew it was dark outside. She'd stayed late again because the defense satellite project was running overtime and over budget and her skills were needed, but she wasn't alone in the building. There were other scientists and engineers in different labs, diligently doing their work.

Or so she believed. Her heart thumped. What if she was wrong and everyone was gone?

Silly. Security would still be there, watching over the building. She was not alone. Nobody was ever alone in Griffin Research Labs.

No, she didn't like the darkness, but she stayed because she needed the code to work. She needed the money this job brought, for one thing. She didn't want to move again, couldn't afford to right now. She had to make a home for her and Nikki. Had to give her sister some stability. Moving would wreck all the progress they'd made over the past year.

Callie focused on the screen in front of her, went over the code line by line. It should work, but it wasn't working. Why wasn't it working?

She didn't know how much time passed before she smelled smoke. She jerked her head up, glancing around like a wild animal caught in the sights of something bigger and stronger.

Then the fire alarm sounded, and she shot up from her chair, fear squeezing her heart as smoke poured into the lab. She was frozen in place for too long before the voice in her head got through to her.

Run! She hit the logout, slapped her terminal closed, and bolted for the door.

But it wouldn't open. No matter how hard she tugged the steel handle, how many times she swiped her card in the reader with shaking hands, the door didn't budge. Smoke swirled around the room, making it harder to see by the second. Her eyes watered and her throat ached.

Callie coughed as she sank to the floor beside the door. Tears of rage and helplessness filled her. The door was barred, and the sprinkler system hadn't come on. She stared up at one of the nozzles she could see through the haze, hoping beyond hope that water would begin to spray.

It didn't.

Because she hadn't been willing to play the game.

And this was the answer.

She was going to die here tonight, and Nikki would be

an orphan. Callie curled her fingers into fists and bowed her head. She wished she'd never gone to Poland, never met Mikhail Volkov. If she hadn't been so completely enamored of him and his attention, she might have seen the signs. Might have understood that he wanted so much more from her than a relationship.

He'd wanted her soul, and she'd understood too late.

Anger sparked as the smoke grew thicker.

"No," she growled. "Not like this."

The alarm still blared, hurting her ears. She looked up defiantly. There was no way he could be watching her, not inside a secure lab, but she had a strong feeling he saw her anyway. He'd told her what would happen if she didn't cooperate. That last time she'd seen him, he'd said she was nearly out of time.

And now she was.

"No," she said more boldly, dragging herself up. "You aren't going to win."

She grabbed the handle again, pulled.

Nothing happened.

Callie lost her cool, tugging and screaming and kicking the door, coughing as she dragged smoke deeper into her lungs.

She would *not* give up.

They would find her with bloody hands and broken toes, and they'd know she'd fought.

At least they would know that.

Above her, there was a small whooshing sound. And then a deluge of water rained down on her.

She sank to her knees, a sob erupting from her throat.

Too close.

Her brain frantically tried to process her options. If she went to the police, would they help her? What about the FBI?

Her gut told her the answer was no. First they needed to believe her, and she wasn't sure they would. Without a confession note from Mikhail conveniently pinned in a place they could find it, why would anyone believe the fire was aimed at her?

She gulped in air and strained to hear sound outside the lab door. Would someone come to rescue her now that the sprinklers were operational? Or would something worse happen?

Callie shivered. If she made it out of this lab alive tonight, there was only one option.

She needed to disappear for good. Not immediately, because she had to make a foolproof plan for her and Nikki, but soon.

Callie had to cease to exist. Before Mikhail made it happen for real.

Chapter Two

Seth woke with a start, gulping air and sweating profusely. He whipped the covers back and lay in the dark, staring up at the ceiling. Why did he keep having this dream? Why now, after all this time?

He got out of bed and went into the bathroom, splashed water on his face, then headed for the kitchen to turn on the coffeepot. It was a little before five, but he could hear his housemate moving around downstairs. If Ghost hadn't turned on the coffee yet, then he would.

When Seth entered the kitchen, the overhead light was already burning. Ghost looked up from where he stood by the counter, the coffee just starting to gurgle. "Rough night?"

Seth dragged a hand over his head and shrugged. "You know how it is. Wouldn't be an operator if we didn't have nightmares sometimes."

Ghost arched an eyebrow and nodded. "Truth, brother," he said before grabbing two mugs from the cabinet.

Truth. Precisely what Seth hadn't admitted.

He didn't dream about missions and mistakes. Didn't dream about the brothers-in-arms he'd lost or the civilians whose lives were cut short by terrorists and tragedy.

Not usually.

What he dreamed about was closer to home. His own life. His own mistakes. The choice he'd made that haunted him to this day.

All he'd lost. All he didn't deserve and would never have.

"Got a message last night from DC," Ghost said.

Seth perked up. Anything to shift his attention somewhere else. Dwelling on all the things that made him a shitty person never got him anywhere except more convinced he was only on this team, close to these men, because they didn't really know him. If they knew what he'd done, what would they think then?

Especially Blaze and Chance, two men who'd found women they adored—and would die for—since moving to Alabama. Chance had a baby on the way with Rory Harper, and Seth had never seen his friend so happy.

Blaze was ridiculously besotted with Emma Grace Sutton, the town doctor, and Seth wouldn't be surprised if they had an announcement of their own one of these days.

He envied them. Hell, even Kane was hung up on Daphne Bryant, One Shot Tactical's uber-competent receptionist-slash-assistant. Not that he'd admitted it to himself, let alone anyone else. He treated Daphne like the little sister he never had while the rest of them could see that, deep down, he wanted her to be more.

Seth hoped he figured it out before it was too late, considering Daphne was seeing Warren Trigg, the manager of the Piggly Wiggly. Or the Pig in local vernacular. Trigg from the Pig. The alliteration was lowkey hilarious in Seth's opinion.

"There was a fire at Griffin Research Labs. Lab Two was destroyed. Lab Three sustained serious damage," Ghost said.

Seth frowned. Lab Three was the secure lab where Chance had switched out a couple of normal cables with spy cables only a couple of weeks ago. "We should have rigged the place with cameras."

He, Kane, and Chance had spent a week at GRL, going over their security while also gaining access to the inner workings of their secure network, thanks to USB cables with a Wi-Fi signal and a keystroke logger onboard. Indistinguishable from a normal cable, but they'd allowed Seth to see everything being worked on in the secure lab where the command and control system for the Athena Project was developed. Who accessed it, who worked on it. He hadn't checked the feed this morning, but he probably needed to. The connection was wonky sometimes because he'd had to rig them to connect to the building's wireless network, and outages affected reliability. Also why he'd put two cables in instead of one. A failsafe. But if they were down because of the fire, he wouldn't be receiving anything.

"Those weren't our orders, Phantom." Ghost sighed. "But we should've and fuck Auerbach."

Ronnie Auerbach was the president's chief of staff. He seemed to have it in for Ghost Ops on some level, though if he wanted them shut down, Seth was pretty sure he could talk President Willis into it. Maybe it was that the president wanted Ghost Ops, and he thought they were a liability. He was the one behind the policy that they weren't going to be acknowledged or saved if they got themselves in trouble. To protect the president's reputation and legacy and give her deniability. It made sense, but it was also a shitty thing to do if you asked him. Nobody had.

"On the other hand," Ghost continued with a sigh, "with the FBI sniffing around, we didn't need to leave anything anyone might find. Rigging Royal Shipping with surveillance was one thing. A top-secret lab is another. The computer hack is enough. Or was."

The coffeepot beeped, and Ghost poured two mugs, handed one to Seth. He took a swig of hot, black coffee, thanking the powers that be that Ghost liked it strong, too. Just what he needed.

"Guess I should power up and see if we still have access."

"That'd be a good start. Caroline Crowell was in the lab when the fire started."

That stopped Seth in his tracks. He'd been heading over to the table to open his laptop. Instead, he turned to look at Ghost. "You think she started it?"

"I don't know. We need the badging records for the labs, see if she exited at any point before the fire started. If she went into Lab Two and then returned, it could have been her."

Seth's gut churned. "She could have wiped the records. She's a programmer. She'd probably know how to do it."

"True. But she nearly got herself killed from smoke inhalation before the sprinklers activated."

Seth pictured the woman he'd only spoken to a couple of times. She'd been standoffish, cool. But she'd also seemed young, maybe a bit scared. He'd attributed that to her fear of getting caught. She was also pretty in that soft way nerdy girls could be, with long brown hair, green eyes behind the glasses she wore when working, and pale skin that told of long nights in the lab or hunched over a computer.

"Maybe she did that too. Made it look like it couldn't possibly be her."

Ghost took a sip of his coffee. "Maybe so. See what you can find out."

Seth sat at the table and opened his computer. "I'm on it."

Chapter Three

CALLIE ALMOST KEPT HER SISTER OUT OF SCHOOL BUT AT the last minute decided to let her go. Nikki slung her backpack and riding gear into the Honda CR-V that Callie had found for a good price used and jumped behind the wheel. Then she looked up, saw Callie watching from the window, and waved before throwing the CR-V in reverse and turning around to head down the driveway.

Callie's heart thumped and her eyes watered. She coughed, a good long fit, and then she was fine. She'd been thoroughly checked last night when emergency crews busted into the lab. Her eyes were scratchy and her voice hoarse, not to mention the cough, but she felt okay. She had a bronchodilator to keep her airways open, and she was staying home to rest.

Not only that, but she *had* to stay home because the lab was uninhabitable at the moment. In fact, the entire building had been vacated while the structure was inspected to make sure it was safe enough for people in other departments to return to work. The leadership at

Griffin Research Labs was probably apoplectic at the delays, but what else could they do?

It'd take a few days before they were cleared to open again, and then she'd find out when and where she was supposed to report for work.

Except she didn't want to report for work. She wanted to get the hell away from here before Mikhail did something else.

There was no doubt in her mind he was the one behind the fire. He'd waited until she was alone, and he'd trapped her. She didn't know how, but he had.

It shouldn't have been possible, but she was learning that nothing was beyond Mikhail Volkov. She hadn't realized it at the time, back in Poland when they'd met, but now she knew. He'd maneuvered her into this job when she needed one and slowly tightened the noose until she couldn't escape without being willing to give up everything.

He pretended to be her friend, but he really wasn't. Whatever he was involved in was far darker than she'd imagined, and her life wasn't worth much to those kinds of people. Mikhail had said as much the last time he was in Huntsville, pushing her to do his bidding. He'd threatened her, and then he'd threatened Nikki if she didn't cooperate.

But she knew, even if she did what he wanted, they were both dead. Mikhail wouldn't leave any loose ends.

Her only option now was to run. She couldn't do that without a plan, though. If she were going to disappear, really disappear, then she needed to take enough time to make sure she couldn't be followed. That meant getting new identities for her and Nikki. It also meant leaving everything behind.

The horses. The Toyota and the trailer. It all stayed.

Callie closed her eyes as despair nearly overwhelmed her. She'd worked so hard to make sure Nikki had a normal life, that she could keep riding her horses and entering competitions, because the kid had lost everything when their parents died. Horses were the only thing that made her happy.

That smile and wave this morning was special because Nikki had finally started coming out of her shell these past couple of months, and Callie didn't want to ruin it. But what was the alternative? If she left Nikki behind, she'd be orphaning her sister all over again. Nikki was sixteen, grappling with being a teenager, a new school, and a new life, and all she had was Callie and her horses. Leaving her behind wasn't an option.

But how was Callie supposed to get new identities? Disappear without being followed? Where would they go? How would they live?

She had some money saved, but not enough because there had been *so* many expenses this past year. Everyone had always thought the Crowells were wealthy when Callie was growing up, but she'd learned the truth when her parents died last year.

Wealth and the appearance of wealth were two entirely different things. Credit cards and loans had kept up the illusion. The vacation her parents had been on in Vail when they died had been charged to a credit card. The house had a second mortgage, her dad's optometry practice was barely solvent. The bank had taken the house, and the rest went to pay off debt. The practice had been shuttered.

Callie wandered into the kitchen to pour another cup of coffee. She looked at the remnants of the breakfast that she'd made for Nikki and her stomach turned. She didn't want food. Couldn't stomach it right now. She put the scrambled eggs in a container and refrigerated them. Same with the hash browns and bacon. No need to waste food when she could reheat it for lunch later or let Nikki have it tomorrow morning.

Besides, though she made a decent living as a programmer, she was always aware that it could end in the blink of an eye. And then what? She was twenty-six, too young to have much of a retirement saved, and living wasn't free. Especially with a teenager and two very large animals to take care of.

She could live off credit cards the way her parents had, but the stress of dealing with their estate had taught her a valuable lesson about things she never wanted to do. It'd certainly put that expensive handbag she'd bought in Europe before her life had changed into a whole new perspective.

She'd sold it on Poshmark back when she was still trying to find a job. It'd fetched a pretty penny, but not what she'd paid for it.

She washed dishes and picked up the mail on the counter, discarding advertisements and putting bills into a stack. The Sutton's Creek Bee, a small local newspaper— really, the word newspaper was stretching it and should be in quotes—sat at the bottom of the stack.

Callie started to toss it, but a square ad at the bottom of the front page caught her eye.

One Shot Tactical - For All Your Security Needs.

One Shot Tactical. She pictured three big, muscular men in navy blue polo shirts with those words embroidered over their hearts.

Those men had been all over Griffin Research Labs a couple of weeks ago, going over their security procedures, suggesting changes to the boss. Her anger kindled. It hadn't been good enough, had it? There'd been a fire and she'd nearly died.

Then again, she could hardly blame them. Security *had*

been tighter since they'd made their changes. Guards who knew her on sight demanded her identification before she entered the building. The codes to the labs were changed on a rolling basis, and everything had been by the book. She'd actually breathed easier when the changes were implemented.

No, it wasn't their fault someone had set a fire. She had no doubt Mikhail was behind it, but in the light of a new day when she wasn't as scared and could reason, she knew he hadn't been inside the lab, secretly starting a fire. He'd had someone do it, which meant he had a spy on the inside.

That thought made her shiver.

She clutched the paper, staring at the ad. She'd talked to all three of the One Shot Tactical employees who'd been at the lab at one time or another. Kane was the nicest. Chance had been nice too, but he'd often seemed distracted, like he'd wanted to be elsewhere.

Seth.

Now that one, he'd been a dick. He'd frowned and growled and been about as unfriendly as a rabid dog.

He'd been gorgeous, though. They were all gorgeous, but Seth, with his coal black hair and iron-gray eyes had been particularly attractive. Until he opened his mouth, and then he'd been downright rude.

Callie sniffed at the memory.

But an idea took hold as she continued to study the small ad. *For All Your Security Needs.*

She didn't know where to start, how to disappear, but she'd bet those guys had an idea how it worked. Not that she would ask outright. Too obvious.

But they were in the security business, former military guys. At the very minimum, they might listen if she said she was in danger, might offer suggestions or even security services. Of course they'd want money, but she could pay them for a few days while she worked on her escape plan.

She swallowed, considering. It was as good an idea as any. Better than doing nothing.

Better than being an easy target.

She'd ask for Kane. She wouldn't need to see Seth at all.

For the first time since the fire alarm blared into the night and scared her half to death, she had the beginnings of a plan.

Chapter Four

"She didn't leave the lab all evening," Seth said to the men gathered in the SCIF attached to the range. To all outward appearances, it was simply a storage room. But this was where all the secret planning and communication happened. Where they got their orders and discussed the mission.

"But our connection is toast now," Kane said.

"For the moment. The building's IT hub was damaged, so there's currently no signal. I won't know for sure until it's back online. Then the cables either connect again or not."

Ghost shoved a hand through his hair and blew out a forceful breath. "The fire seems to have started in the ventilation shaft nearest the two labs. That makes it deliberate."

"Could Ms. Crowell be the target?" Blaze asked.

Seth frowned. "Maybe. Or maybe she wanted it to look that way."

Chance shook his head. "Dude, I know you've settled on her being a suspect for sharing top-secret information about the Athena Project, but just because she speaks Polish and Russian doesn't mean she's the one. We don't even know if the Poles or Russians are the ones behind the threat to Athena. She almost didn't get out of that lab alive. What would be the point in nearly killing herself and potentially shutting down the project before it goes live?"

Seth grumbled. "I'm considering all the options."

"Wilhelm Olkowicz and Cyril Dyka are really Abram Fedorov and Dima Smirnov," Ghost said, dropping a new bomb in the group as he looked up from the screen in front of him. "Just got that information. Russian nationals who have Polish families and roots in Poland. Both are older than they look. They passed for engineering students at UAH, but Fedorov is thirty-two and Smirnov is thirty-five."

"Olkowicz and Dyka have no connection with Caroline. But I have to check the Russian names," Seth said. "And I'm not set on her being the leak, Wraith. I just think we can't ignore the most obvious connection because she's sad and pretty."

"Sad and pretty?" Kane said, arching an eyebrow. "Interesting observation."

Seth wanted to jump up and prowl the room. His skin was suddenly itchy, like if he sat still another moment he'd want to peel it off. "And you didn't notice?"

Kane grinned. "I noticed. I'm just surprised you did."

"Why would you be? She's female and I'm not dead. Yet."

"True. But you're pretty much the only one of us who hasn't hooked up or been on a date since we moved to Alabama. Thought you'd sworn a celibacy oath or something."

"Dude, just because you have to hump everything that crosses your path doesn't mean the rest of us do."

The guys snickered. Kane rolled his eyes. "Whatever. You people are just jealous that I get all the tail."

"Hardly," Blaze laughed. "But you go ahead and tell yourself that if it makes you happy."

Kane shrugged. "It does, so I will."

The meeting went on for another fifteen minutes before they broke up and headed back out to the range before it opened for the day. Seth prepared to do research on Fedorov and Smirnov's potential connections to Caroline Crowell while Kane and Ethan got ready to leave for a security consultation in Research Park. News of One Shot's work at Griffin Research Labs had made the rounds, and they were in demand. Since the money was good and the cover for their mission excellent, they took the jobs.

Though the command and control system software in development at GRL was their current target, it wasn't the only component of the Athena Project being worked on in Huntsville, nor the sole potential target for hostiles. Huntsville was target rich for those who wanted to harm the US, which unfortunately meant Ghost Ops would be needed there for the foreseeable future.

"See you after lunch," Ethan said as they headed out the door.

"Later," Chance said.

"Who's got the church security training at thirteen hundred?" Ghost asked as he perused the schedule.

"It's me today," Blaze said. "That's Emma's parents' church. I said I'd be available for it."

"Then Seth and Chance are range officers this afternoon, correct?"

"Yep," Seth said, looking up from his screen. "I've got the ladies' class at seventeen hundred, too."

He didn't mind teaching personal security and gun safety to civilians, though he certainly wasn't anyone's favorite instructor. He didn't believe in idle chitchat, and some people—women usually, though sometimes men too—always wanted to engage him in conversation. When he didn't reciprocate the nonsense, they left him alone.

Daphne breezed into the break room, her red hair pulled into a ponytail, skinny jeans hugging her curves. Seth noticed and appreciated, but he had no urge to ask her out. Though maybe he should just so he could watch Kane twist himself into a pretzel pretending it was no big deal.

On the other hand, none of them wanted to give Daphne a reason to leave. She ran the range and class schedule with efficiency and speed. He appreciated that about her. And he liked her because she didn't try to engage him in idle conversation.

"Got a customer out front asking for Kane," Daphne said. "A woman."

"Uh-oh," Chance replied. "Does she look pissed off?"

Daphne grinned. "No. She said she met him when he did a security review of her workplace recently. She didn't say what she wants, but I don't think he's managed to piss her off yet. Pretty sure she's here about a class or something."

"Kane just left. He won't be back until this afternoon," Ghost replied. Then he jerked his chin at Seth. "See if you can help her."

Seth closed the laptop, grumbling inside. He'd rather go down the rabbit hole of online networks than talk to some woman with a lady boner for Kane, but when the boss said go, he went. "On it."

Seth strode to the door where Daphne stood. They walked together to the front of the building, and he asked her about the car situation because he thought maybe he should.

She shook her head. "Honestly, I think I'm going to buy Warren's beater he's been letting me use. I don't have time to wait for Kane to finally decide something's a good deal, and the beater drives just fine for what I want."

"Kane's a perfectionist. He wants you to get the most for your money."

Daphne sighed. "I know, but he's so darn annoying about it. I agreed to let him help me because he said he'd worked on cars a lot, but nothing is good enough when we go to look."

Seth was pretty sure he knew why, but he wasn't telling Daphne that Kane just wanted an excuse to spend time with her. "Tell him you're buying Warren's car if he doesn't give you the green light on something else."

"You think I should?"

"Definitely."

That'd light a fire under Kane for sure.

Daphne sighed again. "Fine. But he's going to be a pompous ass about it."

Seth laughed. "No doubt."

They reached the front of the building that housed the store and range entry. A woman with brown hair that fell to the middle of her back stood looking out the window, her arms wrapped around her body, her shoulders hunched. She turned at their entrance, and Seth nearly stopped in his tracks.

Somehow, he managed to keep walking toward her, wondering what the hell she was doing here.

Caroline Crowell gazed at him with wide green eyes in a pale face. A look of dismay crossed her features as she darted a look at Daphne. Seth tried not to let that bother him, but a hot feeling lodged in his chest and wouldn't abate.

He stretched out a hand, reminding himself to smile.

"Hi, I'm Seth. Kane isn't here right now, but maybe I can help you."

She looked wary as she took his hand for a brief shake. Her skin was cold to the touch, and he had an urge to wrap her hand in his to warm it. But she pulled away quickly, stuffing her hand against her body again.

"I, um. We've met. I'm Callie. I work at Griffin Research Labs. You guys were there a couple of weeks ago."

"That's right." He didn't know why he was pretending he didn't remember her, but it seemed a good approach since she clearly preferred Kane to him. Why else ask for his teammate?

The idea that maybe Kane had flirted with her made that hot feeling in his chest bloom. Not that he wanted to flirt with her. He didn't trust her. But Kane didn't need to be hitting on her either. No getting involved with the suspects, for fuck's sake.

"What can we help you with, Callie?"

Nice as pie. That's what Emma and Rory would say. He loved Southern sayings, and that was a pretty good one. Who didn't like pie?

She looked hesitant as she pushed her hair behind her ear.

"Why don't we go into the conference room to talk?"

It took her a moment, but she nodded.

They had a couple of rooms where they ran slideshows for the classes they taught. He led her to one of those, opened the door, and motioned her in. She still didn't take her arms from around her body. She was wearing a pair of loose-fitting jeans and a white T-shirt with a pair of tennis shoes. A small brown purse was slung across her body, so she had her hands free. She looked small and vulnerable, and he stamped down on the kernel of empathy that flared inside.

He closed the door behind him, and her eyes widened a fraction.

"Would you like me to leave it open?"

She appeared to drag in a breath. Then she shook her head. "No, it's fine."

Her voice was hoarse. She started to cough, covering her mouth with one hand. He didn't like the way that sounded. If she'd set the fire, she'd nearly gotten herself killed by staying in the lab. Not very bright of her.

"Would you like some water?"

She nodded, and he turned to open the door and ask Daphne if she could bring a bottle. Then he motioned to the table and Callie dropped into the seat nearest the end. Daphne returned with the water and Seth took it over to Callie, twisting the cap off for her. He sat in the end seat, close but not as close as the chair beside her.

"Thanks," she said after she took a drink. Her voice was still hoarse, but she seemed to have the coughing under control. She did the hair push thing again. "There was a fire at the lab last night. I was there when it happened. Trapped in the lab while smoke filled the room. That's where the cough is from."

"We just heard about the fire. Was anyone hurt?"

She shook her head. "Just some smoke inhalation. I caught the worst of it, but I'll be okay. There were two other researchers in the building and the janitorial crew. Everyone got out safely."

He filed that away to look into later. "That's a good thing."

She lifted her chin a fraction. "It is. B-but I think it's my fault. That it happened, I mean."

He studied her. "Why do you think that? Were you careless with a candle or something?"

"You're making fun of me."

"I'm not. But I don't see how it's your fault unless you started it."

"I didn't."

He told himself to be patient, to let the story unfold. She was here to talk, and that was good. "What do you want from us? How can we help?"

She leaned back against the chair, twisting the water bottle in her fingers. "I think someone set the fire deliberately. Because of me." Her gaze dropped to the table. "Because they want something from me."

His neck prickled as the fine hairs stood up. It was either a good thing she was here, or she knew who they were and she was fucking with them. Not as likely, but he didn't dismiss any possibility.

"What do they want?"

Her green eyes held a mixture of fear and anger. "I can't tell you that. GRL works on many different projects, some of them sensitive and proprietary. This person wants information about a, um, government project."

Bingo. "So why not tell your boss? Or go to the FBI? Why us?"

"Because I can't. He'll know, and he'll do something." She sucked in a breath, her eyes misting over. "I can't let him hurt Nikki. My little sister."

Seth pulled a couple of tissues from the box nearby and handed them to her.

"Thank you," she mumbled, dabbing her eyes. When she was done, she sat up tall, flexing her jaw. It was like watching a tire suddenly reach critical mass. One minute she was soft and flexible, the next strong and firm. "He's been patient so far, but his patience is running out. That's what last night was about."

He wondered if she realized she'd gone from *they* to *he* over the past few sentences. It was an interesting slip. He filed it away.

"Can you tell me who this person is?"

She stared at him a moment. Emotions flashed across her face. Worry, desperation, hope.

Then came fear. That one was strongest.

She shoved her way to her feet, her eyes suddenly wild. "I need to go. This was a mistake. Sorry to bother you."

She rushed toward the door, but he beat her there, barring the way. She collided with his chest, and he reached out to steady her. He didn't think she was faking her fear, but anything was possible.

People were complicated.

"Easy, honey. Nobody's going to hurt you here."

She trembled, her body shaking beneath his hands. "I need to go. I shouldn't be here."

Seth didn't want to feel anything, but that damned empathy flared again. She was truly scared.

"You came to us for a reason," he said softly. "We can help you. If you don't want to tell me who this man is that has you so scared, you don't have to. But don't walk out of here when you're afraid he's going to hurt you or your sister."

The tension in her body eased a fraction. Not enough, but he'd count it a victory. She was listening to him, thinking. He needed to convince her fast.

"Let me call my guys to come hear what you have to say, okay? We're experts in personal security. We'll listen and we'll make a plan. If you still want to leave after that, you can, no questions asked."

He said the words, but there was no way he was letting

her leave when she was as scared as she was. He'd thought she might have come here to lie to them, to ferret them out, but in his experience most people weren't actually that good at acting. Not when it wasn't their profession.

This woman was truly frightened. She might know more than she was sharing, and she might be there on orders from someone with bad intentions, but he had to go with his gut right now and get her to stay.

She dragged in a breath, coughed again long and low. He took that as surrender and walked her over to ease her down into a chair, set the water in front of her, and texted Ghost.

> Caroline Crowell is here, and she says someone tried to kill her.

The reply was instant.

> Be right there.

Chapter Five

CALLIE'S GAZE DARTED BETWEEN THE MEN AT THE TABLE. Four big men, two of whom she'd met before and two she hadn't. Chance Hughes seemed less distracted today. He was kind and made jokes that put her at ease.

Alex Bishop was most likely the boss. She thought so by the way the other three deferred to him. Tall, handsome, and aloof. Intense.

Blaze Connolly asked her how she liked Sutton's Creek, did she eat at The Salty Dawg Tavern often, was she a fan of the Kiss My Grits Café, and what did she think of Colleen Wright's crystal shop and all things woo-woo emporium. That last one made her laugh despite herself.

She hadn't actually been in Colleen's shop, but Nikki had. Her sister was a fan of the crystals.

Then there was Seth King. He was nicer this time, smiled more. He spoke soothingly as he urged her to tell his guys what she'd told him.

She did, but she was beginning to think she'd made a huge mistake. If Mikhail could get to her in the lab, he'd surely know she was here, talking to a bunch of security professionals. Then what?

But she'd started this, so she had to finish it. Then she needed to get the hell out of town.

She didn't miss the looks the men exchanged when she mentioned that someone set the fire to target her. She felt foolish saying it now that she'd done so twice. It sounded outrageous. Griffin Research Labs was a top-secret facility, and though they'd had some trouble with access recently—which these guys had caught and fixed—access to the secure labs had always been well controlled.

These men talking their way past building security, which they'd done, was one thing. Getting into a SCIF behind a coded door was another. The only way Chance had walked into her lab the day he had was with permission and a controlled access card. Thanks to their work those few days, it was even harder to get into the building now.

Which meant they must think she was paranoid.

Four faces looked at her, expressions hard. They didn't look like they thought she was lying though. Her heart pounded in her chest as she waited for one of them to speak.

"We can help you," Alex said. "But you're going to have to tell us who you think did this. And what he wants from you."

Fear spiked. "I-I can't."

"Find a way," Seth said. "You work in a facility with sensitive information. You don't have to tell us specifically about a program, because we understand you can't talk about it outside the security of a SCIF or to people who aren't read in, but you can tell us who this man is and give us an idea what he wants."

He leaned toward her, put his big, warm hand over her

cold one as if realizing he'd sounded brusque. She thought she should pull away, but she was rooted to the spot. For the second time that day, she felt a tingle when his skin touched hers. As if he were made of lightning and she was merely waiting for the spark to make her glow.

"You came here for a reason, Callie. You thought we could help. We can." He darted a look at the other men. Something seemed to pass between them before he spoke again. "We're all former military. Former special forces. We've done protection details for high profile clients, and we've seen a lot of shit in our time. There's nobody else equipped to deal with your situation the way we are."

Hope. It was hope that flared in her soul as she gazed into eyes that were fathomless pools of gray. She wanted to lose herself in those eyes. Wanted to see them spark with that lightning bottled inside him whenever he gazed at her.

Callie shook herself. And then she plunged because she'd already come this far and she couldn't see a way out.

"Mikhail Volkov. That's his name. I-I don't know much about him, not really. I know he's American, and I know he's a fluent Russian and Polish speaker, like me. I worked in Poland for a year, instructing civil engineers in software tools and development. My mother was an immigrant. I learned Polish and Russian from her, and I studied Russian in school along with programming. I sometimes went out for drinks and dinner with my students—I mean as a group. I met Mikhail at one of the clubs we went to. He was also working on the base as a translator for the Dashevsky Group."

She drew in a breath, surprised at all she'd said. And also relieved. It was like she'd been swelling with information, but the pressure had eased. Not completely, because simply speaking his name wasn't fixing anything, but she could breathe again.

Think.

"He was charming. I went out with him a few times. We were just kind of casually dating, getting to know each other. He asked questions about my work, about my background. He talked a lot about changing the world, making it better. One day he told me he knew about a job I should apply for. With Griffin Research Labs."

The room was quiet. She dragged in a breath.

"He knew someone. He said he could give them a call and I'd get the job. I wasn't sure I wanted to leave Poland at that time, but then my parents died and I needed to provide a good home for my sister. I returned home and had to settle their estate, which took some time. I applied for jobs locally, hoping to keep my sister in the town she'd grown up in."

She didn't mention how hard that was when it turned out her parents owed money to so many businesses in their town. People weren't precisely unkind, but they kept expecting to be paid when the estate was finalized. Some of them had been, but many had not. She'd felt responsible enough that she'd used her own money to pay as many as she could.

Which was why she didn't have the savings she'd once had. Mikhail, who'd remained a friend after their relationship went nowhere, told her she shouldn't do it. Maybe she shouldn't have, but she'd grown up with some of those people and it hadn't seemed fair not to try and pay them.

"Nobody was hiring. I needed work so I could take care of my sister, so I let Mikhail help me get the job at the lab because it was one less thing to worry about. Nikki and I moved here ten months ago."

"I'm guessing you don't know who his contact is."

She shook her head, spreading her fingers on the table. Seth's hand was nearby, ready to reach for her again. She pulled her hands back, afraid if he touched her she'd say more than she should.

"I got promoted to a new project, a new team, after a couple of months. That's when Mikhail started to press me for information. I told him the things I could, thinking we were just talking, but he kept asking for more as the months went by. For things I can't talk about. When I didn't tell him what he wanted to know, he got angry."

"Where is he living now?" Alex asked.

Callie closed her eyes a second. It all sounded so stupid, like one of those romance scams that people fell for on Facebook. A dashing man of the world wormed his way into her life, but the currency he wanted was information and access, not to drain her bank account.

"I don't know. He travels a lot, but I know he has an apartment in the DC area where he stays when he's meeting with lobbyists and lawyers for the Dashevsky Group."

"Does he ever come to Huntsville?"

"Yes. He was here ten days ago."

He'd been angry with her. So very angry. He'd given her a simple power cable and told her what he wanted her to do. She hadn't done it. She'd made excuses because she'd needed time to think. When he'd texted her a few days ago, she'd finally told him she couldn't swap it out. She wasn't a hacker, but she knew what that cable could do.

Completely indistinguishable from a normal cable, it had a keystroke logger and a Wi-Fi signal embedded in the connection device. If she replaced any cable in the secure area with that one, Mikhail would have access to the Griffin Research Labs internal secure network. He could steal proprietary information. Share it.

Sell it.

Worse, he would have access to the defense satellite project her team had been working on for the past several months. They were close to debugging the code, which meant the system was that much closer to deployment. There was a lot of pressure from Washington to get it done as quickly as possible. If anyone stole that information, even with the code in the state it was currently in, they could do a lot of harm in a very short amount of time. And if they had unfiltered access to the work Callie was doing? They'd know when the debugging was successful and the project nearly complete.

She didn't know the entire scope of the satellite system because Washington was very secretive about it, but it was incredibly important to national defense. She knew what her instructions were, and she knew the theoretical idea behind the project as an advanced warning system.

She wasn't about to give anyone access to that kind of information. Callie might be a lot of things—a workaholic, a bumbling sister, an incompetent replacement for a mom and dad, a very bad judge of character—but a traitor wasn't one of them.

"If you think the fire last night was in response to your refusal to cooperate, how do you think he staged it?"

Callie swallowed. The more she talked about this, the more unbelievable it sounded.

"I think he probably paid someone. Someone on the janitorial staff, maybe. They're vetted and they have to pass background checks, but it'd be easier to bribe someone, or place his own people there, than to get inside himself."

"We'll look into the backgrounds of everyone who was working last night," Seth said. "Including your coworkers. Just to be thorough."

Callie blinked in surprise. "How will you do that? You aren't cops."

Seth smiled, and her heart did an extra thump. Very inconvenient. She reminded herself that he'd been a dick to her when he'd been at the lab. Not only that, but he hadn't seemed to remember her when she'd introduced herself. Not until she'd told him they'd met before.

"Told you we're equipped to deal with your situation. I have contacts in law enforcement. I'll get the background info."

"I don't even know who was there last night."

"I'll find that information, too."

She stared at him, at the utter confidence in his expression. She believed him. Completely. A little flame of relief burned brighter then.

But not bright enough.

"I'm afraid to go home. To be out there by myself. And later, when Nikki comes home…"

She wasn't sure what she was asking. She just knew she didn't want to be alone if Mikhail came looking for her. He might not kill her yet, but she didn't doubt he'd hurt her. Or hurt Nikki to make her comply. More than anything, that's what she feared would happen next.

"Do you have a security system?"

"No. I'm leasing the farm. It didn't come with anything like that."

"We can put one in for you."

Her throat squeezed. "I'd like that, but I have to get permission from the owner. And a price before I commit."

She couldn't spend much since she suspected she'd need nearly everything she had now to disappear, but an alarm was reasonable for the week or two they had left. She hadn't changed her mind about leaving, no matter what these men said. If they could slow Mikhail down, keep her safe, it'd give her time to make a foolproof plan.

"We don't have to cut holes in the walls to provide you

with security. Give me the owner's contact information, and I'll arrange permission. We'll give you a price before we do any work," Alex said. "Meanwhile, if you've got an extra room, one of us can stay with you for a couple days until the system goes in. Or you can stay in town where we can keep an eye on you if you prefer."

She couldn't burn money on a hotel. She wasn't sure she wanted to spend it on an alarm system either, but she could hardly say no if it meant these guys would help her. If one of them would stay at her place for the next few days, listening for things that went bump in the night, it'd be worth the price.

Callie shot a look at Seth from beneath her lashes. No, it wouldn't be him. They would *not* send him.

"I have an extra room. One of my sister's horses is at the farm with us. We need to feed him, so it's better for us to stay out there."

She'd have to explain to Nikki why there was a man staying with them, but she'd think of something.

"That's fine." He tipped his chin at Seth. "You follow her home, get the lay of the place. I'll take your shift on the range, and Kane or Ethan can take your class tonight."

Callie's stomach dropped. She didn't miss the look on Seth's face either. He was fine being nice to her in the moment, but he didn't want to spend a few days with her any more than she did with him.

If she asked for someone else, would she sound ungrateful?

"I, um—how much will it cost to have personal security like that?"

Because she needed to know. She was prepared to pay them for their help, but there was a limit to what she could spare. She still had board for Nikki's horse at the riding academy, rent and the usual bills, plus feed and hay for the horse at the farm.

"No charge," Alex said. "It's what we do."

She blinked, her gaze sliding over four stern faces. "But you have to make money. Living isn't free."

"It's not," Alex said. "But we're talking an evaluation here. Seth will figure out what kind of system you need, and we'll give you a price for that. The personal security aspect is free of charge. If you need us around the clock for months, that's different and we'll negotiate. But right now, it's part of the service."

A tremor shuddered through her. She wouldn't have to stay awake all night with her dad's old shotgun over her lap and one eye on the driveway and road beyond, praying she didn't nod off.

"Thank you. And thank you for believing me. I know I sound crazy thinking someone set a fire in a secure facility to get to me when I'm nobody important." She paused. "Maybe I am crazy. Maybe I'm just paranoid for no reason."

"Did a man get you a job and then pressure you for information about that job? And did he get angry when you didn't cooperate?" Chance asked.

"Yes," she said, her throat tight.

"Think you were justified in coming here then."

"We've heard crazier things," Blaze said. "It was smart of you not to dismiss your fears."

"If you want to wait here," Seth said as he pushed his chair back, "I'll go grab some things and join you in a few minutes."

Her pulse throbbed. "Of course. Whenever you're ready."

The men stood and each took time to lightly shake her hand and reassure her she'd done the right thing in coming to see them. She felt like she had, but the minute they walked out of the conference room and left her alone, doubts began to creep in.

The voice in her head whispered to her like raindrops on a boulder, wearing the surface away.

Nobody can help you. Run, run, run.

Run. Before he finds you….

She was on the verge of obeying when the redhead named Daphne walked in with a smile on her face and two hot cups of coffee in her hand.

"I thought you might like something while you wait. We have tea if you'd prefer."

Tension gripped her body in icy talons, but she forced herself to smile. "Coffee's fine. Thank you."

She thought Daphne would leave, but she didn't. She pulled out a chair and sat. "Have you been in town long?"

Callie wrapped chilled hands around the mug. "A few months."

"Me too. I was passing through when my car kinda gave up the ghost. The guys offered me a job, and here I am."

Callie took a sip and tilted her head to look at the pretty woman opposite. "They were worried I was going to run out the door, weren't they?"

Daphne nodded and gave her a grin. "They kind of have an instinct for it."

"So you're here to make sure I don't leave?"

"I can't stop you if you want to go. But I can tell you that without these guys looking out for me, I'd have made a lot of mistakes that might have landed me in more trouble than I could handle. But they took one look at me and pulled me into the fold. Gave me a place to stay, food, and security. They're good men. I thought you should know that."

Callie's throat tightened. "I appreciate you saying so." She hesitated. "I don't think Seth likes me, though. He was kind of a dick when I met him before. I wish it was one of the other guys I was waiting for."

Daphne snorted. "Poor Seth. He's so gorgeous to look at, but he's perpetually grumpy. If I had to label him, I'd call him the serious one. He doesn't say a whole lot. He watches though. I don't think he misses much. But don't take the grumpiness personally. He's like that with everyone."

"I'll try not to then."

She suspected it was going to be easier said than done. Especially when the man in question showed up a couple of minutes later wearing a scowl.

"You ready?" he asked.

Callie got to her feet. "Yes."

"Let's go then."

He strode out the door, leaving her to follow him. She shot a look at Daphne, who shrugged and smiled apologetically. "Perpetually grumpy. Told you so. Just remember his bark is worse than his bite."

Chapter Six

Seth strode over to the silver Toyota Sequoia sitting in the parking lot and turned to watch Callie walk toward him. The uncertainty on her face had him taking a mental step back, reminding himself he needed to be friendly. Approachable.

He'd done a good job of it in the conference room, but his guys had been there for back up. He'd been congratulating himself on getting her to talk when Ghost chose him to accompany her home.

Not what he wanted to do. He wanted to be on his laptop, searching the dark corridors of the web for information on Mikhail Volkov and the other two Russians. And her connection to them.

But Ghost had pointed out—rightfully—that Callie was a programmer and he was a hacker, and that meant he was the right man to go with her. Check out her place, see if there was anything suspicious. Break into her computer when he got a chance.

He could do it easily, but in order to do it he had to spend time with her. Be nice. Personable.

It wasn't that he couldn't be personable. He could.

But he wasn't all that good at the polite banter that meant nothing. He never had been. When it was better to be quiet so that nobody noticed you, you learned to be quiet. You learned to sit at the dinner table and not say anything so the grandparents who resented getting stuck with you wouldn't send you to bed still hungry. Which they often did anyway because they said you ate too much. Cost too much.

You learned to be quiet so your grandmother wouldn't call you a burden and a drain on her golden years.

You learned to be quiet so your grandfather wouldn't take a swig of his beer and glare at you, muttering about making a man of you.

You kept your mouth shut and said nothing, praying you'd get the hell out of there someday.

"Do you need to stop anywhere before we go to your place?" he asked, shoving aside thoughts about his damaged childhood. Couldn't change it, did no good to dwell on it. They were dead now anyway.

"The farmer's co-op. I have to pick up another bag of feed and some fly spray."

"Okay." He pointed at his maroon Ford F-150. "I'll follow you there. You need help loading it?"

Her eyes were too big in her face. He wished she'd stop looking scared so he could stop caring that she did. She *could* be the enemy, the leak. Helluva convoluted game she was playing if so, but he knew from his years in Special Ops that anything was possible.

"No, the guys will load the feed. But thank you."

"You're welcome."

His voice was gruff, and she gave him a confused look before reaching for her door handle.

"Anywhere else you need to go?" he added. "Lunch in town? The grocery store? The pharmacy?"

She turned green eyes on him, her glossy hair swaying. She tucked it behind her ears on both sides, something he'd noticed she did frequently. "I don't need anything, but if you want me to stop at the store to pick up things you like while you stay with us, I'm happy to do so."

He waved a hand in dismissal. "It's okay. I'm good."

"You don't even know what I have. What if we're vegans?"

Was she joking with him? He wasn't sure. Best not to laugh in case she got insulted by it. "I'll order pizza. Or one of my guys will drop off some barbecue or a burger from the Dawg. I'll figure it out."

"Good to know." She swung her door open and climbed inside the Toyota. He waited a moment, thinking he should say something else, but in the end he walked away and got into his truck.

He followed her to the co-op, watching as she got out of the SUV and went inside. When she returned, one of the young men who worked there had a bag of horse feed slung over his shoulder. Callie was talking to him. Seth had observed that she had a habit of using her hands to gesture. When she wasn't deliberately holding them flat on the conference table, staring at her fingers instead of making eye contact.

She gave the man a big smile and a thank you as he put the feed in the cargo area for her. He didn't look in any hurry to walk away as he stood there talking and smiling. Seth was about to lay on the horn when Callie turned and walked to the driver's side door.

The man watched her go, his gaze most definitely sliding to her ass. Seth didn't give two shits if the guy found her attractive, so why was there a hot feeling in his chest again?

Must be acid reflux. Wasn't that something that made your chest burn?

Callie backed out and Seth followed her to the road. She hung left and headed south until she took another left on a dirt road that wended between cotton fields, making its way to a thick stand of trees on a small hill. A house and barn appeared once they drove beneath the trees.

There was a field behind the barn. A horse grazed in the pasture, its tail sweeping back and forth to brush away the flies.

He didn't like how isolated she was out here. Not at all. He'd thought Rory Harper's place was isolated, but this property took it up a notch. The only buildings they'd passed for the last two miles had been an abandoned building and a farmer's house that sat back off the road.

Seth turned off the truck and went to help her as she tried to wrestle the bag of feed from the back of her Sequoia.

"I got it," he said, reaching for the fifty-pound sack and slinging it over his shoulder the way the man at the co-op had.

Callie frowned up at him. "I was going to get the wheelbarrow. I was just trying to pull the bag closer to the edge."

"Now you don't have to. Tell me where to put it."

"This way."

He followed her to the barn, watching her ass the way the other man had. It was a nice ass, shapely, though the baggy jeans she wore fooled a man at first. Made him think there were no curves under there when there were plenty. Her white T-shirt wasn't as baggy as the jeans, though. He could definitely see the swells of her breasts beneath the fabric.

She led him to a room in the interior of the barn. It was dark and musty, but he supposed that was just how barns smelled. He'd been in a few, usually while on missions or when they'd been helping Rory at her farm, but he didn't know the first thing about horses.

"You can put it in that wheelbarrow. We still have some other feed to use first."

He tossed the sack down and turned to face her. A shaft of light speared through the slats, tickling her in dust motes that swirled around her head. She looked young. He knew she was twenty-six, because he'd learned everything he could about her, but in that moment she looked even younger.

Made him feel like an old man at the ripe age of thirty-four. He almost felt guilty for noticing her ass and tits in that moment, but he pushed the feeling away. She was old enough, and he wasn't dead. Like he'd told Kane.

"You just have the one horse?" he asked.

"Here, yes. That's Charlie. But my sister has another horse in training at a hunter-jumper stable in Madison. His name is Jack."

"Why two?"

"Because Charlie was Nikki's first horse and she's attached to him. But Jack is what she needs for the next level of competition." She sighed, dropping her gaze a moment. "When our parents died, I couldn't take the horses away from her. It'd be easier with one, but the kid's been through enough. So Charlie lives here and she gets to love on him, but she goes to Madison three to four times a week to practice on Jack. More when there's a competition coming up."

He could hear the love in her voice. The concern. Whatever Callie Crowell might be, she cared about her sister's well-being. He'd never had anyone who cared about him that much. Maybe his mother had, but she'd died when he was three. He'd gone to live with his dad's parents a year later when his dad washed his hands of having a kid and abandoned him on their doorstep.

"Does she enter many competitions?"

"A few. Not as many as she'd like, because they're expensive and time-consuming, though she has one next weekend. She still has to get good grades, or I've told her no horses. She grumbles but she does it. She wants to be a horse-trainer someday. I haven't told her it's not an easy profession. There's time enough for disillusionment later."

"Do you ride?"

"I did when I was her age. There's ten years between us, but we rode at the same stable the last few years I was in high school. Nikki started lessons at five."

"Did you compete?"

She nodded. "I was state champion three years in a row. I loved it, but then you grow up and realize that life is harder as an adult and you don't have as much time. I went to college to study software engineering, programming, and languages, then went to work for the government. How about you?"

He was so focused on asking her questions that he hadn't anticipated her turning the tables on him. "I joined the military at eighteen and I've been there since. Took an early retirement to come here with my bros."

"So you guys are close then."

"We are. Did time in special forces together." He didn't say Special Ops because that was too much information. Too specialized. "Always dreamed of opening our own business, and here we are."

"Why Sutton's Creek?"

"Because it's close to Huntsville and Redstone Arsenal, and because we found the perfect place to open the range and training facility."

"Makes sense."

The sound of an engine approaching at speed reached into the barn. Callie went still, then pressed her hand to her mouth and coughed. Seth watched her as he planned what to do if the visitor turned out to be unfriendly.

"You need a dog," he said when she stopped coughing. "First priority."

"What? No." She shook her head, her voice hoarser than it was a few moments ago. "I don't need a dog to take care of on top of a horse."

"Yeah, you need a dog. One that'll scare motherfuckers off if they think to bother you out here. Don't tell me a dog won't be easier than a horse, either."

"I'm not saying that, but I have enough responsibilities as it is."

"I'm not talking about a fucking lapdog, Callie. I'm talking a big dog. You can let it out to take a piss and not worry it's gonna get snatched by a hawk."

"No, I—"

Seth lifted a hand to silence her as the crunch of tires on gravel got louder. She nodded and he put a hand on his sidearm as he walked to the front of the barn. A red station wagon with a US Mail sign on the roof appeared between the trees and pulled up next to his truck.

Callie breathed a sigh behind him. "It's just Bonnie. She's probably bringing a package that won't fit in the box."

He didn't stop her as she breezed past him and headed toward where a gray-haired woman leaned out the window with a handful of mail.

"Got a package for you, doll," she said as Callie approached. "Take this stuff first and I'll hand it to you."

Callie took the mail and waited. Seth strolled out of the barn, heading for his truck so he could grab his computer and the few things he'd brought. He'd go pack some clothes later, but right now he wanted to get the lay of the place.

Bonnie turned back to Callie, holding a small Amazon box. Her smile went from a hundred watts to a thousand when she saw him.

"Well, well. If it isn't one of Sutton's Creek's newest residents. Which one are you, gorgeous?"

"Seth King, ma'am."

Bonnie winked. "That's right. The strong, silent one. Nice to see you making friends."

Seth didn't know what to say. Callie's cheeks were red as she took the package. "I'm thinking about putting up some cameras to keep an eye on Charlie," she blurted. "When we're not home. Seth is here to give me an estimate."

Bonnie looked disappointed. Then she grinned again before she threw her station wagon in reverse. "You never know, sweetie. Met my Vernon at the gas station. He was on his way back to Decatur after finishing a plaster job for Judy Simpson over at the Bee, but he needed to fill up. I was a cashier back then. Love at first sight. Been married almost fifty years."

She backed up at speed, whipped the wheel, and waved before speeding off down the drive. Callie stared after her, package in hand, as if she was trying to think of an answer that was already too late.

"You want to show me the house?"

She jerked her gaze toward him. "Oh. Right. Of course."

She hurried away and Seth followed. He was supposed to be thinking about where to put cameras. Instead, he was thinking about the way the light had caressed Callie's face in the darkness of the barn.

And wondering what the rest of her would look like with nothing but sunlight stroking soft fingers over her skin.

Chapter Seven

CALLIE PICKED UP HORSE MAGAZINES AND A SHOW PROGRAM
that were scattered across the coffee table. There was a
glass on the end table, too. Not hers, but Nikki's. She
picked it up, clutching it to her as she turned to Seth.

"Sorry. Nikki isn't the neatest kid on the planet. But
neither was I at her age."

Life and cares had worn her down, made her conscious
of her surroundings in a way she hadn't been as a spoiled
kid who had everything. The furniture she'd bought when
they'd moved here wasn't expensive, not like what she'd
grown up with. There were no original oil paintings on the
walls, no custom fabrics, no high-end antiques. Her mother
would be horrified.

Then again, everything she had, she'd paid for. It'd be
a shame to leave it all behind, but what choice did she
have?

Seth only nodded. She didn't know if that meant he
understood or he didn't care. Heat flared. She didn't know
how to handle having him in her space. It was too much,
and yet it was necessary too.

She cleared her throat and went to the kitchen to deposit the glass, along with her package that she knew held scrapbooking supplies. The kitchen, at least, was clean. She'd done that before she'd driven over to One Shot Tactical.

A current of dread snaked through her. Too late now. She'd made the choice to go, and she'd told them far more than she'd intended. It'd been impossible not to.

When she returned to the living room, it hit her how out of place this man looked. Like a Hollywood heartthrob had somehow gotten lost and ended up in the back end of nowhere.

His body was honed, his muscles damn near swoon-inducing. He wore the One Shot navy polo that clung to his chest and arms like a lover. There wasn't an ounce of fat hanging over where his shirt was tucked into his jeans. His waist was trim, and his faded jeans hugged his hips and crotch in a way that made a girl think naughty thoughts.

She did not need to be thinking naughty thoughts about this man. She needed to be figuring out how to get the hell out of town fast.

But it'd been so damn long since she'd gotten busy between the sheets. She and Mikhail had never, thank God. Not that she hadn't wanted to when they'd first met, but he'd never made the move. She'd thought he was just adorably old-fashioned. It'd never occurred to her that he'd had an ulterior motive that wasn't about having a relationship with her. Not that there'd been sparks, but she didn't really believe in them anyway. That was a romance novel thing, not real life.

Seth was looking at a framed picture of her, Nikki, and their parents. They'd gone to Disney that year and they were all wearing mouse ears. She'd been seventeen, Nikki seven. It was one of the most fun trips they'd ever taken as a family.

He turned his attention to her, and her heart thumped. Hard. Why did he have to be so damned beautiful?

Those eyes were intense as he gazed at her. Maybe she'd been staring too long. Callie cleared her throat.

"The house has four bedrooms and two full baths. You can tell which ones Nikki and I are using, so you're welcome to whichever of the other two you prefer."

"Thanks. I'll settle in after I do a sweep."

She frowned as she thought of her sister walking through the door later today. Nikki had been an outgoing kid until the accident that claimed their parents. Now she was far more reserved. Wary. She wasn't going to like having someone she didn't know in the house. And then there was the problem of the gun on his hip. It was ominous.

"I don't know what to tell Nikki about you."

"Why not the truth?"

Callie shook her head. "And scare her half to death? No. No way. She's been through so much already. I'm not telling her about… what's going on."

She couldn't say Mikhail's name again, not here. What if he was listening? He could have planted a device when she was at work. Oh God, if he was listening now….

She picked up her phone and typed in the words, turning it to show Seth. If Mikhail was listening, then he'd already heard what they'd said. Panic clawed into her. Why hadn't she considered it before?

Seth calmly reached into his backpack where he'd dropped it on the floor and pulled out a small black box. "I've jammed any signals. Nobody's listening. If he's put microphones or cameras in your house, I'll find them. But right now, he's not getting any information from them."

Relief was a tsunami inside her. "I guess I didn't give you enough credit. I'm sorry."

His expression didn't soften an inch. "You aren't the security professional, Callie. I am. Trust me, I've got this." He tucked the jammer away and straightened. "As for your sister, I don't know what to tell you. That's not my area of expertise."

"I'll think of something. But, uh, could you maybe not wear the gun so openly?"

"I'll put it in a concealed holster. Will that work?"

She hadn't thought he would agree so easily. "Yes, thank you."

He nodded. "I'm gonna get on with the sweep now. Unless there's something else you want to say?"

"No, it's fine. Sorry to interrupt."

"I need to go into every room. Is this a problem?"

She didn't think Nikki would like anyone in her room without her permission, but it couldn't be helped. "Do what you need to do."

He didn't acknowledge her as he went over to one of the windows at the front of the living room and flipped the lock open and closed. He did it to the rest of the windows then gave her a brief nod and disappeared down the hallway.

Her breath left her like a slow leak from a tire until she found herself sitting on the edge of a chair. What the hell was she going to tell Nikki about this giant of a surly man squatting in one of the spare rooms for a few days? Even concealing his weapon, he wasn't capable of pretending to be anything other than what he was, which was a man primed for protecting others from violence. Maybe even committing some himself.

Who was she kidding? There was no maybe. He was

definitely capable and no doubt had. How did you get to be a security professional if you couldn't fight back?

You didn't. The man had certainly been involved in violence in his life. Many times if she had to guess.

Which was a good thing for her since Mikhail wouldn't shrink from it in pursuit of his goals. She wouldn't have believed it until last night, but now she did. Down to her bones, she knew he'd been behind the fire. A warning shot across the bow. One last chance to dance to his tune.

Callie shoved those thoughts into a box for now. They didn't solve her problem about what to tell Nikki about Seth. The truth was out of the question because she didn't want her sister to withdraw again. If Nikki knew that Callie might be in danger, it'd wreck all the progress she'd made over the past few months. Losing Mom and Dad had been devastating. To know her only remaining family might be in trouble too?

Callie couldn't do that to her. But how could she lie? Their parents had spent a lifetime lying about their circumstances. The shock of dealing with creditors, of finding out how their lives had been built on a house of cards these past few years—it'd been devastating to deal with on top of their untimely deaths. There'd been so many calls from creditors. So many inquiries about repayment.

Her parents had stopped paying their life insurance premiums years ago. They hadn't made provisions for Nikki at all. It still made Callie mad, and it made her feel guilty for being mad. They couldn't have known they weren't going to make it off that mountain.

But that didn't change the fact they shouldn't have been there in the first place because they couldn't *afford* the trip.

"Locks are all functional," Seth said as he walked back

into the room. He stopped at the look on her face. Callie worked to ease the tension and smile.

"That's a good thing, right?"

"What's wrong?"

Callie blinked. "I, uh…. Nothing. Why?"

He tipped his chin toward her. "You've wrapped your arms around your body, and you look upset. Why?"

She dropped her arms. She could make light of it, tell him he was wrong, but it was too much effort to pretend. So she didn't.

"I was thinking about my parents. And how hard it's been for Nikki. I don't want to lie to her about what's going on, but I don't see another way."

She'd have to tell her sister soon enough. Like when it was time to leave town. There was no way she could tell Nikki about that plan before it happened. She couldn't take the risk of her intentions getting out. Of Mikhail knowing.

"So what kind of lie would she believe? You could tell her we're dating, but she'd see through that since you haven't mentioned me before and I'm suddenly moving in. I could be an old friend from college or another job, but that's not going to work because everyone in town knows everything about everyone, and they know I've been here for months. Someone would mention it to her at some point. I don't know shit about horses, so I'm not here for any horse stuff either."

He wasn't wrong. None of those were options. Though her mind was hung up on the dating for some reason. The idea of being romantic with him…

Stop.

She frowned, thinking. "What if you need a temporary place to stay? There's a leak in your ceiling and you can't stay in your place while they fix it. We know each other from my work because you were there, and I said you could stay here with us while the repairs were being done."

"There's nowhere else I could go? Really?"

"Work with me here, dude. I'm trying. You have a better idea?"

He tilted his head back and sighed as if he were the most put-upon person on planet earth. "Fine. If you think that works. I have a leak at my place—"

"No," she said, snapping her fingers. "Lead paint. You live in an old house, and you've got lead paint. You can't stay there while they scrape it off."

"Okay. Lead paint. Whatever trips your trigger."

"It's the best option. You still get to be who you are, you're still going to advise us on cameras so we can keep an eye on Charlie, plus the security system in the house because why not, and that's that. But we have to be friendly. You can't do that silent, moody thing you do all the time."

His eyebrows arrowed down. "Just because somebody doesn't talk a lot of nonsense doesn't make them moody."

Callie huffed a sigh. "I know that, but Nikki's a teenager. Trust me when I tell you she's moody. And whether you are or not, you look like you are because you don't smile much or say a lot." She waved a hand around. "Just act like you like me, okay? Like we're friends—or friendly anyway. If all you do is frown, she's going to know something's wrong."

He forced a smile. "Better, friend?"

"You aren't going to make this easy, are you?"

He looked genuinely surprised. "What? I'm smiling, aren't I?"

"With attitude," she grumbled. "Just pretend to be friendly when I introduce you and then go do whatever you do, okay? You don't have to hang out with us."

"Wasn't planning on it," he said, grabbing his backpack, shouldering it. "If you're done telling me how to arrange my face, I've got work to do."

"I wasn't..." She sighed, frustration hammering into her. Didn't matter what she said because he was already walking down the hall toward the bedrooms.

Daphne said he was grumpy with everyone. But Callie knew, like she knew how to write her own name, that he was extra grumpy with her.

Chapter Eight

Seth chose the room at the front of the house because it was best for seeing who might be coming up the driveway. It was a small room, with a twin bed that wasn't going to be long enough for his frame, but if that was the worst he had to endure, it was still better than long nights in dark, cold, disgusting places while waiting to capture or kill a nest of tangos.

Callie's room was across the hall, surprisingly. She hadn't taken the main bedroom with its own bath but instead had given it to her sister. The main bedroom was an addition at the back of the house. The hall turned to the left after the bathroom next to Callie's room. Nikki's was at the end of it. The other spare bedroom was down that hall, before getting to the main. It was also small so maybe that's why Callie had chosen the one she had instead of being closer to her sister.

He'd gone into all the rooms to check the windows and any doors that provided access to the outside. He knew their layouts and what kind of personal belongings each woman had. Callie had a feminine streak that included a lacy bedspread and roses peppered throughout the decor, whether dried, fake, or part of the many pictures on the walls. Nikki's room was also feminine, but more horsey than rosy.

Hell, no matter which security system Callie put in, there wasn't enough time for emergency responders to make it out this far before an intruder had done whatever they came to do. If Mikhail Volkov wanted to silence Callie, he could do it and be gone before the first cop arrived.

Seth sat back on the bed, crossing his ankles, and fired up the laptop. He still wasn't sure if Volkov really wanted Callie dead or if the whole thing was a con, but that's what he was here to find out. The rest of the guys seemed to have decided Callie wasn't on the wrong side—or at least they leaned strongly that way—but Seth couldn't dismiss her as easily. He had to be sure.

He didn't choose Callie's Wi-Fi network when it popped up. Instead he used his phone and the secure network he'd configured. He used a VPN, because he always did, and logged onto the hidden site where he derived information from a network of contacts. There were no messages waiting for him so he left and returned to the site where he could search records that most people didn't even know existed.

He typed in *Abram Fedorov*. It took a shit-ton of time and a few more rabbit holes, not to mention a lot of masking his trail, but he found what he was looking for. Fedorov was SVR, or foreign intelligence, for the Russian Federation.

Not a big surprise, really. Of course the Russians were snooping around Huntsville. Along with every other foreign nation on the planet.

He suspected Smirnov was the same. He'd save that

search for later, but the record on Fedorov indicated he'd been part of a dead-double operation for the past couple of years. Wilhelm Olkowicz, the real Polish national, was likely dead and had been for some time. In live-double operations, the agent assumed the identity of a living person who had no idea what was going on. But there was nothing on Olkowicz anywhere beyond what already existed, and much of that had been Fedorov assuming the identity in Poland and pretending to be a student. He expected he'd find the same with Cyril Dyka and Dima Smirnov.

Seth shoved a hand through his hair and stared at the green landscape beyond his window. The house sat on a small rise, surrounded by a stand of trees, but he could glimpse the fields beyond whenever a breeze ruffled the lower branches of the trees. Half a mile to the road, at least. Another eight to town.

One Shot Tactical was closer. Six miles away. Might as well be in Siberia for all the good it would do if someone attacked Callie and Nikki out here. *If* the threat was real.

He wasn't saying it wasn't, not with the SVR involved, but he also wasn't willing to move Callie into the innocent victim column yet either. He still needed to find out if she had any connection to the Russians.

Seth navigated back to the hidden bulletin board and left a query worded in such a way that it would catch the right eyes. If there was more information on Fedorov or Smirnov, he'd find it.

That left Volkov. Seth went hunting for him, making encrypted notes to share with his team later. There wasn't much that stood out, but he was able to find photos and a driver's license. Volkov was ordinary on paper. An American citizen, like Callie said, who spoke fluent Russian, Polish, Ukrainian, and Mandarin.

Interesting lineup.

Volkov had spent time in the foreign service but now worked as a translator for a private company called the Dashevsky Group, which is how he was in Poland when he met Callie. The Dashevsky Group specialized in foreign relations and had branches all across Europe and Asia. They were involved in humanitarian work such as building homes for displaced populations and running refugee camps for people fleeing oppression and war. If there was political unrest, the Dashevsky Group was there, preparing for a humanitarian crisis.

As a Hostile Operations Team operator, he'd encountered those kinds of groups before. They were people doing the things nobody else wanted to do, trying to stabilize areas before more people died. Most of them meant well. Not all of them knew what they were doing, which added to the pressure of whatever was going on in the area they occupied.

Seth didn't know anything about the Dashevsky Group. He'd never had dealings with them or crossed paths with any of their operations when he'd been an operator. He grabbed the information, along with the photos of Volkov and a copy of his driver's license, and saved it to an encrypted file. Then he logged out of all the places on his laptop, wiped his trail, and closed the lid.

He didn't fucking know why they were here anymore. President Willis and her team had access to more information than Seth did, but they rarely shared it. Like the mission to Griffin Research Labs to test their security and gain access to their systems. It'd gone as planned, but all the work they'd had to do took time they could have used elsewhere if the chief of staff would have sent the fucking files on all the scientists attached to the Athena Project.

Instead, Seth's team had spent long hours maintaining

a cover and carefully rigging their own access to not only the personnel files, but also to the top-secret Athena command and control system. Access that was now in the toilet, thanks to Callie and her shadowy would-be assassin.

At least until the Wi-Fi went back online at the lab and Seth could determine if his hack was still active.

His stomach growled, and he glanced at his watch. It was nearly one. No wonder he was hungry. He still needed to grab some things from the house where he stayed with Ghost. He'd told her his guys would bring food if he wanted it, but that was before he'd realized how far out in Bumfuck, Alabama, her place was. Probably did need to stop at the Pig and pick up some food for the next few days so he wasn't relying on Callie to feed him or asking his team to bring him things.

He followed the strains of gentle piano music to the kitchen where Callie sat at the table with a bunch of scraps of paper, some photos, and a boatload of different colored pens. Looked like she had tape, too. And glue sticks. What the fuck?

She looked up, seemingly startled to find him standing there, then reached for the portable speaker to turn the music down. "Sorry," she said. "Was it too loud?"

The woman was daft. And adorably geeky in that moment. Her dark hair was in a messy knot on top of her head and a pair of owlish glasses were perched on her face. She was holding a pair of tweezers with a piece of paper in it and blinking at him as if embarrassed he'd found her playing with scraps.

"No. What are you doing?"

There was a stack of books at her elbow and little paper cut-outs of the book covers arrayed on the table, ready to paste into her book.

"I, um, I keep a reading journal when I have time. It's relaxing."

"A reading journal?"

She nodded, fanning her hand over the table. "Yes. I've done so since I was a teenager. I have them all. I keep track of the books I'm reading, what I thought about them, favorite quotes. Things like that."

He was astounded. "Why?"

She frowned. "You're just full of questions, aren't you? Because I *like* doing it. It's relaxing."

"Doesn't look relaxing. You've got paper and glue everywhere."

"I'm catching up on this year's journal. I haven't had a lot of time to work on it lately." She pasted the piece of paper perched in the tweezers into the journal and put the tweezers down. "It keeps my mind off other things."

"Why not just write down your thoughts and move on?"

She arched a brow. "I could, but then it wouldn't be pretty. I like things to be pretty."

He thought of all the roses and lace in her bedroom. It was overwhelmingly feminine. Not what he'd expected when he'd opened the door, that's for sure.

"How did you get into programming?"

She took off her glasses and set them on the table. He noticed she only wore them when doing intense detail work, like on the computer—or, apparently, messing around with scraps of paper.

"That was *not* what I expected you to say." She huffed a breath. "I got into it for a few reasons. One, I'm good at math and I'm detail-oriented. Two, I wanted a job that was in demand when I graduated from college. Three, as much as I wanted to be a professional book reader and journal creator, there's not a market for that. I needed to actually be able to make a living and pay bills. You know, like an adult. Why do you ask?"

He waved a hand at the table. "Seems like you'd rather be an artist."

"Programming is artistry if you do it right. It's just not pretty on the backend. But what you make with it? Now that can be very pretty."

He supposed he couldn't argue with that.

"How about you?" she pressed. "Did you want to be a book cover model but security pays better?"

"A what?"

"Romance novels usually feature a hot guy with his shirt off. It was a joke."

Now he was confused. Was she calling him hot? Or was she saying he wasn't hot and that was the joke?

"I wanted to get the hell out of my grandparents' house. The best way was to join the military, so that's what I did."

There was more to the story about why he'd joined, but he didn't tell anyone that part of it. The part that made him wake up in a cold sweat sometimes.

Her expression softened. "Oh. I'm sorry."

"Nothing to be sorry about. They were assholes."

"I see. And, um, the military prepared you for this career?"

"You could say that." His stomach growled again, and her gaze dropped to his belly. "Yeah, I was thinking about lunch. Can't leave you here alone, so you want to go with me, get a bite at the Dawg? Then I'll swing by the house and pick up some clothes, stop at the Pig for some groceries."

She glanced at her scrapbook shit.

"I should add that it's not really a request. Either you go with me, or I stay here and raid your pantry."

"Guess I can't say no then. Not that I'm bothered by you raiding the pantry. I tend to shop for the apocalypse just so you know. Not that I was always like that, but since coming home and getting custody of Nikki, I've turned into someone who fears not having enough to feed us." She closed her eyes for a second. "And you don't want to hear this. I apologize for the word vomit, but I'm nervous. I talk a lot when I'm nervous."

"Why are you nervous? Did something happen? Did you get a message from Volkov?"

She shook her head. "No, nothing like that. *You* make me nervous. Sorry, but there it is."

He was shocked. "I'm the good guy, Callie. You don't have to be nervous around me. I want to keep you safe. It's my job."

"I..." She sighed, her hands moving in front of her face, and he knew she was about to say something she found uncomfortable. "I don't think you like me much. And you don't have to," she blurted, her hands waving around. "Honestly, why should you have to? We just met. But you don't say a lot, and I feel like you don't really want to be here and maybe you blame me for showing up today and telling you my fears about Mikhail. And I don't know if I'm right, not really, and maybe this whole thing is a waste of your time."

"You done?"

Her mouth flattened into a line. But her eyes were still soft. Still wounded. "Yes. Done. Once more, I'm sorry for the word vomit."

Seth dragged in a breath and dug deep. He didn't do emotions well, but he knew he had to say something to soothe her fear. "You're right, I don't know you. Which means I have no opinion on whether or not I like you. You seem nice enough. You love your sister, probably gave up a lot to take care of her. You're twenty-six, but you don't have a regular social life because you have a kid at home to look out for. Lots of people your age are partying and making bad decisions, but here you are, pasting shit in a journal like you're sitting around a table at the senior center, talking scrapbooking with a bunch of retired ladies."

A corner of her mouth quirked.

"I don't talk a lot," he continued. "Because I learned that listening yields more information in the long run. I've spent the past sixteen years hanging out with a bunch of guys in deserts and jungles. I can talk a woman out of her panties when I want to, and I can talk about the weather, but I don't see the point in it. Not the panties—definitely a point to that."

The pupils of her eyes enlarged. He wondered if she was turned on by the idea of him talking women out of their panties. Or maybe she was imagining him talking her out of hers.

And, shit, that thought made his balls tighten. She was pretty and she had nice tits. He thought she might have a nice ass under those loose-fitting jeans, too. He'd glimpsed one earlier if he wasn't mistaken. Plus her legs were long, though she wasn't very tall. Five foot six, max.

But they'd wrap around his waist and hold him in the cradle of her hips while he rocked into her.

Would she moan in his ear? Or was she more of a screamer? He'd bet she was a moaner. Soft, deep moans that got higher-pitched as she approached her climax.

Seth ruthlessly cut the thread of those thoughts. No. Fucking *no*. He wasn't getting naked with her when he didn't know if she was trying to sell out her country. He believed that less and less, but it was still possible. Which made her off-limits.

"Point being, don't take it personally if I don't say much to you. I don't say much to anyone unless I have to. My guys, their women—I'm comfortable with them. I don't have to think about it. But I have to think about what I say to you. Now, you ready for lunch or what? I've just word vomited a whole lot of shit because you made me, so the least you can do is let me go eat."

She ducked her head. He thought she was smiling as she started to push her paper scraps, glue, and glittery shit into neat piles. "Yes, I'm ready for lunch. Just let me clean this up first."

"Is it gonna take long? I'm expiring of hunger here."

She picked up her piles and dropped them in a plastic case with dividers. Then she snapped the case closed and stood. "Nope, not long. Who's driving?"

"I am."

Five minutes later, they were on the road. She didn't say anything and neither did he. But fuck-all if he wasn't trying to think of the right way to start a conversation all the way to town.

Chapter Nine

CALLIE WASN'T SURPRISED BY THE SILENT RIDE INTO TOWN. For once, it didn't make her uncomfortable. He didn't talk a lot. Not everyone did.

It was just that when a man looked like he did, she thought he'd be so mobbed by adoring men and women that he'd constantly be talking just to fend them off.

Not Seth, apparently. He probably growled and scowled, and they kept on going. She had. The first time she'd seen him at the lab, when he and his guys were conducting security tests, he'd been scowling. Kane and Chance were friendly when introduced. Seth had merely nodded with a clipped hello. She'd channeled what she'd hoped was her mother's cool expression when dealing with some of the mothers at the barn who'd always thought *their* precious little equestrian deserved more of the instructor's attention.

Nobody messed with Anna Crowell more than once. Callie swallowed the lump in her throat. God, she missed her parents. Flawed as they were, they'd loved their kids and wanted them to have the best. Why they'd thought that hadn't included life insurance, she didn't know. But she knew they hadn't let it lapse because they didn't care.

They were simply irresponsible. Something she hadn't realized until they were gone and she'd been faced with the wreckage of their spending.

Seth flipped a right into the One Shot Tactical range and drove around the side of the building to park there. "You can stay here if you want. I'll leave the truck running. Nobody's going to bother you. Or you can come inside. Your choice."

"I'll stay."

He nodded once and got out, then stood with his hand on the top of the door and gave her a look. She tried not to stare. Why was the paler underside of his arm so sexy? And why did the way his muscles corded make her mouth go dry?

"Lock the door and don't open it for anyone but me or one of the guys."

"I thought you said this was safe."

"It is. But you gotta do your part, which is not to open the door for a stranger on the off chance one shows up."

"I can do that."

"Good girl. And don't even think about driving away in my truck. I can cut the engine remotely, and then I'm gonna be pissed."

Her heart thumped. She wouldn't, but she'd certainly thought of running away the first time she'd been here today. The fact he knew it was a little uncomfortable if she were honest. Made her predictable. Was she predictable to Mikhail too?

"Why would I do that?"

"Don't know, but you got spooked earlier and you could get there again. Just don't take off without me."

"Not planning on it."

"Good."

He shut the door and swaggered toward the building. Callie watched his backside, the way it filled out his jeans, and then let her gaze slide down to his thighs. A moment later, he disappeared through the side door. She let her breath out slowly.

She wasn't going to drive away in his truck, but she'd looked up more information on how to disappear after Seth closed himself in the bedroom earlier. She'd read the steps, her heart sinking with every word.

Number one was travel alone to reduce the risk of being found out. Traveling with another person, especially a minor, could be a problem. She hadn't considered it since she had custody of Nikki, but people would notice her sister was gone. Maybe some of them would be worried enough to call the police.

Not good. But school would be out for summer in a couple of days. That meant the only people who'd notice Nikki's absence were the people at the stable. Callie could tell the trainer they were taking an extended vacation, move Charlie over there and pay for a couple of months board for both horses, and be long gone before anyone realized they weren't coming back.

The idea of leaving the horses put a knot in her stomach that wouldn't go away. Nikki would be heartbroken. As if she wasn't already.

But another point on the list was to get rid of possessions they couldn't carry with them. Horses were a big one. They were also supposed to leave personal identifiers like photos and journals behind. And Callie needed to sell her car because it was identifiable.

She could log off all her social media and delete the accounts. That wouldn't be hard. She could also clear the search information on her phone and computer. Getting Nikki to delete her accounts would be harder, but doable.

Callie closed her eyes and leaned her head against the back of the seat, her throat tight. Not just from smoke, either. There was so much more on that list, and it was overwhelming. But what choice did she have?

None.

She had to prepare, had to be ready to take off as soon as she could make it happen. She couldn't hold out for a miracle, and she couldn't do what Mikhail wanted her to do. She'd thought about it. Really thought about it.

But if she did it, he would own her. He would make her do worse and worse things until she either got caught or he decided to eliminate her. The project she was working on was critical to national defense. She didn't know everything, because it was on a need to know basis, but she knew enough to know that the Athena satellite was something big.

Something she didn't want Mikhail to compromise. She didn't know what his plans were, but thinking back on the way he'd talked about a better world seemed ominous instead of admirable to her now. There was a fine line between being passionate about something and being a fanatic.

Setting the lab on fire and threatening her was not the act of a person passionate for their cause. It was the act of someone willing to sacrifice lives to their cause. And that was another matter altogether.

She wanted to tell Seth everything, but she couldn't. He wasn't cleared. As nice as the One Shot Tactical guys were, none of them had the security clearance to discuss Athena. And what could they do about it anyway?

Nothing. They were a temporary solution, not the final answer to her problem.

Seth was back in less than five minutes and then they were driving toward the two farmhouses that sat on the property. He went to the bigger of the two and parked in front of it, then swiveled on the seat to look at her.

"Gotta grab some clothes and shit. You want to stay or go?"

Curiosity got the best of her. She wanted to see where he lived. How he lived. "Go."

Seth turned off the truck without another word and hopped out. She went around to the front and followed him up the steps. The farmhouse was old, white clapboard, with a wide porch that ran the length of the front. The door was off center. He took his phone out and did something on it before he unlocked the door. As if remembering her, he shot her a look.

"I disarmed the alarm system with my phone. You'll be able to do that once we set you up. You can check the cameras before you approach the house, but you'll also get alerts if anyone crosses in front of one."

"Sounds expensive."

"It's not." He stuck his key in the door and twisted the lock, then moved to the deadbolt and unlocked that one too. "You can grab cameras out of any big box store these days, and you can download the app to run them. You'll need your Wi-Fi working, but I can also set you up with a failover in case your primary goes down."

"Using a hotspot."

He opened the door and went inside, holding it for her so she could enter. "Exactly. I'm surprised you haven't set it up yourself. You're a programmer."

The living room was good sized, with original features like shiplap, wooden pocket doors, and wood casings around the windows. There wasn't much furniture. A couple of couches, a plain rug. Two lamps and a television that wasn't nearly as big as she'd have expected for men living alone.

She dragged her attention back to the conversation. "I write code for the government. I'm not an expert in security, other than what I need to know for keeping my work secure. But sure, I could probably figure out how to hook up some cameras and use them through an app. I wasn't thinking about any of that when I went to see you guys this morning. Then you offered to give me an estimate, Alex said someone would stay with me for a few days, and here we are."

"Here we are." He jerked his thumb at the staircase. "I'll be back in a few minutes. Don't go anywhere."

"Where am I going?"

He stopped on the first stair. "Where were you going this morning before I sent Daphne into the conference room?"

Her cheeks heated. "Home probably. Or maybe I'd have driven to the school, picked up Nikki, and hit the road so I could get far away from here."

"That wouldn't work."

Her stomach knotted. "Why not? People disappear."

"People who know what they're doing disappear. Those who don't simply run away. They're traceable though. Easily."

"You can find anything on the internet. Including how to disappear the right way."

"You can, but how do you know which information is right and which is wrong? Make the wrong choice and you're sunk. Think about it."

He disappeared up the stairs without waiting for an answer.

Callie's heart pumped faster as she folded her arms and walked around the room, peering at the books on one of the end tables to distract herself. Mystery fiction and some non-fiction about famous generals and admirals.

Make the wrong choice and you're sunk.

But what was the wrong choice? Besides not traveling alone?

And that wasn't a choice because she couldn't abandon Nikki.

The floor over her head creaked as Seth moved around. She was getting itchy, jumpy, waiting for him. Not that she feared Mikhail would come blazing in the door at any moment, but being alone in an unfamiliar place was amplifying her fear. She'd been alone last night in the lab, and she hadn't been afraid.

Until she couldn't get out. Now she was afraid and jumping at imagined shadows.

Seth had only been upstairs for a few minutes, but she had to keep moving, walking through the house. She went into the kitchen, her breath catching at the sight of original cabinets and wooden countertops.

The counters were scarred in places from years of people using knives to cut food on them and pots being set onto the surface. She'd grown up in a huge house in the suburbs, complete with a chef's kitchen that her mother almost never used, but her grandparents had lived in an old house with acreage when she was a little girl. After they'd passed away, her parents sold it, no matter how she'd cried and begged them to keep it.

She'd been twelve. Nikki had been two, not old enough to remember anything about their grandparents.

She ran her palm over the counter, remembering holidays spent baking cookies with Grandma. Summers spent watching Grandma prepare meals while Callie ate a PB&J sandwich sitting at the counter and thought about riding horses.

"You looking for something?"

Callie gasped as she whirled. "Oh my God, you scared me."

She hadn't heard him come down the stairs. Hadn't heard the squeaking of the floorboards or the creak of the stairs. *And that, missy, is how you end up dead.*

"Expected you to be in the living room. You looking for something?" he repeated.

The heat of embarrassment flooded her. "No, but I like old houses. I wanted to see if the kitchen was original or if it'd been gutted and rebuilt."

She didn't tell him she'd had to keep moving so she didn't freak out.

His gaze slid over the room, though she didn't miss the flicker of suspicion in his eyes. "Looks old to me."

"It is. Nobody's torn it out and replaced everything with shaker cabinets and granite. Yet."

He shrugged. "Don't think any of us actually care what it looks like so long as the fridge and stove work. If you're done poking around, I'm ready to head out."

She started to protest that she wasn't poking around. But what did it matter?

"I'm ready."

It was a short ride to town from the range and soon Seth was pulling into the parking lot behind a row of buildings that faced the town square and the park that lay in the center of it. Callie didn't get to town very often since she worked in the opposite direction. She usually stopped for groceries at the Piggly Wiggly or at a Publix nearer the Redstone Gateway complex where she worked.

Weekends were usually spent doing work projects at home and taking care of Charlie as well as going to watch Nikki take lessons on Jack. In the spring and summer, there were horse shows to attend. Callie didn't go to all of those since someone needed to feed Charlie. If they were within driving distance, she'd go. If they required an overnight, she had to stay home while Nikki stayed with one of the other girls and their mother. Nikki swore she didn't mind that Callie wasn't there, but Callie felt guilty about it.

"Figured we'd eat at the Dawg," Seth said by way of explanation. "Then we'll hit the grocery store before heading back to your place. Do we have enough time before your sister gets home?"

She looked at her phone. It was one-thirty. "She gets out of school in an hour, but she'll go to the stable to take a lesson before she comes home. I don't expect her before five."

Callie had just opened the door of the truck when a woman in a flowing black dress glided toward her. She knew from the cigarette hanging out of the woman's mouth, if not from the giant evil eye necklace, that this was Colleen Wright, proprietor of The Mystic Chick.

"Why hello, Miss Crowell," Colleen said. "I've been hoping to see you."

Callie blinked. "Um, hi."

"Hey there, Ms. Wright," Seth said, walking around the bed of the truck to come to her side. "How's it going?"

"Just fine, young man. Reba and I have been filming the alien craft with her new smartphone. Would you like to see sometime?"

"Uh, sure."

"Wonderful. Stop by the shop and I'll show you on the computer. Well, when I get it working. Damn thing."

"What's wrong with it?"

"I bought a new laptop, and I can't sign in. It keeps asking me for codes and pins and I don't know where to find them."

Callie felt Seth's resignation. "I can have a look at it for you. If you bring it over while we're eating lunch in the Dawg, I'll see what I can do."

"Oh, that'd be great. I'll get it. But before I go—" She fixed the full weight of her gaze on Callie. "Miss Crowell."

"Yes, ma'am?" she forced out.

Colleen's expression was filled with concern. She squeezed one of Callie's hands and it was all Callie could do not to cry. Which made no sense, but there it was.

"The spirits are restless, my dear. They need you to know it's okay to ask for help. To accept that help. And to accept what may come when you open yourself to possibilities."

A chill shivered down Callie's spine. "I've asked." She shot a glance at Seth. "And help arrived."

Colleen's smile was soft. "That's good, dear. Very good. Now don't forget the rest of what I said."

There was no way she could. "I won't. Thank you."

Colleen let her go and turned in a swirl of dark fabric. "You kids go get lunch," she called out as she marched toward her shop. "I'll be along in a few minutes with that damn computer."

Callie stared after the woman who smelled like stale smoke and perfume. She'd never been in The Mystic Chick, though Nikki had, but she'd seen Colleen from a distance. Talking to her was an entirely new experience, however.

"Is she always like that?" she asked, not tearing her gaze from Colleen's diaphanous dress floating in the breeze that stirred as she walked.

"Pretty much," Seth said with a sigh. "Batty as hell."

"And yet you agreed to fix her computer anyway."

"You think I'd say no? She talks to ghosts. And aliens. What if she talks shit about me and then the aliens decide to beam me up and do an anal probe? No thanks."

Callie could only gape at him. Then she burst out laughing. And for the first time since she'd met him, Seth's gorgeous mouth split in a grin that made her belly tighten and her breath almost stop in her chest.

"I'm shocked." She grinned back. "You *can* have fun."

He winked. "Not just a pretty face after all."

"Will wonders never cease?"

"That's me. Wonderful."

Callie shook her head, but she was amused. "Lead the way to lunch, Mr. Wonderful. I think you're probably light-headed with hunger by now."

He put a hand on his belly. "Damn skippy, babe. Now follow me and stay close. I go in first because that's how a protection detail works, got it?"

"Got it."

They headed for the back door of the tavern, and Seth went up the steps first. Callie was having a good time, despite the seriousness of why they were together. She could almost forget her life was in danger when Seth smiled at her.

Almost.

Callie was nearly to the top when she tripped and lost her balance. Her foot slipped off the stone riser and then she was somehow tumbling backward, both feet flying out from under her as she frantically tried to grab the railing.

But it wasn't enough. Her hand slipped from the wrought iron bar, her arms windmilling, her body tilting at a sharp angle.

Her last thought was that Mikhail didn't need to worry about killing her.

Because she was going to do the job for him.

Chapter Ten

SETH WAS IN MOTION THE INSTANT HE HEARD CALLIE scream. He whirled, grabbing for his gun, scanning the parking lot for danger.

In an instant, he realized the danger wasn't out there. It was Callie, who was rocketing toward the ground, her eyes wide and scared. Seth lunged, grabbing one of her flailing arms and jerking her toward him. She was lighter than he'd thought she would be. She flew forward, colliding with his body hard enough to make him grunt.

His arms went around her, and he instinctively turned her away from the stairs. From exposure. He managed to toe open the screen door, push the inner door, and pull her into the hallway that connected the back door to the bar. There was a set of stairs that went up to the second floor and a smaller hallway where the bathrooms were located.

It was dark in the hall compared to outside, and he couldn't see her eyes yet. That didn't stop him from pushing her into the wall, holding her against his body, and waiting for her trembling to subside.

"You okay?"

Her hands were curled into fists in his shirt and her breathing was ragged. She'd dropped her chin so she didn't have to look at him.

"Yes," she whispered.

"What happened?"

"Tripped and lost my balance. I'm kinda klutzy sometimes."

Seth's heart beat fast. Not as fast as hers, but more than usual. She'd scared the ever-loving fuck out of him. One minute they'd been walking into the Dawg, the warmth of laughter still a glow in his chest, and then she'd screamed.

He'd thought she'd seen Mikhail Volkov. That Volkov was lurking in the parking lot, a gun aimed at her heart. That she'd only seen him because he'd moved and sunlight had flashed off the weapon.

But no, she'd been hurtling for the ground. Backward, down six steps, where she'd been about to crash on concrete and hurt herself bad. If she didn't break her head open.

Son of a bitch, that'd been close.

He didn't move to let her go, and she didn't move to step away. They stood like that in the darkened hallway, the sound of classic rock drifting to them from the speakers inside the Dawg. Cool air swirled around them, and laughter occasionally reached down the hall. He almost resented it, like it was interrupting something important.

Callie shifted against him, her body coming in contact with his groin. He barely kept himself from hissing in a breath as blood flowed south of his belt. Surprise rattled around in his brain. Along with a healthy dose of need.

Callie Crowell was soft in all the right places. Her tits against his chest were round and firm. He let his hands skim her sides, the indent of her waist, the flare of her hips. He stopped just there, not missing the intake of breath that matched his a moment ago.

He could kiss her. Dip his head and take her lips. She would let him.

And maybe that was her plan. Let him get involved. Let him strip her naked and explore her curves until he was drunk on her. Until he couldn't be objective anymore.

Seth dragged in a centering breath and took a step back, breaking the contact between them. He put his hands on her shoulders, then tipped her chin up with a finger.

"You sure you aren't hurt? Scrape anything? Bang a knee?"

Her eyes were wounded. Confused. Then she shook her head. "It's okay. I scraped my hand trying to grab the railing, and I think my knee is bruised, but I'll be fine. I tripped on the stairs, that's all. My pride hurts worse than anything."

He shoved a hand through his hair. "Guess I need to let you go up any stairs in front of me, then put you to the side and do a sweep."

Which he probably should have done in the first place. Not that he'd truly intended to sweep the Dawg. He'd intended to walk in first, scan the joint, and go get a table. According to the info Seth had dug up earlier, Volkov was in Washington. Nowhere near Sutton's Creek.

Though it'd take him about twelve hours of driving, give or take, to get here. Seth had talked to Ghost earlier when he'd stopped by the range to tell him what he'd found. They needed phone records on Volkov and location information so they could get more detailed tracking information. Ghost had asked, but so far they didn't have anything.

Fucking DC bureaucrats.

"I'm sorry. I should have watched where I was going."

Seth frowned. "I'm not blaming you, Callie. Shit happens. Just thinking if you're as clumsy as you say, I need to make allowances for it. You break your head open on my watch, that's on me. It's nothing you did."

Her forehead crinkled. "That's nice of you, but believe me, I don't expect you to save me from myself. That's my job."

"Not gonna argue with you. I'm the protector, it's on me." He reached for her hand and tugged her to his side.

She came willingly, but not without some side-eye. "What are you doing?"

"Holding on so I can get you inside and seated without another incident. Now move your ass, honey."

She followed him into the Dawg, her hand anchored in his. Rory looked up from where she was wiping down the bar, smiling big when she saw him. There were a few folks at lunch, but the crowds had moved on at nearly two in the afternoon. They'd return for dinner, though. The Dawg was known far and wide for its menu, courtesy of Theo Harper, who liked to dabble. Besides bar staples like burgers and wings, Theo served up lunch and dinner specials. Today was meatloaf.

"Hey, Seth," Rory said, walking over to where he chose a table in a corner so he could observe everyone coming in and going out. Habit. Even more so with a client to be protected.

"Hey, Rory. How're you feeling?"

She put a hand to her belly. "Just peachy. Doc says my latest bloodwork is good. All is going as we hoped."

"That's fantastic, honey." He leaned in to kiss her cheek when she got close enough to hug him. Chance would box his ears if he were here to see it, but Rory was good people and sweeter than pie. And Seth adored her for making his friend so happy. "Do you know Callie Crowell?"

Rory stepped back to hold out a hand to Callie. "I think I've seen you in the Dawg a couple of times. I'm Rory Harper. My brother Theo and I run the place."

"Rory's engaged to Chance," Seth added. "And they've got a bun in the oven."

Rory swatted him with a bar towel. But she was laughing. "Adorable idiot. Yes," she said, returning her gaze to Callie. "We're expecting a bundle of joy. It's nice to meet you."

"Thank you. It's nice to meet you, too. And congratulations."

Rory beamed. "Thanks." She jerked her head at Seth. "So what are you doing with this dipshit? You look like a nice lady who could do a lot better than Mr. Tall, Dark, and Moody here."

Callie blushed. Interesting.

"We aren't a couple. Seth is giving me an estimate for a little security work. I guess I have to pay him in food for part of it."

Rory laughed. "Sounds about right. What can I get y'all to drink?"

Seth ordered a Coke and Callie asked for water. Rory handed them menus from a table nearby and went to get the drinks.

"I suggest the daily special," he told Callie. "Meatloaf and mashed potatoes with..." He gazed at the printed insert that listed the lunch specials. "Oooh, charred brussels sprouts with balsamic glaze. You don't want to miss that. Unless you don't like sprouts and then you still don't want to miss it because you *will* like them after you eat those."

Callie was looking at him with an arched eyebrow. "I'm

learning secrets about you. One, you're soft enough to fix an eccentric old lady's computer when you don't have to, which then makes you crack alien jokes. And two, food makes you chatty."

He sat back with a shrug. "You aren't wrong. I've got a soft spot for older people who don't understand computers, and I like to eat."

"That's really sweet," she said. "About older people and computers."

Uncharacteristic heat crawled its way up his neck. "We grew up with this stuff. Millennials have almost always had computers. Gen Z doesn't know anything else. And Gen Xers were still young enough to start having to use them at work when businesses started incorporating them. It's the Boomers and Silent Gen folks who have the most trouble. Not all of them. Many are just as good at computers as younger people. But the ones who never had to use them and then suddenly they can't make a doctor's appointment without going to a website and filling something out? It's fucking unfair to ask them to do that. To take away all the phone support and in-person support and demand they use a computer."

Shit, and now he'd said a mouthful. She was staring at him with her mouth slightly open. Hell, he couldn't believe he'd strung that many words together either. That was twice in one day he'd word vomited in front of her.

"You're right. I hadn't thought about it lately, but my grandparents weren't computer literate at all. I can't imagine Grandma trying to schedule a doctor's appointment online. If she had to do it alone with no help, she'd have given up."

"And wouldn't go to the doctor."

"No, probably not."

He sighed, shoving a hand through his hair. "It's a sore

spot with me, that's all. I've been standing in line at clinics where fucking military veterans, people who fought for this country, couldn't figure out how to access a link, and then some snotty assed dickhead behind the counter didn't want to help them. I help."

As if on cue, Colleen came breezing in the back door, her laptop clutched in one hand, a harried look on her face. "Thank you so much," she said as she handed it to him. "I really appreciate anything you can do. You're an angel."

"No guarantees, but I'll do my best. I just need—"

She waved her hands around. "Do whatever you want. You don't have to ask permission. I have to get back to the store. I'm expecting a call about an exorcism. Nasty little demon. Living in an antique wardrobe. Must dash!"

Seth and Callie both stared as Colleen disappeared as fast as she'd arrived. Seth laid the laptop down with a sigh. Without Colleen's email address or access to her phone for codes, it was going to take twice as long to get into the damned thing. He'd do it, though. Just required a bit of hacking.

"Is she serious?" Callie asked. "A demon in an antique wardrobe?"

"Pretty sure she is. She once interrogated me, Blaze, and Chance about if we'd bought any antiques or used furniture. Warned us not to. She said that's how a demon could get a foothold in your house. She never explained what to do if the house was already old or how to check for demons in those originals cabinets you liked so well."

Callie appeared to be biting the inside of her lip to hide a smile. "I don't know what to say."

"Best not even try. It makes sense to her and that's enough. I've learned not to ask questions."

Rory returned with their drinks. "Saw Colleen fly in and out again. What's going on?"

"Demon in a wardrobe," Seth said. "And her computer doesn't work." He pointed at the laptop on the table.

"Did she check it for a demon?"

"I'm going to assume she did. I'll say a prayer just in case."

Rory shook her head. "Just don't let it loose in here, okay? We don't need any more leaky pipes or crumbling plaster. Now did y'all decide what you want to eat?"

They ordered and Rory left to give the ticket to Theo. Seth popped open the laptop and booted it up. Predictably, it was stuck on a startup screen.

"Son of a bitch," he grumbled. But he tapped a few keys and got the computer to start in safe mode. Then he set to work bypassing a bunch of bullshit and getting it ready for Colleen to use.

Callie watched with interest as he monkeyed with the settings. "You're good with computers."

He shot her a look. "You thought I was just muscle?"

"No. I saw you with a computer at the lab a couple of weeks ago. But I thought you were just inputting data."

He typed a command to open a door into the OS. "Mostly," he lied. "But I've picked up a few things here and there."

She sipped her water through the straw. "I get lost in the work sometimes. I love to write new code. I thought this job would be that kind of thing, but it's not as much as I'd like. I write some, but it's mostly checking other people's code, finding the flaws in millions of lines of text. Like combing for a needle in a haystack sometimes."

The skin on his neck prickled. "Sounds interesting. What kind of code are you working on?"

She pulled in a breath as if to speak, then shook her

head. "I can't talk about it. I'm sorry. I shouldn't have said anything."

"Is that what Volkov wanted? For you to talk about it?"

Her gaze darted to the other patrons, but they were out of earshot. She didn't speak, though. She just nodded.

"But you didn't, so he tried to roast you."

"It was a warning."

"Hell of a warning."

As if to confirm it, she coughed, her face going red with the intensity. He was just about to get alarmed when she stopped, grabbing for her water and taking a swallow. "Damn it," she muttered.

"Do you talk to him in Russian or English?" Seth asked when she seemed okay again.

"Both. Why?"

He shrugged. "No reason. I only speak English, so I wondered what it's like. If you have to think about it or if it just happens."

She sighed, spread her hands on the table. "It mostly just happens. But Russian is harder. I have to think more. Polish and English are like breathing. My mom spoke exclusively Polish to me when I was little, my dad English. They wanted me to learn. By the time Nikki came along, they were a lot more lenient."

"They didn't do the same with her?"

"They weren't as deliberate about it. Nikki is fluent, but she relies more on English, especially when she doesn't know something. I should speak exclusively Polish to her, make her practice, but so far I haven't. She hasn't spoken a word of it since we moved here." She dropped her gaze. "I don't want to push her."

Seth clenched his jaw. Frowned.

Dammit, he didn't want to talk about this. But he was gonna because she was worried about her sister.

"My mom died of cancer when I was three. I don't remember her. I was with my dad for a year, until he decided he couldn't handle a kid and left me with his parents. My mom didn't have any family, so they were the only choice. I was four, and four is different than sixteen, but I guess my point is that a kid can adapt pretty fast. You get used to your new normal. And you learn to live with it. She's figuring out her new normal, but maybe it's okay to push her sometimes."

She looked sympathetic, like she was thinking about him as a lost little boy who'd been sent to live with his grandparents. He wasn't about to tell her they were the kind of people who shouldn't be charged with raising a puppy, much less a kid. She'd probably gasp in horror if he did.

"Maybe you can help your sister more than you think by engaging her. Because pretending there isn't a problem doesn't work."

Callie's eyes were suspiciously moist. Her mouth opened, but whatever she might have said was interrupted when Rory came out of the kitchen with a tray and headed their way. By the time she set the food down, made sure they had everything they needed and refilled their drinks, the moment was gone.

He was glad because he'd already said too much.

Chapter Eleven

 around her handsome bodyguard. She wished she hadn't nearly fallen on her ass and broken her head because then she wouldn't know what it was like to have her body pressed up against his.

When he'd held her in the cool, dark back hall of the Dawg, she'd felt like a teenager on her first date again. She'd been enamored of Bobby Bowen since she'd been old enough to be interested in boys. When she was sixteen, he'd asked her to homecoming. That night had been her first kiss, and her heart had thundered so hard she'd thought she was going to pass out.

Callie Crowell was a nerd, and football jocks didn't ask nerds to the dance. But he had, and she'd been positive it was fate. Turned out it was a bet. The moment their mouths touched, a light went on and cell phones flashed as they captured her startled expression. Bobby had laughed.

Then Tara Warren, the head cheerleader and Callie's arch nemesis, only because Tara's mom and hers were rivals at the country club, sashayed up to Bobby and looped her arm in his.

It was like every heart-wrenching moment out of every single teen movie ever made. She'd been the butt of the joke when social media blew up with photos of her stupid expression. Bug eyes behind her glasses—which she no longer wore full-time because yay for corrective contacts— and her mouth open wide. She'd been startled, but it'd looked like she was about to devour poor Bobby's face.

Yet it was still her first kiss ever.

Seth wasn't mean like a high school jock and a prissy cheerleader, but he also hadn't been holding her close out of any real desire for her. He'd held her because she'd been trembling. Then he'd let her go and hauled her inside for lunch.

Sure, he told her things that made her heart ache for him, but that didn't mean he was sharing his secrets with her. He was a man, and whatever emotion he might have felt as a four-year-old left with his grandparents was no longer an issue for him.

He'd been trying to be nice, to tell her that Nikki would be okay, and she appreciated it. Reading anything else into it was folly of the worst kind.

They finished lunch—as amazing as he'd promised it would be—and went to deliver Colleen's computer. Colleen wasn't there, but a note on the door said to leave any packages at Doc Sutton's office and she'd pick them up later. So they'd trudged to the doctor and Callie had gotten to meet Emma Sutton, who'd moved back to town to take over her dad's practice. Emma was engaged to Blaze Connolly.

She was a pretty woman, also nerdy, which meant that Callie liked her right away. Then again she'd liked Rory, and Rory was a girlie-girl stunner in jeans and a white tank top with a plaid shirt over it to keep her warm in the chill of the AC. But she was nice, and she had a comedic streak that Callie admired because she didn't have one herself.

Once the computer was safely stowed and the conversation was over, Seth drove them to the Piggly Wiggly. Callie had been before, many times, and everyone was super friendly and said hello. But this was the first time she'd been inside with a man who attracted the kind of attention that Seth did. Women darted down aisles just to say hi. Older ladies stopped him to talk about how he was settling in and ask did he like the weather, among other things.

The younger women side-eyed her like she was a puzzle they couldn't quite solve. Yet more proof that a man like Seth King would never be interested in someone like her. She didn't have buck teeth and braces anymore, but she knew her limits.

Seth grabbed sandwich meat, cheese, and bread. He picked up milk and cereal and toaster pastries. She resisted the urge to tell him about the toxicity of palm oils and added sugar but made a mental note to make sure Nikki didn't see the box. He also bought steaks, potatoes—she told him she had a bag, but he waved her off—and salad fixings. There were potato chips cooked in vegetable oil (very bad) and soda (ultra-toxic).

"That's enough for the next three or four days," he said. "You need anything?"

She didn't so he rolled to the checkout and paid and then they were on the way again. It was after three when they got back to the farm. Charlie was at the fence, waiting to be fed. Seth wouldn't let her go alone. He checked the house for any intrusions, took the groceries inside and put the cold stuff away, then walked with her to the barn, one hand on his side as he went in before her.

He'd concealed the gun like she'd asked, but now she knew where.

When he was satisfied nobody had been in the barn, he helped her scoop feed into a bucket and grabbed the hay she pointed at. She took it to the run-in stall and patted Charlie as she hooked the bucket to the wall. He shoved his nose into the sweet feed and started to eat.

Her eyes filled with tears, and she cursed beneath her breath, hoping she didn't actually start crying. Because Seth would ask, and then what would she say? That she was worried about what would happen to Charlie when she left him behind? Jack would be fine because he was young and in peak performance shape, but Charlie wasn't. He had Cushing's, and that required regular meds. He could be ridden, and he wasn't in pain, but he would be if he was neglected.

She didn't think Nikki's trainer would do that, but it also wasn't fair to leave Lisa with two horses to support. At least until she could sell Jack. He'd bring a decent price so Callie comforted herself that the money would help take care of Charlie. In fact, she'd write an email saying precisely that, and she'd send it after they'd been gone at least a month. It would be the only email she'd send from that account once she disappeared.

After Charlie was taken care of, they returned inside. Seth put his groceries away after asking her where she wanted them. He took the toaster pastries and chips to his room and stashed them, thankfully. He said he was happy to share, but she'd told him she tried not to feed Nikki those things at home. She knew her sister was going to scarf down some Mickey D's before she came home this afternoon, but she wasn't trying to control everything Nikki ate. She just wanted there to be good, healthy choices at home so maybe the other crap wouldn't do too much damage whenever Nikki indulged.

"So you're a health nut," he said when he returned. "Except you ate meatloaf at the Dawg so that can't be it."

"You didn't read the small print. It was made with grass-fed beef, organic eggs and milk, and fresh onions and bread from local sources. About as good as you can get, really."

"Huh, didn't pay attention."

"I always pay attention to the food I eat. Did you know that in Europe, many of the food additives we use in this country are banned?"

"Nope. Should I?"

"Maybe you should. You look like you work out. Isn't caring about what you put into your body part of that?"

He arched an eyebrow at her. "Honey, I've been shot at, stabbed, and taken prisoner during my time in the military. I've been in situations where I thought I'd die any minute. I've been too hot, too fucking cold, slept in places that would make you shudder. I've jumped out of airplanes, swam through crocodile infested waters, and sewn up my own side on one memorable occasion. If a few Oreos and some potato chips are going to kill me, all I can say is at least I'll enjoy them before I die."

"You swam with crocodiles?"

He snorted. "That's what caught your attention? Yeah, I have. Sometimes we got sent to a jungle. Crocs live in rivers inside those jungles. When you gotta cross the river to get where you're going, sometimes you swim."

"Weren't you scared?"

"No time to be scared. You do what you've been sent to do and you get the fuck out. If you're lucky, you make it back to the transport. If not, well, at least the crocs get a good meal."

Callie shuddered. But beneath her horror was something else. Hope. If he'd done those sorts of things, maybe he really could protect her from Mikhail. Except he wasn't moving in permanently and eventually she'd be back to living alone with her sister and going to the lab every day. Mikhail would find a way to get to her if she hadn't managed to leave town by then.

Her hope slowly flattened under the weight of stress.

Seth's phone rang and he fished it from his pocket. Then he went outside and kept walking until he was far enough from the house there was no chance she could hear what he was saying.

She watched him listen to whoever was on the other end. The hard look on his face. The way he looked like an avenging angel as his expression darkened. Whatever he was being told, he didn't like it one bit. When he tucked the phone away again, he tipped his head back and swore. Then he kicked at the ground, sending a rock flying.

When he turned toward the house, she ducked away from the window. She was paralyzed for a second before hurrying to the kitchen and grabbing her journaling supplies. If she looked like she was busy, he wouldn't know she'd been watching him.

She plopped into the chair, grabbed her reading glasses, and flipped open a box with craft paper and stickers. Then she snatched up her tweezers, threw open her journal, and pretended to be studying the page when Seth stormed back inside.

She looked up as he approached, her heart ramming against her ribs like she'd run a marathon.

"Is everything okay?" she asked.

His expression was black. Concerned? Or just pissed? She couldn't tell, but she didn't like the way it made her feel. Like he had something to say and she wasn't going to like it. In fact, she was going to actively hate it.

But she tipped her chin up and met his gaze, refusing to back down an inch. She'd been threatened, harassed, and nearly burned to death in her lab last night. She wasn't going to cower now. At least not for the next few minutes anyway.

"Depends on your definition of okay. There was a body found in the Potomac a week ago. Cause of death was a bullet to the head."

"That's terrible. But why are you telling me?"

"Because the body was Mikhail Volkov's."

Callie blinked. And shuddered. Her mouth opened. Closed. She finally managed to whisper, "A week ago?"

"That's right."

Ice froze her veins. If Mikhail had been dead for a week, he hadn't set the fire. Or ordered it set. Sure, he could have planned it that far ahead, but he hadn't known she was going to refuse to replace the cable then. She'd still been putting him off with vague talk about people watching her and not having a moment alone in the lab. She'd been trying to think about how to refuse so he'd understand why she couldn't do it.

"He texted me two days ago. But it couldn't have been him, could it?"

Not that she needed an answer to that question. She'd seen him in person ten days ago. Three days after that, he'd been dead.

"What did he say?"

She bit the inside of her lip, thinking about what she could reveal that wouldn't compromise Athena. "He said it was time. That I had to do what he wanted me to do, or things were going to get really bad for me. He said he couldn't protect me from it any longer."

Seth looked like he could chew through nails. "What did he want you to do, Callie?"

She gazed up at him, her heart hammering. She could tell him without revealing anything top secret. She wouldn't be violating her NDA or her security clearance. But the words didn't come. Instead, she got up and went over to her computer case, pulled a cable from inside. Then she went back to where he stood and handed it to him.

He turned it over, studying it.

"It looks like a normal charging cable," she said. "But it's not. There's a keystroke logger and a Wi-Fi chip embedded in the connector. He wanted me to replace one of the cables in the secure lab with this one. I refused."

His eyes burned into her. "You didn't do it."

She shook her head. "No." And then, because she felt like she needed to explain, she said, "You know the lab I work in is secure. You know that Griffin Research has government contracts. If I replaced that cable and gave Mikhail access, I'd not only be breaking the terms of my employment and violating my security clearance, but I'd also be betraying my country. I was born here, but my mother wasn't. She came over as a teenager, first as an exchange student and then later on a work visa. She loved America, loved what it stood for. I was eight when she took the oath of citizenship. My dad and I went with her to the federal courthouse. There were a lot of new citizens taking their oath that day. Most of them wore some combination of red, white, and blue. Mama wore a red dress with an American flag scarf around her neck. She carried a red, white, and blue purse, and she was so happy. The judge read off the stats about where people were from originally and had them raise their hands. They came from all over the world, and they all had stories. I was only a kid, but I'll never forget how it was almost a party atmosphere."

She dragged in a breath, aware she was once more word vomiting a bunch of stuff he hadn't asked to hear. But he watched her intently and she felt like it was something he wanted to know.

"Afterward, we went and had hamburgers, fries, and milkshakes, and Mama kept staring at her certificate. She had a pocket copy of the Constitution in her purse, and she used to read parts of it to me. I was bored, naturally. But she insisted, and then she'd speak Polish and tell me about her family and how hard life had been for them during the Cold War. How she never wanted me to know that kind of deprivation or lack of freedom. I made a mistake getting involved with Mikhail, but I thought he was like me. His parents were immigrants, and my mother was, and I thought we understood each other. I was very, very wrong."

Seth turned the cable over again, his eyes dropping to it. "Thanks for telling me. And thanks for showing me this."

She wrapped her arms around herself, chilled. Mikhail was dead. Someone had sent her a text, she'd sent one back with her answer, and then the lab burned.

"It's scary what kind of tech is out there these days. How many unsuspecting people would plug that thing in and never know it's spying on them, sending someone all their data? Or that somebody could take over their computer remotely and steal everything? I wouldn't have known if I didn't work in the field."

"I don't know who's behind this, Callie, but I'm pretty sure Mikhail was only the tip of the iceberg. He recruited you, put you into play. But somebody killed him, and since you got a text recently, we've gotta assume whoever he worked for still wants access to whatever you're working on."

The chill crawling through her laid icy fingers around her heart. Squeezed.

She was running out of time.

"I need to disappear. Take Nikki and go somewhere they can't find us."

Pity. That's what she saw in his gaze. She'd hoped for understanding. For help.

Not the look he was currently giving her.

"You can't run away. Trust me on this. Witness protection is a thing for a reason. It requires a lot of groundwork, and it requires giving up everything you know and love. It requires people to make sure you're coping with your new life and to keep you from making mistakes. It's not something you're gonna be able to do on your own. Not unless you want to be running for the rest of your life. And not only you, but your sister. You're gonna take her away from every sense of normalcy you've worked hard to build for her, and it'll set her back years. She'll have to give up horses for the next few years, maybe forever, and then there are the new names and passports you'll have to figure out how to get. These days you need a social security number to work anywhere, so how are you getting past that? You can buy a fake number, but you risk getting caught—and that'll land you in worse trouble."

It was like he had a vise around her heart, squeezing it tighter and tighter. Cutting off her oxygen. Her hope. Her wild, reckless, last-ditch attempt to escape and keep her sister safe.

It was in ruins at her feet. Like shattered glass.

A sob welled in her chest, broke free. She spun away so he wouldn't see her lose control. Stuffed her fist against her mouth and tried to contain all the emotion she'd been holding in.

Holding onto for a year now. Since she'd gotten the call her parents hadn't made it off the mountain. She'd had to be strong for Nikki. Had to be the one who took care of them, the reliable one. The one who made it all better.

Her shoulders shook as she worked to contain her feelings.

A pair of strong arms wrapped around her, tugged her backward against his body. She clutched at his arm like a lifeline, her body shuddering with the weight of her tears.

His voice was in her ear. Soft, gentle, and somehow hard at the same time. "I got you, Callie. I got you. You're gonna be okay. I'll take care of you. Both of you. I promise."

She didn't know if she believed him, but the solid weight of him behind her, holding her, felt so very right in that moment. He was the rock she didn't have. The man she'd thought didn't exist.

But he was here, now, and he was holding her firmly, letting her cry and promising to take care of her. She knew he wasn't hers, that this wasn't anything remotely romantic, but for the moment she felt safe. Protected.

"I'm s-sorry," she hissed out brokenly when the tears didn't immediately cease.

His fingers stroked her arm. Softly, gently. "Nothing to be sorry about. Cry it out, honey. I'm not going anywhere."

She wanted to say so many things. That he didn't know her, that he wasn't obligated to soothe her, that she was grateful he did it anyway. That she felt safe with his arms around her, and that scared her too.

He turned her in his arms, pressed her head to his chest, and ran his fingers up and down her back the way he'd done her arm. Soft, gentle, soothing. She clutched him, cried into his shirt, and felt both safe and embarrassed at the same time.

Eventually, her tears gave way to hiccuping little coughs. She closed her eyes tightly and then pushed away from him.

He let her go, his hands falling to his sides. The cable was on the couch where he'd tossed it. She wrapped her arms around her body and stood there, uncertain what came next.

"What do I do now?"

He shoved a hand through his hair, looked away. When he met her gaze again, his eyes were harder than before. Determined. "We stick with the plan. I'm here for your protection and to install an alarm system. I'm not gonna lie to you, though. Alarms aren't going to do much good out here in the sticks. You're far from town, far off the road, and by the time anyone got here, it'd be too late."

Her stomach knotted.

"But you've got me, and that's not insignificant. I did time in special forces, and I've seen combat. I've got the skills you need to keep you and your sister safe, and I'll do it as long as I have to. My guys aren't going to stop me, if that's what you're thinking. We run a range, and we do security and personal safety training, but that's not all we do. You need to tell me everything, Callie. Not the things you can't because of national security, but whenever you get a call, a text, or even a suspicious look from a coworker, I need to know about it. Because you can either try to run, and probably fail, or you can stay here and let me and my friends end this for you. Up to you which to choose. But I highly suggest you choose us."

Chapter Twelve

HE KNEW SHE WOULD CHOOSE HIM. SHE DIDN'T HAVE ANY other options. Not good ones anyway. Seth stalked into the front yard, away from the house, and dialed Ghost.

"How'd she take it?"

Seth could still feel her trembling in his arms. Sobbing her heart out while a knot formed in his throat. He shouldn't have been affected by her crying, but after hearing her talk about how proud her mother had been to become an American, and knowing that she'd lost both her parents so recently, he felt her tears like a rock lodged beneath his ribs.

"She wanted to take her sister and run. I dissuaded her. But I'm going to have to stay with her for now, get her to talk to me. Watch out for her. Probably need to watch the sister, too."

"Copy. I'll put Ethan on the sister. Whenever she's not in school or at home, he'll be there."

Relief was instant. "I'm glad you agree."

"Why wouldn't I? It's a good idea. Callie is the closest

we've gotten to what's happening. She's involved, whether she wants to be or not."

"Truth." Seth blew out a breath, frowned. "If she's actively involved, she's giving an Oscar-worthy performance."

Ghost chuckled. "This mean you don't think she's guilty anymore?"

He'd wanted to believe she was their leak, because it would have been so easy to tie this mission up in a bow, but that scenario was getting less believable by the minute. "Unlikely. But I don't dismiss her completely. There's a chance, however small, that we're being played."

"It's possible, I'll grant you. We need to find out who was pulling Volkov's strings, why they chose Callie in the first place. What they wanted her to do."

"I've got a lead on that last one, boss. At least part of it."

He told Ghost about the cable and the fact she hadn't switched it. He knew it hadn't been one of his own cables being handed back to him because he'd marked them both with a groove across the plug. The Ghost Ops cables were still in place so far as he knew.

"Thank fuck for that," Ghost said. "I'm going to assume you haven't gotten any communications from our rogue cables today."

"No, sir, I haven't."

"I've heard nothing about when the lab will reopen, but I don't expect them to be down long. The pressure to get back to work is enormous. Whoever set the fire wanted to scare Callie into cooperating, but I don't think they're concerned about the timeline. Washington's launch date doesn't matter to them, though it matters a great deal to the president and her closest advisers." He paused a moment. "We need to find whoever set the fire, get some answers. See where it leads us."

"I've got inquiries out on the janitorial staff. The researchers who were there last night are clean." He'd gotten that bit of information a few minutes ago before he'd come outside to call Ghost.

"How many cleaners on last night?"

"Four. Griffin Research contracts out to a local company. Their employees are background checked and cleared before they're hired, and they undergo regular security checks."

Standard procedure for government facilities and top-secret access areas. But if it wasn't the researchers, and it wasn't, that only left the janitorial company and their staff. People were capable of being compromised. Apply the right pressure and even the most law-abiding citizen could fold like a house of cards.

"Copy. Keep digging, Phantom. You need anything out there while you're watching Callie and her sister?"

Seth stared into the distance. He dreaded Nikki Crowell coming home. Dreaded being around her. She was sixteen, same age as Mia. There wasn't a day that went by he didn't think of Mia, but he usually compartmentalized those thoughts pretty well. What was it going to be like when he had to share a house with a girl the same age? Was he going to think even more about the little girl he'd never gotten to see?

He shook his head. He'd handle it. Same as he always did whenever he thought of Mia. So long as she was thriving and happy, that was all that mattered.

"Nah, we're good. I brought weapons and ammo. I've got my own Wi-Fi and a backup. I picked up a couple of trail cameras from our supply, and I intend to mount them when we're done talking so I can monitor the approaches to the house. Callie's planning to tell her sister I'm staying with them because I've got lead paint and it's being removed. She didn't want to scare the kid. Not sure if you need to know that or not, but I'm telling you in case it comes up for some reason."

"Copy that."

Once the call ended, Seth went back inside to get the trail cameras and a drill. Callie was sitting at the table again, playing with her papers and tweezers. She glanced up when he walked into the kitchen. Her eyes were red, puffy, but she had an icepack and a towel nearby. She saw the direction of his gaze and gave him a watery smile.

"I'm hoping there's enough time to stop looking like I'm having an allergic reaction. I don't want to alarm Nikki." She glanced at her phone. "I've got about an hour and a half to go before she arrives."

He didn't want to think about the moment the girl walked in. "Are you allergic?"

"To certain pollens and dust, but that just makes me sneeze. Were you talking about me out there?"

There was no point in lying. "A bit, yeah. We're with you until we resolve this."

"I don't see how you can. You're very skilled, I'm sure. But how are you going to find whoever killed Mikhail? And then make them leave me alone?"

He didn't correct her assumption that Mikhail's killer and the person who texted her pretending to be him weren't necessarily one and the same. It was a logical assumption, because of the phone, but it was also a lot more complicated than that.

"Because we left the military, but we didn't leave the profession. We still have connections, sources. Resources. Besides, whoever's been pressuring you isn't going to stop pressuring you. The communication won't end. They're going to keep pushing, probably even come looking for you, and I'm going to be here when they do. Nobody's getting near you, Callie. Not without going through me."

"I still think it's worth a try to disappear. If you still have those connections you claim, you can help me. Walk me through the process, help me get the identification and the new life. Then you can go back to your life while Nikki and I start our new ones."

She looked hopeful. He understood why, but he couldn't do it and she needed to understand. "I can't help you with that. You need to trust me and let me do my job. I'll keep you alive, and I'll make sure this asshole never gets to you. That's not nothing, even if it's not what you want."

She had the grace to look sheepish. "I'm sorry to sound ungrateful. I'm just… scared, Seth. For me. For Nikki. She's already been through so much, and now I've dragged her into this by being stupid and trusting somebody I shouldn't have."

"Did you know he was going to ask you to do illegal things when you met him?"

"No."

"And did he help you get a job when nobody else would or could?"

"Yes."

"Then how is that being stupid and trusting? It's what anybody would do, Callie. It's usually called networking, and I'd wager it almost never ends up like this."

She tipped her head to the side. A ghost of a smile played at her mouth. "For a guy who doesn't like to talk much, you sure know how to say the right thing sometimes."

"I see no point in talking nonsense. When it's important, I've got things to say."

"I noticed." She sucked in a breath, let it out again. "Thank you."

"You're welcome." He held up the box with the cameras. "Going to install a couple of trail cameras to watch the outside of the house and barn. I'll see anyone who comes onto the property in real time."

"Do you need the Wi-Fi information, or do they use cellular?"

"Cell."

"What information do you need from me to get them running?"

"Nothing. They're already registered to One Shot Tactical. When they aren't needed anymore, I'll take them down again."

"I don't feel like thank you is enough for what you're doing. When I went to the range this morning, I thought I might get some advice. Maybe even an offer to act as personal security for a few days for a price. But what you're doing…"

"For fuck's sake, don't cry again."

Her chin trembled. Her upper lip looked like she was having a spasm. Her red, puffy eyes were shiny. She was a mess, and he still thought she was cuter than hell. Weird.

She laughed and swiped the back of her hand over her eyes. "I'm trying not to. Maybe you should be grumpy again. That'll help."

"I'm not grumpy. What makes you say that?"

She laughed again. "You definitely are. Daphne said so too."

Now that hurt. Sort of. "Daph? She thinks I'm grumpy?"

"She said you were perpetually grumpy but I shouldn't take it personally because you were that way with everyone."

He wanted to protest his innocence like a man on trial for a crime he didn't commit. He wasn't grumpy, dammit. He just didn't talk about bullshit. And hadn't he spent time talking to Daphne this morning about her car situation?

He had. He'd been *friendly*.

Come to think of it, she had seemed a little surprised by the conversation. Like she hadn't expected it. But he was *working* on it. And he liked Daph. Not the way Kane liked her, but enough that he didn't want her leaving the range the way she'd shown up—unexpectedly and clearly hiding from something.

He'd done a background check on her because of course he had. Ghosts Ops wasn't letting someone into their orbit without a full background. She'd come back clean. Unremarkable. Vanilla. Nothing floating around about Daphne Bryant that was concerning.

That didn't mean she hadn't been fleeing demons of her own, though.

Seth sighed. Well, fuck. And here he thought he'd been so ordinary this morning. Not charming in a Chance or Kane way, or conversational in a Blaze or Ethan way. Hell, Ghost didn't talk a lot of nonsense either, and nobody called *him* grumpy.

"I'm not grumpy," he said. Belatedly. And grumpily.

"You're frowning."

He smoothed his face. "I'm not."

"You were." Callie laughed. "It's okay, Seth. You don't have to make small talk with me. I'm going to pretend life is perfectly rosy and glue some stuff into my journal while trying to make this swelling go away. Then I'm going to paste on a smile and lie to Nikki about why you're here—do you remember why?"

"Lead paint."

She gave him a thumbs up and went back to studying

the paper and scraps in front of her. He wanted to ask what the point was in pasting scraps into a book, but he refrained. It wasn't until he was outside, searching for the best location for the cameras, that he realized what he'd almost done.

Small talk.

Chapter Thirteen

CALLIE'S FACE WASN'T NEARLY AS PUFFY BY THE TIME FIVE o'clock rolled around. She checked the location tracking on Nikki to see that her sister was about to hit the Sutton's Creek town limits. A little later than expected, but that often happened when Nikki went to the barn. She lost track of time while she brushed Jack, saddled, took her lesson, and then pampered him again before finally leaving.

Since school was almost over for the summer, Callie was a little more lenient. Final exams had happened last week, and the last day of school was in two days. If Nikki wanted to spend extra time with Jack and her barn friends, Callie wasn't going to say no.

So long as she kept Callie informed of any delays. In fact, Callie was going to have to stress that she needed more communication about delays or changes in schedule. She'd chalk it up to paranoia over her near miss, which Nikki knew about, but without telling her sister she'd been the target of whoever had set the fire. Nikki thought it was an accident, and Callie intended to let her keep thinking that way.

She watched out the window as Seth stood on a ladder, attaching a camera to a tree. She was right that he couldn't look like anything other than what he was, but she thought her explanation would land without question. Nikki cared more about riding and showing horses than anything else besides Callie. She'd probably shrug and retreat to her room to watch show videos. She had a competition next weekend, and she'd be focused on that. Thank God.

It was no hardship to watch Seth work. It was hot outside in the late days of May, and he was sweating. His shirt clung to his chest like a second skin until the moment he dragged it up and over his head.

Callie's breath stopped in her chest. He was tanned, muscled, and perfectly made. She wasn't a big romance reader, not usually, but that body belonged in a novel. She'd teased him about being a cover model earlier, but she wasn't wrong. He could do it. Even with the scowl he so often wore. Give him some pointy ears and armor and he'd be a Fae prince.

Not that she planned to mention that to him. And not that she read those books either, but Nikki had read some books with Fae warriors and had talked about it nonstop at one point.

Maybe Callie needed to start reading some since she could imagine Seth in the starring role.

He lifted his arms to screw the camera into the bracket over his head, and her belly clenched. Worse, something was happening lower down.

Of all the times to start thinking about sex.

A, Nikki was almost home.

B, there was no universe in which Callie Crowell and Seth King would ever hook up. He barely tolerated her, despite saying the right thing from time to time. He was there out of a sense of duty and possibly a Sir Galahad complex. He was not there because he found her irresistible.

Callie made herself walk away from the window. She didn't need to stare like a kid who couldn't afford the ice cream cone. Instead, she checked her reflection again and decided she'd pass, though she might have to tell her sister that she'd cried a little. She'd already decided to use her journal as an excuse. She'd left the whole mess on the kitchen table, and she'd tell Nikki that she'd gotten teary over one of the books she'd read. It wouldn't be the first time, so Nikki would believe her.

The back door opened and closed, and a sweaty Seth came inside. He glistened, his nipples hardening in the cool air. He smelled like sunshine and sweat, and she'd never smelled anything so appealing in her life.

"Nikki will be here in about five minutes or so," she said because she didn't know what else to say.

Seth grimaced. "I'd better take a quick shower then."

They hadn't talked about it, but there were only two bathrooms he could use. One of them was Nikki's because it was in her room. The other was across the hall from his room and next door to hers. Still, rather than assume he knew, she told him to use that one.

He nodded. "Thanks."

He walked away and then she heard the shower go on. Damn if she didn't imagine what he looked like with water sluicing over his toned body, his eyes closed as he stuck his head under the spray.

Oh Lord, Seth King was naked in her shower. He was soaping his body, rubbing his hands over every inch of his glorious form. Every. Inch.

Callie's belly tightened again. And lower, between her

legs. That long-neglected zone of nothingness. Well, other than when she took matters into her own hands, which wasn't often.

"Stop," she muttered. "You barely survived a fire last night, you're still coughing your head off, Mikhail is dead and somebody worse than him is after you, and you're imagining what a naked man looks like in your shower. You need to get your priorities straight, pronto."

She'd lost her mind. That's all there was to it. Stress, probably.

A car door slammed, and her belly clenched again, for a different reason this time. Nikki strolled in the back door a few moments later, her helmet bag and boot bag draped over her shoulders. She'd changed into paddock boots and still had on her jods, which were dusty from the arena.

"Whose truck?" she asked when she walked into the living room.

"It's a friend's. I told him he could stay for a few days."

Callie didn't think her sister could look more surprised if she'd said they were joining the circus.

"*He?* You have a male friend, and I didn't know?"

Callie forced a smile. "Well, yeah. He's just a friend. Not a boyfriend. He lives in an old farmhouse with lead paint. So he needs to stay somewhere while it's being removed."

Nikki looked suspicious. "Why have you never mentioned this friend before?"

Callie cast about for an excuse. "Well, uh, I haven't known him for too long. But he's a nice guy, really. I met him when he did some security work at the lab."

Now that she heard herself saying the words aloud, they sounded ridiculous. Why would she invite a man she'd just met to stay with them, lead paint or not? Was there nowhere else he could stay? No other friends besides a woman he'd met recently? He'd asked her that very question and she'd dismissed it.

Good grief, she was an idiot.

Seth chose that moment to appear. He'd put on fresh jeans and a gray T-shirt with The Salty Dawg Tavern's logo on it. His hair was still damp.

"Whoa," Nikki said as she took in Seth from head to toe. Her gaze jerked to Callie. Callie's heart tripped over itself as she tried to think of what to say next.

But Nikki merely grinned. "Okay, I get it, sis. Say no more."

Callie wanted to wilt with relief. She did not. "Nikki, this is my friend Seth King. Seth, my sister, Nikki Crowell."

Seth seemed frozen in place as he stared at Nikki for a long moment. But then he shook himself and smiled in a way he never had at her. "Hi, Nikki. Pleased to meet you. Your sister's been kind enough to let me crash here for a few days while my house is, uh, remediated. Lead paint," he added.

Callie didn't roll her eyes because this was her fault, but that's how fake the whole thing sounded. Whether it came from him or her.

He extended his hand, and Nikki closed the distance and put her hand in his. She gaped up at him for a long moment while Seth smiled down at her. Then it was over, and he stepped back. Nikki didn't move.

"Hi, um, sorry I smell like a horse. It's nice to meet you too."

"I didn't notice any horse smell," Seth said. Bless him.

"Oh? Well, good. Sometimes I get really hot and stinky when I ride but I'm glad if it's not bad."

Callie wanted to smile at her sister's babbling. And she wanted to tell her not to worry, Seth made her babble too.

"Not bad at all. So you like to ride, huh?"

Nikki was blushing, but her eyes sparked at the question. Soon she was telling Seth about her horses and the competition next week. He didn't show a single hint of impatience with her chatter. He listened to everything, nodding and asking questions, and Callie's heart ached.

He might be a grump sometimes, but he wasn't when it counted. She didn't care if he growled and grumped at her, but the way he treated Nikki with patience and kindness made her heart happy.

"Babe, shouldn't you shower and get ready for dinner?" she asked when Nikki took a breath after she'd been talking for twenty minutes straight.

Nikki blinked. "Oh, right. But I stopped at Burger King on the way home. You said I could get something if I wanted."

"True, I did. You'll want dessert though. I have ice cream with raspberry sauce. But you need to clean up first."

Nikki stood up from where she'd been perched on the edge of a faux leather ottoman, regaling Seth with a story about Charlie bucking her off when he'd still been young and spry.

"I'm going." She gave Seth a smile. "You just let me know if you ever want to take a lesson. My trainer has horses big enough and safe enough for a beginner."

Seth had stood too. "That's a kind offer, Nikki, but I think I'm gonna keep my feet on the ground as much as possible."

She grinned. "Yeah, thought you might say that. It's easier to learn when you're still a kid. The ground doesn't seem as hard as when you're an adult. Or so my trainer says."

She picked up her bags and headed down the hallway to her bedroom. Callie waited until the door closed, then turned to Seth, keeping her voice low. "Thank you for being patient with her. I know you don't like small talk."

He seemed troubled, or maybe it was her imagination, because he shrugged. "She's a kid. I don't mind. Not that I know a damned thing about teenage girls or what they're thinking, but I figured she'd run out of steam eventually."

Callie's eyes prickled again. Nikki was so taken by Seth she hadn't even noticed that Callie had been crying. "I haven't seen her that animated in a while. She gets excited about horse shows, but that's about it. I took her to the company Christmas party because I thought she'd have fun. It was held in the Space & Rocket Center, and dinner was served beneath the Saturn V rocket that hangs there. We had raffles and presents, dancing, Santa Claus. She was ho hum about all of it. We left early and she went to her room."

"That was six months ago, right? Takes time. Six months from now, she'll probably look forward to it."

"I know. But this morning you were at work, doing your job, with no notion of having to spend time with two strangers. Being here with us can't be easy, especially when we both seem determined to talk your ear off."

His silver gaze met hers. "There were times in my military career when I woke up in my own bed and then went to sleep hours later in a new location that wasn't nearly as pleasant. Desert floors. Jungles. Buildings that were mostly rubble. This is a fucking amusement park in comparison. It's fine. Noisy, but fine."

Warmth blossomed. "Well, we're lacking in Ferris wheels at the moment, but we do have a petting zoo. It consists of one horse, a barn cat who makes appearances when he damn well pleases, and a few mice that Sylvester is too lazy to catch."

He stared at her, then shook his head. He didn't grin, but she heard it in his voice. "You aren't what I expected."

"I hope that's not a bad thing." Her heart thrummed as she waited for his answer.

"It's not bad."

She sketched a little bow. "Why thank you, kind sir. Not bad is our goal here at Chez Crowell. We hope you enjoy your stay. Please let our staff know if you'd like to reserve a slot at the petting zoo. Otherwise, the staff needs to do some chores."

He snorted. "Didn't peg you as a comedian when we talked this morning."

"And I didn't peg you as having a soft spot for a chatty teen, but I'm glad you did."

Emotion crossed his face, but it was gone too fast to know what it meant. "About reached my limit of the chit chat. If you're done, I've got some things to do."

Panic flared. "You're leaving us?"

"No. I'm going to my room and getting on my laptop."

Her heart was slow in getting the message he wasn't abandoning them. It kept pounding and pounding long after he'd walked away.

Chapter Fourteen

SETH EMERGED FROM HIS ROOM TO MAKE A SANDWICH AND got caught in the middle of a conversation because of course he did. Nikki pelted him with questions until Callie finally distracted her with a promised TV series viewing.

While the two of them sat down to watch a show about a teenager who wanted to lose her virginity to the high school pretty boy, and whose life story was inexplicably voiced by tennis great John McEnroe, Seth had peaced out. He didn't need that kind of drama in his life. And not when he'd be watching it with two women. Uncomfortable didn't even begin to cover it.

He'd gone to check the cameras at that moment because he wanted to get out of the house. He could have checked from his phone or laptop, but he'd needed to be in the open air where he could breathe.

By the time he was done with the cameras and a perimeter check, Nikki had gone to bed and Callie was no longer watching a teenager try to lose her virginity. Thank sweet baby Jesus.

Callie was in the kitchen, cleaning up the ice cream

dishes, when he walked back in. Her face wasn't puffy anymore. Nikki had finally noticed when she'd returned from her shower, but she'd accepted Callie's explanation that it was journaling about a book she'd read that had made her weepy.

Seth thought it was a bullshit excuse if he'd ever heard one. But Nikki had rolled her eyes and acted like it was a common occurrence. Then she'd asked him if he liked to read. He'd said yes, but when she asked for book titles, he'd had to name magazines about guns and books on cybersecurity. He'd left it vague, and she'd been disappointed before she launched into a description of a book that had horses and romance in it. Then she'd moved on to fairies or some such thing.

Callie had told him when he was establishing their routines that Nikki got up early to feed and take care of Charlie before school. Then she often rode after school at her trainer's barn, cleaned tack, and did chores there. She was worn out by evening time and didn't usually stay up past nine o'clock. He couldn't say he was sorry about that. It was quiet again.

"Sorry about all the questions," Callie said as if she'd read his mind. "Honestly, I think she's crushing on you a little bit."

Seth apparently couldn't hide the horror on his face because Callie laughed and shook her head. "Don't worry, she's not really thinking of you as a potential boyfriend. You're new and interesting, and you're here. Plus you don't actually interrupt her or seem uninterested in what she's saying, so she chatters on. Surprisingly so, I have to admit. But I'd be lying if I said it bothered me. She's almost herself again when she's doing that."

"That's nice." The last thing Seth wanted was a sixteen-year-old crushing on him. "I don't mind her talking. I can tune it out. But you've got me worried with this boyfriend thing."

She finished drying a bowl and hung the towel on the oven handle. "There is no boyfriend thing, promise. But you've got to know you look like you could have rolled off a movie set. It makes people stare."

Seth frowned. A movie set? "I've spent a significant portion of my life not attracting attention. For the job. You're wrong."

She laughed. "If you say so."

"New plan," he said, pointing at her. Because he wasn't taking a chance. Not even a little bit. "I've got lead paint and you were kind enough to invite me to stay here, but now we've gotta admit we're feeling a little more than friendly. You've agreed to go out with me. This could be the beginning of something big."

She stared at him, her mouth hanging open a fraction. "You aren't serious."

"Deadly serious. You're putting an end to any romantic notions your sister may have by staking a claim on me."

"Seth. You're too old for her, and she knows it. Really."

He shook his head. "Not taking a chance that kid's going to get her heart stomped on when I don't reciprocate her crush. You're my new love interest. Congratulations."

Callie gaped, her mouth moving like a fish's as she seemed to be about to say something and then thought better of it. She sighed. "Okay, fine. If it makes you feel better."

"It does."

"Then how's this going to go? You showed up today and asked me out tonight after Nikki was in bed?"

"Sounds good to me."

"Okay. But you realize we can't just *say* we're dating.

You'll have to hold my hand once in a while. Maybe kiss my cheek or something. Just to make it look real."

"Your cheek? Really?"

She looked exasperated all of a sudden. Hell, he felt exasperated, too. This idea had come out of nowhere, and now it was running away with him.

"Then what do you suggest? Bending me over your arm and ramming your tongue down my throat?"

He pictured himself doing just that. Without the tongue ramming, though. He kinda liked the idea.

"I've got more finesse than that."

"Okay, Mr. Finesse. What do you suggest?"

There was a devil in his brain that activated at her question. That was the only explanation for why he strolled toward her, twined his fingers with hers, and tugged her against his body. She gasped as she gazed up at him. He let his gaze follow the contours of her face—the lush mouth, the nose that was slightly larger than it should be, the big green eyes, the pale skin that told the story of how she spent most of her time indoors.

He brought his other hand up to her face, skimmed the line of her jaw, tipped her head back and cradled it. Then he bent and put his nose to her neck, inhaled her.

She was sweet like roses, rich like vanilla. Tart like whiskey, he'd bet.

Her hands lifted to his torso, curled into the fabric of his shirt. A raw, lonely part of him wanted to sweep her up, carry her to the bedroom, and strip her naked until he was buried inside her, taking them both over the edge of oblivion.

The urge stunned him and turned him on at the same time. He'd gotten to a place where he didn't believe she was a traitor, but that didn't mean he trusted her completely. When lives were on the line, he didn't trust anyone except the men he'd served with. The five men back at the range who were his family, his brothers. Them, he'd trust with his life.

Seth ran his tongue across the throbbing pulse point in her neck and growled at the sound of her moan.

He could eat her up. Right now.

He wouldn't, though.

Instead, he lifted his head and gazed down at her. The closed eyelids, the parted lips. The hair that spilled like silk from her top knot. It was askew and he wanted to take it down. Except he wasn't sure if she had hair pins, and he didn't want to pull it.

"Look at me," he commanded.

Her eyes opened. He intended to kiss her, to take the sweetness of her mouth and plunder it. But first he wanted to see those green eyes look up at him in wonder.

They did, too. For all of three seconds.

Then she was pushing him away, stumbling backward, her eyes wounded instead of wondering. He let her go. Stood with his fists at his sides, his dick aching, and wondered where it'd gone wrong.

"Point made," she croaked, turning to grasp the edge of the counter and take a deep breath. He started to apologize, but she whirled to him again, her eyes on fire this time. Sparking, flaring, glaring. At him.

"What point?" He was at a loss. Completely.

Her face was red. She waved her hands. "I don't want to discuss it. Cheek kisses, Seth. A peck on the mouth. Nothing like that, especially when you don't mean it."

"Okay."

She was too upset to explain that he'd meant it, that it was about sex not romance. He got the idea she wanted the romance though. The frilly, girly bedroom and the table full of paper and stickers that she glued into a journal she tried to make pretty told him that.

The anger in her expression ebbed a fraction. She reached up to fix her top knot, winding the hair furiously before snapping the elastic onto it again. "I'm sorry I over-reacted, but I just don't have it in me right now to take things that far when it's all a game to you."

He wanted to growl. He didn't. Maybe. "I'm here because you need me. I'm protecting the two of you because you need me. This is definitely not a game to me."

"I meant the dating part of it. You're suddenly not satisfied unless we pretend to date so my sister's infatuation will die on the vine. I get it. You're uncomfortable with the idea that a teenager can view you as hot. Newsflash, Grumpy Gus, but teenage girls have been thinking you're hot for years now. Trust me, I was one once and I had plenty of crushes on men way too old for me. Usually actors who starred in my favorite shows, but sometimes they were people my parents knew. It didn't mean I intended to do anything about it. Teenage girls mostly want the romance. It's not about sexual feelings, though of course they get those too."

Now how the fuck was she starting to make him feel guilty about the dating idea? "I'm not trying to make it a game, Callie. You have to admit that inviting a man you don't really know to stay at your place just because you're nice isn't a great excuse. A man you're interested in who's also interested in you? Makes a lot more sense."

She sighed. Her top knot listed, but mostly stayed in place. She shoved loose strands behind her ears. "It does. You're right."

"I'll hold your hand. I'll flirt with you and kiss you chastely when appropriate. That work?"

She nodded, her cheeks still red. "Yes. Thank you."

He got the impression somebody had hurt her at one time. He wanted to know who, and he wanted to fucking pound their face in. He didn't ask because it wasn't his business. No matter how badly he wanted to know.

"I don't have any sisters. I don't know the first thing about teenage girls. You think I'm overreacting, but I have no context here."

She huffed. "Actually, I think it's kind of sweet that you're weirded out. Means you aren't a creeper who'd take advantage of a young woman. Nikki is sixteen, but eighteen is the age of consent. To some men that's perfectly acceptable."

Ice formed in his veins as he thought of Mia. Was she safe? Was someone watching out for her and making sure some asshole with a thing for teen girls didn't get close to her?

He closed his eyes as pain stabbed him. He'd never know and there was nothing he could do about it. *Nothing.*

Seth shoved a hand through his hair. It did no good to think about the past. It was done. He'd made a choice because he'd felt like he had no other. He couldn't go back in time and make a different one.

"She's a kid for fuck's sake," he grumbled.

"With the body of a woman."

Sometimes he hated the way the world worked. What the fuck was wrong with grown men who found teen girls attractive?

"I've checked the cameras," he told her, changing the subject before it made him crazy. "Everything's working as it should. If anyone crosses the perimeter, I'll get an alert."

"What about animals?"

"I've filtered it to only ping me on the big stuff. Deer will set it off. Bears. It'll be easy to see that's what it is, though."

She looked worried. "And if a person were to cross the perimeter?"

"Then I'll deal with them."

She went over to the table where all her stuff was laid out, sat down, and stared at it. "I hate the uncertainty," she finally said. "The not knowing if anyone is out there."

He went over and stood with a hand on the back of a chair, made his voice softer. "It's not likely they are. The lab burned last night. Volkov is dead. Whoever did those things isn't waiting in the dark to break in and kill you. Not yet anyway. They haven't asked you for anything, but they intend to. If you don't deliver, that's when they'll act."

Her eyes were wide as she looked up at him. He vaguely thought he could drown in those green pools. He didn't usually think that way with a woman, but her damned frilly bedroom had him thinking about romantic shit.

It needed to stop.

"Do you think the fire was meant for me? Or do you think it was just a coincidence?"

This was territory he understood. He wanted to tell her it was an accident. That it had nothing to do with her.

He couldn't lie, though. Not even to make her feel better.

"Before we knew Volkov was dead, I'd have said it had nothing to do with you. Now I'm not so sure." He dragged the chair out and sat down so he could look at her on her level. "The fire wasn't a risk to the information they want because it's held on the server, and the servers are backed up to secure cloud storage. The only thing they risked was you. But I'm not sure it was a risk to you either. They wanted you scared, pliant, willing to cooperate. So they're going to try again to get you to give them access. If you don't, they'll escalate."

She seemed to take it all in and then nodded. He liked that she didn't fall apart or get that wild animal look that said she wanted to bolt. He knew she was fighting it inside, and he admired that she was.

"I think I'm really glad I went to One Shot Tactical today. You guys were the only thing I could think of."

"It was a good decision."

That was an understatement. Ghost Ops now had a lot more information about who was trying to steal government secrets, and they were acting on it. Without that fire, without Callie coming to see them, they wouldn't have known about Mikhail Volkov for, quite possibly, weeks.

"When do you think I'll hear from them?"

"Soon. They'll use Volkov's phone, pretend to be him. The identity of the body found in the Potomac hasn't been released yet, so they won't know that you know the truth. You can't let on that you do, either. That'll escalate their timeline, which will put you in the crosshairs that much faster."

She swallowed. "I won't."

"Have you heard from your boss about when you can go back to work?"

"Not yet. The last email said that the affected areas would be closed indefinitely, but they're working on accommodation for our team. The building will stay empty for the rest of the week while it's inspected and cleaned. But they don't want us idle for long. They'll make room for us in one of the other SCIFs. I think we'll be back to work on Monday. Nikki will be out of school, though. She has a summer job at the stable, cleaning stalls and exercising horses, so she'll be gone most of the day. But not all of it."

He could see the worry on her face. "We'll watch out for her. One of the guys will shadow her when she's in transit, and we'll put a tracker on her car. I'll be taking you to work and picking you up. You won't be in the building without others around. No more late nights for a while."

"I'm fine with that. I wouldn't have stayed last night, but my boss asked me to finish something up."

"Does she usually ask you to stay?"

She shook her head. "She has nothing to do with what happened if that's what you're thinking. We've got a deadline, and Dr. Robbins has asked other team members to work late before. Including me. The fire happening after she asked me to stay is most definitely a coincidence."

"I didn't say it wasn't. But we have to consider every angle, no matter how remote."

She blew out a breath. "If she were going to ask me to stay in order to set me up, that would mean she's on the side of whoever's pulling the strings. She could just replace the cable herself since she has access."

"True." He watched the play of emotions across her face, the worry. She knew something she wasn't saying. "Is there anything you're doing that nobody else can do?"

She glanced down at the table, fiddled with a pair of tweezers she had lying there for positioning her stickers. Then she looked back up at him, meeting his gaze directly. Coolly.

"No, there's nothing. I'm a junior programmer. I mostly proof the code, like I said."

Seth stared at her for a long moment. She stared back. And then she dropped her gaze.

His stomach bottomed out. He might not know a lot of things in this world, but he did know one thing.

Callie was lying her ass off.

Chapter Fifteen

CALLIE LAY IN BED WITH A BOOK, BUT SHE WAS HAVING trouble concentrating on it. It was almost one in the morning, and she never stayed up that late. But she couldn't sleep.

She dropped the book to her side and blew out a frustrated breath. The scrape on her hand hurt, her knee throbbed where she'd hit it on the steps at the Dawg, and her skin tingled anytime she thought of Seth's tongue on her neck.

Which was pretty much every second since it'd happened. The way he'd tugged her close, bent her back, and pressed his nose to her skin to inhale her had been one of the sexiest things she'd ever experienced.

Okay, *the* sexiest thing she'd ever experienced. The guys she'd had sex with during college and since—a sum total of three men, which wasn't much—had never done anything like that. They'd kissed her, touched her breasts when she'd indicated she wasn't going to stop them, and then things usually progressed to a bit of touching, licking (if she was lucky), and then penetration.

It'd felt good, but not extraordinary.

Seth King had inhaled her, ran his tongue across her pulse, and everything inside her liquified into a molten puddle of need. If he'd kissed her right away, she'd have probably forgotten her name.

He hadn't, though. He'd stopped, and when she'd opened her eyes, he'd been staring at her knowingly. He *knew* the effect he had on her. He'd thought she was his for the taking. She could see it in his eyes, the fact he was going to kiss her and she wouldn't stop him. They'd end up naked, him deep inside her, and she'd lose herself to the sensations.

Her reaction had scared her. And angered her.

It wasn't real—at least *his* part of it wasn't real. He'd kissed her to prove a point—her fault because she'd goaded him—but he wasn't invested. Oh, he'd have taken it all the way to her bedroom, because why turn down free sex, but it wouldn't have wrecked him emotionally.

She felt like it would have left her picking up the pieces of herself and wondering how the hell she'd come apart so thoroughly. She reminded herself she was boring Callie Crowell, the math nerd who spoke three languages, wrote computer code, and always had her nose in a book when she had time, but who really had the soul of an artist and wanted to make pretty things.

It was that artist's soul that threatened to get her in trouble with Seth. Because he was beautiful, and she wanted to explore him. He was too beautiful, in fact, for a math nerd who couldn't figure out makeup to save her life and whose sense of fashion was questionable at best.

Thinking Mikhail was interested in her was what had gotten her into this mess in the first place. She wouldn't make the mistake of thinking Seth was, too.

Besides, she'd lied to him, and she could tell he knew.

He'd asked her if there was anything she was doing that nobody else could do.

She hadn't told him the truth because it was too dangerous. She proofed the code for errors, yes. But she also tweaked the code, wrote new code, made everything work faster and better. She was a junior programmer, but she'd been promoted to the team working on the government satellite project in record time *because* of her skill.

Nobody on the team could do what she did, but because it was a government project, things had to be done a certain way. The protocols had to be followed. Once it got to her, she was supposed to make it better.

And she did. Last night, when she'd been working late, the lines of code hadn't done what they were supposed to do. She'd been perplexed, and she'd run more checks. She'd looked for errors, for ghost code, but she hadn't found anything before the fire began.

She'd wondered in the hours since if someone had sabotaged her work. But why would they do that? And if they had, they hadn't left any obvious trail. That in itself was an ominous thought.

She closed her eyes. She wanted to tell Seth everything. He was here to protect her and Nikki, and she was grateful for that. He was oddly sweet in some ways and supremely irritating in others.

She liked him, but what if she was wrong? She'd signed an NDA, and though she didn't know the full extent of the Athena Project, she knew it was important to national defense. She couldn't tell anyone more than she had already.

She picked up the book again and tried to get back into it. Maybe reading a romance novel hadn't been a good idea after all. It wasn't that she didn't like it, because she did, but the longing looks and sizzling touches the main characters were giving each other was starting to frustrate her.

The creak of a door scraped across her senses, and her heart rocketed into space. Callie sat up in bed, listening hard. Footsteps sounded in the hallway, moving toward the living room. She threw back the covers and got out of bed. It had to be Seth, but it might be Nikki. It was the thought of her sister wandering around at night that made her tiptoe to the door and open it.

Seth's door was closed. She nibbled her lip, then slipped into the hall and trekked toward the kitchen. If Nikki was there, she'd make sure her sister was okay, that she hadn't had a nightmare. Nikki's nightmares had diminished over the past couple of months, but Callie didn't kid herself they were gone.

Nikki didn't elaborate, but the dreams were about their parents. About losing them. And sometimes they were about losing Callie, which broke her heart. She always reassured Nikki she wasn't going anywhere, but Nikki looked at her sadly and said, "You can't promise that, Cal. Nobody can."

It was true, and yet the words always came because there were no other ones she could say.

When Callie hit the living room, the front door was open. Not a lot, but enough to make a chill shoot from her scalp to her toes. She crept over to it, wishing she'd gotten her dad's old shotgun from her closet, her heart a jackhammer in her chest.

Logic told her it was most likely Seth or Nikki who'd walked past her door and stepped outside. Wouldn't Seth have gotten an alert on his phone if someone approached the house?

Fear notched higher. Maybe he had. Maybe he was out there now, searching the darkness for an intruder.

She changed course and went over to the window to look outside. A shirtless man sat on the gravel driveway, his knees drawn up, his head in his hands. He rocked back and forth as if in pain. Or maybe he was trying to soothe himself.

He tipped his head back, his face turned up to the sky, and she got a look at him in the moonlight streaming between the trees.

Seth.

But why? Had he been attacked?

She didn't know, but she couldn't leave him there. She rushed outside, her gaze darting around, looking for whatever could have made him like this. He looked up at the sound of her approach—and then he was on his feet, looming in the darkness like a shadow.

Callie stopped short. She'd stepped off the front porch, but she didn't go further. "Are you okay?"

Seth didn't say anything at first. And then, as if his voice was rusty from disuse, "Callie?"

She took a step. "It's me. What's wrong? Are you hurt?"

He swore and then shook himself like a dog. Alarm prickled beneath her skin.

"I'm not hurt," he said, his voice sounding like it traveled over broken glass to reach her. "Go back inside."

Callie still looked around as if expecting someone to appear, but she wrapped her arms around herself and didn't retreat.

"I can't leave you like this. Did you get an alert? Did you hurt yourself somehow when you were coming outside to look?"

He dragged in a breath and shoved his hand over his scalp. She'd noticed he did that when frustrated. "I'm not hurt," he repeated. "There was no one. I just needed some air. Please go inside."

The air was cooler at night, and a soft breeze ruffled the loose strands of her hair that had escaped confinement behind her ears.

"I can't sleep either," she said. "I'm going inside and pouring a glass of wine. Do you want one?"

"No. Thank you."

"Beer? Water? Tea? Coffee?"

"Jesus," he muttered. "You aren't going to leave me alone, are you?"

"I will when you tell me what you want to drink. I'll go inside and wait for you. Unless you don't plan on coming in?"

He muttered a few more things she couldn't make out. "I'll be in soon. Beer. Thanks."

Callie went back inside, throwing another look over her shoulder at the man who stood with his head tipped back and his eyes closed. His fists were on his hips. A pair of athletic shorts were slung low, showing off the taut muscles of his abdomen. Seth might eat meatloaf and mashed potatoes and drink Cokes, but the man was unfairly ripped.

Callie retreated to the bedroom to slip on a stretchy bra beneath her T-shirt, then went and poured the wine and uncapped the beer. She took the drinks over to the couch and sat with her feet curled beneath her. A few minutes later, Seth came in. He closed the door quietly behind him, then threw himself onto the opposite end of the couch. She handed him the beer and he took it, tipping it toward her in salute before downing a healthy swig.

"I spent sixteen years in the military, much of it in combat assignments. I have dreams sometimes."

Callie's heart ached. It made sense though. "I'm sorry."

He shrugged. "Nothing anybody can do." He was quiet for a moment. "Truth is, I don't dream of combat very often. Most of my dreams are about something else."

"Doesn't matter what it's about if it bothers you."

"I feel trapped and I need air when it happens. That's why I was outside." He took another drink. "You can count on me to do the job I came to do. I'm not going to fall apart when you need me most."

"I didn't think that."

He nodded. They were quiet for a while, drinking in the dark, the sounds of the house creaking around them. The bullfrogs were deafening, their song rising repeatedly along with the crickets and other night creatures. It was peaceful living in the country. Or it had been anyway, until she'd started worrying about assassins attacking in the middle of the night.

Seth took another drink and then leveled her with a look. "I feel like I should explain."

"You don't have to—"

"I do. I don't want you thinking I can't protect you, worrying I won't be on my game if somebody breaks in." He shoved his hand through his hair again. "I had a daughter," he finally said. "I was young, too young, when it happened. She'd be Nikki's age."

Callie's heart throbbed. She didn't even think before she scooted close enough to squeeze his arm. She wanted to hug him. She refrained because she knew he wouldn't like it. But losing a child was unthinkable. She hurt for him, couldn't imagine what he'd been through. And now she understood what had made him dream tonight.

"I'm really sorry, Seth. Being around Nikki can't be easy for you. I'd understand if you want one of your other guys to come stay with us instead. I'm sorry I let her pester you so long tonight, but she was animated for a change. I liked seeing her that way."

His glittering gaze met hers. His skin beneath her hand was hotter than she'd expected, and her palm tingled.

"I'm not leaving. Not unless you want me to because your confidence in me is shattered."

"It's not. I'm trying to be sensitive to your needs."

"I'm fine. If I'd left every time the job got hard, I wouldn't have lasted in the Army. They'd have laughed me out on my candy ass and rightfully so. Nikki makes me think of Mia and that hurts, but it's not her fault. I won't abandon either of you to make myself feel better."

Mia.

Callie let him go and settled in her corner again, though what she really wanted was to sit with her side pressed to his, slip her arm around his neck, and pull his head down to her shoulder. "Okay, but I'll keep her from pestering you. I can redirect her questions when they start."

"No. Leave her be. She's had a tough year, and you said she's opening up again, so don't do anything to endanger that. I'm a big boy. I can handle it."

"Are you sure?"

"I'm sure. I never talk about Mia, so I'll ask you to keep what I've said to yourself. It's personal."

"Of course." *Tread carefully.* "Maybe you should talk about it. It might help. With the dreams."

He twisted the beer bottle in his hands. "Not much point in it. It's in the past."

She didn't know what to make of that, but she knew he was wrong.

"Nikki sees a therapist. About our parents. I think it helps her to deal with her feelings about what happened."

"And what about you? Do you see a therapist?"

Well, shit. She'd walked into that trap, hadn't she? "I don't, but it's not because I don't think it'd be helpful. I haven't had time yet. I will, though."

"When?"

She was starting to squirm. "After this is over. After I don't die and I can maybe have a life again that doesn't involve looking over my shoulder every moment of the day."

His gaze was knowing. "Not so easy is it?"

"No, I guess not."

"Thought so." He stood and finished the beer in one big draft before lowering the bottle. She'd fucked up by pushing the issue. "I'm going back to bed. Thanks for the beer."

"Sure."

Her heart throbbed with the urge to ask him to stay and talk to her about anything he wanted. The darkness and uncertainty wasn't so unbearable when he was near.

But she knew he wouldn't, and then she'd feel even worse because she would have asked for his company and he would have refused.

His bedroom door closed with a quiet snick of the lock. Callie drank her wine, feeling lost and alone as the silence closed in.

And fearful. Couldn't forget that one. It surrounded her, pressed down on her, made her feel like the walls of the house were about to collapse and bury her in the rubble.

She shuddered and took another drink.

Something big was coming. But she didn't know what.

Chapter Sixteen

Despite waking up in the middle of the fucking night to go sit on the gravel and rock like a baby, Seth was up early. The house was quiet when he prowled into the kitchen to find coffee. He'd bought his own yesterday, so he got that out, found the filters, and poured grounds into the basket. Then it was water, pot under the basket, button on.

The thing started burbling right away so that was a good sign. He lifted his head to look out the window. The back of the house faced east, and the first rays of dawn were crawling above the horizon. The sky was pink and orange, and he felt like he could breathe again. Unlike last night.

He scrubbed a hand over his head and yawned. What the fuck had he been thinking last night? He'd *told* Callie about Mia, about her existence. He hadn't even told his teammates about the daughter he'd lost before she was born. The daughter he'd walked away from.

But he'd said the words to Callie. Not all of them. Not the part about walking away before she was born.

Callie had been sympathetic, but he knew what she'd thought. She'd thought Mia died. Seth had been so shocked at the words that came out of his mouth that he hadn't corrected the impression.

He'd said he had a daughter. That he'd lost a daughter. That'd she'd be Nikki's age.

Being around Nikki had ripped off the scab and exposed the wound again. He hadn't expected it to happen that way. He should have known it might. He'd thought about Mia a lot since moving to Sutton's Creek. Probably because the mission, while the most important of his life, wasn't as distracting as his life in the Hostile Operations Team had been.

He'd always been on the go, flying from one war zone to the next, dropping into hostile territory to extract hostages, planning missions when he wasn't actively engaged in one, and thinking every day that this was the day he could die.

Ghost Ops wasn't like that. They *were* ghosts, haunting the perimeter, watching, waiting. Analyzing. He hadn't realized that he wasn't suited to the stillness until it was too late.

If Ghost offered him an opportunity to return to active duty today, he'd take it.

Charlie sauntered into view in the field, taking mouthfuls of grass before sauntering onward. As if he was enjoying the coolness of the day before the sun was high and the flies were biting.

The horse made Seth think of the two women asleep in their beds, and he knew he wouldn't leave yet. Not until they were safe. He'd signed onto this mission precisely because it was so critical, because failure meant that people would die.

People like Nikki and Callie. People like Mia. Rory and her baby, Emma, Daphne, and all the fine citizens of Sutton's Creek. If some megalomaniac dictator on the other side of the world got possession of Athena's technology and deployed it before Athena was active, they could attack the United States with impunity. Northern Alabama would be high on that list because of all the research and development taking place there.

He couldn't let that happen, which meant he was staying right where he was. He had to keep digging for a connection between Callie and the two Russian agents, because he had to be thorough and certain, and he had to keep her safe from whoever had murdered Volkov and quite possibly torched Griffin Research Labs when she was working late.

It was still possible that had been an accident and nothing to do with her, but Ghost Ops wasn't putting that one to bed until they knew for certain. Guesses didn't keep you alive for long in this business. Intuition and gut feelings were a thing, but research was the pillar you could build a house on.

Seth got his coffee and went outside to drink it standing in the cool morning air, feeling the heaviness of the dew that saturated the grass and listening to the morning chirp of birds. He finished the cup and dropped to the grass to do a hundred pushups before he let himself go for the second cup. When he stepped through the back door to the kitchen, Nikki was there in sweatpants and boots, a wrinkled T-shirt half tucked in, a mug of coffee cupped in both hands. Her presence kicked him low in the gut, but it wasn't as hard a kick as yesterday had been.

"Hey," she said when she saw him.

"Hey."

"I gotta feed Charlie." She sounded half asleep. "Coffee first though."

"It isn't too strong for you?"

"Rude. And nope." She popped the p. "It's just right. Callie makes it too weak, so I try to get here first. Hafta admit I was worried when I saw you'd beat me to it, but it's good."

"I'm glad. Sorry I was rude."

Not that he thought he had been, but they'd already established he didn't know fuck-all about teenagers.

She grinned. "Well, you weren't exactly. But you assumed because I'm young—and *that* was rude."

"You got me there. Won't happen again."

She nodded, then leaned against the counter and took a sip. "So... do you like my sister or what?"

Okay, he hadn't expected that one so early in the morning. "Rude," he said with the same inflection she'd used.

She laughed. "Still gotta answer though."

This kid. "You mean do I like her like a girlfriend?"

"Precisely."

He'd been right to suggest they pretend to date. Clearly. "Yeah, I think I do. That okay with you?"

She shrugged. "Callie can make up her own mind about who she goes out with. But if you aren't really into her, if this is just about some easy sex, then you need to move along. I don't want her to get her heart broken by some pretty boy who can't keep it in his pants."

Seth legit choked on his own spit. Once he stopped hacking and knew he wasn't going to die from inhaling liquid into his lungs, he gaped at the teenager standing so casually with her back to the counter. She hadn't moved a muscle. Hadn't tried to help him not choke to death or even looked remorseful.

Diabolical. He kinda liked that.

"You tell it like it is, don't you?"

"There's really no other way. I used to think life was easy. But then I lost my parents, and now I watch my sister work her ass off taking care of me when she's supposed to be living her own life. If you're here for good reasons, then she deserves it. But if you aren't, then you need to move along and find somebody else to get busy with."

Seth finally poured that second cup. He'd been knocked off kilter by this kid and her questions, but he was ready now. Maybe.

"I'm hearing you, but here's the thing. I'm interested in dating your sister. She's interested in dating me. Neither one of us can predict how that's going to go. We might really like each other, or we might find out we aren't compatible after all. No way to know without starting down the path. I'm not looking at her and thinking I want to get married or anything. I'm thinking she's pretty and interesting and I'd like to know her better."

"She is pretty and interesting. She's fluent in three languages, and she's pretty much a computer genius. Did you know she graduated at the top of her class in college? That kind of thing turns guys off sometimes. They don't like it when a girl is smarter than they are."

She frowned and he wondered if she knew that from experience.

"Then they aren't the right kind of guys, are they? Any man who's threatened by a smart woman isn't all that smart himself."

He knew Callie was smart. He'd read her transcripts. Her professors routinely praised her as someone who could go far if she had the right opportunities. For her graduation project, she'd designed and implemented a program to streamline the academic grant process, correcting several inefficiencies and saving the university millions in administrative costs over a period of years. She'd gone straight into government service work, no doubt costing herself a fat paycheck from a civilian company.

Could be because she'd had ulterior motives, but he imagined it was most likely due to the patriotic mother who'd been so proud of her new country.

"Amen, my dude." Nikki set her empty mug on the counter. "Okay, if you really want to date her and see how it goes, I'm on board. If you're just trying to get into her panties, not cool. Take that shizz somewhere else. I can't stop you if that's what you're really up to, but I won't make it easy either. Just so you know."

"I'm duly informed."

"Excellent. And now I gotta feed Charlie and clean his stall so I can get ready for school. Even though tomorrow is the last day and we aren't doing anything anyway. They really should just let us go and be done with the pretense."

He'd already heard from Ethan, who would pick up her trail as soon as she turned onto the road at the end of the long driveway. He would follow her to school and then head to the range until it was time to follow her to the stable in Madison. Seth had put a tracker on her vehicle last night. He'd put one on Callie's Toyota too.

Hopefully they wouldn't need them, but better to have them active if they did. Callie and Nikki had location tracking enabled for each other on their phones, and that was good, but Seth felt better with a backup system in place.

"You need help out there?"

Her eyes lit up and he cursed the impulse that had made him offer.

"That'd be great. Thanks."

Seth followed her outside, coffee cup in hand, wondering what the hell he'd gotten himself into. He soon found out when she handed him a rake, a shovel, and pointed at the wheelbarrow.

It was gonna be a seriously shitty morning.

Chapter Seventeen

"Oh my God," Callie said as she walked into the kitchen and encountered a wall of stench. Seth and Nikki stood by the counter, calmly drinking from coffee cups. They turned to look at her as one.

"Sorry," Nikki said. "Since Seth was helping me, I decided we needed to dig out the stall instead of just pick it out."

Callie knew from experience that digging stalls was a backbreaking, sweaty, smelly job. And these two had tracked some of it in on their clothes, though at least their shoes were outside on the back porch. That was one of her rules, and Nikki was good about following it.

Callie frowned at the man who'd arched an eyebrow at her as if it was somehow her fault he'd had to participate. "Did she drag you into it or did you volunteer?"

"Rude," Nikki chimed in.

"I stupidly volunteered," Seth added.

Callie narrowed her eyes as she slotted them back and forth between the two figures, smelling a rat in addition to the horse crap. "Did you really?"

"Yes, I really did. Not my brightest moment."

Nikki grinned. "He made the mistake of asking if I needed help. So I let him help me."

"Curse my gentlemanly soul," Seth muttered before taking another sip of coffee.

Seth's T-shirt had sweat stains around the armpits, down his abdomen, and over his chest. Nikki's clothes were better but not by much. She set the cup on the counter and straightened.

"Welp, gotta get ready for school. Thanks, Seth. You can come over to the riding stable and dig stalls with me there if you like."

He shook his head. "Sorry, brat, but I'm only falling for that one once."

Nikki snorted. "Ha, we'll see. Charlie's stall needs it about once a week. If you're still here then…"

"Go shower. You stink."

All Callie could do was bounce her gaze between them. Was her typically reserved little sister really laughing and joking with Seth? And was the gorgeous grump really teasing her right back? Maybe she was still asleep and this was a dream.

"So do you." Nikki wrinkled her nose. "Worse than I do, actually."

"Don't remind me."

Nikki left with a chortle that echoed back to them. Callie waited until she heard Nikki's door close. Then she whirled on Seth.

"Are you okay?"

He stared at her for a moment. Then he burst out laughing. "Sorry," he said after a moment. "Are you worried that I can't shovel out a stall? How old do you think I am anyway?"

Callie colored. Well, clearly that had been a dumb

question. "I meant being around her," she grumbled. "Not physically."

"Yeah, I'm fine. Nikki's a badass kid. And you and I are definitely dating because she grilled me about my intentions toward you this morning. Damn near choked to death on my own spit."

"Oh."

"She's not stupid. She figured there had to be more to the story than lead paint."

Callie closed her eyes and sighed. "I should have known. What was I thinking?"

"Dunno, but it's fixed now. She also told me that if all I wanted was a romp in the hay, then I needed to get the hell out. Not in those precise words, but I understood loud and clear."

Callie couldn't help but laugh. And blush, because really? "Okay, I'm really sorry about that, but also kind of flattered. I think."

Seth eyed her. "You should be. She's protective of you. She might be a kid, but she's definitely not oblivious or stupid. Did she ever meet Mikhail?"

Callie shuddered. "No. She knows about him because I used to talk to him on the phone a lot. I told her he was a friend from Poland because that's what I thought he was. But he never met her. The last time he was here, he was waiting for me when I got home from work. But Nikki was at the barn, and he was gone before she got home. Why do you ask?"

It had not been a pleasant meeting, and she'd been shaken by the things he'd said. She'd thought about pulling up stakes then and getting the hell out of town, but he would have found her. He'd said as much, as if he'd known what she was thinking.

"If you're thinking about running away, you need to know it'll be

much worse if you do. Right now you're useful. Leave your job and you won't be. You understand me, Callie?"

"Callie?" Seth said.

She jumped, her attention snapping back to him. "Sorry, I was thinking about something."

He frowned. "You asked why I wanted to know if Nikki and Mikhail had met. I was wondering how she responded to him. If she liked him or not. If she thought he was shady. That kind of thing. She's kinda savvy for a teenager."

Was she? Callie hadn't realized. She'd been so busy worrying about her sister, looking for cracks, that she hadn't examined her strengths.

"Mikhail had the ability to be charming to everyone he met. She probably would have liked him, but we'll never know."

Thank God.

"Nope, guess not." He finished the coffee. "Gotta hit the shower and wash off this horse piss."

"Please do. Hey, I usually fix breakfast for Nikki," she called as he walked away. "Today is egg sandwich day. Do you want me to make one for you?"

He'd paused in the entrance to the hallway. "I feel like I should say no because it's not your job to take care of me, but I'm not gonna. I'm a sucker for home cooking."

"It's just an egg sandwich. Bread, mayo, cheese, and egg. Nothing fancy, so don't get your hopes up."

"Still homemade. Thanks for asking."

"You're welcome."

When he'd gone, Callie got the pan from the cabinet, retrieved the butter, eggs, and bread, and got to work. Nikki was first to stroll in, ready for school in a pair of Capri pants and an equestrian shirt. She took her egg sandwich and poured another coffee, then stood at the counter to eat it while Callie assembled the others.

"I like Seth," she said between bites. "You did good, Cal."

And there was the heat of embarrassment. Or maybe it was the heat of knowing the whole thing was a lie.

"I'm glad you like him. But it's early days, Nik. I don't know what's going to happen or if we'll last beyond a couple of dates."

"You'll last. I believe. He's not the kind of guy who pretends to feel things he doesn't."

Oh, Lord.

"How do you know that?"

"Just a feeling. I mean, he wants to date you, but he didn't try to suck up to me. I like that about him. So I think it's going to last for a while. Maybe not forever, but longer than two dates."

"Maybe."

Nikki rolled her eyes. "Way to be positive, sis."

"Just being realistic."

"No, you're being pessimistic. You weren't always like this."

Callie didn't want to examine who she used to be when she was too worried about survival. She didn't have it in her to have this conversation right now.

"How's Jack these days? Do you feel ready for the show?"

"Way to change the subject, Cal," Nikki said with another eye roll. "I think we're ready. Lisa says we are. We've been taking our fences consistently, and our timing is good. Jack is in peak form. I think Lisa is a better trainer than he had back home. Mary was good, but she was too focused on performance over building a foundation to get to the next level."

"I'm glad you're happy with Lisa. I know moving wasn't easy for you."

Her eyes flashed with emotion. "I didn't want to stay there. I'm glad we left."

Callie reeled. All this time, she'd thought that Nikki missed home. The house she'd grown up in. Her friends. The life she'd had. She'd thought Nikki was homesick, and she'd felt guilty for not being able to find a job to keep her there with everything she knew. Not the house, because Callie couldn't have afforded it, but everything else.

"I didn't know."

"It hurt too much. Being there and knowing nothing was ever going to be the same again."

Callie reached for her sister's hand. Squeezed. "Oh, honey, I'm sorry."

Nikki squeezed back. "I know. But you lost them too. And your life changed because you had to take me."

"No," Callie said fiercely. "I didn't *have* to. I wanted to. Did you want to go to your *ciocia* in Poland instead?"

Nikki shuddered visibly. "No way. Aunt Beata is fun for a few days, but there's a reason she never settled down and had a family."

"You aren't wrong. She's a charming narcissist, but not in the least bit nurturing."

"So true. Plus she resembles Mom too much. That would hurt."

"I think you're right about that."

Nikki took the last bite of her sandwich and set the half-full cup of coffee on the counter. "I better get going. We've got so much to do in school today." She smacked her forehead. "Uh, wait a minute, no we don't. You sure I can't stay here? I won't get in the way of your romantic moments with Seth. Promise."

"No, sorry. You've still got to go, plus there aren't going

to be any romantic moments. You've got today and tomorrow, and then you're free for the summer, so don't complain."

"Okay," she said, dragging the word out into a hint of a whine. "But use protection if you get horizontal, you hear me?"

Callie's skin was on fire. "Nobody's getting horizontal. I've got projects to do, and Seth has a job, which I'm sure he will be going to when he's done showering."

He wasn't going anywhere, but Callie wasn't admitting that to her sister.

Nikki snatched up her keys, backpack, and riding gear before heading for the door. "See ya tonight! Bye, Seth!"

"Bye, kid," Seth said from behind her. Callie's skin prickled at the sound of his voice. How long had he been there?

The door banged shut, and Nikki's CR-V soon started up. Callie turned and went into the kitchen to find Seth looking at the two egg sandwiches she'd made.

"Pick whichever one you want. They're the same."

"Thanks," he said, taking one and biting into it.

Callie grabbed her own and went to the table with her coffee and phone, deliberately not asking how much of the conversation he'd heard.

Seth walked over and pulled out a chair to join her. "Ethan—he's the one with the New York accent—will pick up your sister's tail as soon as she's on the road. He'll follow her to school, make sure she's safe inside. When it's time for school to end, he'll be there and tail her to the stable. Then he'll follow her back here when she's done. She won't know he's there."

The tension in her body ebbed a fraction. "Thank you. I almost think I'm being paranoid, but then I remember

Mikhail is dead—murdered—and whoever he worked for is still out there."

Still wanting her to give them access to a top-secret government project.

"So, does Nikki always tell you to use protection if you get horizontal?"

Of course he'd heard that. Callie wanted to sink into the chair and disappear. "Actually, no. This would be the first time since we started living together that she thinks I might have a boyfriend."

"You haven't been on a date?"

"Not a single one." She managed a smile. "I've been a bit busy with moving, working hard, and making sure my sister is coping with our parents' deaths."

"Gotcha."

"What about you? You date anybody since moving to town? Will I need to keep an eye over my shoulder for a jealous ex?"

"Nope. Now if Kane was here like you originally wanted, you might need to watch yourself. He tends to leave a trail of broken hearts in his wake."

Kane was hot, but not as hot as Seth in her opinion. Still, he *was* nicer. Easier to talk to.

"It wasn't that I wanted him specifically. It's just that he was the nicest to me and I wanted a friendly face."

"And now?"

His iron-gray eyes glittered as they studied her. She didn't think it mattered to him what she said, not really, but she told the truth anyway. "I'm happy it's you. Even if you didn't remember me at first."

"Why?"

He seemed genuinely curious.

"What you see is what you get. You aren't flirting with me or pretending to be nice." She thought of what Nikki had said. *He's not the kind of guy to pretend he feels things he doesn't.*

Other than when they had to pretend to be dating for Nikki's sake, of course.

"Don't see the point in being fake. It's a waste of time. But I am capable of deception, Callie. Everyone is."

She swallowed. "I suppose they are."

"For the sake of full disclosure, I'll admit I didn't forget you. I thought I needed to pretend like I did so I could seem nice and trustworthy since I probably didn't make the best impression the first time. It was a calculated reset."

She gaped at him a moment. Then she laughed. "Damn, Seth, you are not a typical guy, are you?"

He shrugged. "Depends on what you mean by typical."

"I mean that we've known each other about twenty-four hours and you're already dropping truth bombs on me. Most guys wouldn't admit what you just did."

"I'm not most guys."

"Clearly not." She shook her head. "Mikhail pretended from the moment he met me until, I don't know, probably the past couple of months when I kept making excuses not to reveal more information. He pretended a personal interest at first, and we even dated in Poland. When I left, he pretended to have a long-distance relationship with me, but every bit of it was aimed at getting me to take the job at Griffin Research. I can't figure out why, not really. There are a lot of companies in this country working on secret projects for the government. Why this one? What is it about this company and this project he wanted? I've spent a lot of time thinking about that, and I still don't know."

"Think about what you do know. What could interest a foreign state or organization about that?"

She stared at him, wanting so badly to say more. It was only a defense satellite project. There were hundreds of satellites deployed already, with no doubt hundreds more in development. And if Mikhail had known about the project, why not send someone he knew would do his bidding? Why her?

She repeated some of what she'd been thinking to Seth. Not all of it, but the parts that weren't potentially revealing. Seth didn't seem surprised by any of it.

"He knew enough about the project to know he wanted someone on the inside," Seth said. "A programmer, specifically. Maybe he didn't know anyone else who could qualify for the job. Just because he had an informant at the company didn't mean they knew how to analyze code."

"I still don't understand why me specifically. It's not like programmers are rare beings."

"No. I hope you'll forgive me for saying this, but you're also young and female. To some men, that spells weakness. You're potentially more malleable than a senior programmer who's been in the profession for decades."

She ground her jaw. "You're probably right. Still pisses me off though."

She'd spent years proving herself as a talented programmer, both in college and since, and even now she worked on mundane tasks more often than she'd like because she wasn't senior—or male—enough. There were two women on the team. Her and Dr. Robbins, who was in charge. The other six were men, and while most of them were okay, a couple were openly hostile when Dr. Robbins wasn't in earshot.

"The other thing you haven't thought about," he continued, "is that just because Mikhail got you into place doesn't mean he knew what he was after. Spying is like a fishing expedition. You drop a line in the water and hope something bites. You've maybe been told this is a good spot to fish, but you don't really know. So you're casting again and again, trying for that bite. Trying to reel the fish in. Doesn't mean you will, though."

"How do you know so much about spies?"

"Part of my job in the military involved intelligence work. Plus, I like to read about intelligence gathering and cybercrime. It's my jam."

She was thinking about what he'd said. "So you think, potentially, that Mikhail and his employer didn't actually know what they were looking for. They just wanted to put someone in place—someone they believed they could manipulate—so they could gather the information and see if it was worth anything."

"Bingo." He'd finished the sandwich and pushed the plate away. "They probably had enough intel to make them believe they needed to know more, and they had the contacts to make it happen. That's where you came in."

"He began recruiting me long before I had to leave Poland. A couple of months at least." Her blood suddenly froze in her veins. "Oh my God, my parents. It was only after they died that I had to come back to the States and take care of Nikki. I wasn't planning to leave Poland for another year, maybe two. You don't think…"

She couldn't finish the thought. It was horrible. Upsetting. If her parents had died because of her—because somebody wanted her to go to work for Griffin Research in Huntsville—how could she live with that? She'd never considered it before but now that someone had murdered Mikhail….

"Callie." She focused on the handsome face that was suddenly a lot nearer than before. He'd moved his chair until his knees were touching hers. His hand was on hers, holding firmly. She squeezed back, needing the pressure of his grip to ground her.

"Babe," he said, his voice soft and soothing. "I'm not

going to tell you it's not possible, that it didn't happen that way, but I will tell you that thinking it doesn't make it true. Mikhail told you about the job and then your parents died, leaving you open to take it. Doesn't mean he made that happen. Just means it made it a lot easier for him to get you here."

She nodded, thinking. "There was an avalanche that day. They were skiing the back country, possibly not paying attention to the markers… Somebody could have tricked them." She dragged in a breath. "But that's a lot of effort to go through just to get me to take a job where I might not have learned anything useful."

"It is."

"But that doesn't mean they wouldn't have gone that far."

His expression didn't soften. "Also true. It's a lot of effort to get one woman where you want her to be. But not impossible if you want it badly enough."

Callie closed her eyes, her heart pounding. "I hate this. I hate thinking these things. I hate Mikhail and I hate whoever he worked for."

"I know. But I need you to look at me."

She did. His eyes were hard, determined.

"Now listen to me good, sweetheart. You doing that?"

She nodded. She couldn't speak as he leaned toward her, close enough she could see the dark flecks in his silvery eyes.

"I'm going to find who did this to you, who put you in this situation and tried to hurt you. I'm going to find them. And then I'm going to end them."

Chapter Eighteen

Seth took Callie to the range so he could pick up cameras for her house. Ghost had texted that they'd had a new shipment and Seth wanted to get it done ASAP. He'd decided to go with door sensors and cameras, plus cameras in the main living areas. He'd pick up some window sensors too.

No use putting a state of the art system in when the cops were so far away. The most important thing was the ability to call for help and he'd make sure the system could do that. Whether or not they could zoom in and count the hairs on some dude's chin didn't matter as much.

Besides, he'd told her he was going to find the person who'd threatened her while pretending to be Volkov. Whether or not it was the same person who'd murdered Volkov and thrown him into the Potomac was irrelevant. Outcome was the same.

He intended to find the motherfucker and stop whatever the asshole had planned.

Find the mastermind behind Volkov and then Ghost Ops could fulfill their mission. Athena would launch on time, the bad guys wouldn't get the technology, and the nation would be safe from nuclear attack.

Then what? Back to DC to rejoin HOT? Or keep the early retirement and do something else for a change?

But what?

He didn't know anymore. He still leaned toward active duty, but it was too soon to think about anything permanent. Too many variables still in play.

Seth parked around the side of the building and led Callie inside through the staff areas. The guys were all there today. Kane and Blaze were on range duty, but Ethan, Chance, and Ghost were in the stock room, going through inventory. Daphne stood in the door with a clipboard and a pen.

Everyone turned when Seth arrived with Callie bringing up the rear.

"Did we get a lot of fun stuff?" he asked.

Ethan grinned. "You know it. New ammo, new guns, and new security systems. Hey, Callie. How are you today? This guy being a dickhead or is he behaving?"

Seth frowned. "Why would I be a dickhead?"

Callie laughed as she came up to stand beside him. "I'm okay, thanks. Seth is Seth. But I have no complaints," she added.

He thought that last sentence might be an afterthought. He was going to have to ask about that later. Yeah, he'd come on a bit strong when he'd told her he was basically going to kill the assholes who'd manipulated and hurt her, but that's what he was going to do. Why pretty it up?

"No complaints is good," Ethan said.

"Why would she complain?" Seth asked. "I've done a thorough security check, put up trail cameras, mucked a stall, and listened to a teenager talk about fairies. I think I deserve a friggin' medal here."

Callie snorted softly. Ethan blinked. "Fairies?"

Daphne was biting her lip while Ghost looked as if he was trying to solve a Rubik's cube. Chance was shaking his head like the rest of them were ill-informed. "Dude, it's Fae, not fairies."

"How the fuck would you know?"

Chance looked a bit put upon at the moment. "Rory reads all kinds of romance books. I know more than I want to, and I'm guessing a sixteen year-old is reading about Fae romance, not fairies. Wild guess, but I think I'm right."

"You're right," Callie said.

"Way to back me up, Callie," Seth grumbled.

She elbowed him in the side. What the fuck? But she wasn't looking at him, and everybody else was wearing some variation of a smile. Even she was grinning.

Which meant she was comfortable enough with him to joke around. He liked that. Nobody ever did that kind of thing with him. Women didn't, anyway. His guys ribbed the shit out of him, but he ribbed right back. It's what they did.

He didn't usually get that casual with a woman, though. Not enough time to reach that stage. The initial stage was about flirtation. The next stage was the down and dirty sex. After he'd had his fill, he moved on.

Funny thing was, he'd known Callie for all of twenty-four hours and she was already playing around like they'd been a couple for ages. Coulda knocked his ass over with a feather, but he liked it. It was something different than he was used to.

"We should get Rory and your sister together," Chance said. "They can talk all day about that shit. Unless you read it too? In which case I guess the three of you could talk about it."

"I read a little of those books, but not as much as Nikki."

"What about you, Daphne?" Chance said. "You in on this Fae stuff too?"

She held up a hand. "No, I am not. But I'm thinking I need to try it."

"What are you trying to do, Chance? Start a book club?" Seth asked.

Chance arched an eyebrow. "So long as you don't have to read it, what do you care?"

"Guess I don't."

"Rory's a bundle of hormones and she's also dealing with her diabetes. If I can do anything to take her mind off it and let her have a good time, I'm doing it." He shrugged. "Call me whipped if you want, but that woman owns me body and soul."

Seth actually heard Callie and Daphne sigh. It was that loud.

"Nikki would love it," Callie said.

"I'm in," Daphne said. "Somebody tell me where to start and I'll head over to the library and see if they have it."

"I'll text you some titles later," Chance said. "After I ask Rory. I'll send them to you, too, Callie. Then you can see if your sister has read them or not."

"Sounds good to me."

"If Rory's up to it, we'll have a cookout at the house and y'all can talk. Hell, guess I'd better text Emma the list too."

Daphne cleared her throat. "You realize that a book club is usually a thing where women get together, eat snacks and drink, and talk about the book, right? It's not typically held in conjunction with a cookout where a bunch of men are going to sit around a grill and cook—and make a colossal mess, I might add. There's already a club that meets at the library, by the way. They mostly read mysteries and thrillers, though. But they have a potluck lunch in one of the meeting rooms and sometimes they even have guest authors. In case anyone's interested."

"What are you saying, Daph?" Seth asked. "You aren't raining on Chance's parade, are you?"

Daphne's mouth twisted. "Not at all. But I've seen the dirty dishes that result from One Shot Tactical cookouts. Even if y'all promise to do them all, it's a distraction."

Chance waved a hand. "Fine, point taken. Drinks and snacks at our house. The men will purchase barbecue from the Gas-n-Go and eat it outside beneath the oak tree."

"If you guys are done planning book clubs and shit," Seth said, "I want to see what we've got in that shipment. Need to put together a system for Callie."

"Wait. You didn't tell me that," Callie burst out. "You were supposed to give me a price first."

"How about you give me a price."

"Wh-what?" Her eyes were adorably confused.

Adorably?

Odd thought to have. "Tell me what you want to spend, and I'll go from there."

Callie darted a look at the others, who suddenly seemed absorbed in what they were doing. "I don't know," she said, her eyes on his again.

"Tell him no more than a thousand," Ghost said. "And he'll do it for half that."

"That doesn't sound like enough."

"It's enough," Seth said. "We aren't running wires through walls, and you don't need sophisticated equipment. I can still customize it for you, though."

Callie's eyes remained big. "Okay. I can't argue with that."

"Not only can't," Seth replied. "But shouldn't."

He thought she wanted to argue with him, but her trembling lip firmed after a second and she nodded.

While Seth started digging through the new equipment with the guys, Daphne took Callie to her desk in the front office. He heard something about coffee and a chat as they walked away. He had a moment where he panicked about Callie mentioning what'd happened last night when he'd confessed about his daughter, but he'd told her it was private and he knew she'd honor that.

Though it was odd to think this woman he barely knew had personal information about him that none of his guys did. He hadn't told her the full truth, though. He wouldn't be able to avoid that if he started talking about Mia with his teammates. Then what?

"Y'all seem cozy," Chance said when the click of Daphne's heels had faded into the distance.

Seth stopped moving equipment to stare at his teammate with what he hoped was a cool stare. "We are not cozy. She's a client, and I'm her protector."

"Sad and pretty. Wasn't that what you said?" Ethan chimed in.

"You too? Yes, I said that. And she is. Sad and pretty. Doesn't mean I can't be professional about this."

"If anybody can be professional with a pretty lady, it's you."

"Meaning?"

Ethan and Chance exchanged a look. Ghost cut in. "Stop annoying Seth. He's not a robot, and that cool-headed ability to ignore his client's emotional state is an asset, not a detractor. Why do you think I sent him? The last two of my operators to get it into their thick skulls to protect a woman have ended up declaring their undying love while spouting poetry and shit."

Chance looked offended. "I haven't spouted one lick of poetry."

"'That woman owns me body and soul,'" Ghost repeated. "You think that's not poetry to a woman's ears? Hell, you practically had two of them melt into puddles on the floor when you said that. You'd cut off your right arm for Rory. Worse, you'd tell everyone who'd listen that you're willing. Poetry, dude."

Chance looked like a dog hearing a strange noise. "Huh. Didn't think of it that way."

"Blaze is just as bad," Ghost added. "But Seth—I can fucking count on him *not* to make a mushy ass of himself with this girl."

Seth wanted to rewind and ask if anybody really thought he was a robot when it came to emotions, but the conversation had moved way beyond that now. "Not getting mushy, boss," he said because it seemed like the thing Ghost wanted to hear. Telling Callie about Mia wasn't mushy. Not typical, but not mushy either.

"See? No mush, all business. That's what I like to hear. She tell you anything else about what's going on?"

"Only that her boss asked her to stay that night. But she often asks people to stay on a rotating basis, so it might be nothing."

"You'd think if the boss was involved she could do the dirty work herself."

Seth hesitated. "There's something else though." Three pairs of eyes looked at him with interest. "I asked her if there was anything she was doing that nobody else could. She said no. But I think she's lying."

"Why?"

Leave it to Ghost to cut right to the chase. "Body

language. Refusing to look at me when I asked. Fidgeting before she answered me."

"What do you think it is?" Ethan said.

"Don't know. She says she's only a junior programmer, that she proofs the code and searches for mistakes. But her college transcripts indicate she's not your average graduate. Top of the class, wrote a program that saved the university millions for her senior project. I can't imagine the lab is limiting her to proofing code if she's got the talent to do more."

Ghost looked thoughtful. "We really need that cable to come back online."

"We've got everything that was there before we lost communication. It'll take hours—days maybe—but I can isolate her input based on her logins. See what I can learn. I'll set up a secure channel and login remotely. I won't transfer any information, but I can run scripts to analyze the info."

"Didn't we already send the information we downloaded to Washington?" Chance asked, his gaze darting between Seth and Ghost.

"We didn't, in fact," Ghost said, studying a fingernail. "Yet. Network interference or something. I can't quite recall."

"That's right," Seth said. "Not safe."

Which they all knew was bullshit. They were to the point that none of them completely trusted those in power to deal with them straight. So long as Ghost Ops did their mission and kept the Athena Project from being stolen or scuttled before it was launched, then it didn't matter how they did it. Keeping information to themselves was the safe bet at the moment. What they were doing—downloading proprietary and top-secret information from a secure server belonging to a defense contractor—was already illegal as fuck. Didn't need more people knowing about it.

Trust no one but each other. That was their unspoken motto.

"Make it happen," Ghost said. "If we get caught, our asses are grass. But that's true anyway, so why the fuck not? I'm tired of tiptoeing around politicians and wondering whose side they're on. Besides their own."

"Amen," Ethan muttered.

Seth placed the things he'd selected into a One Shot Tactical shopping bag. "I'll get started on it today. After I take Callie to see a dog."

Chance grinned. "Man, I tried to get a dog for Rory, but she shut me down."

"Oh, Callie doesn't want one, but it's happening anyway. Volkov's death shook her up enough that she won't refuse."

Ghost looked troubled. "Yeah, still don't have anything on potentials yet. The man was found with half his head blown off and nobody in Washington's got any ideas."

"So long as it wasn't one of the alphabet agencies," Seth muttered. Because that created a whole new level of fun for everyone.

"Could be," Ghost said. "If we're lucky it's nothing more than an internal squabble with whoever employed him to steal information. If we aren't lucky, then the alphabet agencies are hot on the trail of something that could impact us here."

"Well, fuck," Chance said. "And here I was thinking we might be ready to put an end to this mess now that we've got Callie and access."

"Hardly," Seth replied. "Too many unknowns."

"Yeah, yeah, my parade is officially rained on," Chance said.

"There's one more thing," Seth added. "Callie's parents. Their deaths, her having to return home to take custody of her sister—that's how she ended up at Griffin Research Labs. She said she hadn't planned on leaving Poland until that happened. They were killed on a ski slope when they ignored signs and got caught in an avalanche. Callie made the leap this morning to wondering if their deaths were somehow deliberate."

"Jesus," Ghost said, shoving a hand through his dark hair.

"Yeah. I told her it was possible but not the most likely scenario."

"I'm beginning to believe there is nothing about this mission and the people involved that's the least bit ordinary," Ghost replied with a grim expression.

Seth didn't say what was in his head, but he knew the rest of them were thinking it as well by the way they looked at each other. Were they meant to succeed… Or was somebody hoping they'd fail?

Chapter Nineteen

"Where are we going?"

Callie was having a hard time ignoring the sign up ahead that indicated there was a dog training and boarding center at the end of the driveway. They'd left One Shot Tactical over half an hour ago, and Seth had said he had something he needed to see in Madison. She hadn't asked what since she figured it was none of her business and she was just going along for the ride.

They'd talked a little before lapsing into silence. She'd asked about Rory Harper's diabetes. She hadn't realized Rory had the disease, but she was type one, which meant she'd had it for much of her life. And now she was pregnant, which added a whole new list of potential complications, but so far she was doing well. It was still early days. Callie gathered that everyone at One Shot Tactical was concerned but they all took it a day—a doctor's appointment—at a time.

"Seth, are you taking me to a dog spa?"

Sure enough, he flipped on his signal and turned into the long drive. "You need a dog."

She was going to kill him. "I don't want a dog. I told you I've got enough to do without a dog adding more responsibility."

Seth stopped his truck in the drive and turned to face her. "Babe. Listen to me. Somebody set a fire in the building where you work, perilously close to the lab you were in at the time. You almost didn't get out alive and you're still coughing from the experience. The man who urged you to take that job, and then asked you to do something illegal, is now dead. Do you really want to argue about adding a dog to your protective detail?"

She frowned as a ream of excuses flooded her head. But he was right. Did she really want to refuse anything that might help keep her and Nikki alive?

"Is this permanent?"

"Not if you don't want it to be." He jerked his head toward the direction they were traveling. "This is a rescue and rehab facility. The lady who runs it takes all kinds of dogs and makes them ready for new homes. She has a Belgian Malinois that I think would be perfect for you and Nikki."

"A Malinois? Aren't those police and military dogs?"

"Yep. This one wasn't raised in that environment though. She's sweet, thinks she's a lapdog, but she's also got that instinct to protect. Betty says she was owned by an older woman who recently passed. She had no kids other than this dog and some cats."

Callie's heart thumped. She felt sorry for the dog, but she still didn't know if taking an animal when she wasn't sure she'd keep it was the right thing to do.

"It's normal to try a dog out for a few days, Callie. Betty doesn't want you to commit today. She just wants to place the dog in a good situation."

Callie drew in a breath. If she didn't have to commit, maybe they could try. "Okay. What's her name?"

"Luna. She's four years old."

"Nikki's going to get attached."

"Is that a bad thing?"

"Maybe. What happens in a year when she goes to college and it's just me and Luna?"

"You'll have a companion that will keep you company and look out for you until Nikki comes home on breaks. Then she'll look out for you both."

"You're a bad man, Seth King."

He grinned, and her heart skipped. Why did he have to be so damn attractive? Especially when he was maneuvering her into things she didn't want to do?

"Just doing my job."

He started down the drive again. She folded her arms and tried not to pout. "When did you have time to search up a rescue Malinois anyway?"

"I've got my sources. Betty is highly recommended. I called and she said she had something that might work. I told her you're my girlfriend and I want you to have a dog for protection."

Callie gave him a look. "Seriously?"

"It was the easiest explanation."

He wasn't wrong, and they were already committed to pretending to date for Nikki's sake. Which *was* her fault because she hadn't wanted to tell the truth and scare her sister.

Seth parked and a lady came outside to stand on her porch as they got out of the truck. She was older, pretty, with long blond hair that fell over one shoulder in a big braid. She wore a T-shirt that read *Who rescued who?* with a silhouette of a dog and cat sitting together with their tails forming a heart beneath them.

"Seth King?"

"Yes, ma'am." He looped an arm around Callie's shoulders and pulled her forward. "This is Callie."

"Hi, Callie. Nice to meet you. I'm Betty. Y'all come on over to the kennel and let me show you Luna."

Seth dropped his arm from her shoulder but took her hand in his. Callie couldn't think of anything but his big hand wrapped around hers as they followed Betty into the building that looked more like a house from the outside than a kennel. Inside, it wasn't what she expected. There were no wire cages, no dogs looking sad. Everything was sleek and modern, with clean lines and friendly signs.

Betty stopped before a door and turned to them. "Luna has been here for a month now. I had to keep her in the house the first week, but she's learned to transition to the day spa and boarding suites now. She's incredibly sweet, but she's still a Malinois. Full of energy, smart, and capable of fiercely defending her people if necessary."

"You said she's had some training, but nothing like she'd have had as a working dog," Seth said.

"Right. She can sit and stay and obey commands like *no* and *down*. She has that natural instinct that Malinois have to protect and defend, but you can't command her to do it. She also gets along with cats because the lady had three and Luna was raised with them."

Betty opened the door and led them into another hallway where there were several doors. Then she opened one in particular and a beautiful reddish-brown dog with a wide face brushed in black around her jaw, eyes, and ears hopped off her doggie bed, tail wagging as she hurried over to see Betty.

Her legs were black too, and she looked kind of like a German Shepherd. Though not as big or fuzzy. She was more compact, and that tail was going a mile a minute. Betty dropped to her knees and scrubbed the dog's neck with her hands, telling her what a good girl she was.

Callie's heart cracked. Betty must have noticed because she smiled and nodded. "Call her name and she'll come to you."

"Hi, Luna," Callie said, kneeling with a hand out.

Luna trotted over, ears alert, but the tail was still wagging. Then she licked Callie's fingers and her heart melted even more. She loved dogs, but she hadn't had one since she was a kid and her mom's purse dog died. Not literally a purse dog, but small enough to fit into a tote bag whenever they left the house. Her mother had loved that little beast—Coco, because of course that was her name— to distraction. Callie had loved her too, even if Coco preferred her mother and growled at Callie when she'd had enough attention.

Then there'd been the dogs at the barn, big Great Danes that she'd loved for their size and sweetness. She'd always said she'd get a dog someday, but it'd been impossible when she was working overseas. She'd kept putting it off after they moved here because there was always so much to be done with work and horses, and she hadn't wanted to add a dog to the mix. She worried that a dog would be home alone all day without enough attention.

"She'll be a good dog for you if you give her a chance," Betty said. "Seth told me you live in a remote area and wanted a dog to help you feel safer."

"Yes," Callie said. "It's me and my sister, and a horse and barn cat. I think sometimes it'd be nice to have a dog that could alert us to trouble or scare off anyone who wanted to rob us."

"You can take her home to try her out, see if she's a fit

for your family and situation. I ask you to sign an agreement if you end up adopting her where you promise not to rehome her but to bring her back to me if anything ever changes. There's an adoption fee of one-fifty to help with expenses. You'll get her papers after the fee is paid. Today, you'll get her food, toys, and treats, and we'll have a training session before you leave the premises to make sure you understand her commands and that she listens to you. And if you ever want further training, you get a discount because she's one of my rescues."

Betty's gaze turned to Seth. "You said you were former military. Did you ever work in or around military working dogs?"

"Yes, ma'am, I've been around them. I wasn't a handler, though. But I know how specialized those dogs are. Luna may look like one of them, but she isn't."

Betty nodded. "That's right. We talked about it over the phone, but I wanted to be sure you understood. If you want to take her home because she's a Malinois and they're popular right now, then I'd rather keep her here and find someone else. She's not a dog from the movies. She has all the energy and stamina, but none of the specialized training. She's not going to impress anyone's buddies by fighting other dogs or attacking what she's told to attack."

"Ma'am, if anyone tried to hurt this dog, I'd break every bone in their body. Pets are family."

Betty stared at him. Callie was still petting Luna, but she found herself staring at him too. He'd said it so smoothly, so mildly, but she knew he was deadly serious. A wave of emotion swamped her at how protective he was of a dog they didn't even have custody of yet. And the knowledge that he was that protective of her and Nikki made her eyes sting.

Betty laughed a moment later. "I like you. You're my kind of people."

"And you're mine," he replied. "Anybody who puts in the effort you do for homeless animals is worth knowing."

"Did anyone adopt the cats Luna was raised with?" Callie asked, feeling emotional and weepy and trying not to let any of it show.

"All three went to a family in Madison. I check on them regularly and they're doing well. But that family has little girls and didn't think they could take on a dog Luna's size—or with her energy. As much as I would have loved to keep them together, I just couldn't insist on it."

"I understand." Callie got to her feet while Luna went over to her bed and picked up a toy that she brought back. A set of rubber rings that had been chewed all to hell.

Betty reached for them, and Luna growled and shook her head. It wasn't a mean growl though, and Betty's next move proved it. She pointed at the ground and said, "Drop it."

Luna dropped the rings at Betty's feet and backed up. Betty picked them up and threw them across the room. Luna bounded after them, scooped them up, and shook her head viciously while growling and whipping them back and forth. Then she trotted over and dropped them.

Betty threw them again, and the whole performance repeated as she looked at Callie. "So what do you think? Are you willing to give Luna a try, or is she too scary?"

Callie watched as the dog settled on her bed and chewed the rings. She looked at Seth, who was watching her but said nothing. Then she met Betty's gaze.

"I think she's perfect. I'd love to take her home."

It took another hour of touring the facility, having a training session, talking with Betty about Luna's habits and needs, and loading up Luna and her stuff before they were on the way back to Sutton's Creek. Luna sat in the back seat of the truck, panting but happy, her ears up as she watched things out the window. Callie turned around to look at her from time to time and Luna wagged her tail happily.

It made her emotional for some silly reason she couldn't explain.

"You've been quiet," Seth said after they'd gone about ten minutes without speaking.

She turned to him, eyebrow arched. "I thought that's how you liked it."

"I do. But getting a dog is a big deal. I thought you might have something to say."

"Oh, like I told you I don't need a dog and how dare you take me to look at one anyway?"

"Something like that."

She blew out a breath and shrugged. "Too late now. She's here, and unless she does some crazy shit at the house and I feel she's not safe for me or Nikki, I have a dog for life."

Which would be damned inconvenient if she was still trying to leave town. But she wasn't, though the idea still simmered appealingly in the background. Still, Seth was right. Disappearing the right way took a village. She'd only make herself and Nikki more vulnerable if she went on the run. Their best bet was Seth and his friends.

But for how long? When would this be over?

And then what?

Once Nikki graduated and went off to college, Callie could take a job anywhere. She could go back to Poland, though the idea didn't really appeal the way it once had. When she'd been twenty-four, working as a programmer for a government agency in DC, she'd longed to do something more exciting. An opportunity came up to move to

Poland and teach software development to Polish military for the US government, and she'd jumped on it.

She hadn't wanted to leave that job, despite Mikhail's promise of a fantastic job in Huntsville, because she'd enjoyed the travel she got to do on her off time. A three-day weekend? Go to Paris! A few days off here or there? Fly to Rome!

Being that free again should be something she looked forward to—but she didn't. Returning to the States to take charge of her sister had changed something in her. Not only that, but she liked where they lived. Sutton's Creek was filled with charm, even if she didn't spend as much time in town as she might have liked. Because she worked in Huntsville, she was familiar with the things available close to her workplace. She needed to change that and explore Sutton's Creek.

"I'll pay the adoption fee. It was my idea, so you shouldn't have to."

"You don't have to do that."

"I know. But if you keep her, I want to. Least I could do."

"Okay, then I'll let you."

"Good." He looked smug.

"What now?" she asked.

"You like dogs. I thought maybe you didn't, or that you were scared of them."

"I never said I didn't like them. I just said I didn't want one. I already feel the pressure of taking care of the human and animals in my care. Adding another one wasn't high on my list of priorities."

"You've got Nikki to help you. She's a good kid and she cares about you."

"She is." Callie snorted suddenly. "She's going to freak out. First I bring home a guy who tells her we're dating and now I've got a dog? She'll wonder if I'm having a quarter-life crisis."

"Is that even a thing?"

"It's a thing. Some people feel like their lives aren't adequate or moving in the right direction. Anxiety, depression, FOMO. Lots more symptoms than that, actually. I think I might have one if I wasn't so busy with the life I have right now. Maybe when Nikki goes to college, I'll question everything and decide to join a nunnery."

"Not a nunnery. Get a sports car and shave your head or something. At least you can still have sex that way. Human connection. It matters."

She told herself not to think about all the images his words conjured. No, no, no.

"You mean you can still have sex if you find someone who doesn't mind that you have no hair."

"Trust me, honey, most guys aren't going to care. It's sex with a pretty woman, hair or not."

"Thank you. I think."

"You're welcome."

"Have you ever questioned your direction in life, Seth?"

He seemed like he had it together. She wasn't sure she'd ever felt like she had it together.

He hesitated. "No, never. I've questioned decisions I made, though. But I think we all do that. I never questioned the decision to join the military. It was the right thing for me. Got me out of my grandparents' house and set me free."

He'd said yesterday that they were assholes. It bothered her to think of him as a little boy in that environment. "I'm sorry they weren't nicer people."

"It's okay. Wasn't all their fault. They'd raised their kid, my dad, and then he dropped me off and never came back, though he sent money from time to time. Not enough. So they got to do the child-raising all over again. I think they were resentful. Like he stole their retirement years or something. 'Course they could have had child protective services come get me, but they never did."

"They didn't have to take it out on you."

"They didn't have to, but it was probably the only thing they had in common by then. I think they could stand the sight of each other only a little better than they could me, which wasn't much. They bickered all the time. My grandma watched her news programs around the clock. She hated everyone, thought everyone was out to get her. My grandpa longed for the glory days, whatever those were, and hated everyone too, especially if they weren't white like him. Said they were the cause for all his problems and he'd be happy when somebody taught them a lesson."

Anger bubbled beneath her skin. Her mother had faced narrow-minded people when they didn't like that her English was accented. If it ever bothered her, Callie didn't know because she would sniff and tell Callie that she should never pay attention to bullies or let them get to her.

"They sound like delightful people."

"Soooo delightful. My grandpa died first, and my grandma had the nerve to call and demand I pay to bury him. I told her to fuck off. For all I know he got a pine box and no frills. He didn't deserve that much. Neither did she. They left their property to their church. I didn't expect them to leave it to me, but if they had I'd have sold it as quickly as possible and donated the money to a charity for orphans. Kinda sorry I didn't get to do that, but maybe the church will do something good with it."

Callie was still thinking about all he'd said before she answered when her phone buzzed with a text. She picked it up, assuming it was Nikki telling her about something at school. She'd texted off and on about how boring things were this week in an attempt to guilt Callie into letting her cut the rest of the school year.

But it wasn't Nikki.

It was Mikhail.

Chapter Twenty

Seth could feel Callie go still before he looked
over and saw the whiteness of her skin. She was already
pale, but this was the kind of pale that came with fear.

Rage boiled in his belly. He worked to keep his voice
smooth. "What is it?"

"Mikhail. Or not Mikhail, rather. He says he's in town
and we need to meet."

"Don't answer it yet."

"I didn't intend to. I haven't actually clicked on it so he
—they—won't get a notification I've seen it."

"Good girl."

He whipped a U-turn using a farmer's driveway and
aimed the truck in a different direction.

"Where are we going?" There was an edge of panic to
her voice.

"The range." He glanced at his watch, then hit the
button on the steering wheel to activate the voice
command and told the AI to call Ethan.

"Yo," Ethan said.

"I've got you on speaker. Can you check the locator for Nikki Crowell?"

He felt Callie's eyes on him.

"Just a sec… Car's at the school."

"Can you go early? Callie just got a text from whoever's got Volkov's phone, asking to meet. I'd rather be over cautious than not."

"Copy that. On my way. Where are you?"

"Headed to the range. Give Gho—Alex a heads up, would you?"

He cursed himself for nearly saying Ghost, but to his way of thinking it'd been a ridiculous ask of them anyway. They were former military, guys who'd served in combat. It wasn't unheard of for them to have code names. He got why they had to get used to calling each other by their first names, because that's what civilians did, but the occasional code name shouldn't surprise anyone.

"Stopping there now. I'll shoot you a text when I've got a visual of the target."

"Thanks, brother."

The call ended and Callie said, very quietly, "The target?"

"Nikki. It just means she's the target of observation. Military shorthand."

"It's kind of an ominous word, though. Isn't there a better one?"

A glance at her told him she was keeping it together, but she was also thinking. Hard.

"I guess we could say client. I'll propose it."

He wouldn't, because a lifetime of training wasn't going to change so easily, but if it made her feel better, he'd tell her whatever she wanted to hear.

"You won't," she said, echoing his thoughts. "You're just trying to make me comfortable."

"Truth. Did it work?"

"Not really." She dragged in a breath. "Okay, so Mikhail is dead, but his phone is still active and somebody just asked to meet as if they were him."

She was frowning hard. Thinking, analyzing. He wanted to ask what she wasn't telling him, but he knew if he did, she'd deny it. He'd get it out of her eventually, but he was going to have to ease it out.

"Did he usually text for a meeting?"

"Sometimes. Sometimes he called. He kept it all very casual until the last time when he gave me that cable and said I had to do what he asked or I'd regret it."

Fury was the emotion boiling in his stomach.

"You always met with him?"

"I did. I felt a sense of obligation, I guess. We weren't dating but I thought he was my friend. And he'd helped me get the job. I wasn't comfortable with his questions, but I thought I owed him. I never refused to see him when he was in town. But that last time…" She shivered. "I didn't tell him I couldn't do it. I said it would take time because I wasn't alone in the lab and I had to do it when nobody was looking. I needed time to think, to figure out what to do. Because I wasn't going to be responsible for revealing government secrets like that. He told me I needed to hurry because I was nearly out of time."

"Then somebody texted you from his phone three days ago and told you time was up."

"Yes. I thought it was Mikhail. I said I couldn't do it, that I'd be risking my career and jail time if I did. I asked him to please understand. I appealed to our friendship even though I suspected we didn't really have one. That it'd all been in my mind. There was no response."

"Then the lab caught fire."

"Then the lab caught fire." She turned to him. "I told you

I was trapped in the office, but I didn't tell you I swiped my card repeatedly and the door wouldn't open. The sprinkler system was laggy too. I thought I was going to die in there, but the sprinklers finally came on and the firemen arrived."

He knew about the door because he'd seen it in the badging records. She'd made twenty-two attempts before the door was opened by security.

"Did you swipe it too fast?"

"I thought I had, so I slowed down. Still didn't work. I tried so many times I lost count. I was frantic, ready to claw my way through the door. Then the sprinklers started." She shook her head. "When I was inside the lab, I had the uncanny feeling Mikhail was watching me. Except there are no CCTV cameras inside so he couldn't be. Not to mention he was already dead."

Seth knew it could be paranoia making her think so, but what if it wasn't?

He and his team hadn't searched inside the lab when they did the security assessment. Chance had gotten in and had a look around, but he hadn't been able to remove ceiling panels or inspect the room for signs of surveillance equipment. His mission had been to replace the cables on two computers and gain access to the secure network, which he'd done. That had been their objective, and they'd achieved it. A primary and a backup. In and out. Surveillance equipment hadn't been part of their plan— nor had searching for someone else's equipment.

They should have put their own cameras in and fuck Washington. And they should have checked for others.

Maybe they still could. The lab was closed for repair. They could infiltrate the building and search in the early hours of the morning. If there were cameras inside, maybe having them would lead him to whoever put them there.

But he couldn't be part of the team that went in. He'd have to let others do the work without him because he had to stay with Callie and Nikki. There was no excuse he could make to be gone for a few hours in the middle of the night, and there was nowhere for them to go that he considered safe.

Until he and the team knew what they were dealing with, he wasn't letting Callie out of his sight.

There were a few cars at the range when they arrived. Seth parked around the side of the building where the staff usually parked and looked at Callie.

"Do you want to take Luna or do you want me to do it?"

She glanced behind her at the dog watching them both, her ears swiveling, mouth open in a pant. "I'll take her. We need to get used to each other."

They exited the truck and he waited for Callie to snap on Luna's leash. Then she met him in front of the truck and the three of them headed for the building, Callie telling Luna to be a good girl as Seth held the door and they passed inside.

He led the way down the hall to the offices. Ghost was at his desk. He looked up, his expression giving nothing away as Seth stopped in the door.

"See you got a dog."

"Yep. This is Luna. She looks like a killer, but she thinks she's a lap dog."

"Still, she's a Malinois. They've got the instinct."

"That's what I thought," Seth said.

"What do you think about having a dog, Callie?" Ghost asked, putting down his pen and coming around the desk.

Callie rubbed one of Luna's ears. "Wasn't in my plan,

but she's sweet and she needs a home. I think she'll work out fine."

"That's good. So you got a text, huh?"

"I did."

"Guess we need to figure out what to do next," Ghost said, shooting a look at Seth. "Chance is range officer at the moment, but I'll let the others know you're here. Go ahead and sit. I'll get them to bring more chairs and we'll talk in here."

Ghost disappeared down the hall while Seth and Callie took the two chairs in front of his desk, moving them to make room for two more.

"Luna, sit," Callie said, and the dog dropped to her haunches beside Callie's chair.

Kane, Ethan, and Blaze returned with Ghost. All of them fussed over Luna, who wagged her tail and pushed her face against their hands as if she'd won the doggie attention lottery. Which she probably had. But as soon as Callie called her back to sit, she sat, tongue out as she watched everyone in the room.

"The facts as we know them are this," Ghost said. "Mikhail Volkov is dead. He worked for the Dashevsky Group, a humanitarian organization, as a translator. He recruited Callie to work at Griffin Research Labs, where he presumably had a contact who was able to make certain she was the person hired."

Callie shifted in her seat. "I *am* qualified for the job. It's possible I was the most qualified person who applied."

Ghost nodded. "That's true. Forgive me for suggesting you were only hired as a favor to Volkov."

"I might have been, but it's not the only reason anyone would. That's all I meant."

"Understood, and you're right. I shouldn't have assumed. We know Volkov is dead, but somebody has his phone and they've asked for a meeting with Callie. They haven't admitted they aren't him, just said they're in town and want to meet. Obviously, if Callie were to go through with this meeting, she'd know it's not Volkov. This person is either prepared for it, or they don't care because they don't intend to let her walk away."

Beside him, Seth could feel Callie stiffen. He reached over and put a hand on her thigh, squeezed lightly. She turned big eyes on him, and he gave her a quick nod to let her know he was on her side. That nothing was going to happen to her.

"What we need to figure out is whether we want this meeting to take place," Ghost finished. "What can we learn if we do? What are the risks?"

"Uh, the obvious risk is me," Callie said, her voice soft. Seth could hear the undercurrent of fear, but he was also proud of her for speaking up. Not that he knew why he felt that way. Whether or not she spoke wasn't going to change their handling of the situation. Still, she wasn't sitting idly by and letting Ghost make the decisions.

"We wouldn't let anything happen to you," Seth said.

The others echoed him.

"If you take the meeting, the environment would be controlled," Ghost added. "Unless you refuse, which is your right. If so, I'd still ask you to set it up, make this person think you're coming. They might relax their guard, giving us a chance to intercept."

"That sounds dangerous," Callie said. "Shouldn't we call the police instead? Let them deal with this person."

"We can't do that, Callie," Seth told her gently. "For the reason you said. They *are* dangerous. And we're more equipped to handle them than the police."

She stared at him, her eyes searching his. He could see the doubt there. The disbelief. "You're former military, I get that. But you aren't police. And if anything happens—anyone gets hurt or there's violence—they *will* get involved. Then what?"

Seth exchanged a look with Ghost. Ghost sighed and cleared his throat. "We know how to do this without leaving evidence. We weren't just military. We were Special Operations. We did things for our government that required us not to be seen or heard or leave a trail. We're uniquely equipped to help you deal with this situation, Callie. But you have to trust us."

He could see the understanding begin to dawn. "Oh, you mean like Navy SEALs."

A look of pained resignation passed over Ghost's features. "Yes, like SEALs. All military special operators are trained like SEALs, though they get all the glory for some reason. People know what they are. There are TV series about them, but none about us. Still, I assure you, we're every bit as capable. Maybe more so in some ways."

"The police aren't going to do anything yet," Seth said. "If something happens to you, sure, they'll investigate. But the Sutton's Creek PD is a small operation, meant to take care of the citizens of this town. They have a tiny force and no detectives because the population doesn't warrant it. They'd call in Madison or Huntsville PD for more resources, but it's not going to help you by then. I think what Alex is getting at is that we need to set a meeting with this person and make a plan to either back you up or be there in your place. We want to know who's threatening you and why, and we want to stop them. You came to us, and we're committed to keeping you safe."

Callie looked down at Luna, who'd dropped to her belly and put her head on her paws. She wasn't asleep, but she was relaxed. Callie took a deep breath. Let it out.

"I've known you for less than forty-eight hours. But I trust you."

She looked at him as she said it, no one else. He felt the weight of those words on his soul like she was a magician who'd bound him with a spell.

Seth couldn't help but smile at her. "Glad to hear it. You won't regret it."

She dropped her gaze as if she couldn't hold the weight of their combined stares any longer. Seth shot a look of relief at Ghost—and caught a frown instead of the approval he was looking for.

Blaze smirked. Kane and Ethan looked resigned.

"What?" Seth said because he wasn't any good at keeping his mouth shut apparently.

"Nothing, my man," Blaze replied.

The smirking continued.

For fuck's sake. He got it now. They thought he was somehow enamored of Callie. That she was becoming important to him the way Emma was important to Blaze or Rory was important to Chance. He could see it in their faces now he knew what to look for.

Seth scowled at them all. "What do we do now? That's what we have to decide."

"Are you ready to text and find out when and where this person wants to meet?" Ghost asked Callie.

She nodded. "I can do that. But I really want my sister somewhere safe before I meet anyone. Mikhail knew where I lived, which means this person does too if they have his phone. They might be asking for a meeting, but that doesn't stop them from showing up at my house anyway. I'd rather she's not there, even with all of you around."

"Nikki told me her trainer is going to Kentucky to look at some horses this weekend. Could she go with her?" Seth asked.

Callie chewed her lip and nodded. "Lisa already said she could go, but I told Nikki she was going to the show next weekend so she needed to stay home and help me do household chores, not to mention she's not getting another horse. That was before the fire. I could make sure Lisa is still willing and let her go. Lisa has two German Shepherds she takes with her, and a couple of the other girls are going. Nikki would be in a crowd that went everywhere together. I think the plan was to leave tomorrow afternoon around four and be gone until late Sunday."

"Tell me where in Kentucky and I'll call a friend who's with the FBI," Ghost said. "He'll make sure somebody keeps an eye on the group."

"Lexington," Callie said. "I'll get the address of the farms she's planning to visit and the hotel they're staying in. Will that help?"

"Absolutely. The more information, the better."

She looked as if a weight had been lifted. "When should I answer the text?"

"Answer it now," Seth said. "See if they respond. We'll want to direct the time and location of the meeting if at all possible."

Callie took her phone from where she'd stashed it in her jeans pocket. Then she tapped out a few words on the screen that Seth could see.

When and where?

Short and to the point. He liked that. They hadn't told her what to say because it needed to be natural to her.

The reply came back almost immediately.

Tonight. Bridge Street. Barnes and Noble, 8PM.

Panic flared in her eyes as she looked at him.

"Tell them you can't tonight because you don't feel well enough yet. They'll obviously know about the fire. Suggest tomorrow night, same time." He looked at his guys. Not one of them had a problem with the location. It was public, and that was good. "Same place."

"What if they insist on tonight anyway?"

"We'll worry about that if it happens."

"Okay." Callie typed and the message whooshed away. The answer was swift.

> Tomorrow then. Don't cancel or I'll come looking for you.

> I'll be there.

She set her phone on her leg and let her gaze slide over each of them in the room.

"I'll go to the meeting. But I want to know how you intend to protect me and what I'm supposed to do when whoever I meet clearly isn't Mikhail."

Chapter Twenty-One

CALLIE'S HEART TAPPED A FAST RHYTHM IN HER CHEST. She'd said she could do this, but the closer they got to Bridge Street Town Center in Huntsville, the more nervous she was.

Nikki was on her way to Kentucky with her trainer, Lisa, as well as Amelia and Evelyn, two of the other teenagers who rode at the stables. Fortunately, Nikki liked Amelia and Evelyn, and their moms were reasonable human beings who didn't expect their child to win all the ribbons and get all the attention. When Callie had told her sister she'd changed her mind, after clearing it with Lisa, Nikki was so happy she bounced around the house for a good five minutes. Then she went to her room to start packing what she'd need.

When she'd said goodbye this morning, she'd hugged Callie extra hard and thanked her again. Then she'd whispered in Callie's ear. "Use protection. Remember to hydrate. Bowchickawowow," she'd finished in a sing-song voice.

Callie had blushed and swatted her, but Nikki had

cackled all the way out the door. Seth had been standing in the cased opening to the kitchen, coffee in hand. He'd looked at her with a lifted brow when she'd turned his way, but she'd pretended not to notice. No way did she plan to tell him what Nikki had said.

Luna had followed Nikki to the door, tail wagging as Nikki gave her scratches before she was gone.

At least Nikki had fallen for Luna on sight. She'd wanted Luna to sleep with her, but Seth had said it was better if she stayed with Callie since that was who she'd bonded with at the kennel. He'd then explained that after she'd acclimated to them and the house in a week or two, she'd be able to roam around and choose where she wanted to sleep. Nikki had accepted it with ease, especially when she considered that she'd be gone all weekend and Luna would be sleeping with Callie anyway.

The dog had been a comfort last night. After she'd texted fake-Mikhail back and set the meeting, it was like the gravity of the situation started to press on her. Sure, she'd believed Mikhail had ordered the fire to intimidate her, and Seth and the One Shot Tactical guys had given the theory enough credence that they'd started to help her immediately.

But it'd seemed less immediate somehow, though still terrifying. Almost like she was an observer viewing it from above after the fact.

Now she was down in it, right in the middle, and her nerves were shot raw. Had been since yesterday when the plan was made. Luna had seemed to know something was up because she'd stayed close all evening. Then she'd hopped up on the end of the bed and curled into a ball while Callie tried to read a book before she went to sleep.

She knew that Luna wasn't a trained guard dog, but Seth was right that having a dog was a good idea. Especially a dog like Luna who looked menacing even if she wasn't.

They hadn't left her at the house alone tonight because the situation was still new to her and they didn't know if she'd be anxious. Seth said they needed to acclimate her first, so Daphne had agreed to take her for a couple of hours until they were done at Bridge Street.

"You've got this, Callie," Seth said. "You go in, get a drink, sit at one of the tables against the wall with your back to it. Kane is already there, saving the table for you. He'll give the table to you, throw his drink away, and walk out. Then he'll stand outside and watch the door. I'll be at the magazine rack, observing. Ethan's at another table, reading a book. The other guys are in the parking lot watching the door. They'll follow the target after the meeting."

There was that word again. "And if the goal is to take me with him?"

"He's not going to be able to do it. We'll stop him if he tries. But he won't. That's the point of a public meeting. If he wanted to take you, he'd have suggested somewhere quieter. He's doing this to make you comfortable—and probably to make sure you don't have a tail."

She was supposed to act natural when the person who showed up wasn't Mikhail. Surprised, but curious. Maybe even a little hesitant to talk. All the things she would be if she'd had no prior knowledge of Mikhail's death.

That part worried her. She wasn't an actress, so what if she wasn't surprised enough? Or what if she was too surprised? She'd said that to the guys, but they'd told her it was better to underplay it than overplay it. Just be as natural as she could be. Let them do the rest.

"I feel like I'm in a spy movie. And you know what? I don't like it." She drummed her fingers on the armrest as

Seth turned into the parking lot for the mall. It was an outdoor mall with a central cobbled walkway that ran between shops. There were trees and park benches, performers playing music, restaurants, an upscale hotel, and a movie theater. The bookstore was at one end of the complex, facing the parking lot. You didn't have to walk into the mall area to get to it.

Since it was after five, the parking garage nearest the bookstore, below the main lot, was open, and Seth took the ramp down. That was for the office buildings that sat to one side of the mall during the day. At night and on weekends, the parking was free and accessible without a badge. Callie worked not too far from here and often came over for lunch or to grab new books or do a little shopping, so she was familiar with all the parking areas.

Seth drove to where he could see the stairwell and elevator that led up to the ground level. His eyes speared into hers. "Don't use the elevator. Walk up the stairs and go straight to the store. I'll go back up and park on the ground level."

Callie nodded. They'd discussed this. He was dropping her off so nobody would see them together. He'd come into the store a few minutes after her, but Kane and Ethan were already there. And the other guys were above, watching the entrance to the store.

But what if it went wrong? What if the person who'd killed Mikhail—the person presumably waiting for her—was smarter than they were? What if it really was like a spy novel and somebody stabbed her with a poisoned umbrella tip? She could die, and Nikki would be all alone.

Not acceptable.

She was going to sound crazy, but she didn't care. She only cared about making sure Nikki would be okay.

"If this doesn't work out, take care of Nikki for me. I

don't mean be her parent, but help her and make sure she ends up with decent people—"

She didn't get to finish the sentence because he leaned toward her, hooked her neck with one big hand, and dragged her mouth to his. Then he was kissing her, and Callie's wits scattered to the four corners of the earth.

His tongue was hot, demanding, and she kissed him back with an urgency that surprised her. She was instantly, unequivocally, wet. Ready. So damn ready.

His fingers spread over her jaw, his other hand joining to cup her face between those big hands as he held her and kissed the sense and worry right out of her. He broke the kiss gently, not abruptly, and placed a soft kiss on her forehead. Then he let her go and leaned back.

All he'd done was kiss her and she was ravaged. Her soul ached, craving more than he'd given. Her body was primed. If he tossed her in the backseat and dragged her jeans down her body, she wouldn't stop him.

She should, but she wouldn't. That's how starved she was for touch and connection. How lonely she was.

"Why?" she managed to croak.

He skimmed the back of his fingers over her cheek and smiled. That devastating smile that was so rare. The one that shocked her with its magnificence whenever she saw it.

"Because you needed distracting, Callie. You're going to be fine. I want you to think about that kiss while you walk up those stairs. Think about my tongue in your mouth as you head for the bookstore. Imagine where else you'd like it as you stand in line for your drink. Don't think about bullshit like never seeing your sister again because that's not happening. Think about me and how good it felt to kiss me. How good it'd feel to do more."

Storm clouds brewed inside her, mixing with the feel-good sensations still pinging through her system. That kiss *had* felt amazing, and she wanted more.

But she wasn't some desperate woman needing attention so badly a man could do whatever he wanted to her. She'd been shocked and she'd kissed him back, but she wasn't going to fall into bed with him like he was doing her a favor and she should be grateful.

She started to open her mouth to tell him off, but he stopped her with a finger under her jaw. "Save the pissy attitude for later. Channel your annoyance into battle armor and keep it locked in place. You can tell me to go to hell when we're on the way back to Sutton's Creek. Can you do that?"

There were so many things she wanted to say. But now wasn't the time.

"Yes."

He grinned. "Good. Now get your cute ass up those stairs and march into the bookstore like a queen looking for a throne. You got this."

———

CALLIE WAS STILL FUMING as she made the trip to the store. Tingling too. Arrogant man.

It was a short walk to the stairs, up a flight, a right, past the Cheesecake Factory and then a left into Barnes and Noble. The mall was crowded and it was still light out, though the sun was rapidly falling toward the horizon. People milled around, enjoying the weather. Evenings were nice, though it could get damn hot during the day.

Callie was hot now, but for a different reason. Her skin was on fire from that single kiss. She wasn't a virgin, for heaven's sake, so why had *one* kiss from a man with Hollywood good looks affected her like she was still that awkward girl Bobby Bowen took to the homecoming dance? Like she was filled with hope and happiness and need until the moment it all came crashing down?

But Tara Warren wasn't lurking with a camera, waiting to step in and humiliate her. Nobody cared if she kissed Seth. So why the pounding heart and skin that felt just a few degrees shy of the surface of the sun? The pounding heart might be what she was about to do, but the heat was a different matter.

He'd said to think about him. About the kiss. To stop worrying.

It was the only reason he'd kissed her, and maybe that's why she was so angry about it. It'd felt like heaven to her, but it was part of the job to him. *She* was part of the job. He was with her because he'd been the one sent to be there. It could just as easily have been Kane if he'd been at the range when she'd first asked for him.

Callie steeled her spine and walked with purpose toward the bookstore. She scanned the crowd but recognized no one. Not even the guys from One Shot Tactical. But they were supposed to be inside anyway. The three in the parking lot she wouldn't see unless she went looking for them, and that was definitely not what she was supposed to do.

She entered the store as directed and went to order a drink. The line was long, but it was only seven-thirty. She was supposed to get her drink and take the table. Then she would wait.

She spotted Kane. He had one of the tables against the wall and he sat with his back against it, drinking a coffee and reading a book. She had the idea that he wasn't really reading at all, that he was instead watching the crowd, but she didn't know how he was doing it.

His presence made her feel better, and she could feel her muscles loosen by a fraction.

Ethan was there too. It took her a minute to see him because she couldn't obviously look around, but he was at a table nearer the door, facing Kane, a magazine in his hand.

She didn't have to be here. She could have said she wasn't going to do it. She could have set the meeting up and waited at home with Seth, texting that she was running late, while they watched for the person who was on his phone and annoyed.

But it wouldn't have been as straightforward. And she wanted this person found and stopped so she could live a normal life again.

Except a corner of her brain kept telling her that she should have run when she had the chance. That somebody had killed Mikhail and they weren't playing around. No matter that Seth said she'd be safe, part of her quaked at the idea of coming face-to-face with a potential killer.

She was a computer programmer, not an international spy. She was not cut out for this at all.

Callie managed to get her drink and then sort of wandered into the seating area. The tables were full, but Kane started clearing his like he was about to go. She started toward him but a woman with a determined look suddenly dragged a man in that direction.

Callie wasn't going to get there first. What was she supposed to do if she didn't get the table? She was para-lyzed by the thought as the couple moved closer before she could.

But Kane stopped what he was doing and leaned against the wall again, taking out his phone and scrolling through it. Then he picked up his cup and took a sip. The woman stopped barging her way toward him and turned with a huff before dragging the man in another direction.

Callie waited a few seconds, then started in that direction again. She walked past Kane, who didn't look at her, then turned and looked around again. The café was crowded, and she was beginning to despair of things working the way they were supposed to when she made herself drift past Kane's table again.

"Ma'am? Are you looking for a place to sit?"

She stumbled to a halt. "Y-yes."

He motioned at the empty chair. "Take that one. I'm leaving in a couple of minutes."

"Okay, thank you." She pulled the chair out and sat, then got her phone from her crossbody bag and started to scroll. Kane didn't talk to her, but her heart pounded anyway. She forced herself not to look at him. Eventually, he picked up his book and cup and stood. Then he walked away without a word.

Callie let out a long breath as she picked up her cup with a trembling hand. She really needed to get a hold of herself. Why was she so wigged out? She'd never been that wigged out about meeting Mikhail, though she'd certainly been tense as time went on and it became clear he wanted things from her she wasn't comfortable providing.

She wished she'd never met him. Wished her parents hadn't died—she still wondered if Mikhail had anything to do with it, and that made her sick inside—and that she hadn't had to move back to the US and take custody of Nikki.

She also wished she'd never heard of Griffin Research Labs.

Callie told herself to breathe. She should have grabbed a book to look at, but she hadn't been thinking. So she read on her phone instead while glancing up to check out the store from time to time.

She didn't have to look up to know that Seth was there. She could feel him, which was a weird thing to think. But she could. On her next perusal of the store, she spotted him at the magazine rack, flipping through… Was that a gun magazine? She dropped her gaze again, sipped her drink, and stared at the words on her screen, unable to make them resolve into anything that made sense.

Seth. What the heck was it about Seth—grumpy, handsome, gorgeous, tortured Seth—that had her twisted into knots? He'd been at her house for two nights. She'd spent hours with him, in the same room, or in his truck, riding to Madison for Luna or to the range for equipment and his belongings.

And then there was the first night when she'd found him outside, on the ground, in pain because Nikki made him think of the child he'd lost. That had been the moment when something inside her cracked open.

She wanted to know more. Had he been married? Had it torn through his relationship? What happened to his daughter? None of those were questions she had a right to ask.

She thought he must have been very young when it happened. Barely more than a teenager himself.

Callie sipped her drink and looked at her phone. The minutes ticked by. Eight o'clock came and went, but she remained in her seat because she didn't know what else to do.

She was going to have to pee soon. That was something she hadn't thought about. She looked up again, saw Seth on his phone. He didn't look happy. Ethan was still in his chair, but he wasn't reading a book anymore. He was texting.

Callie's heart beat a little faster as she tried not to panic or stare too much at what Seth was doing. He looked angry. Why was he angry?

By eight-fifteen, her bladder was full and her throat was dry, despite the liquid she'd consumed. If fake-Mikhail didn't turn up in the next fifteen minutes, she was texting Seth and telling him she was done waiting.

Ten more minutes went by, and nobody appeared. There were plenty of people who stood in line at the café, but nobody who seemed to be looking for her. People got their drinks and snacks and either found a table or took them elsewhere. No one asked to sit with her.

When her phone rang, she jumped. But it was only Seth.

"Yes?"

"He's not coming. Need you to send a text asking where he is, because that's what you would do when somebody didn't show up for a meeting, then you need to wait a few minutes and head back down to the rendezvous point. I'll pick you up."

"Okay, but I've been sitting here for nearly fifty minutes with a drink that's completely gone, and I need to head to the restroom before I cause a different kind of scene."

"Understood. Send the text, wait, then go to the bathroom. Ethan will keep an eye on you. Meet me in the garage in—" He looked at his watch. "Twelve minutes. Can you do that?"

"Yes. Did something happen?" He'd looked angry when he was on the phone, and though her bladder was taking up a great deal of her thoughts right now, she remembered to ask.

"I'll tell you in the truck. Do what I told you, Callie. Time for talking later."

Before she could say goodbye, he'd hung up on her.

Chapter Twenty-Two

Callie hopped in the truck and belted herself in, then fixed him with a look. He could see that she was fighting panic. "What happened?" she blurted. "Is it Nikki? Did they get to her?"

"Nikki's fine."

He should have thought to tell her that when he'd called her, but he'd been so focused on shifting the plan that it hadn't occurred to him that's where her mind would go. It should have, though. He swore to himself for not thinking of it and putting her through needless worry.

"Oh, thank God," she breathed, leaning her head back against the seat as he navigated the parking garage and headed for the highway. "When you said you'd tell me in the truck, all I could think was that Nikki was in danger."

"I'm sorry. I wasn't thinking. I should have reassured you."

"It's over now. But something happened. What?"

There was no easy way to tell her, so he ripped the Band-aid off and said the words. "Somebody broke into your house. I got the alerts and checked the cameras. Two men with ski masks. Looks like they tossed things around a bit. They were looking for something. Any idea what?"

Her jaw hung open, her eyes wide. "I… No. I have no idea. Wh-what about Charlie? They didn't hurt him, did they?"

"No. He's in his stall, eating hay. I looked at him through the feed a few minutes ago."

Seth flexed his hands on the wheel. He was trying to maintain his cool here, but he was also pissed that these guys had gotten the jump on them. Whoever set the meeting never had any intention of keeping it. It'd been a distraction, and none of them had seen it coming. They'd been focused on this asshole trying to get to Callie.

"You're hiding something from me, Callie. I asked you if there was anything you were doing that nobody else could do. You said no. Your body language said the opposite."

He was done tiptoeing around. Ghost Ops hadn't been able to infiltrate Griffin Research Labs to look for surveillance equipment, or install their own, because the facility was occupied twenty-four hours a day while they worked to open up again.

But he'd installed the cameras at Callie's place yesterday, the window and door alarms, and he'd set up a script to filter all her input on the computers at Griffin Research Labs. It had filtered a lot of material so far, but none of it made sense to him. He had a good understanding of programming languages, and he could do a lot with a computer, but he didn't know enough to figure out what she'd been doing.

His queries on the bulletin board had only been partly answered. Dima Smirnov was also SVR, no surprise, but there was no word on whether Cyril Dyka, the Polish student he'd been impersonating, was dead or alive.

Seth still didn't know if Callie was tied to Smirnov or Fedorov in any way. He hoped not but he wasn't going to operate on assumptions, especially when she was keeping something from him. He needed cold, hard information.

"It's not something I can share," she said, her voice stiff. "It's sensitive information. I'm not authorized to talk about company projects if you aren't cleared. And you aren't."

"Don't tell me about the project. Tell what you're doing that somebody's interested in."

She was silent, her head turned as they flew down I-565. Her arms were folded over her chest, and she'd slumped down in the seat as if trying to make herself smaller.

Seth bit back a growl. "Callie. I'm *trying* to keep you safe. Somebody just trashed your place looking for something, and you won't tell me what. Doesn't that strike you as more than a bit stupid here?"

She whirled on him. "I don't know what they want! I don't! I don't work on the project at home because it's not a secure facility! There's nothing they could want. Mikhail asked questions, tried to get me to talk about what we were doing, and then he gave me that cable. Maybe they want it back. You ever think of that?"

He had, but it was a lot of trouble to go to for something that any hacker worth his salt could buy on the internet. They weren't proprietary. There would be no identifying information about who wanted her to tap her government computer. All it did was give them a back door into the secure servers the way the Ghost Ops team had installed.

"Nobody cares about the cable. They're easy to buy if you know where to look. There's no identifying information on it. It doesn't record anything. All it does is create a conduit."

She folded her arms and threw herself against the seat again.

"Maybe they don't know that."

"Then they're fucking stupid. And I don't think they're stupid." He was growing angrier by the second. Frustrated as fuck. "You know what? You obviously think you've got this figured out, so maybe you don't need me after all. You can keep the alarm system and I'll send you a bill. But unless you start talking ASAP, I'm out. I'm not risking my ass for you when you can't even give me a straight fucking answer."

She dropped her head into her hands and shook it. "I hate you."

The sound was muffled, and his heart squeezed a fraction at the despair in her voice. He hardened it because he couldn't afford to feel anything except fury.

"It's okay. You aren't the first."

Mandy's parents had certainly hated him. Not that he could blame them. He'd gotten their seventeen-year-old daughter pregnant. He'd only been seventeen himself, and it took two to tango, but in their eyes he'd been a mongrel who'd defiled their princess.

Seth shoved those thoughts away. They weren't productive or useful. That time of his life was miles in the rearview.

Callie didn't speak again until he exited the highway and started down the country roads that led to Sutton's Creek.

"I write code," she said into the darkness between them, her voice soft. "We're working on a satellite. It's top secret so I can't say more than that. But I'm writing the command instructions. Our whole team is, I should say—but there's been trouble with the code, things not working the way they should. I fix it, tweak it, write new instructions. Dr. Robbins knows. If anybody else does, they pretend they don't."

Holy shit. A chill slid down his spine. Callie wasn't just part of the team writing the code for Athena's command system, she was the one actually doing the work. The instructions that, if compromised, would create a back door into a system that could change the world.

Or end it.

"Why would you be the one to write the instructions when you have a team? And why in secret?"

"Because I'm good at it. I pretend to everyone that I don't know as much as I do—but writing code is like speaking another language to me. One I was born knowing. Of course I wasn't born knowing it, but that's how innate it feels. I just... *can.*"

The goosebumps on his arms were still there. "And why don't you want your team to know?"

She snorted. "You already said it once before. I'm twenty-six, Seth. I'm female. You've never been mansplained a day in your life, but if I had a dollar for every time..." She shook her head. "Well, I'd be pretty well off. Men, especially older ones, think they know everything. And computer programming is a science, which means men have always dominated the field. They think they're better at it and, believe me, they have no problems letting me know it. One of the senior programmers has made it his mission to question everything I do. Leo Spinner has been with Griffin Research since they were founded in 2001. He doesn't like Dr. Robbins either, but she's his boss so he takes it out on me. Dr. Robbins is female so she gets what it's like. She's in her forties, so she's had to fight harder than I have. She's a good person. A good boss. The other men on the team resent her sometimes because they all think Leo should be the one leading them. I see it. She knows it, too. How could she not? So, with her permission, I fix what the other programmers do if I see a better way, tweak it, make it work. Usually. Lately it's not working, and I don't know why."

"Did Mikhail know you were writing the code?"

Her body slumped a little lower in the seat, her head turned away from him. "Yes. I didn't tell him what I was working on, but in the early days when I was excited about the job and my promotion to the team, yes, I told him. I shared more than I should. Not classified things. Things about me. The more I told him, the more he wanted to know."

"Jesus," he muttered.

She swung around to look at him. "I was stupid, I know. I was skirting a line telling him that much, but I thought he was a friend. He'd helped me when I needed it. By the time I realized he wanted me to tell him everything, it was too late."

"He knew what the project was about, Callie. Or suspected it anyway."

He could hear the shock in her silence. "I don't see how he could."

"His contact. Somebody at Griffin Research Labs knows what they're working on, and they told Mikhail. Not the technical aspects, because then he wouldn't need you, but enough." He thought about it for a minute. "It's more than that, though. It was you specifically. He knew about your facility with programming languages, didn't he?"

"I told him, yes. We were dating in the early days in Poland, and I wanted to impress him. Plus all that stuff I said before about thinking we had a lot in common with immigrant parents. I thought, back then, that maybe he was the one. There weren't sparks, but there was a comfortable companionship kind of thing going on. He didn't push me for physical intimacy—or, hell, for anything back then. Maybe that's why I was so unprepared when he started pushing about my job."

Seth's anger simmered. "He was grooming you, Callie. He picked you out of the crowd and he groomed you. My guess is he already knew about your ability."

She was quiet as she thought about it. "That fucker," she swore when he'd nearly given up hope of her responding. "Meeting him was never by chance, though I thought it was at the time. We met in the bar one night when I went with my students for a drink. He was there because of me. Because he already knew. I was teaching programming to Polish soldiers. He could have gotten my CV from any of them. I didn't say how easy I found programming, but my accomplishments were there. But how could he know months before it happened that there would be a job in Huntsville on this program?"

"He probably didn't. He just knew you were somebody they could use."

"They?"

"Whoever he worked for."

The Dashevsky Group. The Russian government. The Polish government. Whoever it'd been.

"I don't have anything anybody could want. I don't understand this at all."

He believed her. She was too shocked—and too disillusioned with Volkov—not to.

But it didn't change the fact two men had busted into her house, regardless of the alarm that would have been blaring, and took the time to turn it upside down. They wanted something and they'd known she wouldn't be there because they'd planned it when they'd set the meeting at Bridge Street. They hadn't known her sister wouldn't be home, which chilled his blood—unless they did somehow.

He'd checked for bugs. Cameras, audio. He'd deployed a signal jammer and then swept for equipment. There was nothing. But they knew where Callie lived, and they'd probably been watching. Which meant they also knew about him even before they'd gone inside and seen his duffel.

Sonofabitch.

He wished that Luna would have been there. Then again, not, because they might have shot her rather than be deterred by her bark. He wouldn't want that on his conscience. He'd insisted on the dog because he knew she'd be a good deterrent to ordinary criminals.

Not to determined ones looking for something they desperately wanted. Hell, it was like the Ringwraiths had descended to search for the One Ring. They wouldn't let a dog or a teenager stand in their way.

Thank God neither had been there.

When Seth reached Callie's house and turned to go up the long drive, he knew he'd find Ghost, Blaze, and Chance already there with the police cruiser still flashing its lights. Ethan and Kane were behind him, on his six, making sure nobody tried to attack Callie while they were on the road.

Overkill? Maybe, but considering what she'd just told him about what she was doing at work, he didn't think so. Callie had gone from curiously interesting to vitally important to the mission in the space of a heartbeat.

And he was going to have to tell his team what she'd told him. There was no question of that.

He parked by the house, and they got out. Callie's

Toyota was nearby, the driver's side window shattered. All the doors were open. The alarm had given up already, or it'd been disconnected. Callie made a distressed sound at the sight of it. Seth braced because he suspected that wasn't the worst of it.

"Come on, let's get inside. Nothing we can do about the vehicle yet."

Blaze stood in the doorway as they approached, looking pissed. Seth knew it was bad by that look. He reached for Callie's hand and stopped her. Turned her to him and put his hands on either side of her face.

"Listen to me, Callie. They were in a hurry. They would have upended everything trying to find what they wanted. It won't be good."

She already looked shell-shocked as she gazed up at him. "Okay."

He pressed a kiss to her forehead, just because, and then took her hand again and led the way.

The living room was a disaster. Callie gasped beside him, her free hand flying to her mouth. It was like something from a movie where the furniture had been upended, cushions sliced open, and carpets dragged back. Her knickknacks, which were few, had been tossed carelessly onto the floor. Frames had been ripped open, the photos discarded before the frame was dropped, the glass shattering.

The dishes were broken on the floor, the cabinet doors open. The bedrooms hadn't fared any better.

Callie's reading journal was ripped apart on her bed, the mattress slashed. There was paper everywhere, probably from her other journals. He could see by the look on her face that she was angry and devastated at the same time.

It was part willful destruction and part search mission.

They'd been looking for something but also sending a message.

She'd texted Mikhail's number back at the bookstore but hadn't gotten a reply. He expected she would soon.

Her eyes shimmered as she turned to face him in her bedroom. "I don't have *anything*. I don't take my work home. There's nothing here. Why would somebody do this?"

Seth tugged her into his arms. He didn't know why he did it other than she looked like she needed comforting. She wrapped her arms around him and stood with her face pressed to his shirt. He figured she was drying her tears on him. He didn't care.

"They think you have something. A memory stick or a computer chip maybe."

"I don't. I'd be arrested if I took something like that and the company found out. Prosecuted and thrown in jail for divulging classified information. Why would I do that?"

She wouldn't. He knew she wouldn't. She wouldn't do anything to risk her sister's life being completely uprooted by losing another family member.

He didn't say what else he was thinking. That what was in her head was also valuable. She probably didn't have every line of code perfectly memorized, but there were chunks in there. He'd bet on that.

If these people couldn't get a memory stick, they might decide to come for her instead.

"I don't want to stay here," she whispered against his shirt. "But I can't leave Charlie."

"We can stay somewhere tonight, then come back in the morning and feed him. Then we'll clean up."

She tipped her head back to look up at him. She looked lost, alone, and scared. He hated that for her. After all she and Nikki had been through, he fucking hated that somebody could make her look this way. Like she'd lost something precious all over again.

"I want to say yes, but I also feel like I need to stiffen my spine and refuse to let these assholes make me leave my home."

"It's okay to leave for one night, Callie. It's dark, the police will leave and so will my guys. Then it'll be you and me. And while I'm not in the least worried about my ability to protect you, I am worried about how you're gonna jump at all the shadows and have trouble sleeping."

She seemed to think about it. He could see the relief in her eyes, the *yes* that hovered on her tongue. But then she shook her head. "No. Nikki lost her home when my parents died. I lost it too because it was the one I grew up in. I won't let anybody force me to feel that way again, and I won't let her come home to a mess. I can work on cleaning up as much as possible starting tonight, plus we'll have Luna back and she'll let us know if anyone is coming. You'll be here, like you said. Tomorrow night won't be any different, so why not start now?"

Fucking hell, she was something. Brave, even when she was scared. Fiery, though she wanted to melt into a puddle and let somebody else take the reins.

"If that's what you want."

"It is. When you get thrown off the horse, you get right back up and get on again. You can't let the horse win, because if they know they can buck you off and you won't get back on, then they'll do it every time because they don't respect you. I spent my childhood getting back on even when I was scared. This isn't all that different."

"Nobody would fault you for walking away for one night."

She huffed a breath. "I know. And I want to. Badly. But I won't. Not if you're here with me."

"I'll be with you."

"You swear you're as good as you say? If they come back, you'll keep us safe?"

"Listen to me, Callie. I've got you. Nobody's getting to you while I'm still breathing. I promise you that."

Chapter Twenty-Three

THE POLICE WERE AT HER HOUSE FOR ANOTHER HALF HOUR, taking a statement, investigating the scene, reviewing the video footage from the cameras Seth had installed. Callie felt like she existed in a dream state as she walked around the house, looking at the destruction, and listening to the police's questions.

Nikki was safe in Lexington, ensconced in a Hampton Inn with Lisa and the girls. Seth informed her that Alex's FBI contact had an eye on them and wouldn't stop surveilling until told otherwise.

That made her breathe a little easier.

After the police were gone, Callie thought that Seth's friends would go, too. They did not. They started to help clean the disaster that was her house.

Tears stung her eyes as she swept up stuffing from the couch and chairs and tried to imagine what in the hell Mikhail had thought she had. What he'd told people she had. Because he must have, right? Why else would they think she did?

Ten minutes after the police were gone, a car drove up.

Doors shut and female voices drifted to her ears on the night air. Daphne came inside with Luna, whose tail thumped when she saw Callie. Daphne let her leash go and Luna trotted over to wriggle at Callie's feet.

"Oh my goodness, who's a good doggie?" Callie asked, squatting to scratch the proffered belly and thinking what a contradiction this sweet dog was. A gentle soul wrapped in a deceptively intimidating package. Callie hadn't wanted a dog, or so she'd thought, but the minute she'd seen Luna in her suite at the kennel, she'd felt a connection. Thankfully she'd agreed to a trial period, but there was little doubt she planned to adopt Luna. There'd always been little doubt, which Betty had known. Crafty woman, getting her to take Luna with her for a trial.

Dr. Emma Sutton walked in behind Daphne. Blaze Connolly stopped what he was doing and went over to kiss her like she was the most precious thing he'd ever seen in his life. When the kiss ended, he looped an arm around her waist and seemed reluctant to let go. She whispered something in his ear and he kissed her temple and released her.

"She was such a good girl," Daphne said. "Anytime you need a dog sitter, you can call me."

"Thank you so much. I'm just glad she wasn't here."

Daphne looked around. "Me too. And I'm sorry this happened. Emma and I are here to help."

Emma walked over and stood beside Daphne. "Yes, we are. Rory wanted to come, but it's Friday night at the Dawg. She's a little busy."

Chance grumbled something under his breath.

Emma heard because she snorted. "She's not going to stop, and you should be glad. Rory is healthy and full of sass, like always. If you made her stop moving, she'd topple over like a top that's lost momentum. Also, she said to tell you if you don't stop hanging over her like a mother hen, she's going to glue all your shoes to the floor so you can't follow her out the door and then she's going to put your underwear in the chicken coop so they can crap or lay eggs, whichever they prefer. Which, to be clear, I said eww, Rory, to that one. She remained determined."

"Dude, don't piss off your woman," Blaze said. If smug had a face, his was it at the moment. "Give her what she wants and don't argue."

Emma elbowed Blaze as he came to stand beside her. "Like you never argue with me."

"Barely. Take this morning, for instance, when you said you had to get up and get ready for work. And I very reasonably said you can never have too many org—"

Emma's hand popped over Blaze's mouth as her cheeks turned crimson. Callie could tell that Blaze was laughing behind that hand.

"Hush up, big boy. No examples required."

"Yes, ma'am," he said when she removed her hand. But he was still grinning. Then he winked.

Emma turned and pasted a smile on her face as she looked at everyone watching the two of them. "Carry on. Nothing to see here. As you were. Etcetera."

"As you were, huh?" Kane said. "Blaze teaching you the military lingo?"

Emma beamed. "A little bit. Did I use it right?"

"You absolutely did. Good job."

Emma and Daphne conferred with Seth and then went to Nikki's bedroom to start working there. Callie's heart squeezed. Her sister's photos had been ripped down, her bed given the same treatment as Callie's. Her room wasn't quite as destroyed, probably because it was at the back of the house and the two men would have been conscious of the time and how close the police were getting.

But it still needed cleaning, and Callie was going to have some explaining to do when Nikki got home.

Daphne emerged from the hallway to get a roll of paper towels and nearly bumped into Kane, who put his hands on her shoulders to steady her.

Daphne looked up, her eyes wide. Kane looked down at her. They seemed locked in a staring contest, but then Daphne stepped backward and broke the contact.

Interesting.

Of everyone there, those two were the most awkward around each other. Since Daphne had walked in, she'd only made eye contact with him once when she'd said hello and again now. He stared at her when he thought nobody was looking at him, then jerked his gaze away if anyone so much as glanced at him.

It was almost like they'd had a fling and everything was strained now. Or one of them wanted a fling—or they both did—but neither could figure out how to go about it. Callie made a mental note to ask Seth later. Not that it was any of her business, but it was something to talk about that wasn't about her or Mikhail or this mythological *thing* she had that somebody would want to steal.

By eleven-thirty, the house was tidy again. All the stuffing and feathers were picked up and stuffed in trash bags or back inside the cushions, if it was manageable, and the stuffing was clean. Broken glass had been removed and the floors vacuumed. Photos were retrieved and put back into frames without glass. The broken dishes in the kitchen were swept up and tossed, and the floors were swept and mopped.

The bedrooms were habitable. Sheets were returned to mattresses, papers gathered and neatened or thrown out. Callie's pretty bedroom wasn't as pretty as it had been. It felt dirty. Spoiled, despite the work she and the other ladies had done to return it to the way it was.

Her dried flowers were destroyed, the silk ones ripped off the stems. The lace she'd draped over her lampshade was shredded. Her mother's silk slipper chair, the one piece of furniture she'd managed to keep, had been sliced open, the delicate pink silk gaping to show springs and cotton.

Her journals were a mess, but she'd gathered all the pages and put them into a box. She'd salvage what she could when she had the time. That was the important thing.

If she lost a bunch of book reviews or journal entries, so what? But it hurt anyway. Working in her journal had always given her a place of calm, a few minutes to collect her thoughts and create something pretty. She could still do that, and she could salvage what the intruders had ripped apart. She'd lost her parents and her life had turned upside down. This was minor in comparison, though it felt like they'd ripped into her soul when they'd violated her things.

After Callie thanked everyone profusely and they all said their goodbyes, Seth went outside to see them off. Callie slumped on the couch that was no longer as firm as before, Luna hopping up beside her as she listened to car doors slam and engines roar to life. Then they were gone, and Seth strode back inside with his backpack, which she knew held his laptop, a bigger bag that looked like a gym bag, and a long case slung across his back. It took her a moment to realize it was a rifle case.

Her heart thumped. "What's in there?"

He set it on the floor. "AR-15. Perfectly legal. Though we've got a 50-cal at the range. Unfortunately, I'd blow out a wall as well as a bad guy if I used it inside the house. And probably a cow or two a couple of miles away if they were unlucky enough to be in the path. But believe me, I want to. Not the cows, the bad guys."

She didn't know if he was joking or not and she was too tired to ask questions about a gun. "You were smart to take your computer with you."

Hers was gone. If the thieves could get inside, which they probably couldn't, they wouldn't find anything on it except a bunch of media and harmless programming work. Video games, books, movies, YouTube videos about scrapbooking and journaling. She always closed her internet browser and cleared the information. She doubted they'd get inside. She wasn't entirely stupid on that score. She encrypted everything, not because she was a hacker, but because she was enough of a programmer to understand what hackers could do.

Seth had seemed worried when she'd said it was missing, but she'd assured him she did nothing on it but watch things that interested her and surf social media. Any programming she did was for personal reasons to keep her skills up. There was nothing secret on her computer.

Some of the worry had eased from his expression when she said that.

"I don't tend to leave it in one place," Seth said. "Old habit. If I'm headed out for a few hours, I take it."

"You aren't worried somebody would steal your truck and it'd be gone?"

"Nope. I've got a kill switch. Or have you forgotten?"

"That's right, you did threaten me if I drove away in your truck."

"Not a threat, honey. A promise."

"Makes me wonder if there was an epidemic of people driving away in your truck. Maybe because you exasperated them with your grumpy attitude and no-small-talk policy?"

He arched an eyebrow. "Who's the funny girl tonight, huh?"

Callie rubbed Luna's ears as the dog lay her head on Callie's lap. "It's that or cry, Mr. King."

His expression softened. "I know, baby. It's a bitch what they did, and I'm pissed I never considered it. Could have left one of the guys here and the rest of us could have gone to Bridge Street. We were so focused on who was going to show up at the meeting that we didn't think about what else they might do."

"There was no *reason* for it. That's what I don't understand. I don't take files to work, and I don't bring files home. And even if I did take something with me, like my computer, I can't take it into the secure area. It would stay in the employee locker room. I suppose I could sneak a memory stick in, but a download would be logged. Even if I erased the record, it's not really gone. All activity is in the log, which gets checked by the supervisor, usually Dr. Robbins. Sometimes security does random checks. It's not as simple as walking in and stealing information then walking out again."

"They don't know that," he said. "And even if they did, they wouldn't believe it."

Her throat ached. It was part anger and frustrated tears, part of the smoke inhalation that still crept up on her and made her cough sometimes. "I wish I'd never taken this job."

"I understand. But you did, and we're gonna deal with the situation you're in now."

Callie looked down at Luna and shivered. Why had she been so stubborn about staying tonight? All that bravado and sass about not leaving her home, and now she really wanted to be anywhere but there.

She could tell him. He'd take her away and they could

stay in the Wheeler Inn in town, or they could drive to Madison and get rooms at one of the hotels near the airport.

But admitting it felt like admitting defeat. She'd said she was staying, and now she had to. But not in her room. Not tonight.

"You look tired," Seth said, coming over to hover above her like a guardian angel. A dark, handsome guardian angel with a serious scowl.

"I am tired. I don't want to stay in my room tonight. I'll sleep on the couch."

"Can't let you do that, Callie."

"Why not?"

He swept an arm toward the front door, then the windows, and back to the kitchen and back door. "I want more walls between you and the doors. So either I sleep on the floor to protect you, which isn't my favorite choice though I will, or you go to your bedroom and I'll be across the hall with my door open, ready to move if necessary."

She stared up at him. "You really do think of every-thing, don't you?"

"Not everything, or those fuckers wouldn't have gotten in. But I think tactically, and my tactics tell me you've got to be in a more defensible position."

A tendril of panic uncurled in her belly. "I don't want to stay in my room. It feels wrong in there. I can't do it."

He dropped to his knees in front of her, caressed her cheek softly. "Okay, sweetheart. You don't have to sleep in your room if you don't want to. Do you think you can stay in mine?"

Heat flooded her belly. "I…"

"I don't mean I'll be in bed with you. I'll take the couch. I'm still between you and intruders that way."

Now why did disappointment flare in her brain? This

was not the time to be thinking about sharing a bed with Seth. She was in serious trouble. She didn't have time for her mind to stray to topics like attraction and whether or not he felt it too. He clearly didn't. He'd kissed her earlier to distract her, no other reason.

Same with the things he'd said about imagining his tongue in other places.

"I don't want to take your bed."

"Technically it's your bed, don't you think? I'll be fine. You and Luna take the bed. I'll be out here, protecting you both."

"Okay, I'll try."

He held out a hand and she took it. He pulled her to her feet, but he didn't let go right away. She felt safe with his hand on hers. She didn't want that feeling to end, but it would as soon as he let go.

She prayed he wouldn't let go.

But he did. "Go to bed, Callie. I won't let anyone hurt you. You're safe with me."

She wanted to ask him to go with her, to lay down beside her and not let go, but that was far more than he'd signed on to do. She told herself to move, to walk away, but her body wouldn't obey.

"Go," Seth said softly, as if he knew.

She did.

Chapter Twenty-Four

THE COUCH WAS LUMPY NOW THAT THE CUSHIONS HAD BEEN sliced and some of the stuffing removed. Seth shifted his weight until he found a spot that wasn't quite as bad. He lay on his back, one arm behind his head, looking up at the ceiling, thinking.

After Callie went to bed, he'd fired up his computer and checked for responses to his inquiry on the bulletin board. It'd only been a few hours since he'd last checked, but he had to look again. Nothing more than what he already had. Which wasn't unusual. Information like what he wanted took time to be teased out of the dark corners it resided in.

If she had any connection to Smirnov or Fedorov, he'd find it. Not that he believed she was guilty of anything. He knew the irony of that thought would only make his team laugh uproariously. He'd been focusing on her as the potential traitor in the company from the moment he learned she'd spent time in Poland and was fluent in Russian and Polish.

It'd seemed so obvious at the time. Sometimes if it

walked like a duck and quacked like a duck, it was a duck. Trying to find another explanation because the one you had was too easy wasn't always the correct response.

But he no longer believed she was capable of selling out her country. She'd have to be one cold-hearted bitch to expose her sister to danger, and there was no way he could be convinced she'd do it. Not since he'd spent the past forty-eight hours-plus around the clock with her and saw the way she worried about Nikki.

Callie wasn't guilty of anything but being young and vulnerable when a man singled her out for grooming.

She was also in danger, and he needed to figure out who was targeting her. Then he needed to keep her safe so she and her team could finish their work.

When he'd gone outside with everyone earlier, he'd caught up to Ghost and told him about Callie's work on the code. He'd never managed to hack her computer, because there'd never been time, but he thought the new information probably made up for it. The surprise on his team leader's face had been clear.

"Good work, Phantom."

It hadn't felt like good work to him. He'd pressed her emotional buttons hard to get that confession. She'd been caught against a wall, and he'd been an eighteen-wheeler backing up to flatten her if she didn't spill some truth.

Yeah, they'd needed that information, but he didn't like the way he'd had to get it.

Especially after she walked into her house and saw the destruction. It was one more blow she had to shoulder after a year of blows.

He thought about when he'd pulled her off the couch earlier, telling her to go to bed, and the look in her eyes as she'd gazed up at him.

Lost, scared, alone. Vulnerable.

She'd wanted him to go with her. Not for sex, but because she was scared.

The crazy thing was, he'd wanted to. He'd wanted to tell her he'd hold her all night if that's what it took for her to sleep.

But he didn't do shit like that, and not with someone he was actively responsible for. This was a job, no matter that part of the job was pretending to be dating when her sister was around. He didn't need to confuse those two things, and neither did she.

It was up to him to hold that line, not her.

"Fuck," he muttered. Callie was the last woman he should be thinking about, and yet she was the only one on his mind. He didn't get it. She was pretty, sure. But she was in a heap of emotional turmoil, and he didn't need to take any of that on. He had enough of his own he was still dealing with.

She'd told him he should talk to someone, that it might help. He'd never considered it, but now he kept thinking maybe he could talk to her. She was the only person he'd told about Mia, crazy as that was.

But if he told her the truth, that he'd given Mia up, what would she think of him then? Normal people didn't give up their kids, right? Even when they were seventeen and scared of the consequences the baby's grandparents threatened them with.

Maybe if he'd had people in his life who'd cared for him, he wouldn't have felt so alone. When Mandy's dad, who was a federal judge, had told him he was a good for nothing piece of trash and he'd go to prison for a long time if he dared contact Mandy again, he'd believed it.

When Judge Perry shoved papers in front of him and told him he was giving up all parental rights to the baby, he'd done it, trembling with fear the entire time. He'd been seventeen, working at an electronics store and going to high school, and he'd thought marrying Mandy and taking care of her and the baby was going to be his life.

He'd told Callie that he'd joined the military to escape his grandparents. It wasn't true, though it'd certainly done that. He'd joined at eighteen because Judge Perry had told him that's what he was going to do. His grandparents hadn't argued with the judge, who went to the same church and served as a deacon. They hadn't stood up for him or Mandy, hadn't cared about ever seeing their great-grandchild, and he'd hated them even more for it.

Mandy had given the baby up for adoption because that's what her parents demanded, but she'd at least told him the name she'd given their daughter. Mia.

He hoped she had a great life, that her parents loved her, and that she was thriving. He would never know, and most of the time he was okay with it. Sometimes it killed him because there was one other person in this world that he knew about who shared his DNA, who was his family, and he'd never held her or spoken to her. He tortured himself with thoughts of her unhappy like he'd been, questioning why her birth parents didn't want her. He fervently hoped that wasn't her life, but he'd never know.

That was what woke him in the middle of the night, gasping for air and shaking. The fact he'd never know if his child was unhappy and lonely, if she was well, if she was even alive.

He'd had those thoughts more often lately. He'd considered looking up Mandy's contact info, seeing if she knew anything. Then again, knowing her father, he'd pushed for a sealed adoption so the child would never come looking for her or the family. That would explain why, the few times he'd tried to search the records, he never found anything about a baby.

The Perrys had money, and Judge and Mrs. Perry had plans for their daughter. College at a suitable university with an appropriate professional track, such as nursing, then marriage to someone in their set, a man who would take care of her and let her stay home with the kids while he made a living as a lawyer or doctor. Maybe even a banker. Someone with money and access who fit in at the country club and only wanted the best for his wife and kids.

The door to the spare bedroom opened, cutting into his thoughts. He lay there and listened for her footsteps. She went into the bathroom and shut the door. Luna announced her arrival with a cold nose against his hand. Seth petted her silky fur and waited for her to take off.

But when the bathroom door opened again, she only turned to look. Her tail thumped as Callie's footsteps came closer.

"Luna, don't wake Seth," she whispered.

"She didn't."

"Oh. Was it me?"

"No." He propped himself on an elbow. "Haven't really been to sleep yet."

"Me neither."

She stepped closer and he realized she was still wearing her clothing from earlier. "You didn't change for bed."

She shook her head. "I couldn't." She wrapped her arms around her body. "I wanted to be ready. Just in case."

"Callie," he breathed, his heart squeezing with sympathy.

"You're still in your clothes," she pointed out.

"I'm on the couch with weaponry nearby. Ready. You were supposed to sleep."

"I can't. I feel... anxious. Like somebody's waiting in the woods and the minute I close my eyes, they'll creep closer and closer until I wake up and they're standing over me."

"Unless I have a sudden heart attack or a brain aneurysm and die, that's not happening. Because I've still got the trail cameras and the house alarms, and I'll know if anyone approaches. They aren't getting inside. We patched up the door and boarded it up until we can get the locks changed tomorrow. They aren't waltzing inside without facing a whole lot of firepower."

"I think I need a glass of wine. Maybe that'll help."

He rolled to his feet. "Sit here. I'll get it."

"You don't—"

"Have to. I know. Sit, Callie."

She sat and he went into the kitchen to find a glass that hadn't been shattered, which wasn't all that hard considering there were exactly four left in the cabinet, poured white wine into it, and returned to hand it to her before sitting on the chair nearby.

"You aren't having any?"

"Nope. Gotta keep a clear head."

"Right. Makes sense." She sipped. "You're sure I can't leave town? Take Nikki and get the hell out of here?"

Now why did that thought make the acid reflux in his chest flare again? He was going to have to start taking Pepcid if this kept up.

"I'm sure. Even if you managed to get some of the bigger parts right, like new identities and flying under the radar, you'll need to work. You can't work anywhere these days without a social security number, unless you work cash jobs like picking crops. That's not only backbreaking, it's also not steady. Plus there are a lot of farm workers out there who want those jobs and they can do it better and faster than you can. What's that leave? Your computer skills? How will you advertise for jobs? You don't think these guys won't assume that's the first thing you'll do? They'll haunt all the bulletin boards on all the sites they can, watching for freelancers. Because you'll have to go to the bigger boards. You can't rely on the community center in Nowheresville, pinning your phone number on the board and waiting for calls. And you can't work in a barn because they'll be looking for that, too. You could probably clean houses, but even that has competition these days. And you're inside people's houses without really knowing who those people are. What if somebody assaults you? You going to the police to report it?"

He'd gone through those options rapid fire, and he could see the disappointment in the slump of her shoulders. But she had to know it wasn't going to work even if she thought of something else she could do for money.

"I see your point. But the bad guys can't be everywhere at once. It's a big country."

She sounded defensive, small.

"No, but all they gotta do is be in the right place once. That's all it takes. The odds might be astronomical, or they might not. You willing to take that chance with Nikki's life?"

"No." She sighed. "I just wanted to hear you tell me again why it's a bad idea. When I'm lying in bed alone, I start to think, hey, I'm smart, I can do this. I can disappear. I know how to erase our digital trail, and I'll be careful not to return to any email accounts or sites I've used before. But it's a risk, just like staying is a risk. One day, I'd start to think the risk was gone and I'd make a mistake. I'd think we were in the clear and it'd turn out somebody with a long memory and a thirst for vengeance would have been waiting to find me all that time."

"It's possible."

She sipped her wine quietly. Then her head snapped

up as if she'd remembered something. "Hey, what's going on between Daphne and Kane?"

He snorted. "Helluva gear change, honey. Think you dropped the transmission on the highway back there."

"Cute. Seriously though, they've got a weird vibe thing going. Or is it just me?"

"It's not just you. I think Kane wants her, but he doesn't want her. Treats her like the sister he never had, hovers over her, protects her. Daphne, poor girl, just wishes —speculation here—that he'd act like she's not his little sister for once. She's dating Warren Trigg, manager of the Piggly Wiggly, and Kane acts like it's no big deal when he really wants to twist Trigg's balls off for daring to ask her out in the first place."

"I see. Poor Warren. I think I've seen him before. Tall, scrawny guy. Kane's arms are bigger than his legs. So are yours."

"That's him. I think Daph likes him. I don't think she's only dating him to get a reaction out of Kane. But I also think if Kane were to get his head out of his ass, there might be something there. Or he'd piss her off like he does most women, and we'd lose the best assistant in the world."

"Which you don't want to happen."

"No. Since we hired Daphne, she keeps everything tight. She schedules classes, handles customer service, takes care of the day-to-day bookkeeping, and probably a hundred other things I don't realize. She keeps a running inventory of the supplies, too. Not the guns and ammo, though she has access to those manifests, but everything else. She's indispensable, and it'd be a serious bitch to have her quit because Kane is a dick."

It was hard to remember what it was like before Daphne, but it hadn't been as controlled and smooth. Their main focus was using the range as a cover for Ghost

Ops so everything they'd done had been in service to the mission. But for Daphne, the range *was* the mission. She made them more legit than they'd been on their own.

When Judy Simpson from the Bee wanted an ad for her paper, Daphne took charge and made it happen. When a church group wanted to schedule defense classes, Daphne coordinated everything. When the toilet paper was running low and the coffee was about to run out, Daphne was there with new supplies.

They'd managed fine without her, but they managed much better with her.

Yeah, maybe it was a good idea if Kane kept his head *in* his ass. Because he wasn't the kind of guy who'd ever commit. In all the years Seth had known him, he'd never stayed with the same girlfriend for more than a month. Probably why he treated Daphne like a sister instead of viewing her as a potential hookup. Even he knew he'd wreck it for them all if he got involved with Daph.

Seth decided the dude deserved a medal for his restraint even if it was annoying as shit sometimes. Like when he took Daphne all over two counties looking at cars after hers died but wouldn't actually give her a recommendation. None of them were the right car according to him. The girl was on a budget, so Seth didn't know what the hell Kane expected. She wasn't going to buy something with all the latest bells and whistles. She just needed safe and reliable, but he kept finding excuses why cars weren't right.

"I thought Kane was the nicest one of you guys when you were at GRL."

"That's because he's Kane. Chance and Kane are two of the smoothest motherfuckers you'll ever meet. They say the right things, make you think you're the center of their universe. They excel at conversation."

"You aren't bad at it," she said. "You just take time to warm up."

"For some reason, I've talked more crap to you than I do to most people I know. You're relentlessly chatty."

Her jaw dropped. "I am not. You make it sound like I talk all the time, and I don't."

"You talk a lot to me."

Her gaze dropped to her wine glass. "I told you before. You make me nervous so I can't help myself."

"You said it was because you weren't sure I liked you. What's the reason now?"

"That's part of it."

"And the other part?"

She bit her lip and lifted her gaze. "You kissed me. I know you did it to distract me, but you still did it. And then you told me to think about it, also to keep me distracted, but I *did* think about it. Endlessly. And I know you didn't mean it and I'm probably making a fool of myself here, but yes, you make me nervous, so I talk to cover it up because I'm awkward that way."

He had a choice here. Go in the direction she was leading him, tell her he was sorry for kissing her and hadn't realized it would mean something to her, or tell her the truth, which was that he'd wanted to kiss her.

Yeah, he'd done it to short-circuit her fear, but that wasn't the only reason.

He'd looked at her when she'd walked out of her bedroom earlier and thought, whoa. Her jeans were fitted, finally showing those curves he'd known were there, and she'd put on a white V-neck T-shirt that showed a hint of cleavage when he stood over her and looked down. Her hair was long and silky, parted in the middle and tucked behind her ears, and she wore a delicate chain around her neck with a gold moon and a star.

She didn't have a watch, but wore a slim FitBit. When he'd met her at GRL, she'd had on black pants and low heels with a button up blouse and the same necklace. She hadn't worn the FitBit because it wouldn't have been allowed inside the SCIF where she worked.

Callie was pretty. Not a stunner, but a quiet kind of pretty that unfolded the more time you spent with her. But the more he looked at her, the more stunning she got.

So, yeah, he was attracted, and he'd kissed her because he'd fucking needed to do it.

"I wanted to," he said, because there was no way he was going to agree with her assessment and let that work on her inside. Because it would. She was the kind of person who felt things deeply, like him, and she'd turn it over and over again even when she didn't mean to.

She was quiet. She took another swallow of her wine. "And the rest of it? Did you want to do those things too?"

"You mean when I told you to think about the other places you'd like my tongue?"

She nodded, but she managed to make it look so hesitant that, once more, he couldn't tell her anything but the truth. His dick was on high alert at the moment. Took everything he had to make it stay semi-hard instead of turning to stone.

"I meant every word, Callie. I shouldn't because you're under my protection, but hell, nothing about this situation is ordinary anyway."

"I have to think you'd be bad for me. But I want to go there anyway. I want to stop thinking so much and just feel. It's been a long year of thinking and bottling things up inside and trying to keep a strong front for Nikki because she needed me to be the one who had it together. But I want to let go for a change. I want to do something for *me*. Even if it's bad for me."

His dick was winning the battle with his brain at the moment. "Why would it be bad for you?" he asked, his voice gravelly with need.

"Because you're…" She waved a hand. "Well, look at you. And look at me. I'm not elegant or classy or even very sexy. I'm just me. I write code and I glue scraps of paper and other ephemera into journals. What did you say? I should be at a scrapbooking meeting with a bunch of old ladies? You look like the kind of guy who needs a hot babe with cherry red lipstick, long nails, and a sassy attitude. That's not me. If I put on lipstick, it'll be on my teeth—and probably my shirt—within ten minutes tops. Not that I think you're looking for a girlfriend," she blurted. "Oh lord, I should probably stop drinking this wine. I'm word vomiting again. Embarrassingly so."

"You done?" he asked when her words trailed off.

"I think so. Now I think I should go hide my face beneath my pillow and hope you forget everything I just said."

Fucking hell, this woman got to him. He didn't know why, but when she said shit like that, when she put herself down, he wanted to lift her up and make her believe she was more than worthy of his attention. If anyone was unworthy, it was him.

Seth stood and held out a hand. She stared up at him. Then she set her nearly empty glass down with a sigh and put her hand in his so he could help her up.

He didn't stop there, however. He spanned her jaw with his hand, tilted her head back, and dropped his mouth to hers. She sighed, opening to him, and he thrust his tongue into her mouth, tasting wine. It was sweet, but so was she. He wanted to know if all of her was that sweet.

When he broke the kiss, she put her hands on his arms

to steady herself. He gazed down at her, made sure she was looking at him when he spoke.

"I don't care if you wear lipstick, Callie. You don't need long nails. And I think you're plenty sassy. Sexy too, though you don't think so for some reason. I plan to show you how sexy I find you, but not tonight. Not when you've had wine and your senses are clouded. You still want me to lick all those parts of you tomorrow, then game on, honey."

So much for holding the line. But he couldn't do it anymore. Not with her. With anyone else, sure. But not with Callie. He didn't know what that said about him.

Her breath caught. "I'm not impaired, Seth."

"Can't be sure of that, so not tonight."

"But you want to." She sounded hesitant, uncertain of herself. Like maybe she was imagining the whole thing. It was yet another nudge in the direction they were going. Because he wouldn't let her doubt herself like this.

"I want to."

"You aren't just saying that so I'll go back to bed and leave you alone?"

This woman. He tugged her in the direction of the bedroom. "No, I'm not just saying it. Also, newsflash, I'm going to bed with you because that couch isn't big enough for me. You're getting into the bed, I'm going back for the rifle, and then I'm getting in there beside you. To sleep. That work for you?"

"I—"

He stopped at the door to the bedroom. "Yes or no, Callie? That's all I want to hear from you."

"Yes," she breathed.

Good enough for him.

Chapter Twenty-Five

Callie's heart hammered as she lay on the mattress and waited for Seth to return. She kind of thought he wouldn't, that he was hoping she'd fall asleep. But she wasn't as tipsy or as tired as he thought she was.

But then his footsteps were in the hallway, coming closer, and her heart kicked up again. He walked into the bedroom, dropped the rifle case on the floor beside the bed, and tugged his shirt off.

"Luna, down," he said to the dog, who'd hopped up on the bed to take the unoccupied side.

She immediately obeyed. Seth flipped the covers back and got in beside Callie.

"How do you sleep?" he asked. "Side, stomach, or back?"

"Side."

"Get on your side, facing away from me."

She did as he said. Next thing she knew, his arm was around her body as he tugged her into the circle of his.

And whoa, he wasn't lying about being attracted to her. His dick was hard where it nestled into her behind. She was momentarily paralyzed by that realization, but he put a hand on her hip and pressed her harder into him, leaving no room for doubts to materialize.

"You can change your mind at any time between now and when it happens." His voice was hot in her ear, sending shivers of need down her spine. "But I'm not hiding what you do to me, Callie. Dicks don't lie about what they want even if the men they're attached to do. If all I wanted was to make you feel better and go away, mine wouldn't be aching the way it is. Trust me, I've owned this particular dick for a long time, and I know what it wants."

She laughed softly. "Funny."

She could feel his smile against her ear. It sent another shiver down her spine and she yawned so hard her jaw cracked.

"Glad I could make you laugh. Now sleep, Callie. We've got time to talk tomorrow. You're safe."

"I know."

It was the last thing she remembered before sleep claimed her.

CALLIE JERKED AWAKE, panic stirring in her belly. She was alone, in a strange place—

But no, she was at home. It took her a moment to realize she was in the spare bedroom since nothing was quite the way it was supposed to be.

She'd expected soft light and roses, but she got hard light slanting between the blinds because there were no curtains in this room.

"Charlie," she squeaked, scrambling from the bed. She was late feeding him, and he needed his meds.

She found her shoes where she'd slipped them off, shoved her feet inside, and dashed from the room…

…To find Seth in the kitchen, flipping pancakes. Luna sat at his feet, looking hopeful.

He glanced up. "Hey, babe. You want coffee?"

"Charlie," she began.

"He's fine. I followed the instructions pinned on the wall in the feed room. And Nikki is fine, too. She's at some big horse farm in Lexington, quite possibly planning how to get you to buy her another horse."

Callie blinked as her panic started to ebb and her brain caught up with everything he'd said. "How did you know? Where to look and what to give him, I mean."

"Nikki was very thorough when she coerced me into helping her dig out his stall. Made me help feed, showed me where the instructions were, talked the whole time she scooped everything together, impressed upon me the seriousness of his feeding and medication schedule, and told me he was her baby. She may have intimated that if I was ever tasked with taking care of him and got it wrong, she'd murder me in my sleep."

Callie didn't know whether to laugh or cry. "Wow, I had no idea."

"Yeah, didn't think so. She probably thought she could run me off by making me work hard and inundating me with instructions about horse care. And you know what else?"

She shook her head.

"I don't think she was ever enamored of me. I think you were wrong about that. She's diabolical and protective of you, and she talked my head off that first night to see if I would break. Then she hit me the next morning with hard work and a lecture on my intentions." He snorted. "I like that kid. She's badass. How many pancakes you want?"

Callie's head was still spinning from all he'd said but her heart was beginning to slow down again. Was Nikki that calculating? Maybe so. The fact she was focused on protecting Callie, when Callie thought she was the one doing all the protecting, was probably a sign that Callie needed to stop worrying so much about her sister. Nikki was healing, same as she was. A good thing.

Her gaze slid around the kitchen. If you didn't look too hard, you wouldn't know somebody had trashed her place last night. The pots and pans were fine, there were a couple of glasses left, but the plates had all been shattered. Seth had found paper plates in the pantry, though. And pancake mix.

Except she didn't use pancake mix and she didn't remember him buying any at the Pig.

"Here," he said, pouring coffee for her.

She murmured her thanks and remembered that he'd asked her about the pancakes. "Uh, two pancakes. Those are big."

"And lumpy, but hey, they'll be okay."

"Where did you find pancake mix?"

"I didn't." He put pancakes on a plate, swiping butter between each one, and handed them to her. "The only thing in this world I know how to make from scratch are pancakes. You had the ingredients, so I thought why not?"

Callie poured syrup and then stood at the counter with her plate and cut into the pancakes. "Wow, they're good."

"You sound surprised."

She glanced up at him, wondering if he'd look upset that she had, but his eyes gleamed with humor. Relief sagged its way through her. A knot in her belly reminded her how close they'd been last night. That he'd wrapped his body around hers, his erection against her behind, and held her while sending shivers down her spine as he whispered in her ear that he wanted her.

"Not surprised," she blurted when she realized she'd been staring for too long.

He snorted. "Surprised and distracted, I'd say."

"Sorry." She took another bite. "I feel like I went to bed in a nightmare and woke up in a dream. Not that you were a nightmare, just the part where people broke in my house and you slept all night with a gun at your side in case they came back." She waved the fork around. "These are delicious, and I guess I'm surprised because it's not fair you get to be gorgeous and fit and eat pancakes too."

"You missed the pushups I did before I started cooking. I burn a lot of calories so I can eat them. It's not magic, just hard work."

She had a gym bag. She sometimes went to the employee gym and cycled. Not often enough, apparently. Not since Leo had cornered her in there when they were alone and told her she'd better stay in her lane. He wasn't threatening in a physical way, but it'd rattled her. He'd never been overly friendly in the lab, but that level of anger was something she hadn't seen coming. It made her wonder if anybody else felt that way and just hadn't said it.

"Luna looks like she's starving."

"She's been fed, too. And she had a pancake. Don't let that poor-puppy look fool you."

Callie reached down to pet her head. "Silly girl. It breaks my heart her owner died and her life changed overnight."

"Yeah, but she's here now, and you'll give her all the love she needs."

"I guess I will. Though I'm still kinda pissed at you for taking me to the kennel."

"You needed a dog, living all the way out here in the sticks."

"I know. I thought about it a few times since we moved, especially as Mikhail got angrier, but I didn't take action."

He turned off the stove as he put the last pancake on his plate and buttered it. "I'm guessing you haven't gotten a text from his phone this morning."

She pulled her phone from the pocket of her jeans. "Nope, nothing."

For good measure, she opened the Find My iPhone app and checked on Nikki. Yep, at a horse farm. Bliss Stables. Oh boy. As if Nikki could feel her checking in, a photo pinged onto Callie's phone.

> My next ride…

It was a big German warmblood, chestnut, with a white blaze and two white socks. He was tacked up and ready to go. Nikki stood beside him, grinning big. His withers were over her head.

Callie sent back a laughing emoji and turned the phone to Seth. "You weren't wrong. She's thinking how to get me to buy her a new horse."

He snorted as he led the way to the table and dragged out a chair for her before pulling out his own. "I know you worry about her, but I think she's got a strong mind in there. She's not moping, she's doing."

Callie typed back.

> Beautiful. And big. What would Jack say about you cheating on him?

"Maybe you're right," she said to Seth. "I've been so focused on what she was like at the Christmas party that I hadn't seen the signs. Every little hitch in her mood, every bad day, I hover and try to fix things."

"You should talk in Polish to her again. Maybe she's been waiting for you to make that move, thinking you're the one who was grieving hardest."

I love Jack! And Charlie! I'm not cheating on either of them. Gotta go. I get to ride this big boy after Lisa does!

Be safe! Have fun!

You too. Bowchicka…

Oh lord. Callie put the phone face down and concentrated on breakfast. "You might be right. I never considered it. I thought I was the adult, the strong one, that it was up to me to be those things for her."

"Look, I don't know anything about teenagers, like I said. And I've only known her a couple of days. But that girl strikes me as somebody with a strong idea about what she wants. She's not the sort of person to give up because things are hard. I could be wrong, I'll admit it. Don't think so though."

"When she was seven and riding her first pony over fences—small fences, barely even a hop for the pony—she didn't want anyone to lead them around the course. She wanted to do it herself, and she did. She sat up there, her legs too short to reach past the saddle flaps, and steered that little son of a gun at speed around the arena. And then, on the last jump, he veered sideways and went around. She was clinging to his neck, about to fall off when he reached the gate and stopped. He thought he was done, my parents were white as ghosts, and Nikki dropped to the ground and demanded that I put her up again. I did, and she was off, heading for that last fence. She steered right over it and screamed bloody murder. Not out of fear. Then she rode out the gate and back to the barn. When it was all over, she'd gotten first place." She grinned. "I haven't thought of that in years. But you're right, she's a tough kid and she never gives up."

Seth reached for her hand, turned it over, and skimmed his fingers over her palm. Her skin tingled and her breath shortened. "Seems to me as if both of you are tougher than nails."

"Hardly," Callie said. Wheezed, really. "I'm not tough at all. I want to quit all the time."

"But you don't. Being tough has nothing to do with attitude and everything to do with actions. You want to quit, but you don't. You wanted to go to a motel last night, but you stayed. You didn't want to meet with whoever's using Mikhail's phone, but you set the meeting and you walked into the bookstore, prepared to do your part. And you know what else? The easy thing to do, the simplest thing, would have been to replace that cable like you were told. But you didn't."

Her heart throbbed in her chest. "I don't think replacing the cable would have ended the danger."

"No, I don't either. But it would have been the easy thing to do. It's something a pliable person would have done. It's what Mikhail was counting on when he told you to do it. That you would. He didn't expect pushback."

Emotion knotted her throat. "I don't recognize this brave person you're trying to convince me is inside here, but thank you."

"I don't need to convince you because it's true. You're

just wearing blinders to your own strengths for some reason."

She looked down at their hands, at the way he turned hers over and twined their fingers together. His skin was darker than hers, golden. He was right that she had the pasty white skin of a computer nerd while he looked like someone who spent time outside.

When she looked up again, he was watching her, his expression a mix of emotions she couldn't untangle. "What's wrong, Seth?"

He seemed to hesitate.

"I like you, Callie. There are things I can't tell you, same as you can't tell me, and things I haven't told you but probably should."

"Okay, so tell me."

"You're sweet, you know that?"

"I think a woman likes to be told she's sexy, not sweet." Her heart hammered harder as he stared at her. He was going to tell her they couldn't take this any farther. Why else get so serious all of a sudden? Disappointment was a hot swirl in her chest.

"You're definitely sexy, but I think sweet matters more. And I think, before we go any further, I need to tell you the truth about Mia. I know what you assumed because of what I said, but she didn't die."

"Oh thank heavens. I thought…"

He pushed her hair behind her ear, his touch gentle. "I know you did. I didn't correct you because the truth is so much worse." She didn't see how it could be, but he dragged in a breath, blew it out as if preparing for something big. Traumatic. "I gave her up. Signed away my parental rights before she was ever born. I've never seen her."

"Oh, Seth—"

"I didn't fight for her, Callie. I thought you should know I haven't always done a good job of being there for the people who needed me before we go any further. I'll protect you and Nikki. I'm good at it. But emotionally? I'm not so good at that shit. I give up instead of fight. I disengage. I fail when it's most important."

Chapter Twenty-Six

The pain and self-loathing in his voice was difficult to hear. It made her want to hug him. Hard.

She wasn't certain he'd want that, so she squeezed his hand instead. "I'm sure you had a good reason."

His eyes widened a fraction. "That's it? I tell you I gave up my own kid without a fight, and you think I had a good reason? You don't think it's a terrible thing to do? I bailed on a helpless baby, Callie. You need to understand that."

To hell with it. She scooted her chair next to his and wrapped her arms around him. But he took it a step further and dragged her onto his lap, as if the mere act of touching him had opened up a dam of emotion inside him. Then he buried his face against her shirt as she held onto him. Tears stung her eyes.

"You had a good reason," she said after a while, her cheek on his head. "Whatever the reason, it was a good one."

His head tipped back, his eyes searching hers. "How can you say that?"

She took the liberty of skimming her fingers along his

jaw, tracing her thumb over his lower lip. Because she was this close and she could. "Talk about blinders," she teased.

He looked confused.

"Seth, honestly? You walked into my life three days ago, and you've fiercely protected me—and Nikki—every moment since. You didn't throw up some cameras, give me an app, charge me far too much for the work, and drive away. You *slept* with a gun by your side last night so you could keep me safe. If you'd do that for somebody you hardly know, I can't imagine what you'd do for a child that belonged to you. Give her up because you couldn't take care of her like she needed? Yeah, I can see that happening. I can see you being that *good.* It takes a strong person emotionally to be so selfless. So stop saying you aren't good at emotions."

"Jesus, you're fucking sweet, like it or not. Amazing, too." He sucked in a breath. "I was seventeen. I got my girlfriend pregnant, and her father scared the shit out of me. He was a federal judge and a shark of a prosecutor before that. He terrified me, and I signed the papers without a fight. I should have stood up to him, but I didn't. You're the first person I've ever told any of this to. I don't know why. I fuckin' love my guys. They're my brothers. But they don't know any of this shit."

Callie skimmed her fingers through his hair, hot emotion boiling inside her. She was the first person he'd told about his daughter? The weight of his confession hit her hard, the gravity of it. He'd thought she was going to judge him. Maybe that was why he did it. To push her away.

She wasn't going to be pushed, not when she knew he was so much better than he thought he was.

"First, you can trust me not to tell another soul what you've told me. But I've seen you and your friends together, and they don't strike me as the kind of people who'd fail you when you needed them most. They stayed and cleaned my house, not because of me, but because of you. They'd do anything for you same as you would them. I'm guessing, but I think I'm right." She drew in a breath. "Second, you were a kid yourself. And her father sounds like a horrible human being doing that to you."

"I understand his motivation now, even if I think he did it wrong. He was protecting his daughter. Protecting her future. They gave Mia up for adoption. I only know her name and birthdate because Mandy had a friend send me a message. I joined the military as soon as I turned eighteen because the judge wanted me to."

Anger was a whirlwind in her mind. She imagined someone doing those things to Nikki—because they were talking about teenagers here—and she wanted to go Godzilla on them, smashing the town and making them wish they'd never been born.

"I'm so sorry, Seth. You didn't deserve to be treated like that."

"No. I didn't. But it's okay. I've had a lot of years to get over that part of it. I just can't get over my kid thinking I didn't want her."

"You don't know she thinks that," Callie said fiercely. "Her adoptive family probably loves her and showers her with all the attention and security two kids would have struggled to provide. Because that's what you and Mandy were. I'm not saying it couldn't have worked. But it might have been a struggle."

His forehead dropped to her shoulder. "We were too young and too poor without her parents' money, which they never would have given, to raise a child. Plus we weren't exactly in love. More like teenage lust. We weren't ready for the seriousness of raising a kid. I don't regret that she was adopted, or the path my life took. But I regret I'll never know her."

"You don't know that for sure. There are companies where people put in their DNA and find matches. If she ever goes looking, she'd find you."

He shook his head. "I can't file my DNA like that."

"People do it all the time."

"I know, but I can't. Not yet. And I can't explain, so don't ask."

She considered how to answer. "Okay, so you can't. What if Mandy already did?"

He looked at her in wonder. "I never thought of that. But she would do it. She'd want to give Mia a chance to find her if she ever got curious."

"See? There's a chance you could still meet her someday."

He dragged her mouth to his for a kiss. It didn't last long, but her body sparked to life nevertheless, nerves sizzling with heat and need.

"You're fucking brilliant, Callie Crowell. And not just at computers. Sweet, sexy, and brilliant. Killer combo."

It surprised her how badly she wanted to get naked with this man. She hadn't known him long, but somehow it felt like she had. She was comfortable with him in a way she would have never believed when she'd turned around in One Shot Tactical and saw him instead of Kane. Was that only four days ago? Didn't seem possible.

"I accept your flattery because it's been a rotten week and I've felt like a helpless, frightened idiot for most of it."

"You aren't an idiot, and you aren't helpless. Frightened is a legit response to what's happened, but we're gonna fix that."

"I know. I just wish it was over already."

She looked around the kitchen, thinking about the

destruction of last night. The front door was held to the frame with boards, and while everything was tidy again, it was obvious to her that things were missing. The knickknacks and picture glass that had been shattered. The couch and chair cushions held together by duct tape. She was going to have to buy new furniture again, and that thought depressed her.

Her phone buzzed where she'd laid it on the table and her heart kicked up. Seth gave her a squeeze as if he understood. "Go ahead and check, baby. I'm here. We'll deal with it, whatever it is."

Callie had to leave his lap to reach the phone. She instantly felt less safe, but she told herself to get over it. She couldn't go through life wrapped in Seth's arms. She had to stand on her own two feet because, though he'd shared something painful with her, she didn't know how long he'd be in her life. This wasn't a relationship, no matter how much she might like it to be.

She didn't sit as she checked her notifications. "It's an email from Dr. Robbins. GRL is opening on Monday, but my team reports for work tomorrow evening because we've been down too long and the project timeline's in jeopardy. I'm not surprised, really." She skimmed the message. "We're in another secure lab while repairs continue to the two damaged in the fire. Five until eleven, then back again Monday morning."

Her pulse quickened. Little beads of sweat broke out in her armpits, between her breasts. She hadn't expected to be hit so hard by the idea of returning, but all she could think about was being locked in the lab and unable to open the door while the fire raged. The helplessness and fear were as real as ever. She swallowed as her vision grew dark at the edges.

"Hey," Seth said, tugging her onto his lap again.

"You're okay, Callie. It's okay. I'm not going to let them get to you. I'll take you to work and I'll be nearby waiting until you're done. You won't be alone."

She melted against him, though she told herself she needed to be strong, self-reliant.

"I won't have my cell phone, and I won't be able to contact you if something happens. That scares me." She pulled in a breath. "But there'll be eight of us in the lab, so I have to believe it's safer. They were after me, not all of us."

"Security will be heightened in the building. Standard procedure after an incident like that. Leadership isn't gonna take the chance work grinds to another halt. They have contracts to meet and can't afford more delays. It's a financial decision as well as a security one. There'll be plenty of people on the premises."

"Right. Of course you're right." She pulled in a breath, but the sweat was still there, still working to chill her body as a shiver rippled through her. "I-I don't know what's wrong with me. My chest. It's tight. I'm c-cold."

"It's a panic attack, honey. You can get through it. Breathe deep, let it out slow. That's right," he said as she did what he told her.

"H-how do you know? I've never h-had one."

"Trust me, I know. Seen a million of 'em. Had a few myself. You'll be okay."

He held her for a long time, until the panicky feeling ebbed, until her chest wasn't tight and she was no longer shivering. "I'm okay now," she finally said.

"You sure?"

"Yes." Her clothes felt sticky with sweat, and she started to worry about smelling bad. She'd slept in these clothes, after all. "I want to shower."

His grip on her eased. She stood but didn't move

toward the bathroom. Her pulse raced for another reason now. She'd imagined him under the spray the past couple of days, soaping his body. She desperately wanted to see him do that. She wanted to do it for him.

But telling him was a bold move to make, and she wasn't certain she could. He'd said she was tough. Brave went hand in hand with tough, didn't it?

And why wait anyway? She was in danger, she had no idea who was behind the fire or the break-in and why, and she didn't know how any of it would end.

But she could do this one thing for herself.

Bowchickawow.

Chapter Twenty-Seven

"I think I'd feel safer if you came with me."

Seth's balls tightened. Just because she wanted him to go with her didn't mean she wanted sex. She had a lot on her mind with the break-in, and she'd feel safer if he was there. That's all it was.

But damn, sitting outside the bathroom door and imagining her in the shower, her fingers gliding over her skin, was going to be the end of him.

When he didn't move, Callie held out a hand. He stared at it. Lifted his gaze to hers. She was smiling, but the smile was starting to fade. Like maybe her confidence was taking a beating.

Still, he had to know.

"Let me be sure I understand you. You want me to go with you so you feel safer. Where do you want me? In the bathroom with you or waiting in the hall?"

Her eyes widened slightly. Then she giggled. Flipping giggled. He didn't know why that sound got to him, but it did. Cute. Just like her.

He'd told her his darkest secret, the thing that woke

him up at night, knowing in his gut she'd look at him in horror. Instead, she'd held him close and told him he was a good person. She'd turned him inside out with those words.

Now she was cracking his chest open with her giggle.

He didn't know what it meant, but he wanted more of it.

"I don't think you can do what I have in mind if you wait in the hall. As for where I want you, well, I was hoping I wouldn't have to explain that part."

Ah, now he got it. The surge of blood to his dick would have made him lightheaded if he'd been standing.

Well, maybe not really, but it was an impressive surge.

He got to his feet and took her hand. He felt the tremor in her fingers, and he tugged her toward him, wrapped her in his arms.

"You don't have to do this, Callie. I'm not going anywhere, whether we have sex or not."

Her fingers curled into his shirt. "I know. I want to. It's been a long time for me. I'm not somebody who falls into bed easily, and honestly this feels so fast my head's spinning. But I don't want to wait. I don't want to regret that I didn't take this chance when I had it."

"You'll still have the chance next week. Next month."

She shook her head, her grip on him tightening. "No. I need this now. You." Her gaze dropped to his chest. "I feel like if we don't do this, something bad will happen."

"Callie," he said, his throat tight. "That's not a good reason."

She tugged on his shirt, a growl in her throat. "Look here, mister, you promised me some licking of parts. You promised it today if I still wanted it, and I'm cashing in. I want to take a shower, I want you to go with me, and I want to run my hands over your body. I want to feel your dick inside me, and I want some earth-shattering orgasms because I spent a lot of time thinking about it in that bookstore last night. When I wasn't thinking about murdery people coming after me, that is. Sexy times with you was my reward for going through the hell of waiting for somebody who wasn't Mikhail to show up and stab me with a poisoned umbrella. If I'm going back to the lab tomorrow, I'm going with a smile on my face and an ache between my legs because I've had too much hot sex with my hot bodyguard."

He wanted to laugh and throw her on the nearest mattress at the same time. Strip her naked, bury his face between her legs, and make her scream his name. Fucking hell, this woman turned him on.

Kane was wrong that he hadn't hooked up with anyone since they'd moved to Alabama. There was a woman from Huntsville he'd gone out with a few times. Once they'd had sex, she'd started talking about weddings in an offhand way. He'd noped out of that situation pretty quick.

And maybe he'd nope out of this one if Callie mentioned white dresses and summer weddings, but he couldn't imagine it. Not with the way he wanted her.

She was the last woman he'd ever thought he'd get naked with, simply because of the situation and her involvement in the Athena Project—and his prior belief that she was the most likely person to be their leak—but now she was the only one he wanted.

In four fucking days. He didn't understand it, at all, but that's where he was. His emotions, because he did have them contrary to his team's belief, were caught up in her.

Her sweet vulnerability. Her love for her sister. The way she'd melted for Luna the instant she'd started petting her. Her fucking scraps of paper and her tweezers and her damn reading journals bursting at the seams from all the shit she glued in there. Her feminine bedroom with the pink roses everywhere. It was fucking girly nirvana, and it ought to give him hives, but it was hers and he wanted, more than anything, to make love to her on that bed. To be buried in her, listening to her moans and sighs, feeling her body wrapped around his as they came apart together.

"Well?" she demanded when he didn't speak or move toward the bathroom. He heard the doubt in her voice, the vulnerability. The fear that he was about to tell her no, it was a mistake, he hadn't meant a word of what he'd said to her last night.

So he did the only thing he could do. He hooked an arm behind her knees and lifted her in his arms. She wrapped hers around his neck as he started for the bathroom.

"So this is a yes?" She still sounded vulnerable, uncertain, despite the fact he was carrying her. Like she thought he was going to deposit her in the bathroom and pull the door closed with him standing in the hallway, being noble and self-sacrificing.

Fuck no, he wasn't going to be noble.

He carried her into the bathroom and set her on her feet while pulling her wrinkled T-shirt over her head at the same time. "It's a yes," he growled.

And then he kissed her.

Chapter Twenty-Eight

Callie's pulse pounded in her ears as Seth's mouth met hers. She wanted this, and it scared her too. Not because she was scared of sex, but because she felt way more than she should be feeling. Everything with Seth was amplified beyond what it should be for the amount of time they'd known each other.

She thought of a book she'd read a few years ago. The main point she'd always had trouble with was how two people who knew nothing about each other fell in love instantly and irrevocably, indulged in four stolen days together, and then never saw each other again because they'd had to choose not to wreck the lives of those around them.

It wasn't the affair she found unbelievable. It was the utter conviction *this* was the person meant for them that happened so instantaneously and lasted until the day they died.

She didn't think she felt that conviction about Seth, but she felt something more than she'd ever felt before.

He broke the kiss and reached into the shower to turn

on the water. He'd left the bathroom door open, and Luna walked inside, took one look at them both, and went to lay in the hallway as if she knew what was about to happen didn't involve her but she needed to be close by regardless.

"You showering with those clothes on or what?" Seth asked as he toed off his boots and ripped his shirt over his head. "Or do you need my help?"

He was large in the space. Imposing. But oh my stars, that chest. She'd seen his bare chest before, but she'd never been able to stare the way she was now. His muscles were defined, rippling beneath his skin whenever he made the slightest movement.

"I've got it," she said, unsnapping her jeans and pushing them down her hips while he did the same.

Callie's breath caught in her throat. He wore boxer briefs. Dear heaven. They were gray, fitted, and they strained against the outline of his cock. Big, beautiful, almost spilling from the fabric. Her mouth went dry, and she suddenly found herself unable to speak.

"Come here," he whispered, twining his fingers with hers and tugging her toward him. "Last chance to change your mind, Callie."

But his fingers stroked the skin of her belly, slid under the waistband of her panties, teasing at the edge. He hadn't even touched the sensitive bits and she was ready to melt.

"Not going to," she gasped as his other hand roamed around to squeeze her ass cheek. "More. Please."

"You got it, babe."

Seth unsnapped her bra and slipped it from her arms, dropping it on the counter. Then he pushed her panties down her body and made her turn to face the mirror. Even their reflection turned her on. He was big behind her, dark, and she practically glowed with light and heat. Her lips were parted, her nipples hard peaks. Her pussy ached with the need to be touched by someone other than herself.

She was no stranger to getting herself off, but it wasn't the same thing as having a gorgeous, unbelievably beautiful man do it for her.

With her.

Because this was a participation sport. Seth cupped her breasts with both hands, then tweaked and played with her nipples while pushing his boxer-clad cock against her ass.

Callie couldn't stop the little gasps and breathy moans that squeaked from her throat as he pinched and pulled her sensitive flesh. A moment later his mouth dropped to her shoulder, his tongue licking across her skin to her neck. Shudders of delight rolled through her. She shifted her legs, the wetness between them dripping onto her inner thighs. It ought to be embarrassing, and yet she was completely turned on by it.

"What do you like, Callie?" he asked, his voice a rumble against her ear. Then he nibbled her earlobe and her body turned to putty.

"That. All of it."

"What else?"

She watched his hand glide down her body, his fingers parting her before disappearing in the seam. Callie groaned as Seth swore.

"Fuck, you're wet."

"Sorry," she gasped.

"Are you kidding me?" He stroked her clit and her back arched as her body begged for more. "It's fucking perfect. I could slide inside you right now and you'd take every inch. But this would end much too fast because I wouldn't be able to stop myself. I'd fuck you until we both came and then be pissed I didn't take my time."

"Do it then. We've got time for more."

"You're bad for my control, babe."

He stroked her a little faster now and she leaned forward, hands on the counter, widening her legs so he could reach her better. His other hand skimmed down her spine until he was squeezing her ass.

And then he was gone, and she was gasping for air, disappointment welling inside her. It didn't last long because he took her hand and led her to the shower and opened the door for her. Then he shucked his briefs and stepped into the enclosure with her.

Callie let her gaze drop over his body, her heart hammering against her ribs like a trapped butterfly. He grinned at her. "Love a walk-in shower big enough for two."

He hooked an arm around her waist and dragged her against him, their bodies meeting beneath the spray. He shifted them so their heads weren't underwater and kissed her. Callie had to stand on tiptoe to wrap her arms around his neck as she kissed him back with all the passion beating in her soul.

His tongue against hers was magic. Hot, sweet magic. They kissed until she ached so bad it hurt, until his dick pressing against her abdomen felt like a brand.

"Fuck," he said, dragging his mouth from hers. "Condoms."

She turned his chin from the direction of the door and made him look at her. "I have an IUD. I've had one since college. This one was changed a couple of years ago. I haven't had sex since I left college, so you do the math."

That last part was embarrassing, but it was the truth and he needed to know it. It was also crazy that she was basically initiating a conversation about having unprotected sex with a man she'd known for four days.

His gaze dropped down her body. "Baby, that's a waste. You're so fucking pretty."

She couldn't help but grin. "Thank you. But you realize a woman doesn't need to be pretty to have sex, right? She just needs to be horny and have a willing partner."

"Yeah, but *I* have to think she's pretty or we're not getting lift off."

Callie snorted. "How can you make me laugh at a time like this? I'm confessing that I'm a lonely, practically virginal girl here and you're concentrating on the wrong thing."

He bent to lick a nipple and she gasped, clutching his shoulders for support. When he finished with her nipple, he licked his way up her throat and kissed her.

"Believe me, I know what the right thing is. And I wanted you to laugh because you're embarrassed it's been so long for you. You shouldn't be. It's up to you when you have sex and who you have it with. If you didn't find a guy you wanted in all that time, I'm not judging you." He let his gaze drop down her body, back up again. "Turns me on knowing you've chosen me after all this time. Okay, now me. I've had a handful of partners over the past year, and I always wear a condom. Always. But I want to be bare inside you. Not gonna lie about that. If you're offering, I'm accepting."

Oh God.

"I'm offering."

His smile was beautiful. Heart stopping. "I'm gonna make you feel good, Callie. Promise you that."

She believed him.

He reached for the shampoo and poured some in his hand. Then he made her turn around so he could wash her hair, massaging her scalp in a way that made her moan at how good it felt. "Rinse."

She did so as he got the conditioner. Then he applied it to the ends the way she showed him and got a squirt of body wash. That's when the torture began.

He soaped her body thoroughly, slowly, rubbing her breasts rhythmically, pinching and pulling her nipples until she was a quivering mass of nerves. He soaped the rest of her, careful not to use too much in places where it could itch and sting. She rinsed everything off, including the conditioner, while he dashed the soap across his body much too fast for her liking.

"Slow down and let me."

"Nope, not this time." He finished in record time, then took both her hands in his and turned her to the wall, lifting her arms over her head and pressing her into the tile. "I'm too hard and too eager to let you start rubbing my body. I'd embarrass myself if you tried. A man likes to have staying power when he's trying to impress a woman for the first time."

"I'm already impressed. Nothing you could do would ruin this for me."

He let go of her hands and she dropped them to his shoulders. "Uh-uh, Callie. Hands over your head."

She did as he said, shivering with anticipation. Then he dropped his mouth to hers and dominated the kiss, asking for more and more as his hands roamed her body. He pushed her breasts together and bent to lick and suck her nipples.

"Seth," she said, his name a broken moan.

"I know. I feel it too." He let go of her breasts and gripped her hips. "Up, Callie."

She put her arms around his neck and lifted her legs to wrap around him as he hefted her against the tile.

"I wanted to take it slow, but I can't."

"I don't want you to," she whispered fiercely.

His fingers skimmed against her clit, and she bowed her back, trying to get closer to him. His cock was at her entrance, and she'd never wanted anything so desperately in her life as she wanted him in that minute.

"God, you're wet." He slipped inside her and she wrapped her legs tighter around him, wanting more than he was currently giving. She knew he did it out of consideration for her, but she was ready. She couldn't get any wetter, any more turned on.

"It's okay, Seth. Fuck me. I need you to fuck me now."

He swore and pushed all the way inside her. Callie cried out and he stilled. "Did I hurt you?"

"No, you dork. It feels… oh God… a-*mazing.*"

Chapter Twenty-Nine

Seth had to agree with her. It felt fucking fantastic to have Callie Crowell wrapped around him, his dick buried in her pussy, surrounding him with her heat. He was balls deep inside her, and he felt as if he'd never experienced such a profound connection in his life. Which was crazy, but there it was.

Sex with Callie was like the first time, but with experience and knowledge instead of groping and near-failure. No, this first time with her was about the sensations of being inside a woman, the sheer wonder of it. It felt new and amazing to him.

"Seth?"

"What, baby?"

"You aren't moving."

He laughed, and then he stepped back to tilt her toward the wall. Not to break the connection, but so he could see himself inside her.

"That's a beautiful sight." Her pussy stretched around him, pink and glistening. Her clit was swollen. When he touched it, he knew she'd shudder around him and grip him tighter.

"Are you going to stare or fuck me?"

His gaze met hers. She bit her bottom lip, looking shy. Such a contrast to the words that'd come out of her mouth. The water beaded on her breasts, running in rivulets down her abdomen, her hair was flat against her head, and her lashes held water like dew drops on flowers in the morning.

She was like a water goddess from the mythology he'd liked to read when he was a teenager. The most sensual, beautiful sight he'd seen in a long time. Maybe ever.

"Yeah," he said, moving into her again, pressing her to the tile. "Hang on, baby. It's about to get real in here."

There was no holding back once he started. Seth pushed her against the slippery shower wall and fucked her as hard as he dared. Her tits bounced with his thrusts, and he had to work to keep from blowing before she did. That's how hot the sight of her riding his dick was.

She gripped his biceps, her head rolling back, her legs tightening around him to hold him where she wanted him.

And then she started to moan. Not the soft moans he'd once thought she'd utter. Not a scream either, but something in between. Loud enough to let him know she loved what he was doing. To let him know he'd better not stop.

"Touch yourself, Callie. Let me see you play with your clit."

Her eyes flew open. He thought she'd refuse, but then she put a hand between them and started rubbing. Her moans intensified, her muscles clamping down on his cock as she stroked herself faster.

"Look at me," he ordered when her eyes drifted closed.

She did. "I want to watch you come."

He could tell she was close by the way she shook. His

dick stroked in and out of her, parting the pink flesh and sliding deep, glistening with her juices. His balls tightened and he knew he was close.

But then Callie jerked in his arms, grinding her pussy against him and groaning so loud he was glad she didn't have neighbors.

"That's right, Callie. Come for me, baby."

She did, splintering apart in his arms with a sharp cry that had him losing his tight grip on his own orgasm. He shot jet after jet of semen deep into her body, groaning with the rightness of how it felt to lose himself in this woman. He'd fucked more than his share of women in his life, had some good times and great orgasms.

But none of those compared to this one. This orgasm, this woman's body, this shower enclosure in a house in the middle of the sticks, miles from the tiny town of Sutton's Creek, Alabama. He lost himself and found himself, and he was pretty damn sure nothing was going to be the same ever again.

They stood together, breathing hard, her back still to the wall, him holding her up with arms and legs that were jelly. He eased her legs down until she could stand, then reached over to flip off the water.

"You okay," he asked, reluctant to let her go entirely.

"I think so. You?"

He wanted to laugh. That she'd turn around his concern for her and give it right back to him was a measure of the kind of woman she was. Sweet. Caring. Adorable. He was way bigger than her, way heavier, and though his legs were rubbery, they'd recover quickly because he squatted heavy weights regularly. He also worked out with his own body weight when he wasn't near a gym. He was extremely fit because his body needed to suffer deprivation and hardship on missions. He couldn't afford to be weak.

Yet she worried that he was okay. He loved that about her.

"Yeah, I'm fine." He opened the shower door and reached for a towel, wrapped her in it, and gently dried her body before squeezing the moisture from her hair. She watched him with an expression he couldn't quite decipher, but that was okay.

When she was dry, he grabbed a towel for himself and dried off quickly. Then he took her hand and led her, naked, to the room next door. Her room. She hesitated in the doorway, but he turned to her and pulled her gently forward.

"Can you think of a better way to erase what they did in here than to replace it with a better memory?"

Her eyes were big and green as she stared at him. A smile tugged at the corners of her mouth. "What did you have in mind?"

"Get on the bed and I'll show you."

"Hard to say no to a proposal like that."

She pulled her covers down and climbed onto her bed. Seth joined her, hovering over her on hands and knees before sliding down her body and wedging her legs open with his shoulders. "I've been thinking of this for days now," he said, and then licked her from the bottom of her pussy to her clit.

Chapter Thirty

"SETH!" SHE CRIED AS SHE CURLED HER FINGERS IN HIS hair, lifting her torso to watch what he did to her.

She was still sensitive after her last orgasm, but what he did felt so good she didn't want to stop him. Even if she squirmed beneath his mouth.

She'd had guys go down on her before, but never like this. Never so *intensely*.

He feasted on her. Licked and sucked and ate her like a man starving. She tried to shift away from him when it got too intense, but he held her firmly in place and devoured her. And then, just when she thought she couldn't take another second, he sucked her clit, tugging with just enough pressure to make her explode.

Her grip on his head tightened. She knew she was holding him against her pussy, grinding against him, but he didn't stop. He sucked harder until she saw stars.

And then she fell back on the mattress, her body spent, her head spinning as her heart beat so hard she couldn't hear anything but the blood rushing in her ears.

But then he crawled up her body, his cock nudging her,

and she opened to him, eager for *more*. Coming when his mouth was on her was amazing. But coming with him inside her? Even better.

She spread her legs, inviting him in. He sank into her until he was once more balls deep inside her. Her pussy clenched around him, the remnants of her orgasm still rippling through her.

"Fucking beautiful, Callie. The way you feel, the way you move. The way you moan and then scream a little when you come."

Heat crawled over her. "Scream? Do I?"

He kissed her softly and she tasted herself on him. It wasn't a terrible taste, though not her favorite. *He* was her favorite though. But scream? Did she really?

He chuckled and she felt it to her core. "Yeah, a little. I think it's sexy as hell."

"I guess that's a good thing. It'd be awful if you hated it."

"I don't hate it. No man would hate something that let him know how good he was doing pleasuring his woman. Scream as much as you like. I can take it."

The heat still pulsed over her. "I'm thinking no sex when Nikki's home, then."

He snorted. "Not happening, babe. I'll muffle your screams with my mouth. It'll be hot."

She believed it would be. Good God, Nikki had been right about her getting horizontal with Seth. She didn't know what to think about that just yet. She'd deal with it when Nikki got home. Because one look at her and Nik was going to know Callie was guilty as sin.

But oh, what a way to go.

She thought maybe Seth would lose control again and they'd be wild the way they had in the shower, but it didn't happen that way. He moved slowly, deliberately, their mouths fusing as they made love.

Made love? She wasn't sure she could call it that, because you had to be *in* love didn't you?

But it wasn't fucking, not this time. It was sweet and hot and so incredibly sexy that she never wanted it to end.

"You feel amazing, Callie. You have no idea."

She moaned. "I think I have a pretty good idea."

Because everything about this was amazing.

They kissed long and deep, moving together as if they were one body. It was a dance, a rhythm that could be awkward if you didn't have the right tempo with the other person.

But they did. Their tempo was perfect, matched, as if they'd known each other's bodies a lifetime rather than learning the map of their pleasure with every stroke, every touch.

It was beyond anything Callie had ever experienced before. She didn't know if it was the same for Seth. She very much suspected it wasn't. His experience was infinite compared to hers.

She squeezed her eyes shut, told herself she wasn't going there. Wasn't imagining him with other women, doing what he did to her. It didn't matter. All that mattered was now.

She didn't know how long they stayed that way, moving together like a wave rolling toward shore before the strength of the wave grew into a tsunami. Before they were moving harder and faster, Seth pounding into her as she wrapped her legs around him and held on for the ride.

This time he didn't tell her to touch herself. He did it for her. His fingers found her clit, strummed it until she lost control. Control of her voice, her body. She heard herself moaning, heard herself begging.

And then, because she was desperate and Seth knew how to back off each time before she exploded, she reached down to cup his balls. The way he stiffened and swore made her feel powerful in that moment. She rolled them in her hand, squeezed lightly, and loved the way he shuddered.

"Callie," he groaned. "Damn."

The sexy sound of his voice sent her over the edge. He rode her while she came, thrusting deeper, dragging her orgasm out as her body dissolved into a shower of sparks.

When she was coherent again, she pushed him off her and he rolled until she could straddle him. The bruise on her knee where she'd fallen at the Dawg barely registered. She was that turned on. Still. And she had a wicked idea. He thought she was going to sink onto his cock and ride him, but she dropped to take him in her mouth instead.

"Fuck," he blurted.

His fingers twisted in her hair. She thought he might try to pull her away, but he groaned and then didn't. He lay back on the mattress and let her suck him. She thought vaguely how this wasn't like her, how she was never this bold during sex. She was always afraid of getting it wrong because her experience level was still somewhere in the advanced novice category, but she wasn't afraid with Seth.

Not with the way he had his arm thrown over his face, or the sounds he made in his throat, or the way his fingers tightened in her hair.

She tried to take as much of him as she could, let his cock slide to the back of her throat, then retreated before her gag reflex kicked in. She cupped his balls, kneading them, and then she let his cock slide free and licked his balls instead. That earned her a gasp and a deep groan.

"Dammit, Callie," he said. "You're gonna make me come if you don't stop."

"So come," she said around a mouthful of cock.

She worked him with her fist, sucked him, licked the tip and then tried to deep throat him again. She wasn't so good at that part, so she backed off a little and sucked as much as she could.

"You sure about this?" he asked, his voice sounding strangled.

She didn't dignify the question with a reply. Instead she kept sucking and pumping—and Seth exploded in her mouth. She drank him down, as much as she could, but some leaked down his cock when she couldn't keep up. When it was done, when nothing more came out, she worked her way up his gorgeous abdomen, exploring him as she went. She found the scar where he must have sewn himself up. It was on his ribcage, almost tucked against his side, and she kissed it reverently.

She was still exploring, licking nipples and touching muscles, when he dragged her up and kissed her deeply.

"You've slain me, Callie. I'm dead."

She laughed. "Hardly. But maybe a rest is needed. Recharge so you can do it again."

He grinned. "Yeah, maybe so."

He shifted them until they were on their sides, pulled the sheet over their bodies, and wrapped his arms around her. His cock was still half-hard where it nestled between her cheeks.

"Think I didn't eat enough pancakes," he said against her shoulder before kissing it. "I'm fucking tired. When I wake up, we're going to lunch at the Dawg. Or maybe dinner. Have to see how much energy we've got for round two first."

Callie didn't think she'd sleep, but she did. With a smile on her face and a pleasurable ache between her legs.

Chapter Thirty-One

"Hey, earth to Seth. You hear me?"

Seth jerked his head toward the sound of Kane's voice. "Yeah, I heard you."

Kane snorted. "Somehow I doubt that."

"Doubt all you want. I'm working here. Bother somebody else."

"Work away, stud."

Seth ignored the comment. It was mid-afternoon and they were at the range. As much as he'd wanted to stay in bed with Callie, he had a job to do. They'd slept for a couple hours, partly to make up for the lack of sleep the night before and partly because they were spent after the morning's activities.

Not that he could complain. Sex with Callie was a revelation. She was at turns shy and bold, and both those iterations turned him on and made him crazy for her.

He'd wakened her with a hand on her tit and his dick hard between her legs. She'd purred and turned in his arms before reaching between them to guide him inside her. They'd both gasped at the rightness of it as he slid home. It'd started slow and sweet and ended hot and dirty with her pinned beneath him, legs in the air, taking all of him as he rode her hard and fast.

She was vocal when she came, telling him to keep fucking her *just like that* in that sweet voice of hers. That had been all it took for him to bust a nut inside her, gasping and groaning like he'd just rucked through a jungle in full gear. His heart had been hammering like a drum as he'd claimed her mouth for a hot kiss.

When their breathing had slowed and Luna came in to paw at the side of the bed for somebody to let her out, they'd gotten up and dressed.

Now they were here. Callie and Luna were with Daphne in the front reception area, and Seth was inside the SCIF waiting for the rest of the team to join him. They had a couple of part-time hires who were working as range officers for the shooters, and the counters with weapons and ammo would be watched by Daphne. She could handle most things, but if someone came in looking to buy a gun, she'd have to call one of them to help.

Daph was great, but she didn't know shit about guns. They didn't scare her like they did some people, which was good.

Seth tapped the keys on his computer, checking Callie's inputs that he'd isolated from the coding done by her team. He felt a little weird after everything that had happened between them, but it was the job. The cables that Chance had deployed in her lab were toast. No signal from either of them, which wasn't surprising. The entire lab had probably been gutted so someone could deal with the smoke damage.

But he had everything that had been done in there over the last couple of weeks. That's what he was analyzing.

"Damn," he said, staring at the lines of code.

"What?" Ghost asked, his tone sharp as he walked into the SCIF.

Seth glanced up at the boss. "There's a lot of complicated code here. I can't understand everything because I'm not a programmer, not like this. My skills are hacker based. I can write scripts and perform deep dives for information, but I can't parse this out. And I can't upload it to an AI client for analysis for obvious reasons."

"Obviously," Ghost said. He popped his fists on his hips and looked like a man who'd give up everything he owned if he could be anywhere but where he was. "Seems to me we've got the person who can read it sitting about twenty feet away in this very building."

Seth frowned. "You want to ask her what she's written here?"

The other guys were shifting in their seats. Nobody said anything.

Ghost huffed a breath and threw himself in his chair. "You know, I'm about sick of the restrictions we're operating under. Every fucking move has to be analyzed by the president's staff six ways to Sunday. We've got the programmer in another room, and we're playing with our dicks in here, trying to figure out what the fuck's happening at GRL. Let's just ask her."

"Uh, sir…" Blaze began, reverting to ingrained military protocol when dealing with a superior officer. Especially a pissed-off one.

Ghost fixed them all with a look. "We're HOT operators, boys. When John Mendez was declared a traitor to the unit he'd built, when he was on the run for his life and his reputation while some Pentagon general who knew squat about the Hostile Operations Team was sent to stand us down and dismantle us, I didn't take it lying down. If I had, who the fuck knows what would've happened? I ran ops from the basement of a residential house, and I made decisions that could have gotten everyone involved stripped of our ranks and thrown in a hole somewhere. But we got our commander back and we stopped a traitor. Now the six of us are stranded in Alabama while we get drip fed information from Washington, and we've got at least two women who already know we're more than we seem. What's one more?"

"When you put it that way," Ethan said.

"She doesn't know what Athena is really for," Seth said. "And we're talking about telling her a whole level of things that neither Rory or Emma know."

Ghost shrugged. "Yeah, well maybe she should understand what she's working on. Then she'll know what the stakes are. Not only that, but we're already watching her closely. If she is on the wrong side, we'll find that out, too. And we'll be able to stop her from doing more damage if she is. Might just speed up the process of protecting Athena and bringing this mission to a close."

Seth could only stare, his mind racing with possibilities. He couldn't believe Ghost wanted to bring Callie in. He tried to think of all the ways it might impact her. It was dangerous to involve her. Not to Ghost Ops, because he knew she wasn't a traitor, but to her. The more she knew about Athena, the more vulnerable she was while somebody still wanted information from her.

Ghost waved a hand. "We've got other things to talk about. We can come back to this. Any further information on our Russians and who they worked for?"

Seth shook his head. "Smirnov and Fedorov are former Russian intelligence operatives, but it's possible that's a lie and they're still active. I can't find that either man knew Callie in Poland or had any contact with her here."

And for that he was grateful.

"We could ask her. Show her photos," Chance said, clearly jumping on the bandwagon of involving Callie.

And why not? From a purely rational perspective, it wasn't a bad idea. Seth wasn't sure how she'd react at hearing that he knew what her secret government work really was, but one thing she seemed to understand was not talking about sensitive information to people who weren't cleared for it. Involving her could benefit their mission.

But the danger… He didn't like anything that put her in harm's way.

"I've got info on the Dashevsky Group," Ghost said, clicking his mouse and bringing up a file to the overhead screen. "They seem legit, but there've been rumors about Viktor Dashevsky, the group's founder. They've only started working in the humanitarian space within the past five years. Viktor is a Russian oligarch whose money comes from gas and oil, but he donates to humanitarian causes and funded the group that bears his name five years ago when he wanted to field teams of aid workers to disaster zones. On the surface, it's legit. But the rumors are that Viktor is power hungry, that he'd like to challenge Putin and take his place as the head of the Russian state. He doesn't because nobody survives that kind of open rebellion, but some say that's his ultimate goal. On the other hand, Putin is his kid's godfather, so there's that. Could just be propaganda from people who want to come between Putin and his pals."

Ghost eyed them. "The president's team can be cooperative when it suits their agenda. Also, while we're at it, I've been told there was a phone found on Volkov's body after all. It's the same number Callie's been getting texts from."

"Aw shit," Kane said. "Somebody's spoofed the number."

"That's right," Ghost replied. "They killed him and left his phone, but spoofed the number so she'd think it was him."

"Means they know what they're doing," Seth said, a knot forming in his gut. He already knew Callie was in danger, but the more they knew about the depth of the operation, the more complicated everything got. Not to mention the emotional involvement. She tangled him up inside, made him question everything from a different perspective.

And this was why you didn't cross that line and start fucking the protectee. Because it skewed your judgment.

Yet he didn't regret it.

"Right." Ghost slapped two hands on the table. "So, we bringing her in here and getting her to look at that code or what?"

Chapter Thirty-Two

CALLIE COULDN'T REMEMBER BEING THIS HAPPY, WELL, maybe ever. She'd had a happy childhood and she'd excelled in college. She'd done her best at every job she'd had, and she'd really enjoyed her time in Poland with the troops. The travel and being a part of a different culture— her mother's childhood culture—had been wonderful. She'd been happy doing those things.

But then she got the call about her parents, about the fact Nikki was in Vail with them but hadn't gone skiing that day, and her world had crashed down. She'd been on a plane the next morning—the soonest available—and she'd never gone back to Poland.

She'd lived on the base in housing they provided, and all her personal things had been packed up and sent to storage until she'd gotten the job in Alabama and had it sent there. She'd got up every day since landing stateside, put one foot in front of the other, and made it to the end of the day with her sanity intact and a little more accomplished.

Nikki had been traumatized, inconsolable for weeks, but therapy had helped her learn to cope. Those had not been happy days.

The past few months, happiness crept back in. But it was a quiet, contained sort of happiness. The kind that made you smile because the sunlight was beautiful in the morning or because the cup of coffee tasted just right. Small events, daily events.

But this happiness she felt now was bursting inside her, pushing at her seams, aching to get out.

She was the poster child for a good orgasm lifting one's mood.

"So how is it living with Mr. Grumpy?" Daphne asked when she finished checking a shooter into the range. They'd been sitting down to chat with fresh iced tea that Daphne had poured into lidded cups with straws when the customer came in. But he was gone now, and Daphne was getting straight to the point.

Callie put a hand on Luna's head. She was sitting beside Callie's chair, tongue out, listening to the distant sound of gunfire. She didn't seem nervous, just curious.

"Mr. Grumpy isn't so bad."

She tried to keep her voice casual. Daphne arched an eyebrow. "Not so bad, huh? That's good."

"He even talks sometimes, though reluctantly. But you should have seen him with Nikki. He was patient and kind. She roped him into helping clean her horse's stall, and he didn't back out."

She wasn't mentioning the rest of it: the soulful discussions, holding her last night so she could sleep, the pancakes or—heaven forbid—the sex. That was too much to explain. Especially when she'd only met Daphne a few days ago. But she liked her. Callie had never had a close girlfriend to talk about things with. Her mother had been bold and outspoken in her social circles, which meant many of the girls who might have been her friends were already primed to dislike her because their mothers had disliked hers.

Not to mention that super nerdy thing she'd had going as a kid. No wonder Tara and Bobby had set her up. It'd made for great entertainment to remind the smart girl why she wasn't as smart as she thought she was.

"You're blushing," Daphne said.

Callie blinked. "What? No. I'm just a little warm. Isn't it warm in here?"

Daphne grinned. "No, it's not. See this sweater I have on? It's ninety degrees outside and this is a meat locker. You're blushing."

"Could be a hot flash."

"Hardly. You aren't old enough. What happened? Did Seth kiss you? Or did you kiss him? I could see why you'd want to. No shame."

"No, I did not kiss him." She hesitated. "He kissed me."

Daphne laughed and clapped her hands lightly. "Oh, this is great! What was it like?"

Callie's blush was getting worse. She wasn't embarrassed over a kiss. It was just that she couldn't stop at thinking about a kiss. Her mind had zipped immediately to sex in the shower and then the bed. And again when they woke from their nap. Mercy, that had been hot.

But she seriously needed to get a grip on herself before she said more than she should.

"Honestly, he did it yesterday before I had to go into the bookstore. He was trying to distract me by giving me something else to think about. It worked. Because, yes, he's a fantastic kisser."

"Looking the way he does, you'd hope so. How disappointing if he wasn't, right?"

Callie managed a laugh. "Right."

Daphne leaned back in her chair. She was pretty, with long red hair and green eyes. She was also tall, at least five seven, and almost rail thin. She looked like she'd never been awkward or nerdy in her life. She'd probably been a cheerleader. Bobby Bowen wouldn't have pretended to kiss her. He'd have kissed her for real and to hell with Tara's ideas.

"What about Kane?" Callie asked.

Daphne's gaze dropped to her drink. She fiddled with the straw as if she was pushing the ice around into a better place. "What about him?"

"I don't know. Just seems like there's some tension between you."

"No, no tension." Daphne smiled. "Kane is Kane. He's determined to play big brother to me, so I let him, even if he's annoying as hell. But that one…" She shook her head. "He's a charmer, a player, a manwhore. I'm glad he wasn't the one who went to stay with you for a few days."

She was too but she had to ask. "Why?"

"Seth only kissed you. Kane would have charmed your panties off."

"That bad, huh?"

Daphne nodded. "That bad. I'd never date somebody like that because I'd constantly wonder if he was faithful. I think he just can't help himself. Warren isn't gorgeous, but he's sweet. He's a good man, he works hard, and he believes in treating a woman right." She leaned toward Callie and lowered her voice. "He doesn't want to have sex outside of marriage."

"Wow. Then you've never…"

"No, never." She frowned then. "I wouldn't call him a

good kisser, either. His kisses are very chaste. But he isn't pushy, and I'm happy. It's comfortable with him. Safe. We're more friends than anything. But don't tell the guys. I don't want them thinking Warren is any stranger than they already do."

"Do they?"

She looked thoughtful. "Well, maybe not really. They've never been anything but welcoming and friendly. I think Warren's intimidated though. He's not a big guy, and all of them are. You can't help but think if you needed rescuing, the One Shot Tactical guys are the ones you'd want coming to save you."

Callie couldn't argue with that. She'd been compelled to come here the day after the fire, and though she'd thought it would be more of a temporary thing while she made plans to escape, she couldn't argue that it was the best decision she'd made.

Luna jumped to all fours, her tail wagging happily as she stared at the door. Footsteps sounded in the hallway and then Seth appeared. Callie's insides fluttered at the sight of him.

"Daphne, could you keep Luna for a little bit?"

"Sure," Daphne said, getting to her feet. "She can hang with me as long as you need. Isn't that right, pretty girl?"

Her voice went up a few octaves on that last part. Seth came over to pet Luna and then held out a hand for Callie. Daphne waggled her eyebrows at Callie as if to say, uh-huh, busted.

"I need to show you something," he said, looking serious enough her heart tripped.

"Seth, for heaven's sake, can't you come up with a better line?" Daphne drawled.

He blinked. "What? It's true. I need to show her something."

"So long as it's not X-rated."

Seth's gaze whipped to Callie's. Before she could figure out how to tell him she hadn't said a word, Daphne laughed.

"Oh, you are so busted. And here I thought Kane was the one she'd have to worry about."

"No idea what you're talking about, Daph," Seth said, his hand closing around Callie's.

Daphne shooed them away, still grinning like she'd solved a very amusing puzzle.

"We're adults," Callie said under her breath as they walked down the hall. "Why do I feel like a teenager who's been caught being naughty?"

"Don't say that word, babe. Makes me think of things I shouldn't be thinking of right now." He tugged her into the supply room they'd been in two days ago when he'd gotten the cameras and crowded her into the wall before his mouth came down on hers.

Callie's body melted into his. She wrapped her arms around his neck and stood on tiptoe as they kissed with all the fire of earlier in the shower.

"Shit," Seth said, taking a step back. "Not the place."

"I didn't pull me into this room, you did."

He shoved a hand through his hair. "I know, I know. But I need to prepare you."

"Prepare me? Sounds ominous."

"It's not ominous. It's just… not what you expect. I'm going to take you to a room, Callie. A SCIF."

She tried to process that. A SCIF was a room where top-secret things happened. A hardened facility made especially for that purpose. "A SCIF? Where?"

"Here," he told her in all seriousness.

She looked around the room they stood in, confused.

"Not this room." He huffed a breath. "We have a SCIF. I'm going to take you there. The rest of the team is waiting."

"Team? Seth, what is this? You're scaring me."

He gripped her hand and tugged her in for another kiss. "Nothing to be scared of, Callie. I told you I would protect you, and I am. My team is protecting you. There's nothing more important than that. But there are things you need to know and the only way I can tell you is inside a SCIF."

She stared at him, her mind racing with possibilities. But her heart was the calm one. Her heart knew what her brain didn't want to admit. She let her heart do the talking. "I trust you."

His smile made the butterflies flutter again. He led her down the hall, into the office where they'd talked with Alex. There was a closet, and he opened the door. Inside the closet was another door that led into a short hallway. At the end of the hall stood a door with a keypad and a biometric scanner.

Seth entered a code and put his hand on the scanner while Callie gaped. The door opened and he led her inside.

"Oh my God," she said as she hesitated in the entry. The room wasn't big, about twelve by twelve, but there were overhead monitors at either end, computer terminals, and a central oval table with six chairs placed around it. There was a secure phone sitting on the table, the kind of phone that you only used to call important people. Military people.

Government officials.

Five men she knew sat around the table. She gaped at

them. Clearly, they *were* a team. Not just six friends who'd opened a range together. They were something more.

"It's okay, Callie. Come on in and have a seat."

It was Alex who'd spoken. She stepped across the threshold and Seth followed.

Then the door sealed shut behind them.

Chapter Thirty-Three

Callie dropped into the vacant chair and waited for someone to speak.

She was trying not to freak out. They were on her side, whoever they were.

Weren't they?

Seth dragged a round stool on wheels over and sat beside her. Then he tapped some keys on his laptop and the display appeared on the overhead. "We need to ask you some questions."

Callie's heart sank to her toes. The edges of her vision grew black as panic hovered there.

"That's my code." She whipped her head to Seth. "How did you get my code? What's going on? *Who* are you?"

"You're working on the Athena satellite project," Alex said, and her head whipped to him next. "We're here to protect it. And we need your help."

Her heart was hammering, and her brain was in overload. She had to think, had to process all the information she had and make a decision. Athena was *top secret*. She didn't even know what it was supposed to do when it was done, but she knew what she had to work on.

The ability to maneuver the satellite in orbit, to send commands that told it when to link up with other satellites, and the failsafes that had to be put in place were critical. It was a surveillance system intended to provide early warning capabilities to Washington. Nothing new about that except that it was going to be faster and better than anything they had now.

"I… I don't know what to say." She looked at Seth once more, her heart warring with her head again. Only this time her head had the upper hand because he'd clearly lied to her. "All this time, you *knew* about Athena. All your questions about what I was doing…"

He looked contrite. Or maybe she just wanted him to be. "I couldn't tell you, same as you couldn't tell me. Like Ghost said, we're here to protect the project. It's clear there are bad actors trying to steal it or sabotage it. We can't let that happen. You can help."

"Are you even military?" Tears pricked her eyes. "Has any of this been real?"

His gaze shuttered. That told her all she needed to know. He'd never cared about her. The sex? That was something he'd done because he could. Because she'd wanted him to. Oh, she believed he cared about protecting her. He hadn't lied about that. But the rest of it?

Not real.

She believed Mia was real, but he'd probably told her to elicit sympathy. To make her care much quicker than she would otherwise have done.

Except that didn't make sense, not really.

Still, she was too angry to let go of the theory. The hurt.

"It's real, Callie," he said, his voice rougher than usual.

"We're a team of special operators on a mission from Washington. We report to the highest levels."

"Which I'd prefer we didn't have to prove by making a phone call. Bringing you into this room has painted a giant target on our backs," Alex—or was it Ghost?—drawled. "My ass is so fucked these days it's a wonder I can even get out of bed most mornings."

Callie stared at him. What he did with his face might or might not be termed a smile. She thought it was supposed to reassure her though.

"Not literally," he said. "I love these guys like brothers, not boyfriends. Think they feel the same for me."

"Amen," the rest of them echoed with varying notes of *no way in hell* in their voices. It would have been funny if not for the whole betrayal-of-trust thing.

Callie pulled in a deep breath and huffed it out again. "Okay, fine, whatever. Based on this room, and that secure phone, I'm going to accept this isn't an elaborate hoax. Not to mention you've got my code up there. Which, how the hell did you get that?"

"The security assessment at Griffin Research a couple of weeks ago," Kane said. "We might have hacked into the system while we were there."

Chance raised his hand like a reluctant student. "I entered your lab."

"I remember."

"I may have replaced a couple of connector cables."

"So you knew what Mikhail's cable was when I gave it to you." She did not look at Seth. "Because you guys already smuggled your own inside the lab."

"I'm sorry, but yes," Seth replied. "We needed to know what was going on in there. It was the best way to find out."

"Oh my God, I can't believe this." She put her hands

over her eyes and shook her head. "Did you know about Mikhail? Did you target me?"

"We didn't target you. And we didn't know anything about Mikhail Volkov until you told us. Which was helpful," Alex/Ghost said. "When we said we would protect you, we meant it. I'm gonna be blunt here and say that if you hadn't come to us, you'd be in enemy hands by now. Or dead. That's a possibility too."

Her pulse throbbed with hot anger. And maybe a little guilt for saying they'd targeted her. But it was a path she'd started down, so she had to finish it.

"I'm thankful for your help. But I also have to wonder if maybe you didn't engineer that fire to get me here in the first place."

"Jesus," Seth said. "We're the good guys, Callie. I get you being pissed that I kept the truth from you, but I wasn't at liberty to say, for fuck's sake. Nobody in this room would ever go after a civilian that way. An enemy combatant, a terrorist, a foreign agent? Sure. But not you. There was nothing to indicate you were involved. We checked."

She whipped her gaze to him. "You knew who I was, knew everything about me, before I ever walked in here the other day, didn't you?"

His eyes snapped with anger. And something else?

"Yes. It's my fucking job. I background check everyone who comes within spitting distance of us or this project. Now, are you going to help us with that code or what?"

Their gazes tangled for a long moment. Long enough that she heard somebody whisper, "Is this what I think it is? Because they haven't stopped staring soulfully at each other yet."

"Yep, I'd say so."

"*Our* Seth? Really?"

She didn't know who said any of these things because she was still glaring at the man glaring back.

A banging sound made her look away. Alex/Ghost had dropped his forehead to the table. Repeatedly. "Why? Why me, Lord? What have I ever done to you?"

"Is he going to be okay?" Callie asked, looking across the table at the men sitting on that side.

Kane shrugged. "Probably. Maybe. It's a thing. Don't ask."

"It's a fucking pain in my ass," Alex/Ghost said, sitting up again. "What is in the damned water in this town? Think we need to be investigating that shit too."

"Please, Callie," Seth said. "Just help us out. Tell us what this code does."

"You've got computer skills. You figure it out."

"I'm not a programmer."

"But you do know more than you let on, don't you? The way you fixed Colleen's computer that day." She shook her head. "I was too focused on my own problems to really think about it, but you had to have hacked into it. You can't just bypass the setup screens that easily. You know code."

His eyes flashed. "Yes, I know code. I don't write it like this. I hack into systems. I don't create them."

He was a hacker. Of course he was. Nothing about the time they'd spent together was real. *Nothing.*

He'd been hacking into her, finding her weak spots. Exploiting them.

"Fine, I'll tell you what's in it." Her throat ached. She didn't have the energy to fight anymore. And though she was hurt and pissed, she believed these men were trying to keep Athena safe. "How do you want me to do this? What you've got there is only a section, a big section, but still not the complete code. I can talk you through it or whiteboard it. You tell me."

"Talk us through it," Alex/Ghost said. "If we need something more, we'll address it."

She pointed at the screen. "This section is the initial sequence. I could have made it more obvious, but considering the sensitivity of the project, it's standard procedure to make it obscure. The instructions aren't complicated, but the code looks like they are. Less easy to hack into. Which is exactly what you want with something like this."

She talked them through sections, explaining the process of how she came up with the code for the instructions. A part of her was riddled with guilt for talking about it, but mostly she was relieved. Like when she'd initially come to One Shot Tactical for help. She wasn't carrying the weight on her own anymore.

She was still angry with Seth for the deception. Still hurt. He hadn't needed to make her care about him. He could have just brought her to the SCIF in the first place. If they'd briefed her then, she wouldn't have gotten her stupid heart into a tangle.

"These are your inputs. Is this the full code?" Alex/Ghost asked.

"No. If Seth isolated my inputs, these are the parts I worked on. And I remember a lot about the full code, but I don't have it memorized. I bet you have a copy. You'd have been stupid not to steal it while you were inside the system."

Seth exchanged a look with Alex/Ghost. Nobody said anything.

Callie folded her arms. "It won't do you any good. As a whole, it doesn't work. Yet. I was trying to figure out why the night the fire started. I ran a diagnostic for ghost code, but it returned a negative result. It should be impossible anyway since we have version control systems in place."

"Can you fix it?" Seth asked.

"Maybe. I just need the time and the tools. I might have found the problem if the fire hadn't started and I could have kept working."

"What do you need to work on it here?" Alex/Ghost said.

"At least two monitors. A whiteboard. And I'll need a code editor. But I'm not sure I should be doing this. How do I know you aren't planning to take this code and bypass the company, give it to NASA or MDA? A lot of people depend on Griffin Research for their livelihoods."

"Callie, we're not thieves," Seth said. "This is bigger than you realize."

"Okay. So tell me. What is Athena really? Why is it so damned interesting to everybody? We were told it's a network of defensive satellites. That's nothing new. Why do you care about it? Why was Mikhail trying to get me to give him access to our code? It's an advance, but it's not revolutionary tech."

"That's where you'd be wrong," Alex/Ghost told her. "It is a defensive satellite. But it's the most technologically advanced system this world has ever produced. Once the component parts are finished, Athena will create a net over this country that makes us impervious to nuclear or EMP attack. It's a shield, basically, that deactivates weapons. It doesn't rely on destroying them with lasers or shooting them down. It repels them and then destroys them with their own onboard systems. Can you understand why we're concerned?"

"That's not… How?"

"Yeah, I don't understand it either, but it's obviously critical that we protect it. There are a lot of important parts, any one of which would be a target for spies. Your company is writing the instruction code to control the system. Mikhail's employer, whoever that might be, could sell the technology to the highest bidder. Or, if his employer is actually a rival nation, they could use it to take control once Athena is live. There are a lot of possibilities here, none of them very good."

A chill worked its way through her system, making everything numb. "You're saying Mikhail was a spy."

"Probably. Does that surprise you?" Alex/Ghost asked.

Hurt crawled its way into her heart again.

"Nothing surprises me anymore. You never really know anyone, no matter that you think you do." She swallowed the knot of tears in her throat. "Everybody lies. Especially when they have an ulterior motive for getting close to you."

Chapter Thirty-Four

Seth wanted to take her by the shoulders and shake her. Then he wanted to kiss her, thaw the ice he saw whenever she looked at him.

Which wasn't often because she was pissed.

Pissed at him, and there was nothing he could do. He wanted to talk to her, just the two of them. Explain.

Tell her she'd made him feel things he was still trying to sort out. She wasn't just a job to him. Not anymore.

But they weren't alone, and she was concentrating on the screen in front of her, her fingers flying over the keys. There were two spots of color in her cheeks that told him her anger hadn't abated.

He dropped his gaze to his own terminal and tried to concentrate. His inbox—the secret one attached to the dark web where he did some of his searches—pinged with a message.

Well, fuck. The janitorial staff was clear. Nothing that indicated any of them set the fire. Didn't mean they hadn't, but nobody had a sketchy background or a fake identity.

"What the…" Callie muttered.

All eyes were instantly on her. "What is it?" Seth asked, though maybe he should have let Ghost do it.

Because she didn't look at him or respond. She kept scrolling, reading the code.

"Callie?" Ghost asked. "Anything you want to tell me?"

"Sorry," she said, looking over at the boss. "Something is odd. I didn't see it the other night because I hadn't eliminated the other possibilities. I'd run the diagnostic tools and nothing turned up." She pointed at the screen overhead because they'd been able to watch her work by mirroring what she was doing. "It looks like somebody's inserted unreachable code. That means it's sitting inside conditional branches that can never be satisfied. It's not functional during normal operations. But it shouldn't be there, which means there could be another purpose."

"Such as?" Ghost asked.

"A backdoor, maybe. It would take complex activation triggers, but it's possible this code is meant to activate under specific circumstances."

"Can you tell what those are?"

"Not easily. And not quickly either. It's unfinished, though, because what it's currently doing is preventing the system from functioning. That's why I couldn't get the code to work."

"Okay, so who has access to the code? Who could potentially do this?"

"Anyone on the team. I assume you already know who we all are."

"We do. But tell me who has the skill."

Callie huffed a breath. "Any of us could do it. Everyone on the team is better than average, though not everyone has the same ability."

Ghost shot a look at Seth. A silent plea for help in

cutting through the computer stuff and getting to the meat of the problem. "Rank everyone by ability," Seth told her. "Please."

She didn't look at him, and for some reason it was killing him inside. Like he'd been thrown into a dark room and left to rot. He thought Ghost might end up prompting her again, but she finally started to speak.

"Me. Dr. Robbins. Leo Spinner. Javier Dillon. The rest —Ronald Forde, Charlie Althoff, Blaine Parsons, and Jarrett Mooney are about equal. But all are good. They all have copious experience. They've worked in the field a lot longer than I have, except for Javier, who's only a couple of years older than me. He's still very good, and very creative."

"We've looked at all of their backgrounds," Seth said to the room at large. "Nothing stood out. No radical beliefs, no ties to organizations that are anti-US. The only person with any foreign contacts was Callie."

Her head swiveled to him. Her eyes were glacial. "Oh, so because I spent time in Poland, and because I speak foreign languages—especially Russian, I'm guessing—that made me a potential suspect? Or maybe it was the fact my mother was Polish?"

He wouldn't apologize for doing his job. "Those were factors, yes. You were the most obvious choice. But it's not you. We know it's not."

"Well thank you very much, Captain America. I'm so thrilled you've eliminated me and my dirty foreign ties from suspicion."

Okay, so she was making him feel like shit. Maybe he deserved it. "I did my job, Callie. Same as you're doing yours. And maybe I'm an asshole for it, but I can't apologize for doing what I have to do. But hurting you was never part of it. I'd give anything to change that."

"So would I."

The silence in the room was awkward. It didn't last, thankfully.

"Can you remove that part of the code?" Ghost asked.

"Here, yes. But the real code at GRL? I can, but somebody's going to notice. And maybe do a better job hiding it the next time. Not that they didn't already hide it well."

"We want them to notice," Seth said. "So we can find who did it and what the purpose is."

She turned to him again, her eyes wide behind the glasses she'd put on to work. "If somebody inside GRL is tampering with the code, and Mikhail was after me to provide access to the system, then whoever's on the inside wasn't working for him. Because he wouldn't need me then."

"That's right."

"But anyone tampering with the code would need to know the end goal. What you've told me about the true purpose of the project isn't anything I knew, which means nobody else should either."

He could see where she was headed so he said it for her. "A supervisor might."

She stared at him.

"Oh God," she said softly. Her shoulders sagged. If it was true, it was one more betrayal in a list of betrayals. One more blow to her already fragile trust in those around her.

"I'm sorry, Callie. Doesn't mean it's the answer. But it might be."

She shook her head. "I can't believe it's Dr. Robbins. She hired me, mentored me. Gave me responsibility and autonomy when nobody else would have. There has to be another explanation." She snapped her fingers. "Leo might know what the scope of the project really is. He's her second and he doesn't like me."

Seth opened a file and typed in a search. "We checked the badging records, and nobody from your team was in the building that evening. But they could have erased it. We've got the camera footage from the parking lot. It's a shared lot with the other companies in the complex so the cameras aren't maintained by GRL. It's possible we can find one of them on the feed. Then we'd know."

He sent the footage to Kane and Ethan to study, then put three pictures onto the overhead monitor. Ghost had given him the signal that now was the time.

"Do you know these men?"

He could see the recognition on her face. And the surprise. "That's Wilhelm and Cyril. They're Polish graduate students. They go to UAH and work at the pizza and pasta place in the Gateway. Or did. I haven't seen them lately. I've chatted with them when I was at lunch before. They were happy to meet someone who spoke their native language."

"Did you know them in Poland?"

"No, I did not." Her tone was clipped, and he knew she was annoyed with him for asking. For implying.

"And the last guy?"

She shook her head. "No, I've never seen him. Should I?"

Seth studied her as she gazed at the screen, but there was no hint of deception. No recognition either.

"We thought you would, yes."

She turned to him. "Why? Who is it?"

"It's Mikhail Volkov."

Chapter Thirty-Five

CALLIE WASN'T CERTAIN SHE'D HEARD HIM RIGHT. BUT OF course she had. He hadn't whispered. He said the name with an American accent, but it wasn't garbled or incoherent.

He'd said Mikhail.

She looked at the screen again. At the chubby man with glasses and a receding hairline. He had a friendly smile. "I don't know that person. Are you sure you have the right Mikhail? There could be more than one."

"This Mikhail was born in the US to immigrant parents. He worked for the Dashevsky Group. Had a home base in Washington. His body was found over a week ago, right after you said he came to see you."

"But that isn't the Mikhail I know. *Knew.*"

None of this made sense. Her mind raced over every conversation and interaction with Mikhail. Every nuance, everything he'd said about where he came from and what he'd done.

"Can you describe him?" Alex/Ghost asked.

"He was tall, fit. Not like all of you, but lean. I saw him

run at the base in Poland. He asked if I wanted to join him for his morning runs. I said no." She shook her head in disbelief. "That's not the same man, even if he lost weight and wore a hairpiece. You've got it wrong somehow."

What was happening to her life? How had everything gotten so unbelievably out of control? It was like something out of an over-the-top spy movie. Would James Bond walk into the room, sipping a martini and informing them he'd taken care of the problem so they could rest easy now? Spectre was defeated for another day, cheerio and all that?

God, she almost wished he would just so this nightmare would be over. She was still tired from lack of sleep last night, though this morning's nap had helped, and she was heartsore.

"Do you have any pictures of him?"

It was Seth, and he was being gentle. She appreciated that. She didn't want to, because she needed to keep her heart hardened against him, but she did.

"No."

"Any selfies where he might be in the background?"

"I'm not a big selfie taker, so no, none. Most of what I took would have been to send home to my parents and Nikki so they'd see what a fabulous time I was having in Europe. Or when I visited my aunt and cousins in Gdansk. Mikhail never went along."

"Well, shit," Alex/Ghost said, leaning back in his chair. "So we've got a mystery man who was impersonating the real Volkov. So which one is it they fished out of the Potomac?"

Callie blinked. "They couldn't tell?"

"He was in the water. It does things to the body."

Seth appreciated that Ghost didn't tell her half the man's head was blown away.

"Then wouldn't forensics know? DNA? Dental records?"

"I imagine they're working on it. Nothing goes as quickly as it happens on television, though." He raked a hand through his hair the way Seth did when he was thinking or irritated. "Guess I'd better make some calls. Fuck, I hate talking to bureaucrats."

"If that's the real Mikhail, how could the one I knew get away with impersonating him? I met him in Poland over a year ago. You'd think anyone who knew the real Mikhail would recognize a fake, wouldn't you? Wouldn't people at the Dashevsky Group who'd worked with him know the difference?"

"If somebody went to the trouble to impersonate him, take over his life, they altered the record," Seth said. "It's the kind of thing spies do. They can make fake identities, and do, but sometimes it's more effective to take over someone else's life. Sometimes they kill the person they impersonate. Sometimes they leave them alive, especially if there's no chance their paths will cross. I think the real Volkov was probably disposed of early on. Which means the body is either the Mikhail you knew, or they've tried to make it look that way."

She could only gape at him. "I don't think I want to have anything more to do with spies or codes or any of it. I just want to take Nikki and go someplace we can start over and be left alone."

She wasn't certain, but it looked as if sorrow clouded his gaze for the barest of moments. But sorrow for what? Her? Not likely.

"I understand, Callie. But we have to deal with the situation you're in. I think you also need to consider that you're in a position to do something for your country by sticking with this project and making sure it's done right.

We're talking about the lives and futures of millions of people. You, me, everyone in this room. Your sister. All of us. We can't let Athena fall into the wrong hands. We can't let them win. You hold the key to finishing the command and control system so it can go online and protect us all."

Callie swallowed. Damn him. She closed her eyes, saw her mother on the day she'd taken the oath of citizenship. She'd been so proud. Happy. Giddy even.

She'd loved her mother country—father country if one was translating literally from the Polish—and she was proud to be Polish. Proud of her heritage.

Ah, but America, she would say. *In America, you can be anything you want to be. Anyone can succeed. Anyone can be a movie star or a pilot or a business owner. The sky is not the limit. The stars are. The infinite universe. You must dream big, my little Callie. Be anything you want.*

Callie's throat was tight. She shook her head, fighting memories of a woman she didn't understand as well as she would have liked but would miss forever.

Mama would want her to do this. To stay and be a part of Athena, to make her country safe by doing her job and making sure the code was free of ghosts, back doors, and other malicious sequences meant to do harm. Mama would be proud to know her daughter was doing such important work for the safety of their nation.

"I said I *wanted* to leave. Not that I will," she told him. She dropped her gaze to the computer screen in front of her. "Since you were able to isolate the inputs based on logins, can you isolate who did this one?"

"Not if it was done earlier than our hack. But I can check."

"Thank you. Guess I'd better get back to work then. See if there's anything in here I missed."

The screen blurred a little and she angrily pushed her glasses up and rubbed her eyes.

"You okay?"

"I'm fine. My eyes are tired."

"Take a break then. Nobody expects you to find problems that were likely months in the making inside of a few hours."

"No, but I want to."

"Callie, I—"

"Go away, Seth. Leave me alone. I don't want to *chitchat* with you. You don't like it anyway so stop trying to pretend like you've got something to say."

He shoved his chair back and stood. She didn't turn around as the door opened. As he walked away.

"What?" she practically snarled to the men in the room who'd grown unnaturally silent.

Chance held up both hands. "Nothing. It's fine. Carry on."

"Fuck my life," Alex/Ghost sighed. "I should have made sure you were all neutered before you stepped foot in this state."

Chapter Thirty-Six

THEY DIDN'T SPEAK ON THE WAY BACK TO CALLIE'S PLACE. Seth gripped the wheel tight and imagined a million ways to start a conversation, but he couldn't make the words come out. He was angry and he was sorry, and he wasn't used to existing in both those states at once.

Usually, he didn't get into emotional standoffs with anyone because he never got down in the pit with them in the first place.

He hadn't realized he'd climbed down in it with Callie until she wouldn't speak to him. Until, when she did, she was furiously angry, throwing his own words about *chitchat* back at him. He'd had to walk out of the SCIF or do something that nobody inside there but her needed to witness.

Like drag her onto his lap and kiss her until she was soft and melting. Until she forgave him.

He had a good idea that wasn't going to work, though. Callie might have a soft side, she might enjoying gluing her scraps of paper into her journals and writing about the books she read, but she had a tough side too. She'd lost her parents and she'd taken charge of her sister, working hard to make sure Nikki could keep two horses and continue to ride and train for competitions, though it had to be a big expense. Callie did it because she wanted Nikki to have normalcy in her life, and she protected her sister fiercely. She would not be melted with a kiss.

He glanced over at her. She had her head turned, looking out the window at the sunlit fields. It was almost dusk, and the light was golden. Beautiful. He wasn't looking at the fields though. He was looking at her and the way the light added an orange glow to her hair, her shoulder, places where it touched with the most intensity.

That light made him ache. It was the weirdest fucking thing ever, but the beauty of it almost hurt.

He reached the long driveway to her house and turned. He had his phone lying in the holder in the center console. There were no alerts about intruders. He'd stop and check before driving into the stand of trees where the house sat. Callie knew his routine, so she didn't ask when they stopped. Then he squeezed the gas and they finished the trip.

He parked beside her Sequoia. Kane had taped plastic over the driver's side window last night before he left. He'd gone over the interior, too. The intruders hadn't cut the seats or done any damage beyond the window. They'd emptied compartments and felt beneath the seats. They'd probably been moving fast by the time they got to the Toyota, or it would have been worse.

Callie waited for him to give her the signal before she got out of the truck and followed him to the door. Luna trotted in front of them, always alert. She didn't give any signals that anything was amiss, which was a good sign. She might not be a trained military dog, but she was still a dog and a stranger would ping her radar quicker than

Bonnie the mail carrier could stick her nose in other people's business.

Seth disarmed the alarm and walked into the house, Callie behind him. Then she strode past him without looking at him. Something inside him snapped. He caught her elbow and she jerked away, spinning to glare at him.

"Don't touch me."

He shoved a hand through his hair. He had to say something meaningful, or he'd lose her. She'd keep on walking and hole up in her room and wouldn't speak to him.

"I'm sorry."

She crossed her arms and lifted her chin. Her eyes snapped with fire but he could see the vulnerability in her. The hurt. "For what? Doing your job?"

"No, I'm not sorry for that. I will always do my job, Callie. I swore an oath to my country. I pledged my life in service to its ideals. I'm not sorry for doing my damnedest to protect it. But I am sorry I hurt you."

"You dug into my life. You knew everything about me before I walked in your door and then you pretended you didn't. I told you things and you already knew them. You must have been so bored having to ask questions when you already knew the answers."

"I didn't know everything about you," he snapped. "I knew a lot, but not anything deeply personal. I didn't know about your journals and all that stuff you've got, the way you sit and study a page and then decide what to paste into it. Why the fuck you use tweezers instead of your fingers. The fact you have roses and lacy shit all over your bedroom, or that you've got this weird thing about junk food. I didn't know you'd competed on horses the way your sister does now, or that you'd sound so sweet and hot when you're asking me to make you come. I didn't know I'd crave you or that my fucking heart would feel like there's a vise around it because you're mad at me and refusing to look at me or talk to me about any of it."

He ran out of steam, his pulse pounding, throat aching, breath pumping in and out of his lungs like he'd run a marathon. What the fuck was wrong with him? Why did he feel so damned helpless and powerless at the same time?

Why did he feel desperate?

This was a level of emotion he wasn't accustomed to. No wonder he didn't like feeling them, why he kept himself separate from most people and didn't get involved. How the ever-loving *fuck* did this one small woman get so deep beneath his skin in a matter of days?

She turned her head away from him, arms still folded tight over her chest, hugging herself, but he could see her chin quivering. It made him want to sweep her in his arms and hold her, but he didn't because he couldn't take it if she rejected him.

"I want to believe you," she finally said. "But I don't. You could be saying every bit of this to make me trust you again, to make me let you in. Or maybe you just want to get your rocks off one more time."

She swiped her fingers beneath her eyes and swore beneath her breath.

His heart was a wild thing in his chest. Running scared and desperate. "Tell me why I would do that. Why would I need to make you trust me? We told you what's going on. You're in now. You know more than any civilian should. And you know, no matter how pissed you are, that my goal is to protect you and let you do your work because it's that damned important. So why would I try to make you let me in if all I cared about was the mission? Why, Callie?"

She didn't speak, and he laughed. It was a crazy sound, though. Crazy and hurt.

"You think I care more about fucking than I do this mission? That I'd say anything to make you let me into your bed again? I don't need to do that. I can find a woman to fuck if that's all I want. It doesn't have to be you."

She whirled on him then, her face red, chin still quivering as hot tears slid down her cheeks. "Oh sure, tell me how perfect you are and how you can get any woman you want. Did you lower your standards to be with me, huh?"

Okay, now she was pissing him off.

"What the fuck, Callie? What would make you say that? What I'm telling you is being with you has never been about convenience. If anything, it's fucking *inconvenient*, and this shit right here is why." He threw his arms out in frustration, then slapped a hand to his chest. "I'm supposed to be concentrating on protecting you, but instead I'm getting emotionally involved, and that has the potential to compromise my ability to do what I'm supposed to do."

She dashed those tears away again. Tears that were putting a hole in his heart.

"Stop, just stop. What's the point? Even if we get past this, even if we have sex again, everything about us is temporary. And if I feel this devastated now, what would it be like when you're ready to move on? I don't want to know. I just don't. So we need to be done. Now."

"I don't want to be done."

"But I do."

They stared at each other until she looked away first. She didn't want to be with him. Didn't want more of that bliss they'd had together earlier. Didn't want to sleep tangled up with him. Didn't want pancakes in the morning and sex in the shower. They hadn't even *begun,* and she was done.

Because they'd reached a bump in the road. A single bump and she wasn't willing to keep going.

Why? *Why?*

He was the one who was supposed to not give a shit, who didn't like small talk and useless conversation, who didn't get emotionally involved with anyone. But he was the one whose heart was galloping because he realized he couldn't convince her. Nothing he said was going to work to thaw her ice.

"Who hurt you, Callie? Because it had to be pretty fucking bad to make you give up so easily. Didn't think you were that kind of person. I had you down as a fierce combatant for the things that mattered." He snorted. "Then again, guess I don't matter. Hear you loud and clear, babe. Do what you need to do, and I'll make sure we're safe out here."

He didn't wait for a reply. He headed for the back door, Luna trotting with him.

He needed air.

And he needed to figure out how to make this ache in his chest go away.

Chapter Thirty-Seven

She was a coward.

Callie stood in the living room, hugging herself, listening to the back door open and close. He didn't slam it, which she probably would have done. Luna had gone with him and Callie was alone, the silence an almost physical thing in the room with her.

It was welcome after the emotions that had whipped through a few moments ago. She'd been angry and hurt and wallowing in her feelings, unwilling to give them up because she'd decided it was safer to stay mad than to soften toward him and let him in again.

Seth was so even keel, so cool, that she hadn't expected his whirlwind of emotion to hit her that strongly. He'd been far more upset than she could have thought possible. Didn't mean he actually cared about her. Just meant he was angry he'd lost control of the situation.

Yes.

She breathed in deeply, satisfied.

Yes, that was it. That was the answer.

He was a man who thrived on controlling the situation

because it was his job. He never let her go first into a building. He made her sit in the truck when they arrived somewhere, until he could open her door because that gave him time to check things out, make sure it was safe.

He'd stressed to her again and again that his mission was to keep her safe. To do that, she had to obey his commands on when and where and how. Maybe not at home, in her space, but everywhere else.

She understood and agreed because it would have been suicidal not to let him do the things he was best at.

He'd asked who hurt her. She didn't have an answer for that. Not really. Was she scarred by a high school trick? Or was it a deeper distrust of people because she didn't believe them? Her parents, as much as she loved them, hadn't been what they'd seemed. She'd always had to watch herself, had to dim her talent to make men comfortable in her field, had to hide her ability and pretend to know less than she did.

It wasn't *who* had hurt her. It was a load of people who had in one way or another, and she was afraid—deeply afraid—of it happening again. Especially with Seth. If she let him in again, he would have the ability to destroy her in a way no one ever had.

Because she was so very close to needing him in her life already.

A wave of tiredness slammed into her. It'd been a long couple of days. Coming home to a wrecked house, dealing with that situation and the knowledge someone had violated her space and destroyed some of her things. Not sleeping, sleeping with Seth, then sex with Seth, and then the trip to the range where *everything* she'd thought she'd known about him and Mikhail, and even her own team, had been blown sky high.

Someone on her team, someone she worked with, had

tried to sabotage the code. Had they been the one to set the fire? Who on her team wanted to hurt her? And why? They couldn't have been working with Mikhail because he wouldn't have needed her to give him access to the closed network if he'd had someone else who could do it.

The whole thing was insane. Sheer insanity piled on more insanity.

It was exhausting.

She checked Nikki's location because she hadn't been able to do it inside the SCIF. She'd checked a few times since they'd left One Shot Tactical. Nikki was where she was supposed to be. Callie had sent a text, and her sister blew up her phone with horse pictures. It made her smile when little else could.

Nikki, at least, was having the time of her life.

There had been no texts from fake-Mikhail since the one asking to meet. Not even a reply to the text she'd sent asking where he was last night. Presumably, the original text was meant to get her out of the house so somebody could search for what they thought she had hidden away.

So who was on the other end of his phone, and what did they want? Had Mikhail told them she had a memory stick with the code? That was the only thing that made any sense to her. And since they hadn't found it, would they be back?

Callie shuddered at the idea. But it wasn't like they were going to say *oh well, she doesn't have it, time to move on.*

"What were you up to Mikhail? And who were you really?" she muttered as she went into her room to change for bed.

But walking into her room didn't help at all. Because the bed, while neatly made, conjured images of what had happened there earlier. Callie closed her eyes as memories assailed her.

She was never going to be able to see her bed without thinking about Seth. He'd been right that replacing the memory of someone violating her room with a happy memory was a good idea.

But she hadn't realized the new memory would be a hundred times worse.

She grabbed her pajamas and went into the bathroom.

And, yay for her, it was also bad. She stared at the shower, thinking of everything they'd done in there. It was the first time she'd felt him deep inside her, the first time she'd realized how explosive an orgasm could really be when a man knew what he was doing and worked to get you off before he gave in to his own pleasure.

She could truly say that sex with Seth was the best of her life. Which didn't help matters one bit.

She brushed her teeth with a vengeance, changed her clothes, and padded to the kitchen for a glass of wine because she really fucking needed it. Probably shouldn't have brushed her teeth already, but oh well.

Luna came in the back door first and then Seth. Just the sight of him made her heart skip.

Why did he have to be so damned gorgeous with dark hair and silver eyes and muscles for days? She wanted to climb him, wrap her arms and legs around him, and feel that slice of heaven he'd shown her again.

His gaze slid over her, assessing. He did it every time he came into her presence after being away from her. There was something comforting about it.

"I'm getting wine. You want anything?"

Because it was ridiculous to ignore him. Now that she'd said what she needed to say, she could be cordial.

"I'm good. Thanks."

She poured wine into her glass. "Everything okay out there?"

"Yep. Charlie's fine, too. I gave him some hay. I hope that's all right. Nikki said an extra pad at night wouldn't hurt."

Her heart squeezed that he'd not only listened to her sister, but remembered. "It's fine. He's got a lot of good grass in the pasture, but when he comes in at night it's okay if he has hay."

"The trail cams are working, and I'll get alerts, same as always. I've got the rifle, and I'll stay on the couch if you want the guest room."

She hated the way he sounded so polite and distant, but she'd done that to him. She'd made it happen.

"It's okay. I'll sleep in my room. I'm not afraid."

He nodded. "I've got some work to do, so I'll be at the table for a while with my laptop."

She hesitated, but there was nothing more to say. "Goodnight, then."

"Yeah, night."

Callie took her glass of wine to the bedroom, her heart throbbing with every step. Then she climbed onto her bed, took the box containing her journals and paper from her nightstand where she'd left it, and spread them across the quilt to start repairing what she could.

But it didn't work to distract her like it usually did. She lay back against the pillows, tears pressing her eyelids, and told herself she was doing the right thing.

Except, this time, the right thing felt all wrong.

Chapter Thirty-Eight

Seth worked on chasing down photos of Mikhail Volkov in Poland, but he wasn't having any luck. The fact Callie's version of Volkov was different from the photos he'd originally found was disturbing. Definitely meant a foreign intelligence service was involved. Probably the Russians, though maybe not. But the Volkov Callie knew spoke Polish and Russian in her presence, so presumably it was one of those two.

"Fuck," he said with a groan, putting his head into his hands as he stared at the screen. He heard Callie moving around in her bedroom from time to time, and he wanted to be in there with her.

They'd had sex only hours ago, and he missed it. But worse than that, he missed the intimacy. Lying in bed with her last night, before they'd ever gotten naked together, holding her next to him, had been a revelation. He was the kind of man who didn't get close to people if he didn't have to.

But being close to her had felt right. Callie fit in his arms, fit the curve of his body, and fit into his life.

Maybe it was Blaze's and Chance's influence since they both seemed so damn happy, or maybe there really was something in the water in Sutton's Creek. But for the first time in *his* life, he could envision spending time with a woman beyond a few nights of orgasms and trying to listen to her talk about shit he didn't care about.

He didn't care about some of the shit Callie talked about either, like scrapbooking, but he didn't mind listening to her talk about it. Hell, he *wanted* her to.

Making pancakes for her this morning had been the best way he could think to express how right he felt when he was with her. He wanted to take care of her. He was already taking care of her safety, but he wanted to take care of her in other ways.

He wanted to see her smile. He wanted to watch her glue her paper scraps into her journal and know it made her happy. He just wanted to be with her. Near her, because she made him feel needed and useful in a way he hadn't felt in, well, maybe ever.

Not that he hadn't been those two things most of his life in the pursuit of his job. The people he'd rescued had needed him, and he'd been useful in helping and protecting them.

But it wasn't the same thing as being needed in a personal way. Callie hadn't just needed him to sleep nearby with an arsenal of weapons close to hand so he could keep her safe. She'd needed him to hold her so she could sleep.

Seth straightened and twisted to work the kinks out of this back, then returned to searching for information. He found additional records on Mikhail Volkov, older ones than he'd found before, that featured photos of the same man, though younger. There was an obituary for his dad, who'd died of lung cancer twelve years ago. His mother was in a memory care facility with advanced Alzheimer's. Volkov hadn't married and had no children.

He'd been a great target for a spy who needed a new identity.

Seth's phone buzzed on the table. It was Kane. "Did you find anything?"

"Think so. There's a lot of foot traffic in the area because of the hotels and restaurants, the fitness center, and the lake, but we finally isolated a couple of people who look like they could be headed in the right direction within an hour before the fire started. The resolution isn't fantastic, but it should be good enough to show Callie. One of the suspects is a woman, one a man. We compared photos of Robbins and Spinner, but it didn't help. Both are wearing ball caps, so it wasn't ideal."

"Thanks. I'll show her."

"So, uh, everything all right out there?"

"Fine. Why?" Seth stared at the wall opposite. It wasn't a very interesting wall, but it was something to focus on.

"Don't take this the wrong way, bud, but there seemed to be a little tension between you and Callie today."

"What makes you think that? She was pissed we lied to her—pissed I lied since I'm the one who's been out here with her every day. Not telling her we already knew who she was and what she was working on. I worked to get her to trust me then dropped a grenade in the middle of it. Yeah, I'd say there was tension, and mostly directed at me, but she's mad at all of us. Do you blame her?"

"No, I don't, but there were a few moments where, uh, it seemed a lot more personal than that."

"Kane, I love you buddy, but unlike you I don't want to talk about whether or not I've banged every woman in a hundred mile radius, okay? Even if anything was personal, and I'm not saying it was, it's none of your business."

"Way to turn it around there, Phantom. Not asking for details, man, just wanted to make sure you're all right. Blaze is ridiculously in love. Chance too. Thought it might be nice if the same happened to you. I want all my friends to be happy, even if Ghost is convinced his balls are in a vice with Washington over it."

Seth ground his jaw. "You think it's going to happen in, what, four days? That's not realistic."

"Why not? Chance fell for Rory at first sight, even if he didn't admit it. Not sure about Blaze, but it didn't take him long either. They're both better off for it if you ask me."

"What the fuck, Demon? You been shooting up estrogen on the side? Reading romance novels with Rory? You want to talk about feelings now? Haven't you heard I don't have any?"

"Don't know what you think you're proving other than my point. But okay, I'm done. You do what you gotta do, brother."

Seth was boiling with feelings, and he didn't like it. "You know, before you go pushing others about their personal lives, maybe you need to take a look at your own."

"Meaning?"

"Meaning Daphne. You're crazy for her, and you won't admit it, not even to yourself."

Kane scoffed. "Seriously? Dude, she's like a little sister to me. That's gross."

"Right. Never seen anybody look at their sister the way you look at her."

"Fuck you, Phantom. You're being a dick because you've got yourself tangled up over Callie. She's angry, and you don't know how to fix it. Now show her that footage, figure out if we've got a match, and stop busting my balls."

"You started it."

Now how mature was that? Jesus, he was losing his fricking mind.

"Yeah, whatever. Take your Midol, dude, and get over yourself."

Before Seth could retort, the call was over. He slid his phone across the table and growled as he found the footage and cued it up. The feed was grainier than he'd like so he used a software tool to sharpen it up. Wasn't perfect, but it was better than Kane had sent.

There were two people tagged. One a woman who strolled through the parking lot with an athletic bag. She moved briskly, like she had somewhere to be. The other was a man who wore a backpack. Kane had tagged where they parked, but the lot was full enough that you couldn't see what kind of car they were in. Backing up the footage didn't help because it was dusk and their headlights were on, obscuring the vehicle make. He'd show Callie that too, just in case.

The woman returned to the parking lot forty-five minutes later. The man returned a few minutes after that. Both were potentials, like Kane said. Luna trotted in and licked his hand when he dropped it to pet her, which meant Callie was awake. He didn't have to go find her, though, because she walked into the kitchen on silent feet and set her wine glass on the counter.

Then she turned to face him, arms over her chest, back against the counter. "I can't sleep."

"Sorry."

"You haven't even tried."

"No, I've got work."

She blew out a breath and scrubbed her hands over her face. "Look, I'm sorry for being mean to you. Really. I like you Seth. Too much, if I'm honest, and it scares me. So it's not that you're a terrible person or anything, okay? It's just that I've been through enough already and I don't want to risk something else blowing up in my face. I hope you understand."

"I do."

Because what else could he say?

She chewed her lip. "Was any of what you said real? Mia?"

Hot anger rolled through him. But he wouldn't unleash it on her. It wasn't fair. In her position, he'd probably wonder the same damn thing. "Mia is very real. I have a job to do, it's true, but being such a dick that I'd make up a daughter I've never met isn't something I'd ever do. Everything I told you about that situation is true."

She nodded. "Okay. Thank you. I won't say anything. But you should, you know. Your friends care about you. I think they can handle it."

"Thanks, but I think you gave up the right to offer life advice to me, don't you?"

She swallowed. "I suppose you're right."

"Kane sent over some video. Need you to look and see if maybe you can spot anyone you know." He pointed at the chair nearby and she closed the distance, pulled it out, and sat down. But she didn't move closer.

He turned his computer and started the sequence. "This woman is one of the possibilities. There's a man, too. I'll show you both. I tried to sharpen the picture, but it might be difficult. If you can't tell, it's okay."

She leaned closer, looking hard at the woman. "I... I don't know."

He showed her the man. She studied the screen and then shook her head. "I can't tell. If it was closer, like a bank camera, maybe."

"Yeah, sorry."

The code she'd found had yielded nothing because it'd

been written into the program before Ghost Ops hacked it, so it was impossible to know who'd entered it into the system. Another potential lead fucked all to hell.

"Wait a minute," she said, her brows furrowed. "Can you look at the woman again? Something just occurred to me."

"Sure. First shot or second?"

"Second."

He rewound the video and showed her. She leaned close, so close he could smell the sweetness of almonds. Her body wash they'd both used this morning.

Seth clamped down on the tingle that started in his balls when he thought about the shower. The way he'd rubbed her skin with that soap, fondling her breasts, caressing her ass. The smell of it on her pussy when he'd buried his face between her legs and licked her slick flesh.

Jesus.

"I think..." She sucked in a breath as she stared. "That's a Louis Vuitton athletic bag. Dr. Robbins loves Louis Vuitton. She has several bags, a belt, and luggage. And though she's wearing a ball cap and shapeless clothing, the walk is right. She's told me before that, as women, we have to stride into a room of male programmers like we own it if we want them to take us seriously."

She slumped into the chair and looked sorrowful rather than angry or scared. "I didn't want it to be her. I *like* her, Seth. Why would she do such a thing?"

"I don't know, baby. Money? Idealism? It's hard to know until we get her in custody and talk to her."

"Custody? Who's going to do that? You guys aren't official. If I learned anything today, I learned that much."

She'd been briefed with the kind of intensity that only Colonel Alex "Ghost" Bishop—once a colonel, always a colonel—could provide. Seth had been there for it. They all had. Callie agreed to sign an NDA, which wouldn't be worth shit if she decided to talk because they weren't in any position to sue—no, they'd likely be thrown into a military prison—Guantanamo, probably—but he knew how seriously she took her pledges. He wasn't worried about her talking.

"Not us. Ghost will handle it. He'll make a call, and someone will pick her up. Possibly the FBI. Or the CIA. Maybe even Homeland Security. I don't really know, I gotta admit."

She threw a look at her wine glass. "Maybe I should drink the whole fucking bottle. It's turning into that kind of night."

He wanted to reach over and squeeze her hand, but he didn't. "Do what you need to do. I'll be here to watch your back."

She propped her elbows on the table and put her forehead in her hands. "I wish I'd never heard of Griffin Research. Wish I'd never met Mikhail, whoever he is. Or was. I should have gone to work for a game development company." She turned her head in her hands to look at him. "Is it too much to hope Dr. Robbins is the end of it?"

"Probably. Sorry."

She sighed. "I was afraid you'd say that. You sure that whole disappearing thing is off the table?"

The idea of her and Nikki disappearing made his insides squeeze. She might not want to take this thing between them any farther, but she wasn't kicking him out of their lives if he could help it.

"Yeah, I'm sure."

Chapter Thirty-Nine

Sunday dawned bright and beautiful, but Callie felt the weight of sorrow closing in on her when she woke up alone. She turned to look at the side of the bed where Seth would have been and sighed.

Her choice that he wasn't there. Her decision.

Last night when they'd been talking in the kitchen, she'd wanted so badly to touch him. Just touch his hand, his cheek, sift her fingers through his hair. She'd wanted him to take her in his arms and hold her when she realized Dr. Robbins was the one on the video.

But she'd given up the right to ask him for comfort.

She still couldn't believe Dr. Robbins tried to burn the lab. Joanne Robbins, her boss, her mentor. A woman she admired and had wanted to emulate. What would make her betray her country?

Maybe they'd have answers today, assuming Seth shared them with her. She didn't think he would withhold them out of spite, but he might be ordered to do so by his boss. For national security reasons.

Callie pushed herself upright. Luna wasn't in the room

with her though she had been most of the night. Callie had left the door cracked open enough for the dog to come and go as she liked.

Fresh coffee smells drifted into her space, which meant Seth was already up and taking care of business.

Luna was fed and had been outside. Charlie was fed and medicated.

She didn't expect pancakes this morning, however. She got out of bed, slipped on a bra, brushed her teeth, and wound her hair into a knot, then went into the kitchen for coffee.

Seth wasn't there, but she spotted him outside in the backyard with Luna. He wore athletic shorts and no shirt, his skin glistening with sweat that she realized came from the pushups he did whenever he threw the ball for Luna and then dropped to the ground to pump out a set as she fetched and returned to his side, tail wagging furiously.

He stood and threw the ball again, did more pushups, petted Luna when she returned, and threw the ball for her. Sometimes he stood to do it and sometimes he didn't. He laughed as she licked him, tilting his face away so she couldn't smother him with doggie kisses, scrubbing her fur on either side of her neck and telling her she was a good girl.

Callie's heart did a skip/squeeze thing that left her breathless for half a second. She'd never seen Seth so open and free, and it was a beautiful sight. He was always guarded, though she realized he hadn't been guarded with her in those moments when they'd been tangled together, bodies moving as one. It was a different kind of open then, which was why she hadn't recognized it. Not to mention she'd been lost in her own response to what they were doing. Her own intense pleasure.

A wave of loneliness hit her.

God, she was an idiot. She wanted that back, so badly, and she'd ruined it.

Maybe he was right. Maybe she had given up too easily.

She thought of Bobby Bowen and that moment when he'd kissed her. When she'd thought her entire world had been about to change for the better because a handsome, popular jock wanted *her*, a smart girl, instead of the cheerleader he'd been with before. She'd been so hopeful and stupid at the same time. She hadn't seen the crash coming.

She was still afraid she couldn't see it coming. *That* was why she'd been so mad, why she'd let her anger carry her into ending this thing with Seth before it ever really got started. Because she was *afraid*.

He'd said he craved her, that his heart felt like there was a vise around it because she wouldn't look at him or speak to him. And when she'd said she wanted it to be over, he'd told her he didn't want to be done.

Watching him now, that laughter, the way he cared about making a rescue dog happy—the way he took care of Charlie because he'd listened to what Nikki said—made her eyes sting. And then there was Colleen and her computer, the way he'd fixed it without complaint because she'd been flustered. When he'd told her why he would always help seniors who were confused by technology, she'd thought he was a good guy.

But it was more than that. Seth was beautiful, inside and out. He was grumpy on the outside because it was a protective mechanism, but he was a kind, decent, sweet man that she'd be a fool to let walk away without at least *trying* to make something of it.

Not that he'd appreciate being called sweet. She was sure of that. But he *was* sweet, like it or not.

She watched him play some more then turned away,

her heart pounding with all she felt. Was it possible to fall for someone in a few short days? To think you needed more of them because you didn't know how you'd ever lived without them?

She went to the fridge and took out eggs, bacon, and then got a pan and started the stove. Her heart was full, and she had to do something or burst. She got busy cooking breakfast for two. She heard the door open, heard Luna's nails on the tile, and then Seth stepped inside. She didn't look at him, but she heard his stillness.

He was thinking, wondering what the hell was happening.

"Smells good," he said.

When she trusted herself to turn, she pasted on a smile. "I was hungry. Thought you might be, too."

"Yeah, I am." He was holding his balled up shirt in one hand. Sunlight filtered through the windows and caressed the curve of his chest. He studied her as if puzzled.

Me too, buddy, she thought.

"You have time to shower if that was your plan. I haven't started the eggs yet."

"Thanks."

He left without another word and her heart fell a little as she watched his retreating back. It was like the first day he'd arrived when he'd been silent and brooding, walking away without explanation when he had somewhere he wanted to be.

They were back to being awkward then. Callie finished the bacon, letting it get crispy, then poured most of the grease into a dish so it could cool and she could scrape it into the trash. She put bread in the toaster, started to beat the eggs, and listened to the sound of water falling in the shower.

She didn't have to imagine Seth naked in there now

because she had a very accurate and detailed picture in her head.

By the time he returned, clad in jeans and boots and a fitted T-shirt that read *The Salty Dawg Tavern. You Won't Gag*, she was putting breakfast on the table.

He grabbed the coffee pot and poured fresh coffee into their cups, then sat across from her while she put bacon, eggs, and toast on her plate.

Her heart thumped. She had no idea what to say. How to rewind the tape and start again.

"Charlie seemed happy this morning," Seth said, buttering his toast. "He did that thing—what's it called?—when I walked into the barn."

Callie searched her brain. To be fair, she was scattered because so much of her was focused on not screwing this up, but it finally hit her what he meant.

"Nickered?"

He pointed the fork at her. "Yeah, that's it. He nickered at me, so I scratched his neck and then got his food."

There was a lump in her throat. "Thank you. I really can get up on time and feed him, and I will tomorrow. But I appreciate you taking care of him for me."

"I'm up early anyway. Not a problem."

Silence descended again.

"Food's good," Seth said. "Thanks for including me."

"You're welcome."

More silence while she tried to think of what to say.

"What time is Nikki coming back today?"

"Uh, she's supposed to text me, but I think it'll be later this evening. They're still at the hotel, but they're heading to another farm before they start back."

"That's good. She having fun?"

"Yes. I should have let her go anyway because she's having so much fun, but I guess it doesn't matter how she got there. I'll have to remember it the next time I start thinking she needs to stay home and do chores." She tilted her head to study him as realization dawned. "Seth."

"Yeah?" He looked wary.

She smiled. "You've been engaging in small talk. Initiating it."

He arched an eyebrow. "No offense, Cal, but you've kinda sucked at it this morning. Somebody had to do it."

That made her laugh. And it felt like familiar ground, which was good. "True. Sorry. I was trying to think of what to say but obviously not doing a good job of it."

He looked interested. "Why not?"

And there it was again, the fluttering heart and racing pulse. "I, um—I'm just really sorry for yesterday. I might have overreacted."

He shook his head. "You didn't. I lied to you about a lot of things, because I had to, and then we hit you with a bucketload of shit at once. I'm sorry it had to be that way, but I get why you were pissed."

She wanted to tell him that wasn't what she was talking about, but the awkwardness and fear wouldn't let her put her heart on the line like that. He'd had time to sleep on it. Maybe he'd changed his mind, too.

"Do you know what's going to happen to Dr. Robbins yet?"

"No. I informed command and they're working on it. That's all I know."

"You'll tell me when you do?"

"I'll tell you, Callie. You deserve to know."

She moved her eggs around on the plate, her stomach tense. "Will you be leaving soon?"

He frowned. "I don't know. I guess it depends on what we find out from your boss. If she's involved in the break-in and the texts from Mikhail's phone, then maybe so. But if not, I don't know what'll happen."

"Okay."

"Do you want me gone that bad?"

Her head whipped up, her gaze locking with his. "I…" She was at a loss. A complete loss. If she said she didn't, would she be opening herself for rejection? Or should she play this cool, wait for him to say he didn't want to go again?

"It's okay, you don't have to say it. I'll ask Kane or Ethan to stay with you until this is over. I can shadow Nikki, make sure she's safe going to the barn and back. I'll still be involved, but you won't have to live in the same house with me."

"No," she burst out. "That's not what I mean at all. I…" She threw her hands in the air. "You were right. I've been hurt, and it makes me scared. I like you so much—really like you—and I'm afraid it's not real. That you're somehow punking me, that a film crew will jump out of the closet and yell, 'Surprise!' and there I'll be, looking like an idiot and feeling a hundred times worse."

She ran out of steam as he stared at her, his eyes widening. Then he growled, and before she knew what he was doing, he'd dragged her chair next to his and wrapped his arms around her. Callie turned her face into his chest and breathed him in, heart racing, eyes smarting, soul feeling like she'd found her way home after crawling across a desert.

"Fucking hell, baby, why would you think that?"

"Because it's happened before," she mumbled.

He pulled her onto his lap, and she curled into him, wrapping her arms around his neck. "Tell me. I need to know whose asses to kick."

Callie laughed, a rusty sound. "It was high school, Seth. No need to hunt them down and kick their asses."

"Fuck that. They're adults now. Tell me."

So she did. Every moment, from the invitation to homecoming to picking out her dress and being absolutely giddy. Then the drop to the bottom when Bobby kissed her and the cell phones flashed. She could feel his body tightening beneath her, and it was a beautiful thing. Because he was furious on her behalf. Coiled and ready to strike.

Just knowing it was enough.

"Those stupid pictures are still floating around on social media," she said with a sigh, feeling like she'd let go of a thousand pound weight she'd been dragging around. "They didn't even have the decency to delete them once we were mature enough to leave high school crap behind."

"They're gone, babe. Soon as I get a chance, they're gone."

She tipped her head back. "Bobby and Tara or the pictures?" Because he sounded so serious she wasn't sure if she'd unleashed a beast or what.

"You tell me."

"Seth."

He grinned to let her know it was a joke, but then he was serious again. "I'll wipe every trace from their feeds. Promise you that."

"I'm not sixteen anymore. It's okay."

"Fuck that. Their bullshit almost cost me you. I'm not letting it stand. I've got the skills and the methods, and I'm erasing every mean comment and photo."

She palmed his cheek because she could. It felt so right. "It's okay, Seth. Really. You're right that it bothered me, but I've realized, in telling you about what happened, that it doesn't have power over me anymore. And, honestly, it wasn't just that. It's been a pattern of disappointment in what people say and what they actually do. I've learned it's easier not to trust anyone."

"Including me."

"Yes. But I… I think I'm ready to try now."

He kissed her, and her soul melted.

"I need you, Callie. I don't know why, but I do."

"I need you, too. But why is it breakfast which brings out the feels in us, huh?"

Yesterday it had been pancakes, and today it was bacon and eggs.

"It's the most important meal of the day?"

Callie laughed. "Maybe."

He kissed her again, but it wasn't the kind of kiss that said they were going to end up in bed together anytime soon. It was sweet and hot but not desperately needy like before.

"Finish your breakfast, babe."

"But I thought…"

He shook his head. "Nope, no sex. I'm not going there with you again until I've proven you can trust me. I told Nikki I wanted to date you, and that's what we're going to do. No sex until the fourth date at least."

"Second."

"Fourth. One date for each base and then we're home free."

"Sounds like torture."

"Probably, but a little anticipation will make it sweeter, don't you think?"

Callie sighed. "This is not going the way I'd hoped."

He kissed the tip of her nose. "No, but it's going the way it should."

Chapter Forty

At three o'clock, Seth and Callie walked into the range with Luna at their side. Daphne, Emma, and Rory were sitting in the meeting room with drinks. They'd put plates and side dishes on the console table at one end of the room, and they beckoned Callie in while Seth went to find his guys.

She squeezed his hand before they parted, and he knew she wanted information. To his way of thinking, she deserved it. She'd helped them figure out a major issue with the Athena Project, and she'd been instrumental in identifying the saboteur. He planned to argue for her inclusion in what happened next if it came down to it.

Kane was out back, cooking chicken on the grill. Seth walked out and clapped his teammate on the shoulder. Kane arched an eyebrow, but his smile was friendly.

"Sorry, man. I was being a moody prick."

Kane laughed. "What's new about that?"

"Not much."

"My point. And hey, I was a dick too, so let's call it even and be done. Unless you want to hug it out?"

Seth snorted. "I'm good."

He went inside and found Ghost, who was in his office. "FBI picked her up two hours ago. I've got nothing yet."

Seth sank onto a chair with a sigh. "There's still so much we don't know. Who the fuck is Mikhail? Who trashed Callie's place? I hope she's got the answers because Callie really deserves a fucking break."

Ghost leaned back in his chair, hands folded over his abdomen. "I really thought when I sent you to protect her, I'd cracked the code. No pun intended. But damn, dude, I thought you were the one who'd be impervious to any mushy shit. Then you go and get involved at a rate of speed that's quite frankly astonishing for someone who's always been cool-headed. You want to tell me what's going on with you two?"

Seth shrugged. "Honestly, I don't know. We're figuring it out. It's early days."

Ghost pinched the bridge of his nose. "Fine, fine. Just don't fucking get her pregnant, okay? I don't have time for more of that shit."

"Not planning on it, boss."

Yet. Maybe someday if Callie wanted to.

"I have a daughter though. Gave up my parental rights before I ever joined the military. Probably should have said so before when you told us having no family ties was a requirement for this mission. Not that I've ever spoken to her, or even know where she is. But she's out there."

Ghost looked stunned. "I don't know what to say."

"Nothing to say. I should have told my friends years ago. I'm telling you now, and I'll tell the guys as well. If it changes your opinion of me, nothing I can do about that. It'll be no worse than what I've thought of myself all these years."

"My not knowing what to say was the fact I'm just

learning this about you, not that it happened. I know you joined the military at eighteen, so I'm guessing you were a kid yourself. No shame, brother. No judgment. You probably did the right thing for her. I assume she was adopted?"

"Yeah." There was a knot in his throat. All these years he'd kept it to himself and he'd been wrong. Callie was right that the people who cared about him would understand.

"I was adopted," Ghost said. "My parents were good people who couldn't have children of their own. My birth mother was a teenager. Giving me up was the best choice for *me*. I'm glad she wasn't selfish about it."

Seth blinked. "I didn't know."

"Not something that's ever come up, has it? The conversation now warrants it, so I'm telling you. Maybe don't feel so guilty about it, huh? I know that's easier said than done, but think about what I told you."

"I will. Thank you, sir."

"Knock it off with the 'sir' crap, Seth. I think what we've just shared requires first names, don't you?"

"Yes. Alex. Thank you."

"You're welcome."

Daphne appeared in the doorway. "There's a woman to see you, Alex."

"Doesn't she know the range is closed on Sunday?"

"I think she does. I also think she doesn't care."

Seth had a bad feeling about this. "Is she blond, pretty, and looks like she rips men's balls off for entertainment?"

Daphne's lips quirked. "That about sums it up. Special Agent Diana Corbin asked me not to say it was her."

Ghost groaned. "Well fuck me, how the hell did she escape from Kentucky anyway? She hasn't been gone a month. And what does she want with me?"

"I'm not sure, but she said it was important."

"Okay, fine." He started to get up but then sat back down. "You know what? Wait five minutes and bring her back here. Seth, round up the guys and join us."

"Got it."

Seth hopped up and went to find Blaze, Chance, and Ethan. They were in the stock room, discussing the merits of the new laser sights that had come in. Seth sent them to Ghost's office and went outside to get Kane, who was just putting the last piece of chicken in the foil pan. He turned off the grill and carried the chicken to the meeting room, then he and Seth went to join their team.

They arranged themselves around the room and waited for Daphne to show Diana in. To her credit, Special Agent Corbin didn't blink when she saw them gathered. She strolled in with the grace of a gazelle and took the chair Alex indicated.

"Welcome back, Agent Corbin."

"Thank you. I'm happy to be here."

She was cool, aloof, and so elegant she almost seemed out of place in a shooting range. Which was hilarious because she had to be pretty damned good with a weapon. She wouldn't be an agent if she wasn't.

"Didn't like Kentucky?"

"Oh, I liked it just fine, Mr. Bishop. Turns out I was needed here." She let her gaze slide over them. "It's been decided at levels above my pay grade that our office needs a special relationship with yours. I'll be your liaison."

"Of course you will," Ghost said. "How delightful."

She arched a brow. "I have information. You might want to tone the sarcasm down."

"Duly noted."

She took a notebook from her pocket and flipped it open. "Joanne Robbins cracked like a fresh egg. She set the fire in the building because she wanted to put a stop to the project she was in charge of. She believes that in the wrong hands it could be a tool for harm. She tried to sabotage it from within, but Caroline Crowell is too good at what she does to be fooled for long. So Dr. Robbins wanted to stop the project indefinitely. She wasn't trying to hurt Ms. Crowell, or so she says."

"Bullshit," Seth spat.

Diana's gaze slewed to his. "I happen to agree with you. There's a lot more here, but I'm afraid I'm not able to discuss it. It's too bad you don't have a SCIF. I could talk freely in there because I've been given permission to do so."

She looked meaningfully at Ghost for long seconds.

"Oh Jesus, why don't we just take out an advertisement in the Sutton's Creek Bee? Let everyone know we have special meeting rooms available." He did air quotes when he said *special meeting rooms*. Would have been funny if it wasn't so serious.

"I believe you did take out an ad in the Bee," Diana said. "Though I didn't see any mention of a special room."

"Kane, go tell Daph we're headed into the meeting room for a few minutes. And ask Callie to join us."

Diana frowned. "I don't think having Ms. Crowell—"

"This is my territory, Agent Corbin. I make the decisions."

She glared at Ghost, and he glared back. Then she nodded as regally as a queen. "Of course."

Callie walked in, her gaze going around the room. She went to Seth's side and he put an arm around her. Then Ghost led the way into the SCIF, and they arranged themselves around the table. Seth gave Callie his seat and stood behind her. Ghost indicated that Diana could have his seat at the head of the table while he leaned against one of the computer banks, arms and legs crossed. Seth knew, because he knew the boss, that he wasn't amused in the least.

Diana studied the room. "This is impressive. Looks like some money went into this place."

"You know how it is," Ghost drawled. "Daddy gives, and Daddy takes away. Care to tell us how you found out about this?"

She slid a glance at Callie before deciding to speak. "People in Washington talk. Even when they aren't supposed to. The director is an old family friend, though I don't think you knew that."

"You've got me there."

"I heard it from him when I went to see him about my inconvenient trip to Kentucky."

Ghost laughed. "Son of a bitch, you were holding out on us, Agent Corbin. Friends in high places indeed."

"Maybe not as high as some," she said pointedly. "But good enough."

"Now that we understand each other, what have you got for us?"

"If Joanne Robbins is a foreign agent, she's a very bad one. She's been babbling since we apprehended her. Over the past few months, she's become afraid the Athena Project will be a tool for harm in the future. She said that while President Willis is a good person she believes will use the technology responsibly to protect this nation, she wasn't certain that a future president wouldn't see it as somewhat of a license to attack other countries at will. That's why she sabotaged the code and why she set the fire a few nights ago. To stop Athena from being a tool wielded by tyrants. Her exact words."

Callie made a noise. Seth put his hand on her shoulder and squeezed.

"She said you're too good." Diana directed her gaze at

Callie. "She knew you were going to find the dormant code and figure out who'd put it there. She wanted to scare you, make you quit before it happened. She swears she wasn't trying to kill you, but she also knows if you'd been in the lab another ten minutes without the sprinklers, you'd have succumbed to the smoke."

Diana lifted her gaze to the rest of them. "She's a talented programmer. She interfered with the sprinkler system, and she removed the evidence she'd been in the building at the time of the fire. I'm not sure I believe that she wasn't trying to kill Ms. Crowell." Another look at Callie. "You don't have to report for work tonight. She made that up and sent it to you only. Presumably to try and dissuade you again. Not sure what her plans were this time."

Callie trembled, but was it fear or outrage? "But she hired me! And gave me the freedom to work independently. Why would she do that and then try to scare me away or kill me? She could have fired me. What would I have done then? I'd have left, that's what. What the fuck is wrong with people?"

"We don't know everything yet, but she was ordered to hire you and ordered to put you on Athena. The directive came from the company founder, Dr. Griffin. But she believes someone else convinced him you were the right person. She doesn't know who. She couldn't fire you, Ms. Crowell. She could only make you want to quit."

"Or kill me," Callie muttered. "She knew my story. And she knows my sister depends on me. I guess our lives were worth it to her though, if it stops a tyrant. By all means."

Callie sounded bitter, and he didn't blame her. His own thoughts about Joanne Robbins weren't exactly civilized at the moment.

"Do you believe her?" Ghost asked.

"I believe it's what she believes. Naturally, we'll be watching Dr. Griffin and monitoring his contacts."

"Anything else for us?"

"Yes. The two Russians in custody, Abram Federov and Dima Smirnov, who were picked up impersonating UAH students...."

Callie stiffened, and Seth knew she'd figured out precisely who they were impersonating.

"Federov is being handed over in a prisoner exchange with Russia. But Smirnov... Well, the man we have in custody isn't him."

"Who is he?" Ghost asked.

"Exactly who he says he is. Cyril Dyka. He's been released."

"And where is Smirnov?"

"No idea, unfortunately. We're working on it."

Ghost rubbed a hand over his face. "Okay. Do you have a photo?"

Diana slipped a small paper from her pocket. "It took time to find this because they'd hidden it well, pointed all evidence at Cyril Dyka being Smirnov. But this is Smirnov."

She turned the photo so the group could see, and Seth knew she'd been dramatic on purpose. Looking for a reaction, which she got when Callie shot to her feet with a gasp.

He already knew what she was going to say.

"That's Mikhail."

Chapter Forty-One

"WHAT DO WE KNOW ABOUT DIMA SMIRNOV?" ALEX asked. Callie had reverted to thinking of him as Alex because he'd said it was best if people called him that instead of his military call sign.

She sat again, slowly, her entire body buzzing with fury and fear. Mikhail Volkov was really this Dima Smirnov. The man who'd spent so much time with her, talking to her, recruiting her to work at Griffin Research Labs, had been lying about who he was.

"Former SVR," Seth said. "He hasn't worked for Russian intelligence in a couple of years though."

Callie squeezed her eyes shut as her stomach twisted. A Russian intelligence agent. Great.

"He works for the Dashevsky Group," Diana said, and Callie's stomach dropped even further. "Viktor Dashevsky is bad news, no matter how he tries to look like a humble, kind oligarch with his humanitarian aid and his teams of people who head into disaster zones to help. They *do* help. I'm not disputing that, but it's not his primary objective."

"And what is his primary objective, Agent Corbin?

Because you seem to know a lot about it." Alex was watching her carefully.

"Did I fail to mention that my uncle works for the CIA? How careless of me. Not that Uncle Stephen shares much, but—"

"Stephen Adler? The Deputy Director of the CIA is your uncle?"

"There happen to be many men in this world named Stephen," Diana said with a sniff. "But you're correct. Public service runs in the family."

Alex shook his head and tilted his head back as if having a moment with the ceiling. More likely asking God why him, Callie thought. She recognized the pose because she felt it too. Why her?

"The Dashevsky Group is a front for the arms trade. Not only that, but they make money on those disaster zones. So if they happen to create a few, then what's the harm since they'll be there to help, right?"

"How can you make money on a disaster zone?" Callie asked, dumbfounded. "Mikhail—Smirnov—was a translator."

"And they would need translators, wouldn't they? As to your question, government money," Diana said. "It flows toward the area in need. Dashevsky gives his own money, but he makes it up in the government aid and the connections he forges. He builds armies of loyalists with his aid and his weapons. He's not a nice man. I'm going to assume, since you're in this room, you can be relied on not to talk about anything you hear today."

Callie was slightly affronted. "I'm coding the command and control system for what is apparently a critical military system, so I think I can be trusted. I haven't tried to murder anyone over it either. Yet. I reserve the right if they piss me off."

Seth chuckled behind her. The other guys were smiling too. That made her feel good. Like maybe she was a tiny part of their mission to protect the world.

"I'll take that as a yes. Welcome aboard." Diana looked at Alex again. "We don't have any intel on Smirnov's whereabouts. Because he was operating in this country, and because the body of the real Mikhail Volkov was so recently found, the FBI has jurisdiction. We'd like to find him."

"Has the body been positively identified?"

She nodded. "Yes. He's been dead for approximately two years, though. They put him on ice, then brought him out again when Smirnov needed to disappear. That's our guess, anyway. Somebody shot him at close range to blow half his head off and obscure his features. We don't know why."

Callie put her hand to her stomach. Poor man.

"The phone found with him was registered in his name, but it's too new to have really belonged to him."

"Somebody spoofed his number to text Callie for a meeting," Alex said. "She kept the meeting and we observed, but nobody showed. And they haven't texted since, correct?"

"Correct," Callie said when she realized the question was meant for her.

"While her house was empty, two men entered and trashed it. They appeared to be looking for something," Alex said.

"And didn't find it," Diana mused.

"I don't have anything," Callie added, though nobody asked her.

Diana tucked the photo away. "That's all I have for you today. We'll keep you updated on the search for Smirnov, though we think he's probably fled the country by now."

She gave Callie a grave look. "Thank you for what you did to identify Dr. Robbins as the saboteur. Athena is critical to national defense. It would seem you are too."

"I'm just doing my job."

Seth poked her. She wanted to turn and poke him back but didn't.

"We've got some grilled chicken and sides," Alex said. "If you want to join us."

Diana Corbin rose to her feet in an elegant wave. "No, thank you. I have to get back to the office. Maybe next time."

"Let me see you out," Alex said.

The rest of the guys filtered out behind him. Callie stood, but Seth put a hand on her arm as the others exited.

"Are you okay?" he asked when they were alone.

She sucked in a breath and nodded. "I think so. Mikhail Volkov is dead, but I never knew him. I'm sorry for what they did to him, though. Dima Smirnov assumed his identity and befriended me. Why couldn't he do it as himself?"

Seth sighed. "I don't know. It's a spy thing. The Russian foreign intelligence service is like the CIA. They're always playing games upon games. I'm not even sure they know. Smirnov went to work for Dashevsky and, for whatever reason, they decided Volkov was a better identity. So they killed him. It's possible the real Volkov never worked for Dashevsky. They would have altered the record to make it look like he did, though."

Callie nodded. It was a lot to process, but she was doing so. "I hope Smirnov really is gone. I haven't heard from the number again, so maybe he had to get out of the country quick. But will it ever be safe?"

Seth wrapped his arms around her and pulled her close. "I can't tell you he'll never try to contact you again, but if he's fled, then he's probably cut his losses. Once Athena's live, it'll be too late anyway. So it's best to make sure it launches on time. That's all any of us are trying to do. Keep the timeline and make sure it goes live as scheduled. Then we're free."

Callie pressed her face to his shirt, inhaling his scent. She hoped to God he was right.

Chapter Forty-Two

THEY SPENT THE REST OF THE AFTERNOON EATING GOOD food and laughing together. Seth kept an eye on Callie, worried she was stewing about everything that had happened. Her boss, a woman she liked, had tried to kill her. Whether or not the woman really meant to kill her was up for debate, but the fact that Dr. Robbins had told Callie to report for work tonight and let her think the team would be there too wasn't a good sign.

He'd have been there close by, but he wouldn't have been able to get into the building quickly if something had gone wrong. And how would he have known? Callie couldn't take her phone into a SCIF. She could have been dead for hours before he found out.

The thought chilled him to the bone.

She was important to him. More important than he thought it was possible for anyone to be. Yeah, it was insanely fast, as Ghost had pointed out, but Seth was the kind of man who didn't do emotional entanglements. If he felt this strongly this fast, there was something to it.

Something big.

Callie was looking at her phone, giggling, and his heart thumped. He loved seeing her happy.

She looked up, caught him watching her, and smiled. "It's Nikki. They're in Tennessee, stopping at Cracker Barrel."

"And that's what made you laugh?"

"No." She turned the phone and he found himself looking at three teenagers who were making various goofy faces at the screen. The woman at the wheel of the pickup was smiling but looking straight ahead. "She's having a great time."

"You feeling good about that?"

She shrugged happily. "Yeah, I am. God, so much has happened—but Nikki's happy, and that's a good thing."

"It sure is." He reached for her hand, caught her to him and kissed the top of her head. He knew they were being watched and he didn't fucking care. "I'm with you, baby. I've got your back. We'll get some kind of closure on Smirnov, and then you'll know. I won't leave your side until we do."

"You have a job, Seth."

"I know. Right now, it's protecting you."

Her phone pinged and she picked it up. Then she groaned. "Great, it's an email from Leo. He's in charge of the team while Dr. Robbins takes a leave of absence."

"Remember you're the genius on the team. Show him what you're made of and don't back down."

"And if he doesn't listen?"

"Then I'll come stand behind you with arms crossed and a couple of weapons strapped to my sides. As backup, because you can kick ass on your own. I'm just there if you need me."

"You're fun, you know that?"

His heart skipped. Nobody'd ever called him fun before. "If you think so, honey."

"I sure do."

"Hey," Daphne said, standing, swaying slightly because she'd been drinking wine. "Let's go outside and light the fire. It's almost sunset. Oh, and Warren broke up with me. Just in case anybody was wondering where he is."

Silence descended on the group in the meeting room. They'd had the picnic inside because it was hot out, but it'd be cool enough by now for a fire and sitting in chairs around the pit. Except everyone was focused on Daphne as she swayed slightly.

"You serious, Daph?" Kane asked, looking about as confused as a man could look.

"Dead ser-ous," she said. "Ser-ous. Sri-ous. Fuck it, I'm not kidding. He said I wasn't, um, smart enough. Too vain. Not proper wife material."

The room went silent. Rory shot to her feet and wrapped Daphne in a hug. She looked furious. "Honey, baby, don't cry. Warren Trigg *is* a pig. A male chauvinist pig. He doesn't deserve you."

Emma was on her feet, too. "That's right. What an asshole! Does he have any idea how lucky he was you even looked twice at him?"

Emma motioned to Callie, including her in the female bonding exercise. Callie handed Seth her phone. "Can you plug it in? My battery's nearly dead."

"You got it, honey. Go console Daphne. Take Luna."

She smiled as she stood. Luna was at her side instantly. Then the four women—and the female dog—left the room and headed outside to where the fire pit was located. Seth didn't ask if anybody was going to light it for them because

Rory had it under control. He could see Chance itching to help, but thankfully the dude knew better than to make Rory feel helpless. She'd eviscerate him if he did.

"Warren Trigg dumped Daphne?" Ethan asked with the kind of disbelief they were probably all feeling.

"Apparently."

"Is he stupid?"

Kane snorted. "As a fence post. Daphne's a beautiful girl. Sweet, smart, resourceful." He was fuming the more he talked. "He doesn't fucking deserve her."

"Nobody does," Seth said mildly.

"That's right, Phantom," Kane snapped, pointing at him. "Fuckin' A. Nobody deserves Daphne. She's an angel."

Ghost coughed. "Here we go," he muttered under his breath.

Seth heard because Ghost was sitting beside him. If anybody else did, they didn't let on.

Blaze got to his feet. "Come on, we'd better get out there and sing *kumbaya* or something before it gets worse."

Seth looked at him in disbelief. "What the fuck is worse than singing *kumbaya* in a circle right about now?"

"Uh, four women getting madder and madder and thinking men are shit?"

"That's bad," Ethan said.

"Yeah, but Rory and Emma aren't going to agree. Are they?" Seth asked.

"Fuck no," Chance said. "Not for *real*. But the girl code means they'll agree for now, until the hurt one feels vindicated in her feelings. They'll glare and do a lot of bonding over shared hurts, and we'll be shut out. We get out there now, agree that men are shit, and this ends faster because our women will want to go home with us and show us that *we* aren't shit."

"That's either genius or stupid," Ghost said. "Not sure which. But let's go get this over with and show Daphne our support since she's one of us."

"Sounds like a fucking nightmare," Seth said. He looked at Callie, frowning and nodding in turns while Daphne threw her arms out and gestured. "I'm in. Let's go."

It was cooler outside as the sun fell. Grass waved in the field, waiting to be cut for hay, and deer grazed at the edge of the tree line in the distance. Lightning bugs were beginning to light the night sky around them, and the smell of burning wood surrounded everything, reminding Seth of the Boy Scout campfires he'd had before his grandparents decided that him being in Boy Scouts was too inconvenient and expensive and he had to quit.

The women continued to bolster Daphne's feelings, and the men chimed in from time to time. Blaze was right that it went faster with the men out there offering sympathy because everything calmed down until they were sitting around the fire and the women were planning their book club. Chance chimed in from time to time like a proud parent until they shushed him and told him he was welcome to join but only if he read the books.

That shut him up quick enough that Seth had to stifle a laugh.

Callie drifted over to him, yawning happily. "I'm going to get my phone, see where Nikki is."

"It's in the office, babe. Want me to get it?"

"No, that's okay. I have to pee anyway."

She was only gone a few minutes when the door banged open and she rushed out again. He was on his feet instantly, as was his entire team. Alert. Ready.

"I missed a text from Nikki twenty minutes ago. Her

car's dead, and Lisa's driving her home. I've tried calling to tell them to come here, but it keeps going to voice mail."

His heart rate had quickened, but now it slowed to normal again. The guys relaxed too. He and Ethan had kept an eye on the locator on Nikki's car and it was still at the stable in Madison. Now they knew why. The plan had been to leave when she did so they could be home before she got there. Ethan would head out to meet her vehicle before she reached Sutton's Creek and follow her home down the dark roads she'd have to travel. If anyone were going to try and intercept her, that's where it would happen.

But they'd missed a text, and she was already on the way. She hadn't reached home yet because he'd had no alerts from the alarm system.

"All right, let's get going then. We'll meet her at home."

"I'm sorry," Callie said to the group. "This has been more fun than I've had in a while. I hate to leave, but I need to get home before my sister does."

"We understand," Emma said, standing. "It's been great spending time with you, Callie."

"We'll do it again next week," Rory said, coming over to give Callie a hug. "But at our house. We can talk more about the book club. I have soooo many good books for y'all to read!"

"I'm looking forward to it."

"Bye, Callie," Daphne said, steadier on her feet than had been before. She'd switched from wine to water over an hour ago.

The women had to hug each other, the bros did fist bumps, and they were outta there.

"I like your friends," Callie said when they were in his truck, turning onto the road. "They're good people."

"They are… I told Alex about Mia."

She snapped her gaze to him. He didn't take his eyes off the road, but he felt it.

"And?"

"And you were right. He pretty much said what you did. He was adopted and had good parents, so he thinks giving her up was the right thing. I'll tell the other guys soon. Wasn't going to announce it while sitting around the fire."

She snickered. "You didn't want to upstage Daphne. Poor girl."

He laughed. "That's right. She had center stage. Best leave her to it. Can't believe she was that upset over Warren Trigg though. I didn't think it was serious."

"I don't know if it was or not, but she liked him. Said he was a good man who treated her well."

His phone lit up with an alert. He glanced at it. "Trail cam," he said. "Nikki's home."

Callie tried to call again. "She's not picking up. Her phone must be dead."

They weren't far behind her, so he stepped on the gas a bit to speed up. He wasn't worried anything was going to happen, but he wanted to get there so Nikki wouldn't be alone for very long.

There was another alert, this one the house system disarming as Nikki went inside. The driveway cam alerted that Lisa the trainer was leaving. A couple of minutes later, the camera by the barn alerted. Nikki was going to check on Charlie. He didn't like her going out there alone in the dark, but he wasn't surprised by it. She loved that horse and she'd been gone for two days. She wasn't going to wait until morning to visit him.

A couple of minutes later, he was turning into Callie's driveway. "I'm so going to get after her about keeping her phone charged," Callie muttered as they approached the house. "And maybe I need to get both of us a portable battery since I almost let mine go dead earlier. Pot, kettle."

He parked beside the Toyota. Callie didn't wait for him to walk around before she hopped out and opened the door for Luna.

Luna took off like a shot, arrowing straight for the barn.

Chapter Forty-Three

"What the…?" Callie said.

Seth was at her side in an instant, hustling her into the shadow of the house, weapon out. Fear turned her body to ice as he pressed her against the siding and held her there.

"Quiet," Seth whispered.

"What's happening? Please, Seth. Tell me."

"Maybe nothing. Luna could have scented a rabbit or 'possum, or something."

"Then why—?"

"Shh."

Luna started barking, snarling, and Callie's heart dropped to her toes. "She's in the barn."

"Yes."

"Callie!" It was Nikki's voice, and Callie started for it, but Seth caught her arm and held her back. "Please, Callie! I need help!"

"Seth." His name was half sob, half plea. She pulled against him, but he held her hard.

"I told you I'd take care of you. And I will. Let me do

my job, Callie. Whatever it is, I'm going to get her out of there."

She gulped in air, her brain buzzing with panic as she nodded. "I trust you."

"Callie!" It was a male voice this time. Mikhail's. Smirnov's. Her insides turned to liquid. "You'd better fucking call this dog off and come talk to me, or I'm going to blow your sister's brains out. Tell the muscle to stand down too, or so help me God, I won't be responsible."

"Call Luna," Seth said.

"Luna! Come here, girl. Come to Mama!"

It took a few minutes, but Luna came trotting over, tail wagging. But the hair on her back was standing up like she wasn't soothed yet.

Nikki walked out of the barn with Smirnov behind her. He had an arm around her, his head mostly hidden behind hers, and a gun to her jaw.

"Gonna need you to do some work," he said in Russian. "In exchange for your sister's life."

Seth put his mouth to her ear. "Need you to distract him, babe. Talk to him. Don't approach him. Take Luna and keep her by your side. He won't get close to you, and he can't afford to remove the gun from where it is or it gives me a shot."

She sucked in a breath. "Okay. Do what you need to do. I've got this."

He kissed her swiftly. "I know you do. Now go."

There was nothing she wasn't willing to do to save her sister. If she had to take Nikki's place, she would. If she had to offer herself as a sacrifice, she would. Not that she was about to tell Seth that. If she did, she didn't think he'd let her go. But there was something else she had to tell him before it was too late.

"I think I love you," she blurted.

He hugged her hard. "I fucking think I love you, too. When this is over, I'm moving in. Or we're getting another place. Whatever you want. You, me, Nikki, Luna, and Charlie. Oh, and Sylvester, too. Can't forget him."

She kissed him hard in answer and lurched away, into the open. Luna went with her. Callie kept her hand on the dog's fur, reassuring her it was okay.

"I'm here, Mikhail. What do you want?"

"Where's the muscle?"

"He had to pee. He'll be along in a second." It was ridiculous, but all she could think to say.

"Get him out here. Now. Where I can see him."

"He's coming. Hang on. Tell me what you want."

Luna was growling, her fur standing higher on her back. She might be a love bug, but right now she looked like the guard dog she'd never been trained to be.

"I want that fucking code, and I want access to the system. Like you were supposed to give me in the first place."

"Okay, I can do that."

He snorted. "What, just like that? After you refused so prettily the last time?"

Nikki was being very quiet. Callie could hardly look at her sister's face, but what she saw when she did stunned her. Nikki was angry. She was scared too, but anger seemed to have priority at the moment.

"You didn't threaten my sister the last time."

"I fucking should've, but I thought there was time to convince you. Then shit went sideways."

She didn't ask, but whatever it was had to involve taking the real Mikhail Volkov's body out of cold storage, blowing half his head off, and dumping him in the Potomac. Her stomach roiled.

"Who broke into my house? Was it you?"

"It wasn't me."

"Did you text me for that meeting and then bail?"

"I was being followed. It wasn't safe. Fucking tell that prick to get out here now or I'll start shooting!"

Luna's growls intensified. Nikki looked militant.

Callie didn't know what to do. Her heart pounded, her temples throbbed, and everything felt out of control.

"I, um, I don't feel so good…" Nikki said.

Everything happened at once. Nikki slumped against Smirnov's arm, Luna leaped forward, and the sky exploded.

Chapter Forty-Four

WHILE CALLIE WENT TO TALK TO SMIRNOV, SETH HURRIED around to the other side of the house and scaled the tree that grew close by. From there he dropped onto the roof and crept up the slope until he could see Smirnov and Nikki illuminated in the motion light from the back porch.

Callie was speaking in Russian, and Seth prayed she'd give him the time to get into position. It'd gone against all his instincts to send her into the open, but he'd run through the options and decided that was the best choice. He believed that Smirnov wanted something from her badly enough not to kill her, which was the pivot point his entire plan hinged upon.

If he was wrong, his life was over because he'd lose Callie and any chance at happiness he'd ever have. He'd made it thirty-four years without finding anyone who'd flipped all his switches and lit him up inside, so to find her now and then lose her would destroy him.

But if he didn't rescue Nikki, he'd also lose her. Callie loved her sister, maybe more than she loved herself, and he wasn't going to let her suffer that kind of loss again. Not if he had anything to say about it.

He crouched down and crept closer, studying the trees and terrain. If he tried to climb into the tree and drop onto Smirnov that way, it wouldn't work. The branches would rustle, and bits of leaves and twigs would drop before he did, giving him away.

The roof wasn't as close as he'd like, but if he launched himself at Smirnov, he could take him down and disarm him by landing on him. He'd also take Nikki down, and she might get hurt if he did. Or shot if his trajectory landed him even a hair off balance and he didn't get a grip on the gun before Smirnov could pull the trigger.

It was too fucking close for his comfort, but there was no choice. Smirnov's voice grew louder as he seemed to demand something. Callie answered him calmly, then asked a question. He could tell it was a question because of the lilt and pause at the end.

Smirnov replied. And then Nikki spoke. She said she didn't feel good.

Seth knew, if he was going to act, it had to be now. He didn't know why, but that sixth sense he'd always had about ops kicked in and told him it was go time. He stepped to the edge of the roof and sprung into the air.

Somebody screamed as he landed on top of Smirnov, the breath knocking out of him with the force of his fall. Nikki wasn't there. He didn't know how, but thank God she wasn't, because Smirnov's gun went off and Seth felt the sharp bite of pain explode inside. If it hadn't killed him, it wasn't going to stop him. He grappled for Smirnov's throat.

Smirnov yelled and landed a blow that sent Seth reeling. Then Smirnov scrambled up while Seth tried to catch his breath—and then Luna was there, fifty pounds of snarling beast latching onto Smirnov's arm and clamping down.

He fell to his knees, then spun and tried to kick Luna. She went for his throat next, and he lashed wildly, knocking her to the side before she was after him again.

Seth got to his feet, pulled his weapon from where he'd holstered it before he jumped, and thrust the barrel against Smirnov's head. His body ached, his arm hurt, and he was fucking jacked on adrenaline and itching for an excuse.

"Move again and I'll kill you."

"Call your fucking dog off!"

"Luna! Down!" It was Callie calling her, and Luna backed away, growling as she continued to stare at Smirnov.

Callie knelt in the dirt, her arms around Nikki, who didn't look very sick at all.

"Hands behind your back, asshole."

Smirnov did as he was told. Seth took the zip-ties he'd grabbed from his truck out of his back pocket and wrenched the man's wrists together. They were steel-reinforced, so he wouldn't be able to break free. Then he bound Smirnov's legs with another set.

Blood dripped down Seth's arm from the bullet graze that had sliced across his bicep. It hurt like a motherfucker, but he'd survive. Thank God.

Smirnov was babbling in Russian. Or maybe it was Polish, because Nikki suddenly screamed at him in the same language and he stopped.

"What's he saying?" Seth growled as he took out his phone and dialed the first number that popped up, which was Kane's.

"He was calling me a few names and threatening me with rape and murder," Callie said. "Because he's such a lovely human being."

"In Polish? Or does Nikki also speak Russian?"

"Yo," Kane answered. "What you need, brother?"

"Got a situation at Callie's. Smirnov is incapacitated, but we're gonna need a clean up crew. Call Agent Corbin."

"Damn, everybody okay?"

"Yes, all alive and well. Even Smirnov. Just get out here quick, okay?"

"Cavalry is on the way, brother."

Nikki glared at Smirnov as Seth dropped his phone into his pocket. "To answer your question, I don't know much Russian, but I plan to learn. He was speaking in Polish because he wanted me to know what he was saying. Asshole."

"Are you okay?" Seth asked.

"Yes."

"Not sick?"

"No. I faked it so I could faint and be a dead weight against his arm. Then I stomped his instep and he let me go."

"Jesus," Seth said. "You could have gotten yourself killed."

She shrugged, but he knew she wasn't taking it that lightly. "He was threatening Callie with me. And I didn't know where you were so I thought I should help since Callie was running out of things to say."

"Hey," Callie said. "I was stressed."

Seth's heart hammered as he went over to his girls and hugged them both. They hugged him back. Luna came over for a pet, and Seth reached down to scratch her head for a second. She plopped at their feet, watching Smirnov.

"Never do that again," he said. "Or you'll give your sister a heart attack."

"Fine. And Seth?"

"Yes?"

"Thanks for being here. Also, we don't know each other all that well, but I'm guessing by this hug that things are trending in a good direction with you and my sister. So I'm gonna allow it."

Seth laughed. "Thanks. Appreciate it. Also, I'm moving in and not just because of lead paint. Which was a lie, by the way."

"Yeah, the bad guy and you going all Rambo kind of gave that away."

"Rambo? You know who that is?"

"I mean, yeah. My dad loved those movies. He let me watch with him so long as I didn't tell Mama."

Callie chuckled. "Dad loved anything Sylvester Stallone starred in. Mama used to say he couldn't act his way out of a paper bag, but Dad shushed her and said he was a genius. God, I miss them."

"Me, too," Nikki said.

Callie looked fierce suddenly. She broke away from the circle of his arms and approached Smirnov where he lay on the ground, glaring at the world. Then she asked him, in English, "Were my parents killed so I'd have to take this job?"

Nikki gasped, and Seth squeezed her.

"I should tell you yes," Smirnov spat. "Just to see you suffer. But no. You leaving to take custody of your sister was far more inconvenient than useful. You would have taken the job sooner if that hadn't happened."

"What makes you so sure? I didn't want to leave Poland at the time."

"But you would have. I would have made your work there intolerable until you did. Much easier than killing people, don't you think?"

Callie turned and walked into Seth's arms. He felt her shudder, and he ran his fingers up and down her back, trying to comfort her. "I believe him," she said softly. "Thank God."

Nikki slid her arms around Callie and him and the three of them stood huddled together, Luna at their feet, until Seth's team arrived.

Emma and Rory were there too, which Seth knew Blaze and Chance didn't like, but when help was needed, the whole group went. Even Daphne, who'd been riding with Blaze and Emma. Fucking hell. She stood with arms folded, looking equal parts confused and worried as she watched.

Emma wasted no time grabbing her medical kit. Then Seth found himself sitting on a chair in the kitchen, yelping as she cleaned his wound with something that hurt ten times worse than the wound itself did.

"Stop being a baby," she said as she worked.

"That shit stings."

"Maybe don't go getting yourself shot then."

"Like I planned this."

She grinned at him, and he knew she was just yanking his chain. "Still good advice though."

By the time she was done, Diana Corbin and her team had arrived to take Smirnov into custody. She stood with Ghost, arms folded, staring up at him and looking either furious or detached. Seth didn't know which and didn't much care.

Ghost could handle her, even if the Deputy Director of the CIA was her uncle and the FBI director was a family friend. He had General Mendez in his corner, and Mendez was powerful in his own right. Ghost also had the president's ear, when he could get through her chief of staff, and that wasn't nothing.

It might be fun to watch Ghost and Agent Corbin clash, but then again, it was probably like the Titans of mythology. You didn't want to be around when it happened because things were gonna get destroyed.

Eventually, everyone was gone and it was just Seth, Callie, and Nikki. There was some anger and some tears as Nikki demanded an explanation and Callie gave it, starting with being the target of the fire and not just an unlucky bystander. She didn't talk about the secret things that she couldn't, but she told Nikki everything else that she could.

"You should have told me before." Nikki was furious and pale at the same time.

"I know. I was trying to protect you."

"And you," Nikki said, pointing at Seth. "You went along with her lie about the lead paint."

"What did you expect me to do? Tell you the truth when your sister wanted to let you be a happy teenager and enjoy your summer? Not my place."

Nikki raked a hand over her face. "Argh! You people. Okay, so you didn't really want to date her but now you do and you're moving in. Is there anything else you haven't told me?"

"Nothing that's your business," Seth said, putting an arm around Callie where she sat beside him on the couch.

Nikki's gaze bounced between them. "But this is real? You aren't kidding?"

Callie leaned into him, a hand on his abdomen, her warm body pressing against his side. "It's real. It's fast, but it's real."

"All right then. So, I'm going to bed because it's been a long weekend. I feel fine, and if I have any nightmares about the big scary Russian dude, I'll let you know. I mean it was scary, but it didn't last too long."

Nikki had told them how she'd gone to check on Charlie and Smirnov had been waiting in the barn. He'd approached from the back side of the building and slipped in behind Charlie when the horse went inside. That's why he hadn't tripped the trail cam. He'd been waiting for Callie but took the opportunity to grab Nikki when she arrived.

Then Callie and Seth were there, and he'd used her as a shield. She'd been scared, but she'd decided she couldn't wait for him to kill her. She had to do something.

Seth still shuddered over that, and he intended to teach both his girls self-defense at the first opportunity.

"You sure you're okay?" Callie asked.

"Yes. I'm fine. I'll talk about it with my therapist if that makes you happy."

"I think that's a good idea."

"Okay, going to bed now. I expect no loud noises in the middle of the night. Ahem. Come on, Luna. Let's give these two some privacy."

"Oh my God," Callie muttered when Nikki and Luna were gone. "Where does she get these ideas? It's so embarrassing."

Seth laughed. "She's doing it because she knows it makes you squirm. Stop squirming and she'll quit."

"How can I? My baby sister's teasing me about sex. I may never have sex again. At least until she moves out."

Seth pushed her back on the couch and kissed her until she softened. "That'd be a damn shame, honey. We're too good together. And I don't want to wait that long."

She ran her hands up his back and around to his chest. "I don't either. Maybe we can be quiet?"

"I'm sure we can. Only one way to find out."

Chapter Forty-Five

"Holy shit, you let her do that?"

Callie squeezed Seth's hand as Nikki aimed Jack at the next jump and galloped toward it. Then they sailed over and headed for the next, a triple combination that meant Jack would have to take off, land, gather himself, take off, land, gather himself again, and sail over the last jump before continuing the rest of the course. They'd only jumped two fences at this point and Seth was freaking out.

"Yes, I let her do that. I did it too at her age."

"That's fucking crazy. She's sitting on top of a one-ton animal and hoping she can keep steering it."

"It's a little more than hope," Callie said with a laugh. "Now pay attention. You were the one who insisted on coming to the show."

"Yeah, but I didn't know it was going to be a death-defying act every time."

He shut up and paid attention though, flinching every time Jack's hooves left the ground. Callie leaned into him and squeezed his hand again. She loved how he cared about Nikki. And she loved how he cared about her.

She'd gotten over her hang up about Nikki being in the house and made love with Seth every night in her bed. Their bed. They were capable of being quiet, though if Nikki was gone they got as loud as they wanted.

In the week since Dima Smirnov had been apprehended and taken away by the FBI, Callie had gone back to work and fixed the sabotage Dr. Robbins had done to the code. Leo had tried to bully her, but she'd faced him down and told him if he didn't stop, she was filing a sexual harassment complaint with HR. Then she'd told him that without her, the project wouldn't get done on time and did he really want to answer to the boss why that was.

He'd stopped bothering her and started consulting her, though he didn't seem happy about it. The rest of the team consulted her with coding issues too, which was nice. She'd thought long and hard about the work she was doing, and she'd made a decision. She hadn't told anyone what she'd started working on yet, but she would.

Starting with Seth.

She leaned toward him as Nikki sailed over the last jump. He tensed and then relaxed as Nikki and Jack galloped for the finish.

"You know that kill switch in your truck?"

"Hmm?" He looked down at her. "The kill switch? What about it?"

"Might be a useful thing to have, don't you think?"

He was staring at her, not quite getting it. She could tell when the light dawned. "You think it's possible?"

"I do. I got to thinking about Dr. Robbins. About what she said. I don't know if she's right or not, but if she is, it'd be nice to have that kill switch in place."

She had his full attention now. "Can you do it?"

"Pretty sure I can. I'm working on it."

"We need to tell the guys."

"Agreed."

He kissed her right there on the rail at the horse show, not caring who was watching.

"I love you, Caroline "Callie" Crowell. I love your honesty and loyalty, your sweetness, your fucking paper scraps, and your fierceness. You amaze me."

"I love you, too, Seth. So much. I've never felt like this before."

"Me either. But I know it's right because I want to be with you all the time. I want to talk about shit with you and listen to you tell me everything that's on your mind. That would've been a nightmare to me before you. But not anymore. You make me want to be better."

"How can you be better? You're already perfect to me. You care about people, even if you hide it, and you're the most honest person I know. You'd give your life to protect mine and Nikki's. And not just ours, I fear. Anybody who needed you to save them." She shook her head. "You can't be better than you already are."

His gaze was hot. "If we weren't in public, I'd have you naked and moaning my name."

She gave him a peck on the lips. "Later. Nikki's staying for the after party and then going to spend the night with Amelia. We'll have the house to ourselves."

"That's hours away."

"I know. We'll survive."

"Maybe." He was quiet for a moment. "I'm going to look for Mandy's contact information, maybe send a message in a few months when things are settled."

She knew he was talking about his mission.

"I think that's a good idea."

"Of course it is. I got it from you."

Callie leaned into him, and he put his arm around her. She was so incredibly happy right now. She had a gorgeous man who loved her, her sister was thriving and even speaking Polish again, and Callie was becoming part of the group with Seth's friends and their ladies. Tomorrow, they were going to Chance and Rory's house for a cookout. Their new book club, which Rory had named The Booka-licious Besties Book Club, was meeting for the first time Wednesday night at Emma's apartment. There they would pick their books and decide on a schedule. Nikki already had hers picked out but wouldn't tell Callie what it was.

Something with Fae warriors, no doubt.

Callie looked forward to having everyone over to their place once the new furniture was delivered next week and they got everything decorated again. Whoever had broken into her house and trashed it wasn't coming back. That was according to Diana Corbin, who wouldn't say more.

Seth swore he had no idea and he wasn't just saying that for the job. She believed him. If he couldn't tell her, he would say so. They had that agreement now because they each knew there might be things they couldn't say. Though now that she knew what the Athena Project really was, and his team knew what she did, there wasn't much they couldn't share, though only in the closed environment of the SCIF.

When the last rider finished their round, Callie was on her feet, cheering. Seth surged up with her, not knowing why, bless him, but there for the support.

"She went clean, and her time was fastest. Jack and Nikki won!"

Seth hugged her hard and then put his fingers to his lips and did a wolf whistle that had Nikki waving from the other end of the arena where she was returning to get her ribbon and trophy.

"Damn, that was amazing," he said. "I'm so glad it's over."

"Oh baby," Callie laughed. "You're going to have to get used to this because there's another show in two weeks."

"Aw, hell. Okay, I can do this. I can watch a teenager hurl a giant animal at big scary jumps and not freak out. I can."

Callie laughed. "If anybody can, it's you. I believe in you."

He smiled down at her. "I believe in you, too. Want to go congratulate our champion?"

"Yes, definitely!"

"Too bad we didn't bring Luna," he said as they headed for the stables. "I think she'd like this."

"She would, but Auntie Daphne needed something to do."

Which was why they'd asked Daphne to dog sit while they went to the show. Daphne loved Luna and enjoyed watching her. Plus they'd thought maybe all the horses and activity would be too much for the dog. They needed to introduce her to it slowly by taking her to the stable during lessons first, then branching out to shows if she handled it well.

Nikki came running over to them in her tall boots, her ribbon flapping from where it was pinned to her jacket pocket. Her face beamed happiness as she threw her arms around them both and jumped up and down.

"We won! We won! We won!"

"Noticed that," Seth said, laughing.

"What did you think?" she asked him, her eyes bright. "Did you like it?"

Callie cringed, worried about what he'd say. But he wrapped an arm around her sister and hugged her to his side. "I thought it was the most amazing thing ever. You and Jack were wonderful."

"I'm so glad you enjoyed it! I thought maybe, you know, horses. Ugh. Some guys don't care."

"I care. It was beautiful. Can't wait to see what you do next."

Nikki's smile was wide and happy. "Oh, gotta go take some pics with Jack and Lisa. Don't go anywhere."

She ran off, and Callie turned to the man she loved, shocked once more at how fast it'd happened but also certain it was right. "You didn't tell her the truth."

"Nope. Some things are better kept quiet. No way am I dimming that kid's sparkle over my shit. What?"

He stared at her suspiciously, but she couldn't contain the giddiness of her smile. "Nothing. I love you, that's all. I always will."

"That's all I need, baby," he said, looping his arm around her and tugging her close while they watched Nikki ham for photos. "I can't wait to see what life brings us."

Neither could she. Because she knew it was going to be good.

———

THANK YOU FOR READING SETH!! I hope you loved their story as much as I did. Kane and Daphne are up next and I just can't wait to bring them to you!

SCAN THE QR code to join my newsletter list! Get information on sales, new books, and free content.

Seth

Books by Lynn Raye Harris

Ghost Ops

Book 1: BLAZE - Blaze & Emma

Book 2: CHANCE - Chance & Rory

Book 3: SETH - Seth & Callie

Book 4: KANE - Kane & Daphne

Book 5: ETHAN

Book 6: ALEX

The Hostile Operations Team ® Books
Strike Team 2

Book 1: HOT ANGEL - Cade & Brooke

Book 2: HOT SECRETS - Sky & Bliss

Book 3: HOT JUSTICE - Wolf & Haylee

Book 4: HOT STORM - Mal & Scarlett

Book 5: HOT COURAGE - Noah & Jenna

Book 6: HOT SHADOWS - Gem & Everly

Book 7: HOT LIMIT ~ Ryder & Alaina

Book 8: HOT HONOR ~ Zane & Eden

—

The Hostile Operations Team ® Books
Strike Team 1

Book 0: RECKLESS HEAT

Book 1: HOT PURSUIT - Matt & Evie

Book 2: HOT MESS - Sam & Georgie

Book 3: DANGEROUSLY HOT - Kev & Lucky

Book 4: HOT PACKAGE - Billy & Olivia

Book 5: HOT SHOT - Jack & Gina

Book 6: HOT REBEL - Nick & Victoria

Book 7: HOT ICE - Garrett & Grace

Book 8: HOT & BOTHERED - Ryan & Emily

Book 9: HOT PROTECTOR - Chase & Sophie

Book 10: HOT ADDICTION - Dex & Annabelle

Book 11: HOT VALOR - Mendez & Kat

Book 12: A HOT CHRISTMAS MIRACLE - Mendez & Kat

—

The HOT SEAL Team Books

Book 1: HOT SEAL - Dane & Ivy

Book 2: HOT SEAL Lover - Remy & Christina

Book 3: HOT SEAL Rescue - Cody & Miranda

Book 4: HOT SEAL BRIDE - Cash & Ella

Book 5: HOT SEAL REDEMPTION - Alex & Bailey

Book 6: HOT SEAL TARGET - Blade & Quinn

Book 7: HOT SEAL HERO - Ryan & Chloe

Book 8: HOT SEAL DEVOTION - Zach & Kayla

———

HOT Heroes for Hire: Mercenaries
Black's Bandits

Book 1: BLACK LIST - Jace & Maddy

Book 2: BLACK TIE - Brett & Tallie

Book 3: BLACK OUT - Colt & Angie

Book 4: BLACK KNIGHT - Jared & Libby

Book 5: BLACK HEART - Ian & Natasha

Book 6: BLACK MAIL - Tyler & Cassie

Book 7: BLACK VELVET - Dax & Roberta

———

The HOT Novella in Liliana Hart's MacKenzie Family Series

HOT WITNESS - Jake & Eva

———

7 Brides for 7 Soldiers

WYATT (Book 4) - Wyatt & Paige

7 Brides for 7 Blackthornes

ROSS (Book 3) - Ross & Holly

———

About the Author

Lynn Raye Harris is a Southern girl, military wife, wannabe cat lady, and horse lover. She's also the New York Times and USA Today bestselling author of the HOSTILE OPERATIONS TEAM ® SERIES of military romances, and 20 books about sexy billionaires for Harlequin.

A former finalist for the Romance Writers of America's Golden Heart Award and the National Readers Choice Award, Lynn lives in Alabama with her handsome former-military husband, one fluffy princess of a cat, and a very spoiled American Saddlebred horse who enjoys bucking at random in order to keep Lynn on her toes.

Lynn's books have been called "exceptional and emotional," "intense," and "sizzling" -- and have sold in excess of 4.5 million copies worldwide.

To connect with Lynn online:
www.LynnRayeHarris.com
Lynn@LynnRayeHarris.com